Merkland by Margaret Oliphant

Or, Self Sacrifice

Margaret Oliphant Wilson was born on April 4th, 1828 to Francis W. Wilson, a clerk, and Margaret Oliphant, at Wallyford, near Musselburgh, East Lothian.

Her youth was spent in establishing a writing style and by 1849 she had her first novel published: Passages in the Life of Mrs. Margaret Maitland.

Two years later, in 1851 Caleb Field was published and also an invitation to contribute to Blackwood's Magazine; the beginning of a life time business relationship.

In May 1852, Margaret married her cousin, Frank Wilson Oliphant. Their marriage produced six children but, tragically, three died in infancy. When her husband developed signs of the dreaded consumption (tuberculosis) they moved to Florence, and then to Rome where, sadly, he died.

Margaret was naturally devastated but was also now left without support and only her income from writing to support the family. She returned to England and took up the burden of supporting her three remaining children by her literary activity.

Her incredible and prolific work rate increased both her commercial reputation and the size of her reading audience. Tragedy struck again in January 1864 when her only remaining daughter Maggie died.

In 1866 she settled at Windsor to be closer to her sons, who were being educated at near-by Eton School.

For more than thirty years she pursued a varied literary career but family life continued to bring problems. Cyril Francis, her eldest son, died in 1890. The younger son, Francis, who she nicknamed 'Cecco', died in 1894.

With the last of her children now lost to her, she had little further interest in life. Her health steadily and inexorably declined.

Margaret Oliphant Wilson Oliphant died at the age of 69 in Wimbledon on 20th June 1897. She is buried in Eton beside her sons.

Index of Contents

CHAPTER I

"But may not Mrs. Catherine's visitor belong to another family? The name is not uncommon."

"You will permit me to correct you, Miss Ross. The name is by no means a common one; and there was some very distant connexion, I remember, between the Aytouns and Mrs. Catherine. I have little doubt that this girl is his daughter."

"Mother! mother!" exclaimed the first speaker, a young lady, whose face, naturally grave and composed, bore tokens of unusual agitation. "It is impossible; Mrs. Catherine, considerate and kind as she always is, could never be so cruel."

"I am quite at a loss for your meaning, Anne."

"To bring her here—to our neighborhood," said Anne Ross, averting her eyes, and disregarding her step-mother's interruption, "where we must meet her continually, where our name, which must be odious to her, will be ringing in her ears every day. I cannot believe it. Mrs. Catherine could not do anything so barbarous."

Mrs. Ross, of Merkland, threw down her work, and pushed back her chair from the table:

"Upon my word, Anne Ross, you turn more absurd every day. What is the meaning of this?—our name odious! I should not like Lewis to hear you say so."

"But Lewis does not know this terrible story," said Anne.

"And never shall," replied Mrs. Ross. "Neither can your brother's crime make my son's name odious to any one. I fancied you knew that Norman was called by your mother's name; and this Aytoun girl, if she knows anything of it at all, will have heard of him as Rutherford, and not as Ross."

"But Mrs. Catherine—she at least cannot be ignorant, cannot have forgotten: who could forget this? and my mother was her friend!"

"The friendship has descended, I think," said Mrs. Ross, with a sneer, "as you seem to imagine feuds should. I suppose you think this girl's brother, if she has one, would be quite doing his duty if he demanded satisfaction from Lewis, for a thing which happened when the poor boy was a mere infant? But be not afraid, most tender and scrupulous sister. People have better sense in these days."

Anne Ross turned away, grieved and silenced; her conversations with her step-mother too often terminated so: and there was a long pause. At last she said, timidly, as if desirous, and yet afraid of asking further: "And my father never knew how he died?"

Mrs. Ross glanced hurriedly at the door: "He did not die."

Anne started violently. "Norman, my brother? I beseech you to tell me, mother, is he not dead?"

"Ah, there is Duncan back, from Portoran," said Mrs. Ross, rising. "Letters from Lewis, no doubt. How slow they are!" And she rang the bell vehemently.

The summons brought in a maid, struggling with the buckle of Duncan's letter-bag, which was opened at length, and gave to Mrs. Ross's delighted eyes the expected letters from her only son: but Anne sat apart, shivering and trembling with a great dread—a secret, most sad and terrible; a tale of dishonor, and crime, and misery, such as might chill the very heart to hear.

"And there's a letter from the Tower, Miss Anne," said the maid, giving her a note. "Duncan got it at the Brig, from Johnnie Halflin, and Johnnie was to wait, till Duncan got back with the answer, if there was to be any."

"There is no answer, May," said Anne, glancing over the brief epistle; and May withdrew reluctantly, having obtained no news of Maister Lewis, or his wanderings, wherewith to satisfy her expectant audience in the kitchen.

The letter of Lewis was a long one, and Anne had time to travel listlessly again and again over the angular and decided characters of her ancient friend.

"My friend," said the singularly-folded black letter-looking note, "you will come to the Tower to-morrow. I am expecting Alison Aytoun at night; and seeing the world has gotten two new generations (to keep within the truth) since I myself was done with the company of children, I am in need of your counsel how we are to brighten the bed-chamber and other apartments, so as will become the presence of youth. For undoubtedly in this matter, if I am like any mortal person, it is like Issachar in the prophecy (not to be profane,) for there is Elspat Henderson, my own woman, that would have out the old red satin curtains (that are liker black than red now, as you will mind,) to put upon the bed, and Euphan Morison, her daughter, is for no curtains at all, for the sake of health, (pity me, Anne, that have doctors among my serving-women!) and Jacky, Euphan's daughter (bethanked that she has but one!) has been gathering dahlias and sunflowers, and such other unwholesome and unyouthful things, to put in the poor bairn Alison's room, wherewith I have near brought a fever upon myself, first with the evil odor of them, and then with flying upon the elf Jacky. So mind you come to the Tower, like a good bairn, as you are, and have always been, as early in the day as you can; and before twelve of the clock, if possible, seeing that I have many things to say to you.

"CATHERINE DOUGLAS."

For the third or fourth time, Anne's eyes had travelled down to that firm and clear signature, when an exclamation from her step-mother roused her. "Lewis will be home before his birthday! Lewis will be here on Friday! I believe you are more concerned about that girl coming to the Tower. Do you hear me, Anne? On Friday your brother will be home."

There were only two days to prepare for his coming; and before Anne had finished her hasty perusal of the letter which Mrs. Ross permitted her to see, the house was full of joyful bustle and unwonted glee— for the frigid soul of its mistress melted under the influence of her son, as if his words had been very sunbeams. By nature she was neither amiable nor generous; but the mother's love, in its first out-gushing, almost made her both.

And she had known the details of that dark mystery too long, and had too little liking for her husband's unhappy son, to sympathize at all with Anne's horror and agony. And so Mrs. Ross, of Merkland, bustled and rejoiced in her selfish gladness, while Anne, longing to ask, and yet afraid of rude repulse or angry reprimand, sat silently, with a heavy heart, beside her. At length, when they were about to separate for the night, Anne took courage.

"Mother," she said, "I do not wish to disturb you, in so happy an occupation as this, but only one word— Norman, poor Norman, you said he did not die."

"Upon my word, Anne, I think you might choose a better time for those disagreeable inquiries," said Mrs. Ross, impatiently.

"He is my brother," said Anne, "and with such a dreadful history. Mother, is Norman alive?"

"How can I tell?" cried Mrs. Ross. "You ought to desire most earnestly, Anne, both for his sake and your own, that he may be peacefully dead. Your father, I know, received a letter from him, secretly, after the ship was lost. He had escaped the wreck; but that is seventeen years ago."

"And did he confess?" said Anne, eagerly.

"Confess! Criminals do not generally do that. No, no, he professed his innocence. I may find you the letter sometime. There, will not that do? Go to your room now."

"And will you not tell Lewis?" said Anne.

"Tell Lewis!" exclaimed Mrs. Ross, "why should I grieve my boy? He is but his half-brother."

Anne turned away without another word and went quietly up stairs—not to her own apartment first, but to a dusty attic lumber-room, seldom entered, except by herself. In one dark corner stood a picture, its face to the wall. Anne placed her candle on the floor, and kneeling down turned the portrait—a frank, bold, generous face, half boy, half man, with its unshadowed brow and clear eyes, that feared no evil.

"Lewis is but my half-brother also," said Anne Ross, replacing the picture with a sigh; "but Norman was my mother's son."

The house and small estate of Merkland were situated in one of the northern counties of Scotland, within some three or four miles of a little post-town which bore the dignified name of Portoran. The Oran water swept by the side of its small port, just before it joined its jocund dark-brown waters to the sea, and various coasting vessels carried its name and its traffic out (a little way) into the world. The parish in which Merkland stood, boasted at least its three Lairds' houses—there was Strathoran, the lordliest of all, with its wide acres extending over three or four adjacent parishes. There was the Tower, with its compact and richly-cultivated lands, the well-ordered property of Mrs. Catherine Douglas; and, lastly, there was Merkland—the home of a race of vigorous Rosses, renowned in former generations for its hosts of sons and daughters, and connected by the spreading of those strong and healthful off-shoots, with half of the families of like degree in Scotland. The children of the last Ross of Merkland had not been vigorous—one by one, in childhood, and in youth, they had dropped into the family grave, and when the infant Anne was born, her worn-out mother died, leaving besides the newborn child, only one son. His mother's brother long before had made this Norman, his heir. At the same time, in consideration of his independent inheritance, and his changed name, he had been excluded from the succession to his father's lands. So Mr. Ross of Merkland, in terror lest his estate should have no worthier proprietor than the sickly little girl whose birth had cost her mother's life, married hastily again. When Lewis and Anne were still only infants, Norman Rutherford left his father's house to take possession of his own—and then some terrible blight had fallen upon him, spoken of in fearful whispers at the time, but almost wholly forgotten now. A stranger in the district at the time our history begins would only have learned, after much inquiry, that Norman, escaping from his native country with the stain of blood upon his hands, proved a second Jonah to the ship in which he had embarked, and so was lost, and that grief for his crime had brought his father's grey hairs in sorrow to the grave. But the difference of name, and the entire silence maintained by his family concerning him, had puzzled country gossips, and restrained the voice of rumor, even at the time. Now his remembrance had almost entirely passed away, and in another week Lewis Ross, Esq., of Merkland, would be of age.

But the whole dreadful tale in all the darkness of its misery had been poured into Anne's ears that day. She had known nothing of it before. Now, her stepmother thought, it was full time she should know, because—a reason that made Anne shrink and tremble—Mrs. Ross felt convinced that the girl who was so soon to be a visitor at the Tower, could be no other than the daughter of the murdered man.

"The south room, May—he had it when he was a boy," said Mrs. Ross, as Anne entered their breakfast-room the next morning. "I wish there had been time to get some of the furniture renewed; but I dare say Lewis will like to see it as he left it. Do you not think so, Anne?"

"He was always such a kindly heart," interposed May.

Mrs. Ross looked dubious.

"You must remember, May, that my son is no longer a boy. This day week he will take the management of his affairs into his own hands. He left us a youth, but he returns a man."

"And I was just thinking that myself, ma'am," said May; "and Duncan says it behoves us to call the young Lord by his own name, Merkland,—and not Mr. Lewis; but I always think the old way's the kindliest."

"Lewis will be changed, if he does not like the kindliest best," said Anne.

"Ah, that may be," said Mrs. Ross; "but there is something due to—Well, where were we. Ay, the south room. I know you keep it in good order, May, but we must have it on Friday shining like—"

"Like a new pin, ma'am," said May, as Mrs. Ross paused for a simile; "and so it shall, and you may trust that to me."

"Yes, Lewis will be quite a man," said Mrs. Ross, leaning back in her chair with a smile. "I should think he would be a good deal browned, Anne—I have been thinking so all the morning."

"Oh! and he'll have a lordly presence," said May, "like his father before him. The Rosses have always been grand men to look upon. They say the young Laird—"

"Was not in the least degree like what my son will be," said Mrs. Ross, stiffly, while Anne grew pale. "You will see that my orders are strictly attended to, May, and let Duncan come to me whenever we have had breakfast. Take your place, Anne."

Discomfited by her abrupt dismissal, May took her departure, muttering between her teeth:

"One would think it was a crime to speak a good word of the old lady's bairns! Well, if one but knew what became of him at last, I would like to see the man in all Strathoran like the young Lord."

"Anne," said Mrs. Ross, somewhat sternly, as May withdrew, leaving Anne's heart vibrating painfully with her indiscreet reference; "was it to-day that Mrs. Catherine expected her visitor?"

"Yes, mother."

"And to-day you are engaged to go to the Tower?"

"Yes," said Anne. "But I can send Duncan with an apology, if you wish it. I did not know that Lewis was likely to arrive so soon when I received Mrs. Catherine's note."

"Send Duncan! no, indeed!" said Mrs. Ross. "There would be little profit in wasting his time to save yours. Duncan is the most useful person about Merkland."

"And I the most useless," said Anne, sighing. "It grieves me deeply, mother, that it should be so."

Mrs. Ross threw back her head slightly, expressing the peevish scorn which she did not speak, and Anne returned to her tea-making; and so they sat till their joyless meal was ended: each the sole companion and nearest connexion of the other, and yet so utterly separated in all that constitutes true fellowship.

The clear light of the October sun was shining on the waters of Oran, and its tinted, overshadowing leaves, when Anne emerged from among the trees that surrounded Merkland, and took her solitary way to the Tower. Her heart was heavy within her, her step irregular, her brow clouded. The great secret of the family had fallen upon her spirit with all the stunning force of a first grief, and vainly she looked about her for comfort, finding none.

How many times had May's admiring mention of the "young Laird" called forth upon her lips a sad smile of affectionate sorrow for the dead brother whom she never saw. How often had she marvelled at the old nurse's stern summary of his end: "He died a violent death!" How often lingered with sorrowful admiration over his picture in the attic lumber-room! And now his name had become a name of fear! The stain of blood was upon him! A Cain! a murderer!

Not dead! Anne's hasty steps passed quick over the narrow pathway, with its carpeting of fallen leaves. In what pain—what misery, must that blighted life have passed! Whither might that guilty soul have wandered, seeking, in crowd or in solitude, to hide itself from its own fearful consciousness, and from its angry God! In privation, in danger, in want in sin, unfriended and accursed, and alone, with none to speak to him of mercy, of hope, of Divine forgiveness! And this was her brother! her mother's son!

It was like some dreadful dream—but not like a dream could it be shaken off. How often in her childish imaginings, long ago, had she dreamed of the dead Norman living again, her friend and protector! Now how bitter and strong that unavailing wish, that God had indeed stricken him in his early youth, and laid him in the peaceful family grave unstained. Again and again those dark particulars rolled back upon her in bitter waves, swelling her grief and horror up to agony. And that the daughter of the slain man should come here—here, to have daily intercourse with the nearest kindred of her father's murderer! The idea was so terrible, that it produced a revulsion. She tried to believe that it was not so—that it could not be possible.

Again and again she stopped, and would have turned back, and yet a strange fascination drew her on. There was a link of terrible connexion between herself and this girl, and Anne's spirit throbbed to bursting with undefined and confused purposes. She could not trust herself alone, therefore she put force upon her struggling heart, as she had learned to do long years ago, and passed on to the Tower.

For the step-daughter of Mrs. Ross, of Merkland, had small reason to think of this many-sided world as a place of happiness. In a household which had barely means enough to support its station, and provide for the somewhat expensive wanderings of its heir, she was the one dependent, and Anne had ripened into some three-and-twenty years, and was no longer a girl. She felt how useless she was in the eyes of her clever step-mother; she felt the lethargic influence of having no aim, and deep down in that hidden heart of hers, which few others knew, or cared to know, sorrow and pain had been dwelling long, like Truth, in the well of their own solitary tears.

She was now proceeding to the house of her most dear and especial friend: an ancient lady, whose strong will swayed, and whose warm heart embraced all who came within their influence, and whose healthful and vigorous spirit was softened in a manner most rare and beautiful by those delicate perceptions and sympathies which form so important an element in the constitution of genius. Mrs. Catherine Douglas had seen the snows of sixty winters. For more than thirty of these, her strong and kindly hand had held absolute dominion at the Tower, yet of the few admitted to her friendship and confidence, Anne Ross, the neglected step-daughter of Mrs. Ross, of Merkland, an ill-used child, a slighted woman, held the highest place.

The Tower was a gray, old, stately place, defiant alike of storm and siege, with deep embrasures on its walls meant for no child's play, and a court-yard that had rung to martial music centuries ago, in the days of the unhappy Stuarts. Deep woods stretched round it, tinted with autumn's fantastic wealth of coloring. The Oran ran so close to the strong, heavy, battlemented wall, that in the old warlike days, it had been the castle-moat, but the drawbridge was gone, and there was peaceful access now, by a light bridge of oak. A boat lay on the stream, moored to an over-hanging rock, by which Mrs. Catherine herself was wont to make the brief passage of the Oran. It was a favorite toy of Anne's also, in her happier moods, but she was too heavy of heart to heed it now.

"Mrs. Catherine is in the library, Miss Anne," said Mrs. Euphan Morison, the portly, active housekeeper, whose medical propensities so frequently annoyed her mistress; and threading the dark passages familiarly, Anne passed on alone.

"Mrs. Catherine is in the library, Miss Anne," repeated a dark, thin, elfin-like girl, who sat on the sill of a deep window, reading, and hiding her book beneath the stocking which she ought to have been knitting, as she threw furtive glances to the door of the housekeeper's especial sanctum: "but there's gentlemen with her. It's a business day."

"I suppose you may admit me, Jacky," said Anne. "Mrs. Catherine expects me."

"Mr. Walter Foreman's in, Miss Anne," said Jacky.

"And what then?" said Anne, smiling.

"And Mr. Ferguson, the factor from Strathoran," said the girl, gravely, taking up, with a look of abstraction, some dropt loops in her neglected stocking.

"Then I will go to the drawing-room," said Anne. "Tell me, Jacky, when Mrs. Catherine is disengaged."

"And Miss Anne," said Jacky, starting, as Anne was about to pass on, "the young lady's coming."

"So I have heard," said Anne.

"And she's to get the mid-chamber," said Jacky, "and the chairs have come out of the big room in the west tower. You never saw them, Miss Anne. Will you come?" And Jacky jerked her thin, angular frame off her seat, and threw down book and stocking.

"What have you been reading, Jacky?" said Anne.

The sharp, dark face owned an involuntary flush, and the furtive eyes glanced back to the housekeeper's closed door. "It was only the Faery Queen."

"The Faery Queen! Jacky, these are strange studies for you."

"There's no harm in it," muttered the girl, angrily.

"I did not say there was," said Anne; "and you need not transfix me with those sharp eyes of yours, because I wondered. But, Jacky, your mother would not be pleased with this."

"It's not the chief end of woman to work stockings," murmured the girl.

"No, surely," said Anne; "nor yet to read poems. Come, Jacky, let me see the mid-chamber."

Jacky seized the book, deposited it in a dark niche below the window, and glided away before Anne up the broad stone stairs, to the room which the united skill of the household had been decking for a bower to little Alice Aytoun. The mid-chamber, as its name imports, occupied the front of the building, between the two round towers, that rose grimly with their dark turrets on either side. It was a room of good proportions, with two deep windows, looking out on the windings of the Oran, and commanding a view of the little town, seated on the point where the river poured itself into the sea. The country looked rich and gay in its russet coloring, and here and there you could see the harvest labourers in a half-reaped field—for the harvests were late beneath the northern sky of Strathoran. A little way below, the unpretending house of Merkland stood, peacefully among its trees; on the left hand, the plain church and substantial Manse basked in the sunbeams; and the broad sea, flashing beneath the light, belted its blue breadths around the landscape. Anne stood at the window, and looked out, as in a dream; dim, misty, spectral visions floating before her, in which were ever mingling her unhappy wandering brother, and the unconscious girl who should look forth on that same scene to-night.

"It's not so much here," said Jacky, glancing round, and looking complacently on a great bunch of dahlias and hollyhocks, rudely inserted in an uncouth china vase. "The room's just as it always is, except the flowers—will you come in here, Miss Anne?"

Anne followed, thinking little of the arrangements which she came to superintend. The room they entered was small and rounded, occupying as it did, a corner of the eastern tower. Its deep-set window was toward the sunrising—towards the hills, too, and the sea—and Anne paused upon the threshold, in wonder at the unwonted preparations made for this youthful visitor. In one end of the room stood a great wardrobe of richly-carved oak. There was an ancient piano, also, and little tables laden with well-chosen books, and the antique chairs looked richly sober in their renovation, heightening the air of olden romance which hung about this lady's bower. The blooming plants in the window were the only things new, and pertaining to the immediate present. Graceful and pure in its antique delicacy, the small apartment was a bower indeed.

"But Mrs. Catherine," said Jacky, "would let me put no flowers here—only a big branch of barberries that I slipped in myself."

The branch of barberries was, indeed, projecting fantastically from the rich frame of the mirror on the wall.

"I think you may let Mrs. Catherine have the whole merit of this, Jacky," said Anne, taking it down; "and do you have a ramble through the garden, and find something more fragrant than those sunflowers. You will get some roses yet—run, Jacky. Mrs. Catherine—"

"Is troubled with undutiful bairns," said the lady herself entering the room. "Wherefore did you not come to me, Anne, and me in urgent need of counsel? And wherefore did you not open the door, you elf, Jacky, unless you be indeed a changeling, as I have always thought you, and were feared for learned words? Come down with me this moment, Anne! You can fiddle about these trifling things when there is no serious matters in hand. I am saying, Come with me!"

Mrs. Catherine Douglas was tall and stately, with a firm step, and a clear voice, strong constitutioned, and strong spirited. In appearance she embodied those complexional peculiarities which gave to the fabled founder of her house his far-famed name—black hair, streaked with silver, the characteristic pale complexion, and strongly-marked features, harmonising perfectly in the hue—she was dark-grey. It seemed her purpose, too, to increase the effect by her dress. At all times and seasons, Mrs. Catherine's rich, rustling, silken garments were grey, of that peculiar dark-grey which is formed by throwing across the sable warp a slender waft of white. In winter, a shawl of the finest texture, but of the simple black and white shepherd's check, completed her costume. In summer, its soft, fine folds hung over her chair. No rejoicing, and no sorrow, changed Mrs. Catherine's characteristic dress. The lustrous silken garment, the fine woollen shawl, the cap of old and costly lace remained unchanged for years.

"It is a new vocation for me, child," said Mrs. Catherine, as Anne followed her down stairs, "to set myself to the adorning of rooms; but when my serving-women must have their divers notions concerning them, I should put to my own hand, unless I had wanted the stranger to be terrified with the aspect of my house—which I do not, for—Look back, child, is that elf Jacky behind you with her sharp eyes. But I have matters more important on my hand to-day."

They reached the library door as Mrs. Catherine spoke, and she entered, while Anne lingered behind. Another voice, the brisk one of Walter Foreman, the young Portoran writer, began to speak immediately, but was summarily interrupted by Mrs. Catherine's clear tones:

"I tell you you're a fool, Walter Foreman, as was your father before you—it's in the blood. You say he was a kinsman. Ay, doubtless, as if I did not known that. And was not James Aytoun as near of kin to him as me, and Ralph Falconer nearer. To think of any mortal, in his senses, passing over the promising lads, to leave siller to me! Me, that have an abundance for my own turns, and none to be heir to either my land or my name. Speak not to me. Walter Foreman, I say the man was crazy!"

"But even if he were," said Mr. Walter Foreman, as Anne entered the library, "you would surely never think, Mrs. Catherine, of contesting the validity of a will made in your own favor."

"And who said I would not, if it seemed right in my own eyes?" said Mrs. Catherine, indignantly. "Come here, Anne; you are not blinded with the sight of siller, as this youth is. Robert Falconer, the merchant (the third son of old Falcon's Craig,) is dead, and passing over his own near kin, that needed it (besides leaving the most part of his siller to hospitals, which may be was right, and may be not, I have not time to enter upon it,) the auld fool—that I should speak so of a man that is gone to his account—has left by his will a portion of siller, ten thousand pounds, no less, to me: me, that have no manner of use for it; that know not even what to do with it. I am thankful to you, Mr. Ferguson, you would learn me an easy way of putting it out of my hand; but I must consider, first, with your permission, whether I have any right to take it in."

Mr. Ferguson, the Strathoran factor, smiled. "It is not often, Mrs. Catherine, that people receive legacies as you do."

"No—neither, I am hoping, are there many left like this," said Mrs. Catherine; "but truly, gentlemen, that is no fault of yours, that I should fall upon you for it. Come back to me this day week, Mr. Ferguson; and you can come also, Walter Foreman, unless your father, who has more discretion, has the time to spare; and in that space, I will have taken counsel what I should do."

Mr. Ferguson and the young lawyer took their leave; and Mrs. Catherine turned to Anne: "Heard you ever the like of it, child? To leave siller to me! You did not know the man; but Ralph Falconer, of Falcon's Craig, is his grand-nephew, and James Aytoun is also allied to him by the mother's side: and I, that am but his cousin, three times removed, and having my own share of this world's goods, and none to come after me—undoubtedly the man was crazy!"

CHAPTER II

The October sun rose brilliantly upon ancient Edinburgh, throwing the strong radiance of its russet gold upon the noble outline and antique grandeur of the historic city, and shone joyously into a family room, where a small household round their breakfast table were discussing the journey which that fair-haired, smiling girl, half-timorous, half-exultant, was to undertake that day. The white hair upon the mother's placid forehead was belied by the fresh cheek and dewy liquid eye, from which time had not taken the brightness. Her son was entering upon the strongest years of manhood, with sense and intelligence shining in his face. Her daughter was a girl, just emerging from the child's mirth and unrestrained gaiety, into those sensitive, imaginative years, which form the threshold of graver life—

"Standing with reluctant feet,
Where the brook and river meet,
Womanhood and childhood sweet."

"But, mother," exclaimed Alice Aytoun, suddenly, "Miss Douglas will see at once that Bessie has not been my maid at home."

"Miss Douglas!" cried her mother. "Alice, did I not tell you that you were on no account to call her Miss. Remember always, Mrs. Catherine. And she knows very well that we are not able to keep a maid for you, and will understand that Bessie is for a companion on the way, and in some sense a protector. If you stay long, you can send her home."

"And be alone in the strange place, mother," said Alice, the sunshine fading, for a moment, from her face.

"How long will it be strange, Alice?" said her brother. "How many acquaintances will you make in a week?"

The sunshine flushed back again.

"And Mrs. Catherine—is she very eccentric, mother? I hope I shall like her."

"I hope still more, Alice," said Mrs. Aytoun, smiling, "that she may like you. Mrs. Catherine has many friends who could serve James; and then, you know, she has no heir. So be as fascinating as possible."

"Mother!" exclaimed James, "this worldly wisdom sounds strangely from your lips. We do not send Alice away to pay court to Mrs. Catherine Douglas for her estate's sake."

"By no means," said Mrs. Aytoun. "I have heard Mrs. Catherine spoken of often as a most kind, loveable person, in her own peculiar way; and I accepted her invitation to Alice gladly, not because she has an estate unheired, but because—for various reasons, indeed—but the other, by the way. You are a landless laird yourself, James, and I am not quite so stoical as to despise a good inheritance."

"Do you know any of Mrs. Catherine's neighbors, mother?" said Alice, whose attention, sadly distracted by anticipation, had altogether wandered during this discussion of motives. "The people I am likely to meet, do you know any of them?"

"No," said Mrs. Aytoun, "I never was at the Tower; and my mother left the neighborhood young, and died so soon, too, that I have had very little connexion with her friends or native place. Indeed, it surprised me, that Mrs. Catherine should remember our relationship at all: but she is one of the most generous persons possible, I have heard often; and no doubt wishes to give you a glimpse, Alice, of the world you should enter on now." And Mrs. Aytoun gave a very quiet sigh.

"Nonsense, mother!" said her son, energetically. "Alice stands in no need of generosity: and I should fancy a set of North Country lairds could be very little superior to the society we have here, landless though we be."

"There are most gentlemanly and intellectual men in the North Country, James," said Mrs. Aytoun, quietly shifting her premises.

"No doubt of it, mother; but not better than we have in Edinburgh."

Mrs. Aytoun drew her hand over her daughter's fair curls, and made no answer; confessing to herself, that a North Country laird would be, in her eyes, a more suitable partner for her Alice, than any rising W.S., or poor advocate of all James Aytoun's friends.

Alice's trunks were standing, corded and ready. Little Bessie, the daughter of a woman who had been Mrs. Aytoun's nurse in better times, and who was her humble agent and assistant in all emergencies now, sat in the kitchen in all the glory of a new shawl and bonnet, a brevet ladies-maid; and it was nearly time to start. Mrs. Aytoun had yet to pack some small, forgotten tendernesses in a basket, with tremulous mother-anxiety, half-pleased, half-sorrowful, while James stood, watch in hand, warning her of the flight of those quick moments and of the possible starting of the coach before her cares were at an end.

At last, they left the house, established Alice in the cosiest corner, set little Bessie by her side, gave the guard all manner of instructions to attend to their comfort, and waited till the vehicle should start.

"Mind, Alice," whispered Mrs. Aytoun, anxiously; "always to call her Mrs. Catherine," and, in a moment more, Alice had lost sight of the compelled smile on her mother's pale face, and had started on her first journey from home.

She was seventeen only, and her heart was bounding high within her. The October morning was so bright and invigorating, the beautiful world so new and so unknown. A transitory qualm passed over the unclouded, youthful spirit, as she thought it not right, perhaps, to rejoice at leaving home, but that passed speedily. A temporary anxiety as to the unknown Mrs. Catherine, whom she was hastening to see: but that disappeared also. The brilliant dreams that had been rising by day and night, since that momentous invitation came, floated together in indistinct brightness before her. The red October sunbeams, the bracing October breeze, the beautiful landscapes on that northern road—though these danced but indistinctly in her eyes, a part of the exhilaration of spirit, yet scarcely things rejoiced in for their own beauty—filled up her gladness to overflowing. The little heart at her side danced too, in its degree, as blithely, for after the young lady herself, in the great house to which they journeyed, was not the young lady's maid next in dignity.

At one of the stages of the journey, a hypochondriac old gentleman, who had been the only other tenant of the coach, became faint, and declared himself unable to remain in the inside; whereupon, after some delay, an outside passenger was prevailed upon to exchange. A by no means unpleasant exchange, for the new comer was a young man of good looks, and frank, prepossessing manners, to whom the innocent, youthful face, with its blue eyes and fair curls might, or might not, have been an inducement to descend.

The beauty of the road became more articulate after that, as the polite stranger, apparently well-acquainted with the way, took care to point out to his young fellow-traveller its various points of interest, and imperceptibly, Alice scarce knew how, they glided into confidential conversation. For Strathoran, the stranger said, was his home and birth-place, whither he was returning after a long absence, and Mrs. Catherine Douglas was one of his oldest friends—he had known her all his life. So the hours went on, quick and pleasantly, and the long miles gradually dwindled down. Her new friend talked, Alice thought, as few could talk, and interspersed his comments on their present road so gracefully, with anecdotes of other roads, world-famed and wonderful, which she had read of often, but which he had seen.

He told her of her kinswoman, too, and of the Tower, and hinted how her own gentle presence would brighten the old walls and recall its youth again, till Alice, with all these magic influences about her, began to discover that this journey, instead of the weary means of reaching a wished-for destination, was in itself a young Elysium, unthought of, and delightful—the first homage rendered to the youthful woman, no longer a child: the first sign of her entrance into that fair world of more eventful life, whose air seemed now so golden with smiles and sunshine.

The dim lights of Portoran began to blink at last through the mists of the October night, and by and bye, the coach stopped at the door of the principal inn, in the main street. Already Alice could perceive various individual loungers without, touching their hats as they caught a glimpse of her companion, and while she herself began to wonder how she was to travel the remaining five or six miles to the Tower, the head of a tall and gaunt, elderly woman, dressed in stiff old-fashioned garments, looked in at the coach window.

"Is Miss Aytoun here?" said a harsh voice.

Alice answered timidly to her name.

"Quite safe; but very weary I am afraid," said the gentleman, "Mistress Elspat, you have forgotten me, I see. How are they all at the Tower?"

"Bless me, Mr. Lewis, is't you?" said the stately Mrs. Elspat Henderson, own woman to Mrs. Catherine Douglas, of the Tower. "Who would have thought of meeting you here? They're a' well, Sir. I left Miss Anne there even now; but the carriage is waiting for the young lady. The carriage is waiting, Miss Aytoun."

And, beginning to tremble, with a revulsion of all her simple apprehensions and timidity, Alice Aytoun was transferred to Mrs. Catherine's comfortable carriage, and leaving Lewis Ross at the inn door, looking after her, rolled away through the darkness to the Tower.

It was not a pleasant change; to leave the cheerful voice and vivacious conversation of Lewis, for those formal questions as to her journey, and the terrified stillness of little Bessie, as she sat tremulously by Mrs. Elspat's side. Alice had scarcely ever seen before the dense darkness of starless nights in so wide and lonely a country, as she looked out through the carriage window, and saw, or fancied she saw, the body of darkness floating round about her, the countless swimming atoms of gloom that filled the air, her bounding heart was chilled. The faint autumnal breeze, too, pouring its sweeping, sighing lengths, through those endless walls of trees; the excited throb of her pulse when in some gaunt congregation of firs, she fancied she could trace the quaint gables and high roof of some olden dwelling-place; the disappointment of hearing in answer to her timid question that the Tower was yet miles away! Alice sank back into her corner in silence, and closed her eyes, feeling now many fears and misgivings, and almost wishing herself at home.

At last the voice of the Oran roused her; there was something homelike in its tinkling musical footsteps, and Alice looked up.—Dimly the massy Tower was rising before her, planting its strong breadth firmly upon its knoll, like some stout sentinel of old. The great door was flung wide open as they approached, and a flood of light, and warmth, and kindliness beaming out, dazzled and made denser the intervening gloom. Foremost on the broad threshold, stood a young lady, whose graver and elder womanhood, brought confidence to the throbbing girlish heart; behind stood the portly Mrs. Euphan Morison—the elfin Jacky, and furthest back of all, a tall figure, enveloped in the wide soft folds of the gray shawl, Mrs. Catherine's characteristic costume. Little Alice alighted, half stumbling in bashful awkwardness, the young lady on the threshold came forward, took her hand, and said some kindly words of welcome. Jacky curtsied; the tall figure advanced.

"I have brought ye the young lady—Miss Aytoun, ma'am," said Mrs. Elspat Henderson, and Alice lifted her girlish face, shy and blushing, to the scrutiny of her ancient kinswoman. Mrs. Catherine drew the young stranger forward, took her hand, and looked at her earnestly.

"A right bonnie countenance it is," she said at last, bending to kiss the white forehead of the tremulous Alice. "You are welcome to my house, Alison Aytoun. Anne, the bairn is doubtless cold and wearied. Do you guide her up the stair."

Up the fine old staircase, into the inner drawing-room, which was Mrs. Catherine's especial sanctum, with its warm colors, and blazing fire, and shining tea equipage. Little Alice had to close her blue eyes perforce, dazzled as they were, that no one might see the happy dew that gathered in them. The contrast was so pleasant, and forthwith the bounding of that gay heart, and all its bright dreams and sunshiny anticipations came flushing back again.

"And so you had a pleasant journey," said Mrs. Catherine, kindly, when after half an hour which Alice had spent arranging her dress, half in awe, and more than half in pleasure, in the beautiful apartment called her dressing-room, they were seated at table—Anne Ross presiding over the massy silver tea-pot, and hissing urn: "and were not feared to travel your lane? Jacky, you elf! what call had you to open that door, and let in a draft upon us? The bairn will get her death of cold."

"If you please, Miss Anne," said Jacky, resolutely holding the door of the outer room open, as she kept her ground.

"Come in, ye fairy, and shut the door," commanded Mrs. Catherine.

The girl obeyed, casting long sharp glances from under her dark eye-brows at the wondering Alice.

"If you please, Miss Anne, my grandmother says—"

"What, Jacky?"

Jacky had paused to ascertain who it was that the young stranger was like, and muttered a private memorandum of her discovery before she went on.

"It's the little picture in the west room—my grandmother says, Miss Anne, that Mr. Lewis—but she bade me say, Merkland—"

"What of him, Jacky?" said Anne, rising hastily.

"If ye please, Miss Anne, he came to Portoran in the coach with a young lady to-night."

"Came to Portoran to-night!" repeated Anne, "then you must let me leave you immediately, Mrs. Catherine. I must hasten to tell my mother, if indeed Lewis is not at home already."

"Away with you down the stairs, you elf," cried Mrs. Catherine, "and see if the horses are put up yet; and if they're not, let Simon be ready to drive Miss Ross to Merkland. Anne, doubtless you must go, but mind the bairn Alison is not used to such company as a staid auld wife like me, and be soon back again."

"I will bring Lewis to see you to-morrow, Mrs. Catherine," said Anne, as she hastily bade Alice good night.

"It must have been your brother who travelled with me, Miss Ross," said Alice. "He said he had been abroad, and knew Mrs. Catherine—and he was very kind. Will you thank him for me?"

Anne Ross felt herself shrink and tremble from the touch of the small soft hand, the innocent frank look of the girlish face—the child of the slain man, whose blood was on Norman's hand.

A strange contrast—the little throbbing happy heart, whose slight fears, and shy apprehensions, scarcely graver than a child's, had trembled and palpitated so short a time before, in the same vehicle which carried down to Merkland, so grave a burden of grief, so few hopes, so many sorrows, in Anne's maturer spirit—for before her there lay no brilliant heritage of unknown good to come. One vision was in her very heart continually—a wandering, sorrowing, sinning man, buffeting the wind, striving through the tempest, enveloped with every physical attribute of misery, and carrying its essence in his soul. It is only those who have mourned and yearned for such, who can know how the sick heart, in its anxious agonies, conjures up storm, and blast, and desolation, to sweep around the beloved head, of whose sin and wanderings it knows, yet knows not where those wanderings are—the pain without, symbolizing and heightening the darker pain within, with one of those touches of tragic art, which grief does so strangely excel in.

Lewis had not arrived when Anne reached Merkland, but he came shortly after; and the stir of joy incident on his arrival united the family more closely together than was usual for them. Mrs. Ross's cold bright eyes were wet with tears of joy that night, and her worldly spirit melted into kindliness; and the presence of Lewis gave his only sister a greater share in the household and its rejoicings. He stood between her step-mother and her, the nearest relation of each, linking them together. Lewis had been two years away. He had gone, a fairhaired youth, with a gay party from Strathoran, who, seizing the first opportunity of restored peace, set out to those sunny continental countries from which mere tourists had been excluded so long. He was a man now, bronzed and bearded, and with the independent manners of one who had been accustomed in all matters to guide and direct himself. There were various particulars of that same independence which jarred upon Anne's delicate feelings. A considerable remainder of boyish self-importance, and braggadocio—a slight loudness of tone, and flippancy of expression; but there was the excitement of his home-coming, to excuse these faults in some degree.

"And the Duncombes, Lewis," asked Mrs. Ross, when the first burst of welcome was over, and they were seated by the fireside, discussing his journey—"where are they now?"

"Oh, Duncombe's in Gibraltar," said Lewis, "with his regiment of course. Duncombe can't afford to choose his residence—he must have his full pay. A dull life they have of it, yonder."

"And how does Isabel Sutherland like that, Lewis?" said Anne.

"Isabel Sutherland? Mrs. Duncombe, do you mean? Why you don't think she's one of the garrison! She's not such a fool, I can tell you!"

"Where is she then, if she is not with her husband?" said Anne, wonderingly.

"What an innocent you are, sister Anne!" said Lewis, laughing. "Why, she's one of the 'unattached,' as Gordon says. I left her in Paris with Archie. You have no idea what a moody, gloomy fellow Duncombe's grown. I should think he was enough to frighten anybody!"

"He was always a bilious-looking man," said Mrs. Ross; "and yet Isabel ran away with him."

"Ah! there's no accounting for the taste of young ladies," said Lewis, lightly. "I should think she would be more likely to run away from him, than with him, now. But you should see their menage in Paris! Archie's the man for all that."

"How do you mean, Lewis?" said Anne.

"You used to like him—eh, Annie?" said Lewis. "Don't break your heart—it's all up with that now. But, I can tell you, he makes the money fly finely."

Anne's face flushed deeply—perhaps with the faintest shadow of pain at that intelligence, more than did merely belong to her regret for the folly of an old neighbor and early companion—but certainly with a painful feeling of the levity and carelessness of Lewis.

"Well, Lewis," said Mrs. Ross; "I should think Archibald Sutherland could afford it pretty well. The old people must have saved a great deal, they lived so quietly. Strathoran is a good estate. Archie does not need to be so frugal as you."

"Frugal!" echoed her son. "I wish you only saw. But, unless you did, with your quiet Scotch notions, you could have no idea of it. If Archie Sutherland is not poorer than we are, I'm mistaken."

"Oh!" said Mrs. Ross; "that will be the reason they are thinning the woods. Then why don't they come home and economize?"

"Come home!" cried Lewis. "Home to this dull Strathoran after Paris! It's not such an easy thing, I can tell you, mother. But, to be sure, one never knows the true reason. I've heard Archie often wishing for home—perhaps he is afraid of falling in love with Anne."

"At all events, Lewis," said Anne, gravely, "whatever Archie Sutherland fears, you are not afraid of giving me pain."

"Don't be absurd, Anne," said Mrs. Ross. "The poor boy's first night at home, to begin with these airs of yours!"

Lewis saw the painful flush upon Anne's face—the look of deep humiliation with which she turned away her head, and his heart smote him.

"I did not think you were so easily hurt. Nonsense, Anne! It was mere thoughtlessness, I assure you. I would not give you pain for anything."

Alas! there were many things for which Lewis Ross would have been content to pain any one in the world. But Anne was easily mollified, and he ran on:

"I met a little fairy of a girl in the coach, to-day. She was going to the Tower, to visit Mrs. Catherine. Hallo! what's the matter, Anne?"

"Nothing," said Anne, forcing a smile on the lip which she had felt quiver a moment before.

"How pale you were!" said Lewis. "I thought you were ill. I must go up to see Mrs. Catherine to-morrow. How does she wear, the old lady? She must be getting very ancient now. But that girl is a pretty little thing. Who can she be—do you know, Anne? I thought of her being a companion, or something of that kind; but there was a little maid with her."

"A relative of Mrs. Catherine's," said Anne, faintly.

"A relative—oh! What if she cuts you out!" said Lewis.—"I should have thought you sure of a good place in Mrs. Catherine's will, Anne. But there is no saying what a little fairy like that may do."

Anne Ross felt the pang of dependence bitterly that night. Lewis was too like his mother to make it light to her; and portionless, with her plain face, and fastidious taste, what could she ever look for but dependence. Marriage, that necessity, often enough an unhappy one, to which so many young women in her position must look, as to a profession, for home and means, could never be a matter of mercenary convenience to Anne, and honorable earning of her own bread was an impossibility. And from her own sombre prospects she could turn for relief to so few of the things or people around. Lewis, so carelessly unfeeling and indifferent, so blunted in perception—Norman, whose very life was so great a dread to her, remaining before her mind's eye for ever—and even the sunny, youthful face at the Tower, which had lifted its blue eyes so trustfully to her own—why did its remembrance, and Lewis's light words of comment on its girlish comeliness, strike so deep a chill of fear into her heart? Ah! clouds deeply gathering, heavily brooding over this nook of still and peaceful country, what new combinations were your dark mists to form?

Alice Aytoun by this time was snugly settled in the Tower, and had already written a little note, overflowing with innocent pride and joyousness to her mother at home, describing that most cheerful of all inner drawing-rooms, and dwelling fully upon the glories of her own apartments, the carved wardrobe, the old piano, the beautiful flowers; mentioning, too, in the postscript, in the very slightest manner, a "young gentleman," who had pointed out all the places to her on the way, and who turned out to be Miss Ross's brother, though who Miss Ross was, Alice did not stay to particularize. And after the letter was written, Mrs. Catherine, whose eyes had been lingering on the youthful face with most genial kindliness, began to play with her in talk, half childish, and wholly affectionate, as with some toy of unknown construction, whose capabilities she did not yet quite see. Jacky, too, with those quick, sidelong glances, as she went jerking in and out at every possible opportunity, had commenced her study of the young stranger's character, and quickened by admiration of the simple pretty face, was advancing in her study as quickly as her mistress. The minds of the stately old lady and the elfin girl came to conclusions strangely similar. There rose in them both an instinctive impulse of kindly protection, natural enough in Alice Aytoun's aged kinswoman, but contrasting oddly with the age and position of Jacky Morison.

Anne and Lewis visited the Tower next day. In the Sutherlands, of whom Lewis brought tidings so unfavorable, Mrs. Catherine was deeply interested, and listened while he spoke of them, with many shakings of her head, and doubts and fears.

"Trysted to evil," she exclaimed, as Lewis told her in his careless way, of Mrs. Duncombe's Paris life. "Did I not say nothing good could come of the bairn that left the sick bed of her mother, for the sake of a strange man; ay, and made the sick-bed—a death-bed by the deed. Lewis, is't the lad's fault, think you, or is't hers?"

"Oh, I don't know that there is much fault in it," said Lewis. "It's not a formal separation, you know; only Isabel's living with her brother, because it is, beyond dispute, pleasanter to live in Paris than in Gibraltar. You don't know really—you can have no idea."

"Think you so?" said Mrs. Catherine, quickly, "but maybe there are folk living who knew such places and things, before you were born! Why does Isabel Sutherland not return to the house of her fathers, if she cannot dwell with the man she left father and mother for?"

"There is no accounting for these things," said Lewis, with a slight sneer.

"Lewis Ross," said Mrs. Catherine, "hold your peace; you are but a boy, and should leave that to your elders. Anne, I am sore grieved for Archie Sutherland; if evil comes to the lad, it will be as hard to me, as if evil were coming upon you."

CHAPTER III

During the following week there were great preparations and much bustle in Merkland, for Lewis's birthday was to be celebrated with unwonted festivities, and all Mrs. Ross's energies were aroused to make an appearance worthy the occasion. All the Lairds' families round about had received invitations to the solemn dinner-party, at which Lewis Ross was, for the first time, to take his father's place. There was to be a dinner, too, in the Sutherland Arms, at Portoran, of the not very extensive tenantry of Merkland, at which the landlord and his underlings laughed in their sleeves, contrasting it secretly with the larger festivities which had hailed the majority of the youthful Sutherland of Strathoran, whose continued absence from his own home, gave occasion for so many surmisings. But yet, on a small scale, as they were, these same Merkland festivities were a matter of some moment in the quiet country-side. Alice Aytoun's gay heart leaped breathlessly at the thought of them, and many anxious cogitations had risen under her fair curls, touching that pretty gown of light silk, which was her only gala dress. Whether it was good enough to shine in that assemblage of rural aristocracy, and how it would look beside the beautiful robes which, Bessie reported, the Misses Coulter, of Harrows, had ordered from Edinburgh for the occasion. Alice had serious doubts—her only consolation under which was Bessie's genuine admiration; and thought within herself, with a sigh, that if she had to go to many parties, the same dress would not do always, and her mother, at home, could not afford to order beautiful robes for her, as Mrs. Coulter could; however, that was still in the future, and but a dim prospective evil.

Lewis Ross, in those busy days, had many errands to the Tower, and on his fine horse, looked, as Alice thought, the very impersonation of youthful strength, and courage, and gay spirits. And Merkland was a pretty house, with its deep bordering of woods, and its quiet home-landscape, of cultivated fields and scattered farm-houses. Alice almost thought she preferred its tamer beauty, to the wide expanse of hills and valleys, of wandering river, and broad sea, upon which she looked out, from the deepest window of her chamber in the eastern tower.

All the parish was stirred to welcome Lewis, and other parishes surrounding Strathoran, added the pressure of their kindliness. He was in the greatest request everywhere. From gay Falcon's Craig to the sober Manse, from drowsy Smoothlie to the bustling homestead of Mr. Coulter, of Harrows, everybody delighted to honor the youthful heir of Merkland. Lewis did all that goodwill and good horsemanship could do, to renew his acquaintance with them all. He gallopped to Falcon's Craig, and spent a gay night with the bold Falconers. He met Ralph by appointment next day, to follow the hounds. He made a visit to Smoothlie, and curbed his horse into compulsory conformity to the sober paces of Mr. Ambler's respectable pony, as that easy, quiet old gentleman, who was conjoined with Mrs. Ross in the guardianship of her son, accompanied him to Merkland. And Lewis inspected the stock at Harrows, and dropped in at the Manse, to chat awhile with Mrs. Bairn's father; yet, with all these labors on his hand, did yet insist, in the excess of his brotherly solicitude, on accompanying his reluctant sister Anne to the Tower, the day before he became of age.

Mrs. Catherine sat in her library, that day, in grave deliberation—with young Walter Foreman, and Mr. Ferguson, the Strathoran factor, again beside her. The table was strewed with papers, and the two gentlemen were pressing something to which she objected, upon the firm old lady.

"The siller is mine," she said, "be it so. The man (I will say no ill of him, seeing he was a kinsman of my own, but that he was a fool, which is in no manner uncommon) is dead, and his will can have no more changes; frail folk as we are, that can never be counted on for our steadfastness, till we are in our graves! But allowing that the siller is my own—is it a lawful purpose, I ask of you, Mr. Ferguson, to build up with it, the foolish pleasures of a prodigal—alack, that I should call his mother's son so! while I may have other righteous errands to send it forth upon?"

"It is to build up the old house of Strathoran. It is to save your friend's son," said the factor, with an appealing motion of his hand.

Mrs. Catherine was moved, and did not answer for a moment.

"The lad was left well in this world's goods," she said, at last. "A fairer course was never before mortal man. An honorable name, a good inheritance, the house of his fathers over his head, and a country-side looking up to him. What could he seek more, I ask you, Mr. Ferguson? And where is the lad? Revelling in yon land of playactors, and flunkies, and knicknackets: consorting with a herd of buzzing things, that were worms yesterday, and will be nothing in the morn. Speak not to me; I have seen suchlike with my own eyes. He must have his feasts, and his flatterers, forsooth! and the good land, that God gave him, eaten up for it. Bonnie-dyes, and paintings, and statues said he? And if it were even so (and the youth, Lewis Ross, says otherwise,) should he take the poor man's lamb for that, think ye?—the farmer's honest gains, that he toils for, with the care of his mind, and the sweat of his brow?"

The lawyer and the factor exchanged glances.

"I beg you to do us justice, Mrs. Catherine," said Mr. Ferguson, deprecatingly: "that was done in no case but in Mr. Ewing's; and the land is really worth considerably more now than when he got his former lease."

"And whose praise is that?" said Mrs. Catherine, sharply. "Not the laird's, who never put a finger to the land. Do you not know well yourself, Robert Ferguson, that Andrew Ewing's lease had but four years to run, when by the good hand of Providence, giving him a discreet wife, with siller, he was set on improving the land? Has he not spent his profits twice told upon it? And, before he has time to reap a just harvest, the prodigal must come in, to take a tithe off the gains of the honest man. I take ye to witness, that the welfare of the lad, Archie Sutherland, Isabel Balfour's son, lies near my own heart, but I cannot shut my eyes to this evil."

"It was done in no other case," repeated Mr. Ferguson.

"Was there any other lease out," retorted Mrs. Catherine, "that the hunger of siller could have its aliment on? You are a discreet man, Mr. Ferguson, and you, Walter Foreman, with your business-breeding, should have some notion of the value of siller. Is it not a deep sea that ye are asking me to throw this portion into? A hungry mouth that, the more ye fill it, will but gape and gaunt the more? So far as the siller is mine, have I not gotten it to use it well, as my light goes?—to succour the widow and fatherless, maybe—not to pamper the unnatural wants of a waster and a prodigal?"

"Mrs. Catherine," said the factor, "hear me speak before you make this decision. I do not, by any means, defend Strathoran. I have taken it upon me, indeed, both to warn and to entreat him to give up this ruinous—I will not say criminal course, he is embarked on: and I have received from him, in return, letters that would melt your heart. Why he persists in what he acknowledges to be wrong, I cannot tell; and I do not defend him. He has got into the vortex, I suppose, and cannot extricate himself. But his father built up my fortunes, Mrs. Catherine, and so long as anything can be done, I will not forsake his son. This seasonable relief may save him: without this, his affairs are hopelessly entangled, and Strathoran must cease to be the home of the Sutherlands."

Mrs. Catherine leaned her head upon her hand, and did not speak. At length, looking up, she saw, through the opposite window, Anne Ross and Lewis coming up the waterside, to the Tower.

"You will leave me a time, for further thought," she said, slowly. "Put the papers out of yon keen gallant's sight, or go into another room. You will hear tidings of your prodigal from Lewis, Mr. Ferguson; and doubtless you know him well enough, Walter, being birds of a feather. Euphan Morison, send lunch for the gentlemen into the dining-parlor, and tell Miss Ross I am waiting for her, in the little room."

So speaking, Mrs. Catherine rose and left the library, her face shadowed with deeper gravity than was its wont—her step slow and heavy, and proceeded through many winding passages, to a locked door, in the furthest angle of the western wing. She opened it with a key which hung from her neck, and entered a small apartment furnished with the most meagre simplicity. It contained but two chairs and a small table, and from the deep diamond-paned window, you could only see the steep side of a hill, rough with whins and crags, which sprang sheer upward from the back of the Tower. Upon the wall hung a fine portrait—a noble, thoughtful, manly face, resembling Mrs. Catherine's except in so far as its flush of strong manhood was different from the aspect of her declining years. It was her brother, whose untimely death had cast its heavy shadow over her own womanly maturity; and the room was Mrs. Catherine's especial retirement, whither she was wont to come in her seasons of most solemn and secret prayerfulness, or at some crisis when her deliberations were grave enough to require the entire attention of her whole earnest mind. Upon the table lay a large Bible—other furniture or adornments there were none. In elder days, when the Douglases of the Tower professed the faith of Rome, it might have been called the lady's oratory; in these plainer times it was only "the little room;" yet was surrounded with the awe, which must always environ the strugglings of a strong spirit, however faintly known to the weaker multitude around. Mrs. Catherine paced up and down its narrow limits, moved in her spirit, and expressing often her strong emotion aloud.

"Isabel Balfour," she murmured to herself, stopping as she passed, to turn upon the picture a look of deep and sorrowful affection. "Ay, Sholto, it is her bairn, her firstborn, the son of her right hand. If ye were here, Sholto Douglas, where you should have been, but for God's pleasure, what would you spare for Isabel's son, that should have been yours also, and a Douglas? I envied you your bride and your bairns, Strathoran, for his sake that I left lying in foreign earth, and now your home is left to you desolate—woe's me! woe's me!"

Mrs. Catherine turned away and paced the room again, with quick and uneasy steps: "Unrighteous? I know it is unrighteous; but if he had been Sholto's son, what would I not have done for him, short of sin? and he is Isabel's—"

A footstep approached, through the passage, as she spoke, and controlling herself instantly, Mrs. Catherine opened the door to admit Anne Ross.

"What is the matter?" exclaimed Anne, as she entered. "What has happened, Mrs. Catherine, that you are here?"

"Nothing, but that I am in a sore strait, and am needing counsel," said Mrs. Catherine, closing the door; "sit down upon that seat, child, that I may speak to you."

Anne silently took the chair, and Mrs. Catherine seated herself at the other side of the small table, with her dead brother's picture looking down upon her from the wall.

"Anne," she said, gravely, "you have heard the history of Sholto Douglas, and I need not begin and tell it here again. Look upon him there, in the picture, and see what manner of man he was. And you have heard of Isabel Balfour, the trysted bride of the dead, and how, when he had been in his grave but two twelvemonths, she was wedded to Strathoran. I blamed her not, Anne, though I myself was truer to the memory of my one brother; but wherefore am I speaking thus? There are two lads, Anne, to whom I may do service. One is, as I have heard, an honorable and upright young man, born to better fortune than he has inherited, and toiling manfully, as becomes the son of a good house; besides that, there is a kindred of blood between us. And the other is a rioter, wasting his substance, and dishonoring his name in a strange country. I am in a strait between, the two, which will I help, and which will I pass by?"

"Mrs. Catherine," said Anne, anxiously, "what can I say? I fear that I can see whom you mean; but how can I advise?"

"The well-doing lad is James Aytoun, the brother of the bairn Alice," said Mrs. Catherine, "who is working an honorable and just work to win back the inheritance of his fathers. The rioter is Isabel Balfour's one son—that might have been your first-born, Sholto Douglas! and I am in a sore struggle between my reason and my liking. The boy has gotten in to my inmost heart, as if he had been truly Sholto's son, and I cannot see him fall."

There was a long silence—for many motives deterred Anne from attempting, what at any time she would have done with reluctance, to offer counsel to the clear and mature judgment of Mrs. Catherine; and she rightly judged that her ancient friend had all the strength of secretly-formed resolution to combat the scruples which Anne could not help sympathizing with, though in her also, so many kindly feelings pleaded for Archibald Sutherland—a prodigal, indeed, but still the frank and joyous comrade of her childish days, the "young Strathoran" of her native district.

At last, Mrs. Catherine rose.

"It must be done," she exclaimed. "Bear me witness, Anne, that I do it against my judgment. I take the siller to feed the false wants of the waster, that should help the honorable man in his travail. I do it, knowing it is ill, but I cannot see the lad a ruined man. Let us away. I will blind myself with no more false reasonings; the thing is wrong, but we must do it—come!"

Anne followed without speaking. Mrs. Catherine locked the door, and, leaning on her heavily, led her up stairs. Alice Aytoun was in the drawing-room; Mrs. Catherine sent Anne thither, and went herself to seek for something in her own room. She had intended offering substantial help to James Aytoun, and now, when the warmth of her feelings for Archibald Sutherland baulked her benevolent intent, she turned with an involuntary impulse to make some atonement to Alice.

It had been a very dull morning for Alice—Mrs. Catherine was unusually grave at breakfast, and since breakfast Alice had been alone—then she saw Lewis and Anne walking arm-in-arm up Oranside to the Tower, and for a long half-hour had waited and wondered in tantalising loneliness, vainly expecting that they would join her, or she be summoned to them. But they did not come, and Alice, wearied and disappointed, was venting some girlish impatience on the piano, and indulging in a sort of fretful wish for home—quiet, affectionate home, where such slight neglects and forgetfulness never could take place—but, while the thought was being formed, Anne stood beside her.

"Oh! Miss Ross," exclaimed Alice, "I thought you were never coming," and through the fair curls the slightest side-glance was thrown to the closed door, which testified that Anne now came alone. "I saw you coming up by the water, and I have waited so long."

"Mrs. Catherine had some business with me," said Anne: "and Lewis, I think, is detained below with other visitors. And what do you think of our Strathoran now, Miss Aytoun?"

"Oh! a great deal," said Alice; "only I have not seen Strathoran itself—Mr. Sutherland's house—yet. I am to go to Falcon's Craig, Mrs. Catherine says, after to-morrow. Miss Falconer was here yesterday—riding."

"And you liked her, did you not?" said Anne, smiling.

Alice looked dubious.

"Yes, very well. But is she not more like a gentleman than a lady, Miss Ross?"

"Tell her so yourself to-morrow," said Anne, "and she will think you pay her a high compliment."

Alice shook her head.

"I should not mean it for that, Miss Ross; but Mrs. Catherine said you would perhaps go with me to Falcon's Craig. Will you? I should be half afraid if I went alone."

"Feared for Marjory Falconer!" said Mrs. Catherine, entering the room. "If once she knew her own spirit, it is not an ill one; and I see not wherefore she should scare folk. I know well you are not feared, Anne. See, bairns, here are some bonnie dyes to look at, while I am away. Ye are to wear them the morn's night, Alison Aytoun, according to your pleasure. They belong to yourself. And see you go not away, Anne, till I come back again. I will send Lewis up to hold you in mirth. For myself, I have things to make me up, other than mirthful."

Alice advanced timidly to the table as Mrs. Catherine left the room. What might be within that mysterious enclosure of morocco? Anne smilingly anticipated her. Rich ornaments of pearls, more beautiful than any thing the simple, girlish eyes had ever looked upon before. Alice did not know how to look, or what to say; only her heart made one great leap of delight—all these were her own! How pleased and proud, not for the gift alone, but for the kindness that gave it, would be the mother's heart at home!

Mrs. Catherine descended slowly, and, resuming her seat in the library, called the young lawyer and the factor to her presence, and dismissed Lewis to the pleasanter company up stairs. Mr. Ferguson, one of those acute, sagacious, well-informed men, who are to be met with so frequently in the middle class of rural Scotland, came with looks of anxious expectation, and Walter Foreman, of whom his independent client did not deign to ask counsel, took his place again, with secret pique, fancying himself at least as good an adviser as the plain and quiet stepdaughter of Mrs. Ross, of Merkland.

"Mr. Ferguson," said Mrs. Catherine, "I have made up my mind. You shall have the siller. Thank me not. I do that which I know is wrong, and which I would have done for no mortal but Isabel Balfour's son. You can get the papers made out at your convenience, and tell me the name of his dwelling. I will write to the ill-doer myself."

"Oh!" exclaimed Mr. Ferguson, eagerly, "I beg you will not give yourself so much trouble, Mrs. Catherine. I will myself write to Strathoran immediately, and tell him of your kindness."

"Doubtless," said Mrs. Catherine: "but wherefore should I not have my word of exhortation, as well as another? Write me down Archie Sutherland's address. I could get it from Lewis Ross, but I do not choose that; and let the siller be paid to Mr. Ferguson, Walter Foreman—that is, when the papers are ready— for mind that I do not give this siller, I only lend it."

"On the lands of Lochend and Loelyin," said Mr. Ferguson. "Of course, Mrs. Catherine."

A slight smile of triumph hovered about the factor's mouth.—Mrs. Catherine perceived it.

"On which I will have the annual rent paid to a day," she said, with some sternness, "as if I were the coldest stranger that ever heard of Archie Sutherland's needs or ill-doings, and, I trow, that is a wide word. If I had not purposed so, I might have given him the siller, for what is it to a woman of years like me? Truly, my own spirit bears me witness, that I would give that threefold, if it were mine to give, with a light heart, to restore the prodigal to the house of his fathers, as innocent as he went away. Let the business be done, Walter Foreman; doubtless, you will be taken up with the ploy to-morrow, and will be putting it off till after that."

"We can get it done immediately," said Walter, somewhat sullenly.

"What ails you, sir?" said Mrs. Catherine. "Should I have taken counsel with you on the secrets of my own spirit, think you?—I that am given to take counsel of no man. Be content, Walter Foreman—you are not an ill gallant, but have overmuch favor for your own wisdom, as is common at your years. If you live to count threescore, you will be an humbler man."

"Our success is a most fortunate thing for Strathoran," said Mr. Ferguson, as they left the Tower. "But the letter—I would not receive such a letter as Mrs. Catherine will write, on such a subject, for the half of his estate."

Walter Foreman shrugged his shoulders.

"And yet she has the greatest regard for him. Mrs. Sutherland was betrothed to Mrs. Catherine's brother, when he died, people say; and it is her strange adoration of his memory that makes her so fond of young Strathoran. A singular consequent, one would think."

"Mrs. Catherine is altogether singular," said Mr. Ferguson, "and not to be judged as people of the world are."

And when the night was far spent, and Alice had carried her bounding heart, and her new possessions, into her own bright apartment, and was electrifying little Bessie there, with a glimpse of the wonderous beauty of those pearls, and trying them on before the mirror on the walls, and listening with bursts of gay laughter to Bessie's guesses of their value—sums immense and fabulous to the simplicity of both, yet, nevertheless, in truth, not greatly exceeding their true worth—Mrs. Catherine sat in the library alone, writing her letter, her strong features swept by deep emotion often, and her steady hand shaken. The course which the young man was pursuing, was in every way the most repulsive to her feelings. Sin it appeared in the eyes of her strong, unswerving, pure religion—dishonor to her nice sense of uprightness and independence. His foreign residence and likings shocked her warm, home-affections, her entire nationality, and the possible alienation of his lands from the name and family in whose possession they had been so long, alarmed alike fear and prejudice; for Mrs. Catherine, boasting her own pure descent from the "dark-grey man," was no enemy to the law of entail. His sister, too, and her separation from the husband for whom she had left her mother's sick-bed—all these things poured in upon Mrs. Catherine's mind, increasing her agitation, and hallowed, as all her fears were, by that strange visionary tenderness, so thoroughly in unison with her strong character, despite its romance, which clung around those who might have been the children of that dearest brother Sholto, whose mortality, so much as remained of it, lay treasured in yon lone burying-ground in far Madeira, upon whose sunny shore he died.

"Archibald Sutherland," wrote Mrs. Catherine, "I have been hearing tidings of you, which have carried a sword into my inmost heart; and though I might well write in anger, seeing that though I am not of your kin, you were in my arms a helpless bairn, before you were in the arms of any mortal—it is in grief rather that I speak to you. Wherefore is there neither firelight nor candlelight in the house of Strathoran? Is the home of your fathers not good enough for a son that puts in jeopardy their good fame? Is the roof that sheltered Isabel Balfour in her bridal days, too mean for Isabel Sutherland? or wherefore is it, that with your fair lands and good possessions you are dwelling in a strange and ungodly country? Father and mother you have none to warn you. Answer to me, Archie Sutherland, who have known you all your days, wherefore it should be so. Think you that among the flattering fools that are about you, there is one that would lose a night's sleep, if Strathoran and all belonging to it, were swept into the sea? Come back to your own dwelling-place: witless and prodigal as you have been, there is not a hind in the parish but would lament over the desolate house of your fathers. Think you that it is a small thing, the leal liking and respect of a whole countryside, come down to you as a heritage? or is it your will to give up that for the antics of a papistical and alien race? I say to you, come back to your own house, Archie Sutherland. There is neither healthfulness nor safety—let alone good fame and godliness, a man's best plenishing for this world and the next—in the course you are running now.

"Think not that I write this because I have served you with siller. Over the son of Isabel Balfour, the sister of Sholto Douglas has a right of succor and counsel, warning and reproof. Boy! if you had been my own—if in God's good pleasure you had borne the name of my own brother—the dearest name upon this earth to me—what is there that you might not have claimed at my hands? What is there now, that would be for your own good, that I would hesitate to do?—but far be it from me, who mind your mother's travail for the new birth in you, the which in all mortal seeming has not yet been granted to her prayers—to prop up your goings in a way of ill-doing. Of what good is it to the world, I ask you, Archie Sutherland, that you have been made upon it, a living man with a mind within you, and a heaven over you? Who is the better for the light that God has put into your earthen vessel? A crowd of dancing, singing fools, that know not either the right honor, or the grave errand of a man into this world. Shame upon you, the son of a stalwart and good house, to be wasting in bairnly diversion, the days you will never see again, till you meet them before the Throne. Listen to me, Archie Sutherland—return to your own house, and to such a manner of life as becomes an honorable and upright man, and I give you my word—the worth of which, you may be known—that for disentangling you from the unhealthful meshes of borrowed siller, the means shall not be to seek.

"Unto your sister Isabel, I have ever been a prophet of evil; nevertheless, she bears the name, and, in a measure, the countenance, of Sholto's Isabel and mine. If she will not return to the lawful shelter and rule of her own house, let her come to Strathoran, or, if it likes her, to the Tower. Do you think, or does she think, that the very winged things that are about you, their own sillie selves, honor the wife for disregarding her natural right? The bond was of her own tieing; she liked him better than father and mother once—does she like him less now than she likes ill-fame, and slight esteem? If it is so, let her come home to me, her mother's earliest and oldest friend. Bairns!—bairns! there is more to provide for than the pleasure of the quick hours that are speeding over ye. Purity before God, honor in the sight of men: are your spirits blinded within ye, that you cannot perceive the two?

CATHERINE DOUGLAS."

CHAPTER IV

The festive morning dawned at last, a vigorous, red October day, and all about and around Merkland was bustle and preparation.

"Duncan," cried Bell the cook, her face looming, already red and full, through a mist; "when was that weary man, Bob Partan, to send up the turbot?"

"Punctual at eleven," said the laconic Duncan.

"Eh! man, Duncan," said May, "have ye tried on your new livery yet?—isn't it grand?"

"Hout, you silly fool," responded Duncan, "has the like o' me leisure, think you, to be minding about coats and breeks?"

"Eh!" exclaimed Bell, "what has possessed me! There's no clove in a' the house and they need to be in—I kenna how mony things. You maun off to Portoran, Duncan, gallopping; there's not a minute to be lost."

"Duncan," cried Johnnie Halflin, the boy at the Tower, who, with sundry other articles, had been lent for the occasion, "I've casten doun a jar o' the Smoothlie honey, and it's broken twa o' the bottles. Man, come afore the leddy sees't."

"Duncan," said Barbara Genty, Mrs. Ross's own especial attendant. "You are to go up to the parlor, this minute. You were sent for half an hour ago."

"Conscience!" exclaimed the overwhelmed Duncan, "is there two of us, that ye are rugging and riving at a man in that gate? Get out o' my road, ye young sinner, or there shall be mair things broken than bottles! I'm coming, Bauby. Woman Bell, could ye no hae minded a'thing at once?"

Above stairs, Mr. Lewis's servant, who had left Merkland a loutish lad, and returned glistening in Parisian polish and refinement, a superfine gentleman, was condescendingly advising with Mrs. Ross, as to the garniture of the dinner-table. Things were so arranged in the Hotel de ——, John said; for Monsieur Charles, Mr. Sutherland's major-domo, had a style of his own. But for the country, John fancied this would do very well. Mrs. Ross had dismissed Anne, an hour before, to her own room, as useless; and half-offended with the airs of her son's dignified servant, was yet not above hearing the style of the Hotel de ——, and in some degree making it her model, certain that Parisian fashion had not penetrated to any other house in the district, and well-pleased to take the lead. For the gay parties at Falcon's Craig, and the stately festivities at the Tower, had an individuality about them which had always been wanting in Merkland, and Mrs. Ross had resolved to outshine all to-day.

Anne, meanwhile, sat up stairs, busied with her ordinary work. She was the seamstress of the family, and the post was not by any means a sinecure.

The guests began to arrive, at last. Mr. Ambler, of Smoothlie, emerged from his dressing-room, neat as elderly, finical gentleman could be, with his carefully arranged dress, and wig, savoring of olden times. Mr. Ambler had been in India once, and alluded to the fact on all occasions; albeit, an indulged only son, with the snug enough of his lairdship to fall back upon, he had returned in the same vessel which took him out. But though Mr. Ambler was too fond of slippered ease to try his fortune under the burning sun of the East, his voyage supplied him with an inexhaustible fund of conversation, innocently self-complacent, in which India and its wonders had a place all incompatible with his brief experience of them.

Dashing in, full gallop, came the Falconers—the gay, bold brother and sister, fatherless and motherless, and entirely unrestrained in any way, whose wild freaks afforded so much material for gossip to the countryside. Then in a methodical, business-like trot, came in the sleek horses and respectable vehicle of Mr. Coulter, of Harrows; the Manse gig; the stately carriage of Mrs. Catherine, and other conveyances, whose occupants we need not specify by name. The room was filled. Alice Aytoun had never in her life been at so great a party.

She could distinguish on yonder sofa, in the corner, Mrs. Bairnsfather's black satin gown, side by side with the strong thrifty hued silk of Mrs. Coulter, of Harrows. The Misses Coulter, in their Edinburgh robes, were near their mamma. They were very well-looking, well-dressed girls; but Alice's own silk gown bore a comparison with theirs, and their ornaments were nothing like those delicate pearls. The discovery emboldened little Alice Aytoun, and took away her sole existing heaviness. She was fully prepared to enjoy herself.

The stately dinner, and all its solemnities, were over at last. The real pleasure of the evening was commencing; the company forming into gay knots; and Lewis doing the honors, with so rare a grace, that his mother almost forgot her own duties in admiration of her son. Alice Aytoun admired him, too.

The pretty little stranger had become a sort of centre already, with the gayest and most attractive of all those varied groups, about her—and Lewis let no opportunity pass of offering his homage. Even on Mrs. Catherine's strong features, as she sat near her charge, there hovered a mirthful smile. Mrs. Catherine herself was not displeased that the debut of her little stranger should be so much a triumph.

"A pretty girl—there is no doubt of that," said the good-humored Mrs. Coulter. "James, do you not think she is like our Ada? See, the heads of the two are together, and Jeanie is behind them, with young Walter Foreman. I declare that lad is constantly hovering about Jeanie. Ah, Mrs. Bairnsfather, we have many cares who have a family!"

"No doubt," said the little, fat, round-about Mrs. Bairnsfather, the childless minister's wife, whose cares, diverted from the usual channel of children-loving, expended themselves upon the many comforts of herself, and her easy, comfortable husband. "You must be troubled in various ways now that the young people have got to man's estate, and woman's. But what were you calling Miss Adamina, Mrs. Coulter? I noticed a change in the name."

Mrs. Coulter looked slightly confused.

"You see, Mrs. Bairnsfather, it is a cumbrous name—four syllables—and we must have some contraction. When they were all bairns, they used to call her Edie, poor thing; but that would not do now; and at school she got Ada, and it really is a prettier name, and quite a good diminutive: so we just adopted it."

"Dear me! is that it?" said Mrs. Bairnsfather. "When I got the last note from Harrows I saw it was 'A. M. Coulter.' And that's it!"

"Yes," said Mrs. Coulter. "Ada Mina—they are two very pretty names."

Mrs. Bairnsfather coughed a short sarcastic cough of wonder, and Mrs. Coulter continued:

"Oh! there is John beside little Miss Aytoun. Is he not like his father, Mrs. Bairnsfather? James, did you not say that Miss Aytoun was a relative of Mrs. Catherine's?"

"Ay, my dear," said Mr. Coulter. "Mrs. Catherine told us so herself—you recollect? or was it to me she said it? So it was—when she was looking at yon new patent plough of John's."

"I wonder," said Mrs. Bairnsfather, "who is likely to get the Tower? In the course of nature, it cannot be very long in Mrs. Catherine's hands, and it's a good estate."

"Wonderfully improved in my time," said Mr. Coulter. "Mrs. Catherine is not without a notion of the science of agriculture, which, to the shame of landed proprietors, is generally so much neglected. The low lands at Oran Point were but moor and heather in my memory, but they grow as fine barley now as any in the country."

"Well, I suppose no one can say that Mrs. Catherine neglects her carnal interests," said Mrs. Bairnsfather, with a professional sigh. Her husband was known among his shrewd parishioners to be greatly more observant of temporal than spiritual matters, and his wife, conscious of a failing in that respect, was wont to assume at times a technical solemnity.

"I believe Mrs. Catherine is a very excellent woman in every respect," said the good-humored and uncensorious Mrs. Coulter, "and cares as little about money, for money's sake, as any one can possibly do; but she thinks it a duty to use well and improve what Providence has given her, as you do yourself, James, though, to be sure, we have more motive, with a young family rising round us."

"I was very much struck yesterday," said Mr. Coulter, "with the contrast between the Tower fields, and the adjoining lands within the bounds of Strathoran. There is a place where the three estates meet— Mrs. Catherine's, Mr. Sutherland's and mine. You recollect the little burn, my dear, which that silly maid of yours fell into last Hallow-e'en? well, it is there. Mrs. Catherine's stubble-fields stretch to the very burnside—mine are turnips—uncommonly fine Swedes; but, on the other side, spreading away as far as you can see, is the brown moor of Strathoran, miles of good land wastefully lost, besides breeding by the thousand these small cattle of game, to destroy our corn."

"Ay," said Mrs. Bairnsfather, mysteriously, "I hear the Sutherlands are not in the best way."

"Poor things! they are young to be out in the world alone," said Mrs. Coulter; "and Isabel was a wilful girl at all times. I gathered from what Lewis Ross said, that they were living very gaily; but perhaps you have heard more?"

Mrs. Bairnsfather shook her head.

"It is a melancholy thing to think of the downfall of an old family!"

"Hout! Mrs. Bairnsfather," said Mr. Coulter; "you are taking it too seriously. Strathoran can stand a good deal. It will take more than one lad's extravagance to bring down the family, I trust; and young Sutherland used to have good sense and discretion. I spoke to him of draining Loelyin before he went away, and he really had very just ideas on the subject. No, no; let us hope there will be no ruin in the case."

Mrs. Bairnsfather shook her head again.

"I have no objection to hope the best, Mr. Coulter; but it is no uncommon thing to be disappointed in hopes; and, if what I hear be true, there is more room for fear."

"What's this," said Mr. Ambler, approaching the little group, as he made a leisurely, chatting, circuit round the room—"hoping and fearing, Mrs. Bairnsfather? Is it about these happy-looking young people of ours, and the future matches that may spring from their pairings—eh, Mrs. Coulter?"

Mrs. Coulter smiled, and glanced over to where Walter Foreman lingered by her Jeanie's side. They were a handsome couple, and Walter had a nice little improvable property, inherited from his mother. There was no saying what might come to pass.

"No, Mr. Ambler," said Mrs. Bairnsfather, "we were speaking of poor young Strathoran;" and, from the depths of her fat bosom there came a mysteriously pathetic sigh.

"Strathoran! what's happened to the lad?" exclaimed Mr. Ambler. "Lewis Ross left him well and merry— no accident I hope; but Lewis has not been a week at home yet: there is little time for any change in his fortunes."

"Ah, Mr. Ambler," said Mrs. Bairnsfather, "it is not aye well to be merry. I have heard from those who know, that young Mr. Sutherland's gay life is putting his lands in jeopardy; they say he'll spend a whole year's income sometimes in a single night, poor ill-advised lad! I happened to mention it to Mrs. Catherine, but she turned about upon me, as if I was to be any better of Strathoran's downfall, which I am sure I never meant, nor anything like it."

"Bless me!" said Mr. Ambler, "I am concerned to hear that—I am grieved, do you know, to hear that. Is it possible? Why, I always thought Archie Sutherland was a wise lad—a discreet lad of his years."

Mrs. Bairnsfather shook her head.

"Archibald Sutherland ruined!" continued Mr. Ambler, "no, it's surely not possible—it must have been an ill-wisher that said that. Why, Strathoran is as big as Falcon's Craig and Smoothlie put together—ay, and even ye might slip in a good slice off Merkland. Ruined! it's not possible. When I came home from India I heard of old Strathoran saying—I do not recollect the amount, I always had a bad memory for figures—but a great sum every year. It must be a false alarm, Mrs. Bairnsfather."

"Very well, gentlemen," said Mrs. Bairnsfather, "it's no concern of mine; but a little time will show that I am correct."

"Bless me!" repeated Mr. Ambler, "then the lad must go to India, that is clear—he may do great things in India. You see when I was there myself, there was the best opening for a lad of talent that could possibly be; but I had a yearning for home. I was always uncommonly fond of home, and so I am only a country Laird, when I might have been a Nabob. But if he were once in India I would have no fear for him—he would soon get up again."

"India, Mr. Ambler!" exclaimed Mr. Coulter, "no doubt there are fortunes to be made in India; but I fancy it's a shame to us to send our sons away to seek gold, when it is lying in our very fields for the digging—agriculture—"

"What's that you're saying, Mr. Coulter?" exclaimed the Laird of Smoothlie. "Gold! where is't man? we'll all take a hand at that work, if it were but for poor auld Scotland's sake, who has ever been said to have but a scanty providing of the precious metal."

"There are harvests lying in the cold breast of the great Strathoran moor," said the agriculturist, energetically, "of more import to man, Mr. Ambler, than if its sands were gold. If what we hear of Archibald Sutherland is true, he may never be able to do it now; but a sensible man, with sufficient capital, might double the rent-roll of Strathoran."

Mr. Ambler looked slightly contemptuous.

"Well, well, Mr. Coulter, I'll not gainsay you; but to tell the truth, I've no notion of making young lads of family and breeding amateur ploughmen—I beg your pardon, Mr. Coulter, I mean no affront to you— you look upon it as a science, I know, and doubtless so it is; but—you see if Archie Sutherland could fall in with such an opening, as was waiting ready for me when I went to India, he might be home again, a wealthy man, before your harvests were grown."

"James," interposed Mrs. Coulter, "you are not looking at our young people—how happy they all seem, poor things. I do not think you have seen my Ada, Mr. Ambler, since she returned from Edinburgh."

Mr. Ambler adjusted his spectacles, with a smile. "No, I dare say not. Is that her with Lewis Ross? No, that's Mrs. Catherine's little friend. Ay, ay, I see her—like what her mother used to be, in my remembrance. Mrs. Coulter, you must have great pleasure in your fine family."

Mrs. Coulter smiled, well pleased.

"Do you know, Mr. Ambler," said Mrs. Bairnsfather, "who that Miss Aytoun is?"

"Who she is? No, indeed, except a very bonnie little girlie. She is that, without dispute; but Mr. Foreman will know. Mr. Foreman, can you tell Mrs. Bairnsfather who that young lady is, at Lewis Ross's hand?"

"Miss Aytoun, ma'am, a relative of Mrs. Catherine's," said the lawyer.

"We know that," said Mr. Ambler. "Is that all her history? Aytoun—Aytoun—I have surely some associations with that name myself."

"Very likely," said Mr. Foreman, dryly. "She comes from the south country; her mother lives in Edinburgh, I believe, and is of a good family. I do not know anything further of the young lady, Mrs. Bairnsfather; that is, nothing at all interesting."

"Which means," said Mrs. Coulter aside to her husband, as their little group increased, and the conversation became more general, "that Mr. Foreman knows something very interesting about that pretty little girl. Mrs. Catherine is a client of his. Perhaps he thinks of Miss Aytoun for Walter. James, will you call Jeanie to me?"

And so, in quiet talk, in that bright drawing-room, these ladies and gentlemen—all possessing their average share of kindliness—had decided upon the ruin of Archibald Sutherland, who sat this same night in yonder brilliant Parisian saloon, with the fatal dice trembling in his hand, in all the wild, delirious gaiety of a desperate man; and in their flood of easy conversation, had touched upon another centre of crime and misery, darker and more fatal still, the facts of which lingered in the lawyer-like memory of Walter Foreman's father, and even attached some dim associations, in Mr. Ambler's mind, to Alice Aytoun's name. Strange domestic volcano, over which these slippered feet passed so heedlessly! How often, in quiet houses, and among quiet people, are mighty sins and mighty miseries passed by as lightly!

CHAPTER V

Sleepy, weary, and uncomfortable, the household of Merkland reluctantly bestirred itself next morning. Mrs. Ross rose ill-humored from very weariness. Duncan, and May, and Barbara, were all more than ordinarily stupid; and Mr. Ambler, of Smoothlie, with all his neatness and finicality, was still in the house.

The imperturbable Mr. Ambler was first in the breakfast-parlor, joking Anne on her pale cheeks, and Lewis on his last night's conquests—fully prepared to do justice to the edibles of the breakfast-table, and not, in any degree, inclined to forgive the sleepiness which had mangled these delicate Oran trout, and sent up the eggs hard-boiled; for Mr. Ambler, by right of his comfort-loving old bachelorship, was excused everywhere for discussing matters of the table more minutely than ordinary strangers were privileged to do, and had besides, as Lewis Ross's guardian, a familiar standing at Merkland.

"Bless me, Madam," said Mr. Ambler, "your cook must have been up all the hours of the night. Sleepy huzzies! Why, I myself was not in bed till two o'clock, and here I am, as fresh as ever I was. And just look at this trout—as beautiful a beast as was ever caught in water—broken clean in two! It's quite shocking!"

"Are there never any such incidents in Smoothlie, Mr. Ambler?" asked Mrs. Ross, somewhat sharply.

"Accidents, Madam! Do you call that an accident—the massacreing of a delicate animal like a trout? No, I send Forsyth to the kitchen every morning to superintend; and Forsyth, by long practice, has arrived at perfiteness, as the old proverb says.—Better try a bit of one though, Lewis, mangled though they be, than hurt your stomach with these eggs; they're indigestible, man—like lead. Send me your plate; here is not a bad bit."

"There is a kipper beside you, more carefully cooked, Mr. Ambler," said Anne, smiling.

"Thank you, Anne, my dear; but I never take kippered trout when I can get fresh, fit for the eating. Lewis, man, what makes you yawn so much? It's very ill-bred."

Lewis laughed. Mrs. Ross looked displeased. "Poor boy, he is fatigued. No wonder, after all his exertions yesterday."

"Fatigued! Nonsense. What should fatigue him?" said Mr. Ambler. "Take my word for it, Mrs. Ross, it's just an idle habit, and not genuine weariness. A young man, like Lewis, fatigued with enjoying himself!— on his one-and-twentieth birthday, too! Who ever heard the like? When I was in India (which is neither the day nor yesterday) I have seen me up till far on in the night, and yet astir and travelling a couple of hours before sunrise.—What would you say to that, Lewis? No; so far as I can see, our young generation are more likely to be spoiled by indolence than overwork."

"Indolence! that's quite too bad, Mr. Ambler," said Lewis.—"Bear me witness, Anne, how I have been running about since I arrived at Merkland. I don't think I have had a couple of hours to myself since I came home."

"Lewis," said Mr. Ambler, "what was yon I heard last night of Archie Sutherland? That little round body, Mrs. Bairnsfather, was enlightening us all as to Strathoran's affairs. She says the lad is ruined."

Lewis shrugged his shoulders.

"I can't say, Mr. Ambler. I am not so deeply read in economics as the good lady. Archie's an extravagant fellow: but—oh! if I say any more, I shall have Anne upon me. Never mind, he's a fine fellow, Archie."

"Anne?" said Mr. Ambler, inquisitively. "Ay, what is Anne's special interest in Archie Sutherland? Well, I will ask no questions."

"My special interest in Archie Sutherland, is a figment of my brother's lively imagination, Mr. Ambler," said Anne, quietly, "produced by what inspiration I do not know; but repeated, I suppose, because it annoys me."

"Well, you can pay him back in his own coin," said the old gentleman. "Oh, you need not look innocent, Lewis. Do you think nobody noticed you last night hanging about that pretty little girl of Mrs. Catherine's? Bless me! Anne, my dear, what is the matter?"

Anne had turned very pale, and felt a deadly sickness at her heart, as she saw the color rising over Lewis's cheek, and the conscious smile of pleasure and embarrassment hovering about his lip. But Mrs. Ross spoke before she could render any reason for her change of countenance.

"Miss Aytoun, indeed! Upon my word, Mr. Ambler, your ward is indebted to you—after all the pains that have been bestowed upon him, and all the advantages he has had, to think he could be attracted by yon little animated doll. Nonsense! Lewis will look higher, I confidently hope."

"Upon my word, you dispose of me very summarily," said Lewis, half laughing, half angry. "Mr. Ambler, will you put my mother in remembrance of those cabalistic forms of yesterday, which made me master of my own person and possessions. I suppose I may be very thankful, though, that you did not make me over to Miss Falconer—eh, Mr. Ambler?"

"Miss Falconer would not take you, Lewis," said Mr. Ambler, coolly. "I will trouble you for the toast, Anne, and—yes, I will take the marmalade, too—do not alarm yourself, Lewis, you are in no danger from Miss Falconer."

Lewis looked piqued. It was more agreeable to feel himself a prize, than to be told so very coolly that he was in no danger from Miss Falconer, and the pleasant flattery of those blue eyes of Alice Aytoun's, which had looked up to him so gladly last night, returned upon him in consolatory fascination. His mother's interference, too, excited a spirit of opposition and perversity, which stimulated the remembrance; and when Mr. Ambler had happily ridden away, Lewis beguiled Anne into going out with him, and, before long, their walk terminated at the door of the Tower, whither Alice Aytoun had seen them approaching, from her high window, and glided softly into the drawing-room, with her gay heart fluttering, that she might at once meet and welcome Miss Ross.

"Anne," said Mrs. Catherine, "Alison Aytoun has a petition to make to you. She wants you to protect her when she goes to Falcon's Craig. I, myself, as you know, am not given to visiting; besides that, at this time, I am taken up with graver matters. I would like you to take the bairn there to-morrow."

"Oh, if you please, Miss Ross," pleaded Alice.

"For the Tower is dreary enough for a young thing," continued Mrs. Catherine, "At all seasons. Lewis, they are always quickening the speed of travel: how soon could a letter be answered from Paris?"

"Oh, in a week or two," said Lewis, carelessly. "A fortnight, I dare say. But no one ever accused me of punctuality, Mrs. Catherine, so I cannot say exactly."

"The more shame to you," said Mrs. Catherine. "A silly youth bragging of a short-coming! Truly, Anne, I count it an affliction that folk must bear with the lads through their fool-estate, before ye can find an inkling of sense in any man. Alison, has Miss Ross consented to take charge of you? and will you go, Anne?"

"I shall be very glad," said Anne, as Alice hung round her. "But is not Marjory related to Miss Aytoun?"

"It's past counting, that kindred," said Mrs. Catherine; "we could reckon it in my generation, that is with Alison's grand-mother and the last family of Falconers passing the father of Ralph and Marjory, who was an only son, and died young—a poor peasweep he was, that might never have been born at all, for all the good he did!—and it was only a third or fourth cousinship then. I want the bairn to go to Falcon's Craig, more for a diversion to her, than any other thing: and doubtless we must have festivities of our own, also. I will borrow your French serving-man from you, Lewis, to teach us a right manner of rejoicing."

"You shall have him, with all my heart," said Lewis, with some offended dignity; "only, I fear John would not take his orders from Mrs. Morison. He is too sensitive."

"Set him up!" exclaimed Mrs. Catherine. "Sensitive, truly! Then you must e'en keep him and humor him yourself, Lewis. I am plaguit enough in my own household. There is Euphan Morison waylaying me with herbs. I caught her my ownself, this very morning, wileing the bairn Alison into poisoning herself with a drink made from dockens: the odor of them has not left me yet."

"It was only camomile," whispered Alice.

"Never you heed what it was," said Mrs. Catherine. "Unwholesome trash that she calls good for the stomach, as if a bairn like Alison had any call to know whither she had a stomach or no! I have no patience with them. Jacky, you evil spirit, what are ye wanting now?"

"If you please," said Jacky, "It's Mr. Foreman—"

Mrs. Catherine started.

"Where is he?"

"And a strange man with him, dressed like a gentleman," continued Jacky. "They're in the library, Mrs. Catherine."

Mrs. Catherine rose hurriedly.

"Bairns, you will tarry till I come back. I am not like to be long."

Mr. Foreman, the acute, and sagacious writer of Portoran, was seated in the library when Mrs. Catherine entered, and a man of equivocal appearance, bearded like the pard, who had been swaggering round the room, examining, with an eye of assumed connoisseurship, the dark family portraits on the wall, turned round at the sound of her step to make an elaborate bow. Mrs. Catherine looked at him impatiently.

"Well, Mr. Foreman, have you brought me any tidings?"

"I have brought you no direct tidings, Mrs. Catherine, but this,"—Mr. Foreman looked dubiously at the stranger—"this gentleman, whom I met accidentally in Portoran, is charged with a mission, the particulars of which I thought you would like to know, being deeply interested in Mr. Sutherland."

"Maiden aunt," murmured the stranger. "Ah! I see."

"You seem to have clear eyes, Sir," said Mrs. Catherine, sternly. "Mr. Sutherland will be a friend of yours, doubtless?"

"Ah! a fine young fellow—most promising lad!" was the answer. "Might be a credit to any family. I have the honor of a slight acquaintance. Nothing could be more edifying than his walk and conversation, I assure you, Madam."

"I will thank you to assure me of what I ask, and trouble your head about no more," said Mrs. Catherine. "Are the like of you acquaint—I am meaning, is Archibald Sutherland a friend of yours?"

"Very intimate. My friend Lord Gillravidge and he are. Astonishing young man, Madam, my friend Lord Gillravidge—missed church once last year, and was quite overcome with contrition—so much comforted by Mr. Sutherland's Christian friendship and fraternity—quite delighted to be a spectator of it, I assure you."

"I was asking you about Archibald Sutherland, Sir," said Mrs. Catherine, standing stiffly erect, as the stranger threw himself into a chair unbidden, "and in what manner the like of you were connected with him. I am waiting for your answer."

"A long story, Madame," said the stranger, coolly, "of friendly interest and mutual good offices. I have seen Mr. Sutherland often with my friend Lord G., and was anxious to do him a service—my time being always at my friend's disposal."

"Mr. Foreman," exclaimed Mrs. Catherine, "know you the meaning of all this? You are a lawyer, man; see if you cannot shape questions so as they shall be answered."

"Your friend Lord Gillravidge is intimately acquainted with Mr. Sutherland?" interrogated Mr. Foreman.

"Precisely—delightful; dwelling together in unity, like—"

"And Mr. Sutherland is in embarrassed circumstances?" continued Mr. Foreman, impelled by an impatient gesture from Mrs. Catherine.

The stranger turned round with a contraction of his forehead and gave a significant nod.

"A most benevolent young man—kind-hearted people are always being tricked by impostors, and made security for friends—merely temporary—does him infinite credit, I assure you, Madam."

"Assure me no lies!" exclaimed Mrs. Catherine. "What have you to do—a paltry trickster as you are—with the lad Archie Sutherland: answer me that?"

"Madam!" exclaimed the stranger, rising indignantly, and assuming an attitude.

"The lady is aware of Mr. Sutherland's embarrassments," interposed Mr. Foreman, "and is putting no inquiries touching the cause. Your friend, Lord Gillravidge, Mr. ——"

"Fitzherbert, Sir," said the stranger.

"Mr. Fitzherbert has served Mr. Sutherland in a pecuniary way?"

Mr. Fitzherbert bowed.

"And you are charged with a mission of a peculiar kind to Strathoran. Might I beg you to explain its nature to Mrs. Catherine Douglas, a lady who is deeply interested in your friend's friend, Mr. Sutherland."

The stranger looked perplexed, gracefully confused, and hung back, as if in embarrassment and diffidence.

"The fact is, Madam, I am placed in quite a peculiar position—a mission strictly confidential, intrusted to me—friendly inquiries—which I have no authority to divulge. I beg I may not be questioned further."

"Mr. Fitzherbert, fortunately, was less delicate with me, Mrs. Catherine," said Mr. Foreman. "Mr. Sutherland, Madam, is in treaty for the sale of Strathoran—for some portion of the estate, at least, and this gentleman is commissioned to report upon it, as he tells me, before the bargain is completed."

"Not fair—against all principles of honor," exclaimed Mr. Fitzherbert. "A mis-statement, Madam, I assure you; merely some shooting-grounds. Mr. Sutherland is no sportsman himself, and my friend, Lord Gillravidge, is a keen one. Amicable exchange—nothing more."

Mrs. Catherine stood firmly erect; gazing into the blank air. The shock was great to her; for some moments she neither moved nor spoke.

"I appeal to yourself, Madam," resumed the stranger. "I investigate farms and fields. I, fresh from the most refined circles: do I look like a person to report upon clods and cattle?"

The voice startled Mrs. Catherine from her fixed gravity.

"I will come to you by-and-by, Mr. Foreman," she said. "Gather the story as clear as may be—at present, I cannot be troubled with strangers."

A slight, emphatic motion of her hand conveyed her desire that the friend and emissary of Lord Gillravidge should be dismissed as speedily as possible, and turning, she left the room.

"Spoilt it all," exclaimed Fitzherbert, as the door closed, "never have any commerce with lawyers—bad set—Scotch especially—keen—ill-natured. What harm would it have done you, old gentleman, if I had pleased the old lady about her nephew, and got her, perhaps, to come down with something handsome? I always like to serve friends myself—wanted to put in a good word for Sutherland—but it's all spoiled now."

"You expect to see more of Strathoran, I suppose," said Mr. Foreman; "good sport on the moor, they tell me, Mr. Fitzherbert, and you say Lord Gillravidge is a keen sportsman."

"Keen in most things," said the stranger, with an emphatic nod. "Sharp—not to be taken in—simple Scotch lad no match for Gillravidge—serves him right, for thinking he was. But I say, old gentleman, don't be ill-natured and tell the aunt—let him have a fresh start."

"It is to be a sale, then?" said the lawyer, "is your friend really to buy Strathoran?"

The stranger laughed contemptuously.

"Has Sutherland got anything else, that you ask that? all the purchase money's gone already—nothing coming your way, old gentleman—all the more cruelty in you preventing me from speaking a good word for him to his aunt."

"Was the bargain concluded when you left?" said Mr. Foreman.

"Very near it," was the reply. "Why, he's been plunging on deeper in Gillravidge's debt every night. I say it was uncommonly merciful to think of taking the land—an obscure Scotch place, with nothing but the preserves worth looking at; but Gillravidge knows what he's about."

Half an hour afterwards, Mrs. Catherine re-entered the library. The obnoxious visitor was gone, and Mr. Foreman sat alone, his brow clouded with thoughtfulness. He, too, had known Archibald Sutherland's youth, and in his father had had a friend, and the kindly bond of that little community drew its members of all ranks too closely together, to suffer the overthrow of one without regret and sympathy.

"Is it true—think you it is true?" said Mrs. Catherine.

"I can think nothing else," said Mr. Foreman, gravely; "there is but one hope—that strange person who left the Tower just now tells me that the bargain was not completed. Mr. Ferguson's letter, telling Strathoran of the advance you were willing to make, Mrs. Catherine, may have reached him in time to prevent this calamity."

"I cannot hope it—I cannot hope it," said Mrs. Catherine, vehemently. "It is a race trysted to evil. Do you not mind, George Foreman, how the last Strathoran was held down all his days, with the burdens that father and grandsire had left upon him? Do you not mind of him joining with his father to break the entail, that some of the debts might be paid thereby? and now, when he has labored all his life to leave the good land clear to his one son, must it be lost to the name and blood? George Foreman, set your face against the breaking of entails! I say it is an unrighteous thing to give one of a race the power of disinheriting the rest; to put into the hands of a youth like Archie Sutherland, fatally left to his own devices, the option of overthrowing an old and good house—I say it is unrighteous, and a shame!"

Mr. Foreman made no answer—well enough pleased as he might have been that in this particular case, the lands of Strathoran had been entailed, he yet had no idea of committing himself on the abstract principle, and Mrs. Catherine continued:

"What is he to do? what can the unhappy prodigal do, but draw the prize of the waster—want. I cannot stand between him and his righteous reward—I will do no such injustice. Where did you meet with the ne'er-do-weel that brought you the tidings, Mr. Foreman? a fit messenger no doubt, with his hairy face, and his lying tongue." Mrs. Catherine groaned. "You are well gone to your rest, Isabel Balfour, before you saw your firstborn herding with cattle like yon!"

"I think," said Mr. Foreman, "that you are anticipating evil which is by this time averted, Mrs. Catherine. At the very crisis of Strathoran's broken fortunes, your seasonable assistance would come in; and, on such a temperament as his, I should fancy the sight of the precipice so near would operate powerfully. I know how it has acted on myself, who ought to have more prudence than Mr. Sutherland, if years are anything. I came here to advise you to withdraw your money, when there was such imminent danger of loss—and here I am, building my own hopes and yours on the fact of its being promised."

Mrs. Catherine was pacing heavily through the room.

"What care I for the siller," she exclaimed, sternly. "What is the siller to me, in comparison with the welfare of Isabel Balfour's son? Doubtless, if all the rest is gone, there is no need for throwing away that with our eyes open; but what share in my thoughts, think you, has the miserable dirt of siller, when the fate of the lad that might have been of my own blood, is quivering in the balance? George Foreman, you are discreet and judicious, but the yellow mammon is overmuch in your mind. What is it to me that leave none after me—that am the last of my name?"

"I think we may depend on the last statement of that strange messenger—that Fitzherbert," said Mr. Foreman, endeavoring gently to lower the excitement of his client, "that he came down to examine, and would have his report to make, before the transaction was finished. Your letter must reach Strathoran, Mrs. Catherine, before this fellow can return. Depend upon it, the immediate danger is averted. Mr. Sutherland has good sense and judgment: he must by this time have perceived the danger, and receded from it."

Mrs. Catherine seated herself in gloomy silence.

"And if he has," she said, after a long pause, "if he has saved himself for this moment, what then? He has sown the wind, and think you he can shun its harvest? What has he to trust to? principle, honor, good fame, the fear of God, the right regard to the judgment of his fellows which becomes every man—has he not thrown them all away? What is there then, to look to in his future, if it be not a drifting before every wind, a running in every stray path, a following of all things that have the false glitter upon them, whatsoever ill may be below? I am done with hope for the lad: there is nothing to guide him, nothing to restrain him. I must e'en take fear to my heart, and look this grief in the face."

"He is quite young," said Mr. Foreman; "there is abundant time and room for hope, Mrs. Catherine. I feel assured we have erred on the side of fear. A shrewd lad, like Strathoran, surely could not be fascinated to his destruction, in society which can tolerate that man, Fitzherbert. Depend upon it, we have overrated the dangers; and that, by this time, Mr. Sutherland has taken warning, and withdrawn. A pretty counsellor I am, after all!—I should have sent Walter—coming here to advise you to withdraw your money, and now felicitating myself that it is given."

Mrs. Catherine became more cheerful at last, before the kind-hearted Portoran writer took his departure, and admitted the chances in favor of his hopes. Archibald had been shrewd and sensible, and could not surely be so ruinously involved as to put his whole estate in peril; nevertheless, dreary visions, such as he had read in books of modern travel, of haggard gamesters risking their all upon a cast—staking wealth, and hope, and honor, in the desperate game, and marking its loss with the ghastly memento of blood, the hopeless death of the suicide—rose darkly before the lawyer's eyes, as he rode home—home, to pleasant competence and unobtrusive refinement, and to a family of sound principle and cultivated intellect, in whose healthful upbringing and clear atmosphere fictitious excitement had no share.

And Mrs. Catherine went up stairs, gravely, to her cheerful inner drawing-room, and looking on the youthful faces there—the peaceful household looks, suggesting anything rather than misery and crime—forgot her terrors for Isabel Balfour's son, warm as her interest in him was.

Haggard, desolate, hopeless, with no roof which he could justly call his own to shelter him, and with a dreary blank before him, where the teeming dreams of a bright future were wont to be, Archibald Sutherland stood that night, in the strange alien country, a ruined man.

CHAPTER VI

Tiresome as the manifold preparations for a feast may be, there is something especially dreary and full of discomfort in the bustle of setting to rights, which comes after: dismantled rooms undergoing a thorough purification, before they can once more settle down into their every day look and aspect; servants, in a chaos and frenzy of orderliness, turning the house into a Babel—a kitchen saturnalia; mistresses toiling in vain to have the work concluded bit by bit; and all this without the stimulant of expected pleasure to make it bearable.

Mrs. Ross rather liked such an overturn, and had it commenced gaily in the first relief of Mr. Ambler's departure; so that when Lewis and Anne returned from the Tower, there was no place of refuge for them, save in the small library, which Lewis had already appropriated as his own peculiar place of retirement.

Mrs. Ross had long taken a malicious pleasure in excluding Anne from all share in the economies of Merkland, in which, indeed, her own active habits and managing disposition could brook no divided empire; and it was not, therefore any super refinement of feeling which called Anne Ross out after her daily task was over, into the silent evening air, upon the quiet side of Oran. It is true that there were delicate tones of harmony there, which few ears could appreciate as well as her own; but the first yearning of these human spirits of ours, is for the sympathy of other human spirits, and it is oftenest disappointment in that, which at once makes us seek for, and susceptible to, the mild pity and silent companionship of the wide earth around us.

A long invigorating walk she had, the little river modulating its voice, as she could fancy, to bear her musings gentle company. Strangely accordant was that plaintive harmony of nature. Wan leaves dropping one by one, the stillness so great that you could hear them fall: the wide air ringing with its tremulous, silent music; the pleasant voice of Oran blending in low cadence, "most musical, most melancholy." These graduated tones had been significant and solemn to Anne's spirit all her life long—from the dreamy days of childhood, so strangely grave and thoughtful, with all their shadowy array of haunting ghosts and angels, those constant comrades of the meditative child—up through the long still years of youth, unto this present time of grave maturity, of subdued and chastened prime. Other and mightier things, springing from heaven and not from earth, the presence of that invisible Friend, whose brotherhood of human sympathy circles His people, no less tenderly than His divine strength holds them up, were with her in her solitude; and the lesser music of His fair universe wrought its fitting part in the calming of the troubled spirit; pensive, shadowy, calm, and full of that strange spiritual breath, which Time has, in his momentary lingering between the night and day.

A lonely unfrequented path, winding by Oranside, to a little clump of houses, not very far off, almost too few to be dignified by the name of hamlet, ran close to the high, encircling hedge, which shut in at that side the grounds of Merkland. Not far from the principal entrance was a little gate, across which the branches nearly joined, and which was never used, except by Anne herself, in her solitary rambles. She lingered at it, before she entered again—her dark dress scarcely distinguishable from the thick boughs behind her, as she leant upon the lintel. There was some one approaching on the road, whom Anne regarded with little interest, thinking her some resident of the hamlet, returning to her home; but as the passenger came in front of Merkland, she suddenly stopped, and standing still upon the road, gazed on the quiet house. Her head was turned towards the gate, and Anne, startled into attention, looked upon it wonderingly—an emaciated, pale face, that spoke of suffering, with large, dark, spiritual eyes, beaming from it, as eyes can beam only from faces so worn and wasted. Wistfully the long, slow look fell upon Merkland; standing there, so firm, serene, and homelike, its light shining through the trees. And then Anne heard an inarticulate murmur, as of muttered words, and the cadence of a deep, long sigh, and the stranger—for the wan face, and thin, tall figure, were too remarkable to have escaped her notice, had the passer-by been other than a stranger—went forward upon the darkening path, scarce noting her, Anne thought, as the figure glided past her, like a spirit.

The image would not leave her mind. The pale, worn face—the wistful, searching eyes—haunted her through that night, and mingled with her dreams. Strange visions of Norman, such as now filled her mind continually, received into them this stranger's spiritual face. Dangers, troubles, the whole indefinite horde of dreaming apprehensions and embarrassments clung round those wistful eyes, as round a centre. Anne could scarcely believe next morning, when she awoke, with the remembrance so clear upon her mind, that it was not some supernatural presence, lingering about her still.

The morning was very bright and clear, and cold, for October was waning then into the duskier winter; and Anne, remembering her engagement with Alice, laid her work by early, and prepared to walk up to the Tower. She met Lewis, booted and spurred, at the door.

"Are you going to the Tower, Anne?" he asked.

"Yes," was the answer.

"Well, don't be surprised if you find me at Falcon's Craig, before you."

"At Falcon's Craig, Lewis! What errand have you there?"

"May I not make a friendly call as well as yourself?" said Lewis, gaily. "Besides, I shall take care of you, on the way home. How do I know that the Strathoran roads are quite safe for young ladies?"

"But I thought you were afraid of Miss Falconer?" said Anne.

"Oh, Mr. Ambler relieved me of that fear, you know. She wouldn't have me, he said. Very fortunate, for she will never get the offer."

"Mr. Ambler was quite right," said Anne, uneasily. "But, Lewis do not go, pray—take another morning for your call at Falcon's Craig. Your mother will be grieved and irritated—do not go to-day."

"My mother!" Lewis drew himself up with all the petulant dignity peculiar to his years. "Upon my word, Anne, you are perfectly mistaken if you think I have come home to be restrained and chidden like a schoolboy! Grieved and irritated! because that pretty little Miss Aytoun happens to be of the party, I suppose. You are a foolish set, you women, forcing things upon a man's consideration, which, if you had but let him alone—." Lewis drew himself up again, and let the end of his sentence evaporate in a smile.

"I was not thinking of—I mean it is not for Miss Aytoun," said Anne, anxiously; "but your mother wants to consult you, Lewis. There are so many matters of business to attend to that you should manage yourself. Do not go to-day."

"Don't fear me!" said Lewis, confidently. "I will attend to my business, too. We shall soon see who is strongest in that respect. Here, Duncan!"

Duncan had brought his master's horse to the door, and stood at some distance, holding the bridle.

"Good morning, Anne!" cried Lewis, as he mounted and cantered gaily out. "I am off to Falcon's Craig."

Anne would gladly have broken her appointment now, had that been possible, but, as it was not, she too set out on her way to the Tower. A comfortable pony-carriage—Mrs. Catherine's favorite vehicle—stood at the gate as she entered, and up stairs in her bright dressing-room Alice Aytoun was hastily wrapping herself in the costly furs—Mrs. Catherine's latest present—which she had already spent so much time in admiring.

"Child," said Mrs. Catherine, during the moment in which they were left alone together, "let Lewis come to me the morn; or is he with you to-day?"

"He spoke of meeting us at Falcon's Craig, and returning with us," said Anne.

"Bring him to me, then, when you come back," said Mrs. Catherine. "I am feared there is little hope for the lad, Archie Sutherland, child, and I am solicitous to hear from Lewis what kind of friends his sister Isabel has. If the lad is ruined (which the Almighty avert, if it be His pleasure!) what is the wilful fool of a girl to do? A man may win back good fame, even if it be once lost—and that is a sore fight—but a woman can never; and if she be left in that narrow place, with an evil-speaking world that judges other folk as it knows it should be judged itself, I say to you, child, what is the inconsiderate fuil to do?"

"Captain Duncombe will surely come to take care of his wife," said Anne.

"What know you about Captain Duncombe?" exclaimed Mrs. Catherine. "I will go myself to bring Isabel Balfour's ill bairn home to my own house, child—the fittest place for her to be. I will leave her to the tender mercies of no ill-conditioned man, well though she may deserve it; that is if things come to the worst with Archie. Bring Lewis to me when ye come back, child. I would know what kind of folk she has her friends among."

In a few minutes after, attended by Johnnie Halflin, the two young ladies drove over the bridge on their way to Falcon's Craig.

The road was pleasant, and Alice was so very gay and full of happiness, that Anne's heart expanded in involuntary sympathy. The girl had been so tenderly guarded through all her seventeen years, so hedged about with domestic love and protection, and did so trustingly rely now upon the kindness of all about her, that few could have been harsh enough to disappoint the reliance of the youthful spirit, or teach it suspicion. It was, besides, an altogether new enjoyment to Anne, to have anything loveable looking up to her as Alice did. It suited her graver nature to be trusted in, and leaned upon. The depths in Anne's spirit began to stir; tenderness as of a mother's to spread its protecting wing over the "little one" beside her. Might she not make some secret atonement—might she not by tenderest care, and sympathy, and counsel, in some slight degree, make up the loss which her brother's hand had inflicted upon that unconscious girl?

They reached Falcon's Craig at last. It was a great, rambling, gaunt, old house, standing high and bare, with inartistic turrets, and unsightly gables, on the summit of a rock. The perpendicular descent behind was draped with clinging shrubs and ivy, but the situation gave a bleak, cold, exposed look to the house. Nor had any precautions been taken to amend this. Trees and shrubs before the door grew rough and unkempt as nature had let them grow. The grass upon the lawn waved high and rank, great rows of hollyhocks and sunflowers shed their withered leaves and ripe seed below the windows. The much-trodden path, at the further end which led to the stables, and the presence of one or two lounging grooms, told the enjoyments of the Laird of Falcon's Craig, and explained, in some degree, the inferior cultivation of the neighboring fields—fields over which Mr. Coulter, of Harrows, with a good-humored desire to see all around him as prosperous as himself, shook his head and groaned.

The visitors alighted, and were shown into Miss Falconer's heterogeneous drawing-room. The lady herself lay upon a sofa near the fire, with a newspaper in her hand. Alice Aytoun did not like the appearance of the reclining figure, in its bold, manlike attitude, and kept close to Anne's side.

"Anne Ross!" exclaimed Miss Falconer, springing up with an energy which made the room ring; "why, I should as soon have thought of Merkland coming to see me bodily, as you. How do you do? How are you, little Miss Aytoun? Tired of the Tower yet?"

"No," said Alice, drawing back, instinctively.

"Don't be afraid; I won't hurt you," said Miss Falconer, with a laugh. "Well, Anne, how do you get on in Merkland? Mrs. Ross will be good and dutiful now, when Lewis is at home."

"You must ask Lewis himself," said Anne; "he is here now, is he not?"

The face of Alice, which had been somewhat in shadow, brightened.

"Oh, yes, Lewis is here," said Miss Falconer; "gone with Ralph to these everlasting stables. Take notice, Miss Aytoun, that when gentlemen come to Falcon's Craig, it is Ralph's horses and dogs they come to see, and not his sister. I say this, that you may not be jealous."

Little Alice blushed, and drew up her slight young figure, with some budding dignity. "I have nothing to be jealous of, Miss Falconer."

Miss Falconer laughed again. "Well, we will not say anything before Anne. Anne is taking lessons from Mrs. Catherine, in state and gravity. How did you come? In that little phæton, I declare, with these two sober ponies, that I have known all my life. You never ride now, Anne?"

"I do not remember that I ever did," said Anne. "We keep few horses in Merkland; and besides, Marjory, there are not many ladies of your nerve and courage."

"Miss Aytoun," said Miss Falconer, gaily, "do you ever flatter? Anne, you see, knows my weak point, and attacks me accordingly. She thinks I rather pride myself on these two unsafe qualities of nerve and courage. Well, and why should we be cooped up within four walls, and sentenced to do propriety all our lives? The bolder a man is, the more he is thought of; but let one of us hapless women but stir a step beyond the line, and we have 'improper, indecorous, unwomanly,' thundered in our ears from every side."

"Then you will not acknowledge the proverbial truth of what everybody says?" said Anne.

"Not a bit," said Miss Falconer, boldly. "Why should not I follow the hounds as briskly, and read that political article," she pointed to the paper she had thrown down, "with as much interest as my brother? I do, it is true; but see how all proper mammas draw their pretty behaved young ladies under their wings, when I approach. You all desert me, you cowards of women; I have only men's society to fall back upon."

"But did you not tell us just now that you liked that best?" ventured little Alice Aytoun.

"No, not I. Perhaps I do, though; but I did not say it."

"Then, after all," said Anne, "the mistake is not in what we quiet people call decorous, and proper, and feminine; but only that you, with your high spirits and courage, have the misfortune to be called Marjory, instead of Ralph; that is all; for here, you see, are Miss Aytoun and myself, and all the womankind of Strathoran to back us, who have no ambition whatever to follow the hounds, nor any very particular interest in the leading article. It is merely an individual mistake, Marjory. Acknowledge it."

"Not I," exclaimed Miss Falconer; "it is a universal oppression of the sex. They try to reason us down first, these men; and failing that, they laugh us down: they will not be able to accomplish either, one of these days. There! how you turn upon me, with that provoking smile of yours, Anne Ross. What are you thinking of now?"

"Do you remember a little poem—I think of Southey's," said Anne, smiling—"about the great wars of Marlbro' and Prince Eugene, long ago? I was thinking of its owerword, Marjory—'What good came of it at last? said little Wilhelmine.'"

"Ah, that is just like you," said Miss Falconer; "coming down upon one with your scraps of poetry, when one is speaking common sense. Oh, you need not raise your eyebrows! I tell you I am speaking quite reasonably and calmly; and we shall see, one day."

"But, Miss Falconer," inquired Alice, timidly, "what shall we see?"

"See! Why, a proper equality between men and women, as we were created," said Miss Falconer, vehemently. "No more bandaging up our minds, as they do the feet of the poor girls in China—oppressing us for their own whims, everywhere! No more shutting us out of our proper share in the management of the world—no more confining us in housekeepers' rooms and nurseries; to make preserves, and dress babies!"

"Are the babies to be abolished, then?" said Anne. "For pity's sake, Marjory, do not sentence the poor little things to masculine nurses. Farewell to all music or harmony, then. If we are to dress babies no more, let it be ordained, I pray you, that there shall be no more babies to dress!"

"Nonsense, Anne!" exclaimed Marjory Falconer, loudly; "you want to ridicule all I say. You are content with the bondage—content to be regarded as a piece of furniture, a household drudge, a pretty doll."

"Hush!" said Anne; "spare me the abjective. I am in no danger of your last evil. And see how Miss Aytoun looks at you."

"Never mind," said Miss Falconer; "Miss Aytoun will sympathise with me, I am sure; every true woman must. See how they smile at our opinions—how they sneer at our judgment—'Oh, it's only a woman.' I tell you, Anne Ross, all that will be changed by-and-bye. We shall have equal freedom, equal rights—our own proper dignity and standing in the world."

"And how will it change our position?" said Anne.

"How obtuse you are! Change our position! Why it will make us free—it will emancipate us—it will—"

"Particulars, particulars, Marjory?"

Miss Falconer paused.

"We shall not be thought unfit any longer to do what men do; our equal mental power and intelligence shall be recognised. We shall have equal rights—we shall be free!"

Anne looked up smiling.

"'And what good came of it at last? said little Wilhelmine.'"

Miss Falconer started from her seat in anger, and walked quickly through the room for a moment, Alice looked on in wonder and alarm. At last Marjory approached the table, looked Anne in the face, half smiling, half angry, and replied, in a burst:

"'Nay, that I cannot tell,' quoth he, But 'twas a glorious victory?'"

Conversation less abstract followed, when Lewis and Ralph joined them; and not long after, Anne and Alice resumed their places in the phaeton, and turned homewards, Lewis riding by their side. Anne's spirits had wonderfully lightened during their drive, and now she defended Marjory Falconer, almost gaily, against the laughing and half-contemptuous attacks of Lewis.

"Marjory arms all the silly lads in the parish with flippant impertinences about women and their rights, Miss Aytoun," she said. "I did not mean you, Lewis, so there is no occasion for drowing yourself up. Yet Marjory has some strength, and much kindliness of spirit. And when she has once got rid of those foolish notions, which she will when she has matured a little—"

Anne stopped abruptly. She had noticed before the tall, stooping figure of a woman advancing towards them, and could recognise now, as the passenger approached, the wan face, and wistful, melancholy eyes, which had made so deep an impression upon her imagination, when she saw them on the previous night, looking so sorrowfully on Merkland. A very remarkable face it was, which the stranger now lifted to them, as she passed slowly on, speaking in its emaciated lines of mental struggle more than bodily sickness; and with its strange habitual look of wistful search, as if its eyes had been exercised by constant watching, and had sought about vainly for some hope or gladness never to be found again. Anne met her steadfast, melancholy look for a moment; in another she had passed on.

"What is the matter, Anne?" said Lewis.

Anne drove on awhile, in silence.

"Did you not observe that face?"

"What face? I saw a woman passing, who stared at you, as you did at her; don't be sentimental, Anne: some shopkeeper's wife, from Portoran, who has been at the mill. What were you saying of Marjory Falconer? Go on."

Anne went on.

"She will mature by-and-by, and come out of these follies a sensible woman. You shake your head, Lewis. She will never be of the gentlest; but sensible, and kindly, and vigorous, I believe she will be, one day. There is often some eccentricity about strength, in its development."

"Hear, hear," cried Lewis. "Do you observe how Anne turns her periods, Miss Aytoun? Marjory will keep a chair for you, Anne, in some of her feminine colleges, when she has accomplished the rights of women. Moral philosophy! I hope they will give you an LL.D."

They reached the mill as Lewis spoke. It stood near the spot Mr. Coulter had spoken of "where three lairds' lands met;" and the burn was intercepted for the uses of the mill, just before it joined its waters to the Oran.

Anne drew up her ponies at the end of the little bridge, which gave access to the miller's dwelling. Alice had never seen this picturesque corner of the Oran banks, and Anne proposed giving her a glimpse of the bright interior of Mrs. Melder's pleasant house: she was anxious herself to ask the miller's wife if she knew anything of the singular stranger, whose appearance had interested her so much.

So Johnnie Halflin scrambled down from his perch behind, to hold Lewis's horse, much wondering what motive they could have for calling on Mrs. Melder; and Alice lingered on the grassy bank, that sloped down to the riverside, from Mrs. Melder's door, to ask questions and to admire. The grey mill buildings, and mighty revolving wheel, and rush of foaming water, as the bairn, like some brown mountain urchin, ran, boisterous, from its labors into the placid Oran, giving life and animation to the stream it increased, were worthy of admiration even more genuine than that of Alice, whose little heart was beating very pleasantly, from various causes, which she had not skill, if she had had inclination, to analyze.

But the cottage door was suddenly flung open, a loud scream startled them, and, turning round alarmed, they saw a child flee out, its little frock blazing, its face distorted with pain and fear. Alice screamed, and clung to the arm of Lewis, Lewis called to the boy, and sprang irresolutely forward himself, not knowing what to do; Johnnie Halflin scampered off in terror, holding firmly the bridle of his charge, and the child, blinded with fear, and scorched with pain, flew forward madly. Anne snatched from the carriage a large, rough plaid, threw herself before the little girl, and wrapped it closer round her. The child struggled—Anne pressed the long, wide folds closer and closer round her, extinguishing the flames with her hands. The terrified miller's wife ran to her assistance—so did Lewis, and at last, very much frightened, and considerably scorched, but with no serious injury, the child was carried into the house, where Alice followed timidly, pressing the small hand of the sufferer within her own, and murmuring kindly words to still its weeping. It was a little girl of some six years, and moaned out its childish lamentations in broken words of some strange, sweet, foreign tongue. The remnants of its burnt dress, too, were not like the ordinary garments of peasant children, and Mrs. Melder herself had no family.

"God be thankit ye were passing by, Miss Anne!" exclaimed Mrs. Melder. "I am the silliest body mysel that was ever putten in a strait. Eh! do ye no hear my heart beating?—and the stranger bairn!"

"Whose is it, Mrs. Melder?" asked Anne, as they undressed the moaning child, and laid her on the wooden bed which formed part of the furniture of the homely apartment.

"And that is just what I cannot tell ye, Miss Anne," said the miller's wife. "It was left wi' me by ane—ye wad meet her on the road. She wasna put on like a lady, but she wasna a common body either—it was clear to see that. We've had a dreary house, Robert and me, since little Bell (ye'll mind her, Miss Anne?) was ta'en from us, two years syne come Martinmas, and the stranger leddy had heard tell o't, and thocht, as she said, that I wad be guid to the child—as I will, doubtless, puir, innocent thing!—who could be otherwise?"

"And where did she come from?" inquired Anne, as she assisted in applying some simple remedies.

"The bairn? Na, how can I tell you that Miss Anne, when I dinna ken mysel?"

"No, no; I mean the lady," said Anne, hurriedly. "I saw her—a very remarkable-looking person she is. Is the child her own?"

"Na; she said no, any way," said Mrs. Melder. "Whaever it belongs to, they think shame o't, that's sure. Woes me, Miss Ross! the ill that there is in this world! She has been living at the brig for a day or two back, and the bairn wi' her. I am doubtful it was but a foolish thing, taking a bairn when one kens nought of its kindred. But the house was dreary. Where there has been a babe in a dwelling, it makes great odds when the light of its bit countenance is lifted away, and my heart warmed to the puir wee thing, sent out from its own bluid. So I took it, ye see, Miss Ross, and Robert he didna oppose. It's to bide two years—if we're all spared as long—and the stipend for it is twenty pound, and the siller's lying in Mr. Foreman the writer's hands—so we canna come to any loss. It's an uncommon bairn a'thegither o't, and speaks in a tongue neither Robert nor me can make onything of. It maun have come from some far part—was ye speaking, my lamb?"

Anne beckoned Lewis forward as the child murmured again some incoherent words.

"What language is it?—I do not recognize the tongue."

"It is Spanish," said Lewis. "Strange! Where did the child come from, Mrs. Melder?"

The miller's wife repeated her story, and, promising to call at the house of the doctor on their way homeward, and send him up to the little patient, her visitors left her, and proceeded on their way, disturbed by no further incident, except in Anne's mind, by the strange excitement of interest with which this story moved her. She could not banish the stranger's pale face from her mind, nor forget the pitiful look of the little child, in whose soft features she thought she could trace some resemblance, moaning out its feeble complaint in that strange language, uncomprehended, and alone.

CHAPTER VII

These days passed on in suspense and anxiety to Mrs. Catherine. Uncertain what to believe or disbelieve, concerning the young man in whose fortunes she was so deeply interested, her strong spirit chafed and struggled in its compulsory inactivity. Nor did Lewis's report of Mrs. Duncombe's friends, in any degree still her anxiety. Fashionable ladies stood low in Mrs. Catherine's opinion at all times; and her strong nationality aggravated tenfold her dislike to fashionable ladies in Paris—French or semi-French. Had it not been for Alice, Mrs. Catherine herself would have been on her way to Paris ere now. But unwilling to send the girl abruptly home, and riveted besides by a hundred little ties, which made her absence from the Tower (she had not left it since her sorrowful journey, thirty years' ago, from Sholto's island grave) seem an impossibility; she waited—we are constrained to admit, not patiently—for further tidings, inclined to hope sometimes that Mr. Foreman's benevolent surmise might be well-founded; and anon, cast down, and venting her grief in a show of bitter indignation at "the prodigal that could sell his birthright."

Many solitary hours were spent during that anxious fortnight (for mails travelled tardily thirty years ago) in the little room—and many wrestlings of secret, silent prayer these narrow walls were witness to. Jacky, gliding hither and thither in her elfin ubiquity, could hear Mrs. Catherine's step shake the floor; and listened in tremulous awe and reverence sometimes to those often-repeated words, the burden of Mrs. Catherine's anxiety: "Isabel Balfour's one son—that might have been your firstborn, Sholto Douglas!" But Jacky, with a sentiment of honor peculiar to herself, kept her knowledge of Mrs. Catherine's trouble, jealously within her own mind, and in the intervals of her heterogeneous occupations, and no less heterogeneous studies, wove dreams of that young Laird of Strathoran, over whom Mrs. Catherine prayed and mourned—and creating for his especial service, some such wondrous vassal as the Genii of Aladdin, conjured Sholto Douglas back to life and lands again, and made the prodigal his heir and son.

Little Bessie, Alice Aytoun's maid, did not know what to make of that strange, thin, angular girl, with her dark keen face, and eccentric motions, and singular language. Bessie, plump, rosy and good-humored, looked on in wondering silence as Jacky sat on the carpet in the library, bent almost double over some mighty old volume from those heavy and well-filled shelves—was inclined to laugh sometimes, yet checking herself in mysterious reverence, revolved in her mind the possibility of Mrs. Catherine's frequent epithet "you elf"—having in it some shadow of truth. Bessie had read fairy tales in her day, and knew that in these authentic histories there were such things as changelings—could this strange Jacky be one? The flying footsteps, and bold leaps and climbings, which Bessie did not venture to emulate, gave some color to the supposition, so did these out-of-the-way studies and singular expressions; but Jacky withal was not malicious, nor evil-tempered, and Bessie paused before condemning her. On consulting Johnnie Halflin on the subject, she found him as much puzzled as herself.

"For ye see," said Johnnie, "she was never at the schule—and look till her reading! I was three—four year at it mysel, the haill winter; for ye ken in this part, Bessie, it's no' like a toun—there's the beasts to herd all the summer and other turns, till the shearing's by; but I wad rather hae a day's kemping with that illwilly nowt that winna bide out o' the corn, than sit down to the books wi' Jacky. She kens best herself where she learnt it."

"And look how she speaks," ejaculated Bessie.

"Speaks! ye have not heard her get to her English—it's like listening to the leddies. No Mrs. Catherine ye see, for one canna think what words she says—ye just ken when ye hear her, that ye maun do what ye're bidden in a moment; but Jacky! ye would think she got it a' out of books—whiles, when ye anger her—"

"Eh, Johnnie! yonder she is, coming fleeing down the hill," cried little Bessie in alarm, as a flying figure paused on a ridge of the steep eminence above them, and drew itself back for a final race to the bottom. "Look! ye would think she never touched the ground."

"Whist, whist," said Johnnie, apprehensively, "she can hear ony sound about the place, as quick as Oscar, and Oscar's the best watch in the parish—be quiet, Bessie."

The youthful gossips were standing, during their gloaming hour of leisure, at the back of a knot of outhouses, barns, and stables, and Jacky came sweeping down upon them out of breath.

"Are you there, Johnnie Halflin? is that you, Bessie? Has my mother been in the barn yet?—whisht, there she's speaking."

"No, it's Jean," said the lad; "the cow's better, and Jean said she would never let on there had been onything the matter wi't, or else the puir beast would be killed wi' physic. Ye needna tell on her, Jacky—ye wadna like to harm a bonnie cow like yon, yoursel."

"And we'll no' tell on you," added Bessie.

"I'm no caring," was the quick response, "whether ye tell on me or no—only if you do, Bessie, I'll never be friends with ye again; and if you do, Johnnie, ye'll catch grief. Guess where I've been."

"Scooring ower the hills on a heather besom," said Johnnie, "seeking the fairies—they say ye're one yoursel."

A sweep of Jacky's energetic arm sent Johnnie staggering down the path.

"I have been down at Robert Melder's mill, and there's a bairn there—a little girl—Bessie, ye never saw the like of it!"

"Is't a' dressed in green, and riding on a white powny?" said Mrs. Catherine's youthful servingman, returning to the charge.

"Ye're a fuil," retorted Jacky, flushing indignantly, "how do the like of you ken what's true and what's a fatle? There was a lady once, that led a lion in her hand—you dinna ken what that means—and if there were gentle spirits lang syne in the air, what do you ken about them? Bessie, come with me the morn, and see the little bairn. I like to hear her speak; she says words like what you hear in dreams."

Jacky's companions indulged in a smothered laugh.

"Has she wings?" asked the lad.

"I will throw ye into the Oran, Johnnie Halflin," cried Jacky, in wrath; "if ye do not hold your peace in a minute. Miss Anne saved her life, and she speaks a strange language that naebody kens; and she's from a strange country; and she's like—"

"On, I saw her mysel," interrupted Johnnie, "a bit wee smout, wi' her frock burning—saved her life! how grand we're speaking! I could have done't mysel, a' that Miss Anne did, and made nae work about it—on y I had Merkland's horse to haud."

"I have seen a face like it," said Jacky, thoughtfully, "a' but the eyes."

"Eh, and isna Mr. Ross a fine young gentleman?" said little Bessie. Bessie was glad to seize upon the first tangible point.

"How would ye like to bide constant in Strathoran, Bessie," said Johnnie Halflin, "down bye at Merkland? Eh, disna Mr. Lewis gie weary looks up at the easter tower?"

Bessie bridled, and drew herself up with pleased consciousness, as her mistress's representative.

"I wonder at ye, Johnnie! how can ye speak such nonsense?"

"Is t Miss Aytoun Mr. Lewis looks up for?" inquired Jacky.

Her companions answered with a laugh.

"I think," said the boy, "for my ain part, that there's not a young leddy in a' Strathoran like Miss Aytoun. She's out-o'-sight bonnier than Miss Anne."

Jacky pushed him indignantly away.

"A fine judge you are. Like a big turnip your ain sel. A clumsy Swede, like what they give to the kye. But, Bessie, do you think Mr. Lewis is in—" Jacky hesitated, her own singular romance making it sacrilege to speak the usual word in presence of those ruder comrades: "do ye think Mr. Lewis likes Miss Alice? he's no courting her?"

Bessie smiled, blushed, and looked dignified.

"O, Jacky, how do I ken?"

"Does Miss Alice like him?"

"Jacky, what a question! Miss Alice disna tell me."

Jacky looked at her inquisitively, and finishing her share of the conversation in her own abrupt fashion, shot into the byre to see the ailing cow, from whence she soon after stole into the Tower, where an irksome hour of compulsory stocking-knitting, in the comfortable housekeeper's-room of Mrs. Euphan Morison, awaited Mrs. Euphan's reluctant daughter. The room was a very cosy room in all things, but its disagreeable odor of dried and drying herbs; and Jacky, after a reproof from her mother, so habitual that it had sunk into a formula, took her customary seat and work. Bessie joined her, by-and-bye, with some little piece of sewing that she had to do for Miss Aytoun, and Johnnie Halflin, less dignified, betook himself to the kitchen fire, to read, or joke, or doze the evening out.

The time drew near when Mrs. Catherine's doubts concerning Archibald Sutherland were to be solved. The strong old lady grew nervous on these dim mornings, and opened her letter-bag with a tremor in her hand; but when the latest day had come, there was still no letter from Paris. Impatiently she tossed them out. There were two or three letters of applicants for her vacant farm, the closely-written sheet of home-news for Alice, business-notes of various kinds, but nothing from the prodigal, whose interests lay so near her heart. She lifted them all separately again, turned out the bag—in vain. Her clear eye had made no blunder in its first quick investigation. Mrs. Catherine's brow darkened. Alice hardly dared to approach timidly, and withdraw her own letter from the little heap. Not that the face of her kinswoman expressed anger, but it bore the impress of some unknown mental struggle, which Alice, in the serene light of her girlish happiness, did not even know by name.

So Alice stole up stairs to the fireside of her bright dressing-room, to read the long mother's letter, overflowing with tender counsel and affection, and to weave fair dreams—dreams of joy and honor to that gentle mother, and all things pleasant and prosperous to James—round one unacknowledged centre of her own. Pleasant are those bright dream-mists of youthful reverie, with their vague fairy-land of gladness—pleasant to weave their tinted web, indefinitely rich and glorious, over that universe of golden air, with its long withdrawing vistas—the wealthy future of youth.

But Mrs. Catherine sat still alone, her head bent forward, her keen eyes looking into the blank depths of a mirror on the wall, as though, like the hapless lady in the tale, she could read the wished-for tidings there. The door opened slowly. Jacky, with some strange intuitive knowledge of her mistress's anxiety, had been on the outlook from the window of the west room, and had now glided down stairs to report. Mrs. Catherine raised her head sharply as the girl's prefatory "If you please!" fell on her ear.

"What ist', you elf?"

"If you please," continued Jacky, "it's Mr. Ferguson, the Strathoran factor, gallopping up the waterside like to break his neck!"

Mrs. Catherine started to her feet.

"Take him to the library—I will be down myself in a moment. Are you lingering, you fairy? Away with you!"

Jacky vanished, and Mrs. Catherine walked hastily through the room.

"He will have gotten tidings!" And then she was still for a moment, in communion with One mightier than man, nerving herself for the "tidings," whatever they might be.

Jacky stood at the open door as Mr. Ferguson gallopped up, but he did notice the unusual haste with which he was hurried into the library. A cold dew was on his honest forehead; regret and grief were in his kindly heart; the familiar ordinary things about him bore a strange look of change. The difference was in his own agitated eyes, but he did not think of that. Mrs. Catherine stood before him, calm and stern, in the library.

"Mr. Ferguson, you have gotten tidings?"

The firm, strong figure reeled in Mr. Ferguson's dizzy eyes.

"Mr. Ferguson, you are troubled. Has the prodigal done his worst? Sit down and calm yourself. I am waiting to hear?"

The factor sat down. Mrs. Catherine did not, but, clasping her hands tightly together, stood before him and waited.

"I have bad news, Mrs. Catherine," said Mr. Ferguson; "worse news, a hundred times, than ever I suspected—than ever you could expect. Strathoran is fallen—ruined! No hope—no possibility of saving him! It is all over!" And the strong man groaned.

"How and wherefore?" said Mrs. Catherine, sternly.

"He has sold his estate—parted with his home and his land to some titled sharper in Paris. Sold! he has done worse—still more dishonorable and fatal than that, he has gambled it away; what his father spent years to redeem, and set free for him, he has staked on the chances of a game. Bear with me, Mrs. Catherine, if I speak bitterly. The young man has disappointed all my hopes—ruined himself—what will become of him?"

Mrs. Catherine stood with her head bowed down, but otherwise firmly erect, and silent.

"What will he do?" repeated the distressed factor, "what can he do? land and name, fortune and character, all lost. What has he left, as he says, but despair—with his prospects too, his fair beginning. O, it is enough to make a man distracted! What have they done, that unhappy race, that they should be constantly thus—father and son, a wise man and a prodigal, the one wasting his substance and his inheritance, the other denying himself the lawful pleasures of a just life to win it back again."

"Comfort yourself, Robert Ferguson," said Mrs. Catherine, bitterly, as drawing forward a chair with emphatic rapidity, she seated herself at the table, "there will be no son of the name again to waste years in building up the house of Strathoran: their history has come to an end—fitly ended in a rioter and a prodigal."

The factor looked up deprecatingly, the very words which his excitement brought to his own lips, sounding harsh from another's.

"Mrs. Catherine, Mr. Archibald is young. When other lads were leaving school or entering college, he was launched upon the world his own master, with a great income and a large estate.—You know how easily the light spirit of youth is moved, but you cannot know how the way of a young man is hedged in with temptations—Mrs. Catherine!" the factor raised his hand in appeal.

"Speak not to me," said Mrs. Catherine, "I know! yes truly, I know more than you think, or give me credit for. Temptations! and what is obedience that has never been tried, or strength that has not been exercised in needful resistance? I bid ye listen to me, Robert Ferguson—was there not a test appointed in Eden? and would you set youself to say that the fool of a woman (that I should say so, who am of her lineage and blood!) might be justified for her ill-doing, because the fruit hung fair upon the tree, and tempted the wandering eye of her? Think better of my judgment and bring no such pleas to me."

"What can I bring? What can I say?" said Mr. Ferguson, in a low voice. "Is he to be left to live or die, as he best can, in yon strange country? Are we to let him sink into a professional gamester, like the men who have ruined him? I speak wildly.—He would never do that. I myself must seek, in some other place, a livelihood for my family; and I will get it; for my work is clear before me, and it is known that I can do what I undertake; but for him, Mrs. Catherine, with no friend in this wide world but yourself, who can give him efficient help—with not an acre but these poor lands of Loelyin and Lochend, which are still entailed; and, worse than all that, with his best years lost, his principles unsettled, and a stain upon his name—what is to become of him?"

"He will drink the beverage he has brewed," said Mrs. Catherine, harshly. "He will have the reward of the waster, as I have told you before now. Let him take his wages—let him want now, as he has sinfully wasted. It is his righteous hire and reward."

"And you can see that, can think of that, and not stretch out a hand to him?" cried the factor, nervously, as he rose from his chair. "Except my hand and my head, Mrs. Catherine Douglas, I have no inheritance; and your estate yields gold to you, greater every year; but, before I see want come to Strathoran's son, I will labor night and day. The professions are open to him yet.—His mother's uncle was a Lord of Session; his father's cousin was the greatest physician in Edinburgh. I bid you good morning, Mrs. Catherine. I have to write to Mr. Archibald, without loss of time."

"Sit down upon your seat, this moment," said Mrs. Catherine, authoritatively, "and do not speak to me like a fool, Robert Ferguson. Let me hear Archie Sutherland's story, the worst and the best of it; and spend a pound of your own siller on the rioter, at your peril! As if I did not know one lad at the college was enough for any man. Sit down upon your seat, and tell me the whole story, as I bid you, this moment; or I vow to you, that your young advocate, if he had his gown the morn, shall get no pleas of mine!"

Mr. Ferguson sat down, well pleased, and taking out a letter, laid it silently before Mrs. Catherine. The letter was long, blurred, uneven, and written, as it seemed, in hurried intervals, with breaks and incoherent dashes of the pen between. It was not either very clear or very coherent; but it told how rent and distracted the writer's heart and spirit were, and what a ceaseless struggle raged and contended there. The large soft folds of Mrs. Catherine's shawl shook as if a wind had stirred them, but she did not speak; the moisture gathered thick beneath her large eyelid, but was not shed, for Mrs. Catherine was not given to tears. At last she closed the letter carefully, occupying much more time in the operation than was necessary, and endeavored to assume her former caustic tone to hide her graver emotions. "A fine story to come to a gentlewoman withal! well, Mr. Ferguson, and what is it your purpose that I should do for your rioter?"

"I do not know—I have not been able to think," said the factor, himself moved even to weeping: "that something must be done, and that immediately, is clear. If I had not been coming to you for assistance, Mrs. Catherine, I should have come for advice, for how to proceed I cannot see."

There was a considerable pause—at length, Mrs. Catherine started from her seat and resumed her quick pacing of the room.

"Wherefore are we losing time—send a message home, to Woodsmuir to bid them put up a change of apparel for you; ride into Portoran and get what siller will be needful—do not be scrupulous—and go your ways this very day, or, if it be too far spent, at the latest the morn, to the prodigal. I would go myself, but the witless youth, as I see by his letter, is feared for me, and you can maybe travel with less delay. Bring him home. Strathoran can shelter him no longer, but the dwelling-place of Sholto Douglas can never be closed upon Isabel Balfour's son. I say to you, lose no time, Robert Ferguson." Mrs. Catherine rang the bell energetically. "Write to your wife about the needful raiment. Archie Sutherland has slept in young Robert's cradle. She will not grudge the trouble."

Mr. Ferguson did not wait to reflect, but with all speed, drew paper and ink towards him and began to write.

"Let Andrew or Johnnie be ready in a moment to ride to Woodsmuir," said Mrs. Catherine, as Jacky appeared at the door; "and tell your mother to send in refreshments for Mr. Ferguson. Begone, you imp—what are you waiting for?"

"If you please," said Jacky, "it's Mr. Foreman himsel in the gig—will I bring him in?" and, without waiting for an answer, the girl disappeared.

"Mr. Foreman himself," repeated Mrs. Catherine. "What new trouble is coming now?—they are ever in troops."

Mr. Ferguson raised his head uneasily and paused in his writing. The excited curiosity of both suggesting some further aggravation of the great misfortunes they already knew.

Mr. Foreman entered the room gravely, and with care in his face—greeted Mrs. Catherine in silence, and starting, when he saw Mr. Ferguson, asked; "It is true, then?"

"True?—Ay, beyond doubt or hoping," said Mrs. Catherine, bitterly. "The prodigal has made an end of his house and name. I was right, Mr. Foreman, and you were wrong. The hairy fool had been sent on no less an errand than to see the value of the prey. Grant me patience!—how am I to see daily before me, some evil animal, such as could herd with cattle like you, reigning in the house of the Sutherlands?"

"How have you heard, Mr. Foreman?" said the factor, anxiously. "Has Mr. Archibald written to you himself?"

"No," said Mr. Foreman, "I have got my information from a most disagreeable source. I received a letter to-day from the solicitors of Lord Gillravidge, touching the conveyance of the property. Have you the intelligence direct from Mr. Sutherland? I came up immediately to let Mrs. Catherine know."

"I have a letter," said Mr. Ferguson. "It is indeed all over. He has lost everything except the entailed lands of Loelyin and Lochend, and the farm of Woodsmuir, upon which my own house stands, and it, you know, is mortgaged to its full value. All the rest is gone. Mr. Archibald is ruined."

There was a pause again, broken only by the sound of Mrs. Catherine's footsteps, as she walked heavily through the room.—These grave, kind men, Archibald Sutherland's factor and agent, who had known him all his life, were almost as deeply affected with his sin and misfortune as though he had been an erring son. Mr. Foreman broke the silence by asking:

"What do you intend to do?"

"Mrs. Catherine advises me to start immediately for Paris," said Mr. Ferguson. "We all of us know how bitterly Mr. Archibald will reproach himself, now that all self-reproach is unavailing. I will endeavor to bring him home—to the Tower, I mean; and then—I do not well know what we are to do. But we must try to rouse his mind (it is a vigorous one, if it were but in a purer atmosphere,) to shape out for itself another course. I was about to ride into Portoran to make immediate preparation for my journey."

"Your letter, Mr. Ferguson," said Mrs. Catherine, as Jacky again appeared at the door. "Let Andrew—is it Andrew?—lose no time! Here, you elf! Have you anything else to advise, Mr. Foreman? I myself would start in a moment, but that I think Mr. Ferguson would do it better. The lad's spirit is broken, doubtless, and I might be over harsh upon him. Give me Archie's letter."

Mrs. Catherine's large grey eyelid swelled full again, and she seated herself at the table.

"I have nothing else to advise," said Mr. Foreman, abstractedly. "I think it is very wise, and you should start at once, Mr. Ferguson. But—" The lawyer paused. "Is it not possible to do anything? Could no compromise be made? Better mortgage the land (it was mortgaged heavily enough in his grandfather's time—I remember how old Strathoran was hampered by paying them off,) than suffer it to pass altogether out of his hands. Could nothing be done? Mrs. Catherine, if such an arrangement were possible, would you not lend your assistance?"

Mrs. Catherine raised her eyes from the letter.

"To what end or purpose? That he might have the freedom of losing the land again, if it were won back to him by the spending of other folks' substance? George Foreman, it is not like your wisdom to think of such a thing. A penniless laird—a shadow, and no substance—with a false rank to keep up, and nothing coming in to keep it up withal? I will not hear of it! Gentlemen, I have made up my mind; out of yon hot unnatural air of artificial ill, the lad must come down to the cold blast of poverty, if he is ever to be anything but a silken fule, spending gear unjustly gotten, in an unlawful way. I say I will have no hand in giving back plenty and ease to Archie Sutherland, till he has righteously wrought and struggled for the same. Bring him back to my house, Robert Ferguson. He has lost the home and the lands of his fathers. Let him see them in the hands of an alien, and then let him gird his loins to a right warfare, and win them back again. With God's blessing, and man's labor, there is nought in this world impossible. I hope to live to see him win back his possessions, as I have seen him lose them. If he does not, he deserves them not."

"Write to him so," said Mr. Ferguson, eagerly. "It is the spur he needs. Let me have a letter, so hopeful and encouraging, to carry with me, Mrs. Catherine. Mere reproach would do evil, and not good. You are perfectly right. A struggle—a warfare—that is the true prescription. Write to Mr. Archibald yourself—it will have more effect than anything I can say."

Mr. Foreman sighed, and felt almost inclined to withdraw his adherence from those reformers who aim at the abolition of entails. At length, and slowly, he signified his consent.

"Yes—yes: Mrs. Catherine is right. I believe it is the wisest way. But—"

Mr. Foreman paused again. A strange master in Strathoran—the kindly union of the country broken in upon by one who, if they judged rightly, had done grievous ill to Archibald Sutherland. A painful film came over the lawyer's eyes. It seemed like treason to the trust reposed in him by "Old Strathoran" thus to suffer his son's downfall.

"You are losing time," said Mrs. Catherine. "Robert Ferguson, the day is wearing on. Ye will not be able to leave Portoran the night. Start with the first coach the morn's morning. Do not tarry a moment. Mind how long the days will be to a spirit in despair; and come to me when you are returning from Portoran if there is time. I will write to the unhappy lad."

Thus dismissed, both gentlemen took their leave, the factor receiving a parting adjuration to "take sufficient siller—be not scrimpit. Ye will have many charges in so long a journey; and, as I have said, Robert Ferguson, lay out a pound of your own siller upon this dyvour at your proper peril! I will visit your iniquity upon the head of your young advocate, if ye venture to do such a thing.—Mind!"

Mrs. Catherine seated herself at her library table as the factor and the lawyer rode away together, and began to write to Archibald Sutherland—a hurried letter, swiftly written. It ran thus:

"I have heard of your transgression and calamity, Archibald Sutherland, and write as I need not tell you, in sore grief. Nevertheless, I have neither time nor leisure to record my lamentations, nor do I think that tears from old e'en—the which are bitter in the shedding—are things to make merchandise of for the mending of young backsliders. At this moment, I have other matters in hand. I see by your letter to Mr. Ferguson (a better man than I fear you will ever be), that you are yourself cast down, and in grief, as it is meet you should be. See that it be for the sin, and not for the mere carnal consequences, and so there will be the better chance for a blessing on your repentance.

"And boy, rise up and come back to the country that brought you forth, out of that den of sin and iniquity. The house of your fathers is open to you no longer—the house of Sholto Douglas can never be shut upon Isabel Balfour's son. Come back to me—you shall not be my heir, for the lands of my fathers must descend to none that cannot keep them firmly, and guide them well; but whatsoever is needful for you to begin your warfare, lies ready for your claiming. I say your warfare, Archie Sutherland, for I bid you not come home to dally through an idle life or waste more days.—Come home to fight for your possessions back again—come home to strive in every honorable and lawful way to win back the good land you have lost—come home, I say, Archie Sutherland, to redeem your inheritance by honest labor, and establish your house again, as it was established by the first Sutherland that set foot on Oranside. The road is clear before you. You have gotten all the siller wasted now that you can get to waste. I command you, as there is anything in this life you set a value on, to throw these evil things behind you, and gird yourself for a warfare—a warfare that will be neither light nor brief, but that will be—what your past life has not been—just and honorable, a work for a man, not a witless and sinful dalliance for a silly youth, a play for a fevered bairn.

"I have a burden of years upon me as you know, and may have but a small distance between me and the kirkyard of Strathoran, therefore I lay my charge upon you to be speedy with your labor. My kin and youthful neighbors are round about me, Archie Sutherland, (all but Sholto my one brother, that I left lying in the cold earth of a strange country,) but they are dwelling in silent cities, where no living thing can tarry. Boy! let me see hope breaking upon you, before I lay down my head beside them. My time is short. Turn to this work, Archie Sutherland, that I may carry better tidings with me, to your father and your mother, in the good land where they are resting from their labor. To your warfare I command you, young man, that I may see your prosperity as I have seen your down-come. Come home to the house of your mother's oldest friend, come home without delay (and I charge you that what honor remains to your name may be preserved—to bring home to me that wilful girl, your sister Isabel) to your just work, that I may not go down with a sore heart to my last dwelling-place.

"CATHERINE DOUGLAS."

Mr. Ferguson returned to the Tower on his way to Woodsmuir, and received this letter, with many messages and charges besides, especially addressed to Isabel Sutherland, whom Mrs. Catherine, in the excitement of her grief for Archibald, had almost forgotten. Mr. Ferguson was to leave Portoran with the night-coach for Edinburgh; and, again, the perforce quietude of waiting fell upon the aged lady of the Tower.

CHAPTER VIII

Other two weary slow-paced weeks wore through, before Mrs. Catherine heard any further tidings of her prodigal. At last Mr. Ferguson's hurried intimation of his arrival in Paris came at once to satisfy and to stimulate her anxiety—for Mr. Ferguson's brief epistle said emphatically that it was well he had lost no time in setting out upon his journey, and that he found "Mr. Archibald" in sorest need of some steadfast friend about him. A few days after there came a more explicit letter. Mr. Ferguson had found poor Archibald Sutherland in the strong grip of despair. Loss of fortune had brought loss of friends—not one of all his former guests or flatterers remained to comfort him in his poverty; and save for the jealous solicitude with which he guarded his sister, Mr. Ferguson believed that his reckless desperation would have laid him ere now in the grave of the suicide. But Isabel, wilful, impetuous and admired as she was, bound her fierce guardian to his hated life—still courted in these gay circles, for the wit and beauty which all this burden of calamity could not diminish, the ruined man stalked by her side everywhere, like some intruding spectre, casting a blight upon the smiles that woke no congenial sunshine in his ghostly face. The treachery which he had felt surrounding himself—the warning of Mrs. Catherine's letters had awakened him to a wild anxiety for Isabel: he could not bear her absence from him. Regardless of sneers and inuendos—regardless of contempt and indifference, he followed his sister wherever she went, and scowled away from her in his gaunt pride and anger, whosoever ventured upon any show of admiration. But no human spirit could bear that fierce tension long; and when his factor's home face looked in upon him, so clear, upright, and manlike, with all its respectful kindliness of sympathy, the heart of Archibald Sutherland burst from its compulsory hardihood, and melted into very weakness. None knew or could appreciate better than he, the thoroughly honorable character of Mr. Ferguson—none better knew the warm kindliness of that pleasant home of Woodsmuir, which the factor had left for the discomforts of a long journey and a strange country, to aid and succor him—him, the prodigal, the destroyer of his father's house. Tears, strange to the eyes of the broken man, fell copiously over Mrs. Catherine's letter—a time of strange incoherence followed, and when Mr. Ferguson wrote again, it was from the sick room where Archibald Sutherland lay, prostrate in body and mind, in the wild heat of fever, struggling for his life.

Mr. Ferguson wrote with unwonted pathos of that strange phantom of terror for Isabel, which haunted his patient's mind by night and day—the one consistent thread through all that delirious chaos—of how the wilful sister in the pride of her wit and beauty heard it first from her brother's raving lips with indignant anger, haughtily blaming the manly watcher by that brother's bedside whose place she did not offer to take; but how, at last, the "weeping blood of woman's breast" was reached by that wail of agony, and Isabel gave up her gaieties, and took her place in the sick room, soothing the sufferer by her very presence. But Mr. Ferguson did not tell, how unweariedly he himself watched by that bed of fever, and when doctor and attendant despaired, still hoped against hope—nor how, when feeble, and pale, and worn out, the convalescent could raise his head again, it was the strong arm of his Strathoran factor that held him up—it was the kindly tongue of home that gave thanks for his recovery.

But long weeks had lengthened into months during Archibald's illness, and the dark short days of December were rising, in their chill alternations of frost and rain, upon the northern skies of Strathoran, when Mr. Ferguson returned home. He came alone, for Captain Duncombe had joined his wife and brother-in-law in Paris, and was to be their escort to England. Captain Duncombe had got a considerable accession of fortune, by the death of some friend, during the time of Archibald's convalescence, and had managed to effect an exchange into a regiment stationed near London, whither his wife had no objection to accompany him. The saturnine Captain was something touched by his hapless brother-in-law's emaciated appearance, and had no objection to travel leisurely home for his convenience, though protesting many times, with unnecessary fervor, that, when once at home, he could do nothing for him; and Mr. Ferguson, whose own affairs imperatively called for his presence, and whose strength had been wasted by long confinement, reluctantly left his patient, and returned to Strathoran alone.

In the meantime, changes had taken place there: bevies of English sportsmen had arrived with Lord Gillravidge at his newly acquired property—gamekeepers and grooms, a whole village full, overbrimmed its quiet precincts. Rough Ralph Falconer, condescendingly noticed at first, in acknowledgment of his kindred pursuits, was shrinking from the neighborhood already fairly over-crowed and put down, endeavoring to hide his mortification under bitter laughter. Bitterly upon them, "pilgarlic dandies," "hairy fuils," "idle cattle," poured the full flood of Mrs. Catherine's derision. The countryside was stirred with unwonted excitement. An Englishman, alien to their blood, and contemptuous of their Church—the supplanter, besides, of an old and long established family, in a district peculiarly tenacious of hereditary loves and hatreds,—the new Lord of Strathoran had all the strongest feelings of his neighbors arrayed against him.

The new Lord of Strathoran was supremely indifferent. The countryside and its likings and dislikings, were not of the remotest consequence to him.

And little Alice Aytoun was beginning to receive gentle and tender hints from Edinburgh, that the original limits proposed for her visit, had been considerably overpassed. She had forgotten, in the unconscious selfishness of a light heart, how lonely the Edinburgh parlor would be, during the long days which her mother spent there alone—for Alice's entree into the festivities and party-givings of that quiet district, which her inexperience called "the world," had been a triumph—and with so much homage laid at her little feet, and so much girlish delight and laughing wonder, in receiving that strange, new tribute of admiration, it was scarcely wonderful that the Edinburgh parlor, with its quiet dwelling at home, and brief domestic circle, seemed almost sombre in the contrast. It was arranged, however, that Alice should return home after the new year, and, her conscience eased of some compunctions it had, respecting neglect of her mother, Alice looked forward to the especial merry-makings of that blythe season with a light heart.

Meanwhile, Anne Ross's ingenuity was vainly exercised in devising expedients to occupy her brother, and divert him from those frequent visits which it had become his pleasure to pay at the Tower. Lewis found numberless errands—alleged consultations with Mrs. Catherine, at which his mother fumed silently in sullen dignity—pretences for advising with the shrewd factotum of Mrs. Catherine's finely-cultivated home-farm, concerning those fields immediately adjoining Merkland which Mr. Coulter advised, putting on some scientific regimen—or even a rare fungus, or delicate moss to show to Miss Aytoun, who began to be interested in that beautiful science of botany which Lewis himself had taken up so suddenly.

These visits, and the too certain end to which they tended, pained Anne deeply, overpowered her, indeed, sometimes with sick bewilderment, the more that in the present state of matters, she was perfectly powerless. Any step of her's might precipitate Lewis, so jealously alive to interference as he was, and make that certain, which was now only feared and deprecated, so Anne, like her friend in the Tower, had to wait perforce for the regular course of events, and with an anxiety still more intense and painful than Mrs. Catherine's. What but woe and mishap could come from this unhappy intercourse? What but pain and disappointment and sorrow to these two youthful hearts.

Anne could perceive that it annoyed her step-mother; that Mrs. Ross, with her overweening partiality for, and pride in her only son, was inclined to take his attention to Alice Aytoun as a personal slight and injury to herself. But it was not because a connection so terrible existed between the families already—Alice had no friends to elevate the standing, nor portion to increase the wealth of her future partner, and therefore Mrs. Ross frowned upon the growing devotion of Lewis, and already, in many a peevish altercation and sarcastic allusion, had brought in Alice Aytoun's name—fanning thereby the flame which she hoped to extinguish.

And during these months, the little girl, so strangely brought to Oran Mill, was learning the tongue of her new home rapidly. A strange junction, the liquid Spanish, which fell on Jacky's visionary ear so pleasantly, "like the words folk hear in dreams," made, mingled with these soft syllables of the homely, Scottish tongue, broken from what harshness soever might originally be in them, by the child's voice of lisping music. Mrs. Melder had been told to call her Lilias, and affection had already contracted the name into the familiar diminutive of "Lilie." A strange exotic lily the child seemed with her small, pale features and olive-tinted cheek, and flood of dusky silken hair, and she had become already a wonder in the parish.

Mrs. Coulter sent for the miller's wife on some small pretext of business, that she might see her little lodger, and Lilie returned from Harrows laden with fruit, and toys, and sweetmeats, and leaving little Harry Coulter, the agriculturist's Benjamin, struggling with desperate energy to follow her, and hopelessly in love. Lilie had even been taken to the Tower, and half smothered with caresses from Alice, had received from Mrs. Catherine strange looks of musing melancholy, and one abrupt expression of wonder—

"Who was she like?"

Miss Falconer herself had gallopped a couple of miles out of her way, and stopped at the Mill, with her horse in a foam, to make acquaintance with the little Donna. Jacky had constituted herself her bodyguard and attendant, and carried her off whole days on solitary rambles among the hills. There were few of all the circle round who were not interested in the stranger child.

But no one received so great a share of Lilie's regard, or was so powerfully attracted towards her, as Anne Ross. There was a new pleasure now in the long walks, which had a half hour's playful intercourse with Lilie to make them cheerful; and Anne again and again repeated her inquiries concerning the stranger who had left the child with Mrs. Melder, without however eliciting anything new.

"She wasna put on like a lady," repeated the miller's wife. "My ain muckle shawl, wi' the border, was worth twa o' the ain she had on, and naething but a printed goun. But I have seen folk in silks and satins, Miss Anne, that had a commoner look—no that she was bonnie—but you saw her yoursel."

"Yes," said Anne; "she was a very remarkable looking person."

"Na' but the eyes of her! They made me that I near sat down and fainted—they had sic a wistful, murning look in them. The bairn's are no unlike. Haud up your head, Lilie, my lamb—only it wad tak watching and sorrow, if I'm no far mistaken, to gie her yon look. Waes me, Miss Anne! it spoke o' a sair heart!"

"But Lilie's are bright and happy," said Anne, drawing the child closer to her, and looking affectionately upon the little face, from which shone eyes deep enough in their liquid darkness to mirror forth great sorrows. "We must not let grief come near Lilie."

"Lilie blythe—blythe?" said the child, clinging to her side. "Lilie no like happy. Blythe is bonnier! Lilie go the morn—up—up!"

"To the hills, Lilie?"

"Up—up!" said the child, imitating with feet and hands the motions of climbing. "Lilie look away far—at the water."

"At the Oran, Lilie?"

"Where he go to?" asked Lilie, pointing through the window to the brown, foaming water—"rinning fast? Where he go to?"

"To the sea, Lilie," said Anne.

"Yes—yes," said the child. "Lilie once sail upon the sea; row—row—in a big boat. Lilie likes to look at it."

"Were you alone, Lilie?" said Anne. "Was no one with you?"

The child did not understand.

"A big boat—big—big—bigger than yon!" Lilie had seen Mrs. Catherine's little vessel on the Oran, and had been greatly interested in it. "Lilie ran about," and the child eked out her slender vocabulary with the universal language of signs, "and saw the sea; but the water did not come upon Lilie."

"And was there no one to take care of Lilie?" said Anne.—"No one to put on her little frock, and to comb these pretty curls?"

The child looked up thoughtfully for a moment, and then, hiding her face in Anne's lap, burst out into a passion of tears, moaning out in her own language a lamentation over her "good nurse, her Juana," with all the inconsolable vehemence of childhood.

"She has done that before," said Mrs. Melder. "Can ye make onything o' the words, Miss Anne? I hae gotten to ken the sound o' them, though neither Robert nor me can make ony sense o' the outlandish tongue. Lilie, my lamb, whisht, like a guid bairn, and dry your eyes. See what a bonnie book Miss Anne has brocht ye, and pictures in't!

"There's mony o' the neighbors wonder at us," continued Mrs. Melder, as the child, when its fit of weeping was over, clambered up upon the table in the window, and sat there, in enjoyment of the picture-book, "for taking a bairn we ken naething about; and ye may think it foolish too, Miss Anne. But the house was waesome wi' Robert out a' day, and the bit thing had a pitiful look wi't, and the leddy—for she bid to be a leddy, though she was plain enough put on—pleaded wi' me in sic a way that I couldna withstand it; and we're clar o' a' loss, wi' the siller being in Mr. Foreman's hand; and the bairn—puir wee desolate thing, cast off by its ain bluid—is a fine bairn, now that she's learning to speak in a civilized tongue. My ain Bell, if the Almighty had spared her, would hae been about Lilie's age. Eh, Miss Anne! a young lady like you canna ken what a sore dispensation that was! But we maun hae our ain way."

"And do you think the lady could be Lilie's mother?" said Anne, after a pause.

"It's hard to say," said Mrs. Melder; "but I am maistly inclined to think no, Miss Anne, for ye see the bairn disna greet after her the way she did the now, when ye asked her wha came hame wi' her; and the leddy hersel, though she beggit me to be careful o' the bairn, did not keep her in her sight till the last moment, as a mother would have done; and when she went by the Mill, Robert says—for he was watching—that she never stopped to look back; sae I think she may have been a friend further off, Miss Anne, but she couldna be Lilie's mother."

"Strange!" said Anne, "that any friend, above all a mother should send away a child so interesting!"

"Ay, Miss Anne," said Mrs. Melder; "but the like o' you disna ken. There are bitterer things in this world than even grief.—One canna tell. It may be a shame and a disgrace to some decent family, that that wee thing, pleasant as she is, has ever drawn breath—and the lady may be some kin of the mother's, bringing it away out o' the sight o' kent folk and friends. The like of that is ower common. Eh, pity me! there's nae counting the wiles o' the enemy! There's Strathoran, ye see, and the gentlemen that's in't playing at their cartes and their dice, they tell me, on the very Sabbath day itsel! Is't no enough to bring a judgment on the country-side? If auld Strathoran—honest man—could but look down into his ain house now, I canna think but what it would make his heart sair—even yonder. He was a guid man, auld Strathoran, though he did put Mr. Bairnsfather into the parish."

"Was that wrong, Mrs. Melder?" said Anne.

"The Apostle says we're no to speak evil o' the ruler o' our people," said Mrs. Melder; "but, eh, Miss Anne, he's wersh and unprofitable. When I was in my trouble and sorrow (and who can tell how dark the earth is, and a'thing in't, when one is bereaved o' their first-born—their only lamb!) Robert brought the minister, thinking he could speak a word o' comfort to me; and what think ye he said, Miss Anne? No that I was to look to my Lord that had gathered my lamb to his ain bosom, out of a' the ills o' this world, but that I was to be reasonable and calm, and bear the trouble wi' fortitude, because it couldna be helpit. That was a' the comfort he had to speak to a distracted woman, whose only bairn was in its grave! But he never had ony little ones himsel."

"And you do not come to the Church, now?" said Anne, holding out her hand, as Lilie descended from the table, and came to her side again.

"Na; we were once gaun to the Meeting, Robert and me, for the Seceder minister preaches guid doctrine, but we couldna think to leave the Kirk. My father was an elder for twenty year—sae we aye waited on till Mr. Lumsden came to Portoran. Eh, Miss Anne, he's a grand man! They say there's no the like o' him in the haill Presbytery!"

"What is this, Lilie?" cried Anne.

Lilie had brought her new "Shorter Catechism," that much-prized text-book of Presbyterian Scotland, to point out the lessons which she was to repeat to Robert Melder, on the Sabbath afternoon, according to the venerable and excellent custom of such religious humble households; and insisted upon repeating her former "questions" and the first Psalm she had learnt in her new language.

Anne took the book, well pleased, and listened, while Lilie repeated that beautiful proposition in which all Scotland for centuries has learned to define the chief end of man, and then, with some slight stammering and uncertainty, went on:

"That man hath perfect blessedness, Who walketh not astray."

The first verse was repeated, and Lilie stayed to remember the second.

"Eh," cried Mrs. Melder, "hasna she come uncommon fast on? but I wish ye would speak to Jacky Morison, Miss Anne, she's learning the bairn nonsense ballants and—"

"He shall be like a tree that grows, Near planted by a river,"

burst out Lilie triumphantly.

"Which in his season yields his fruit, And his leaf fadeth never. And all he doth shall prosper well—"

The child paused—accomplished the next three lines with prompting, and then made a stop.

"Lilie no mind now—Lilie show you the tree."

Anne suffered herself to be drawn out—the tree which Lilie fancied must be the one meant in the Psalm, was an oak which stood upon a swelling hillock close by the Oran. When they came near, the child's wandering attention was caught by some carving on the rude and gnarled trunk.

"What's that?" she asked.

Anne read it, wonderingly:

"Norman R. R. Marion L."

Beneath were two longer lines:

"Like autumn leaves upon the forest ways, The gentle hours fall soft, the brightest days Fade from our sight."

and a date. The carvings were near the root, and might have been done by some one sitting on the grassy bank below. Anne had some difficulty in deciphering them, and when she had led her little charge home, returned alone to trace the moss-grown characters again. The date was seventeen years before—Norman R. R. Could it be possible that some other bore that name—or was it indeed a record of some bygone pleasant musing of her unhappy brother's, before name, and fame, and fortune were lost in that dark crime—before the mark of Cain was sealed upon his brow.

And were there yet greater depths in this calamity than she knew, and more sufferers; the Marion who shared his happier thoughts—who was she? or how had Norman's blight, so much more dreadful than death, fallen upon her?

The dusky December weeks passed on, and, on the last night of the year, a tall man, closely enveloped in a plaid, walked softly up the dark avenue towards the house of Strathoran. He seemed to know its turns and windings well, as keeping under covert of the thickest trees, he hastily approached the house;— once near it, he crossed the path quickly to gain the obscurity of its shadow, and then walked round it several times without manifesting any desire of entering. It was a very dreary night—the ground was thoroughly soaked with recent rains, and heavy clouds drifted in dark masses over the sky, of whose dull leaden surface, and wading afflicted moon you could see occasional glimpses, as these gloomy hosts of vapors were parted by the wind. A fitful glance of the moon fell now and then upon the stranger's face. It was pale and resolute, and rigid, like the face of one undergoing some terrible surgical operation, to endure which manfully his every nerve was strained. He paused at last opposite a brilliant window, and retreating backward, raised himself by aid of a tree, so that he could look in. Through the closed curtains he could see a party of gentlemen sitting at their wine—the sound of their laughter, and gay voices, reached him on his watch. With keen eyes he surveyed the unconscious revellers, marked every face, took in, as it seemed, every particular of the scene, and then descending, took his way again through the solitary avenue, and turning as before into a side path, reached the highway unseen. Onward he went, walking very quickly for full two dreary miles, and arrived at last not at any dwelling of man, but at a solitary graveyard, still and solemn, lying upon Oranside, in the midst of which rose the ruined walls of an ancient chapel, moss-grown, and clad with clinging ivy.—The alarm which called forth the parishioners of more southern districts, night after night, to watch their dead, had not reached the distant stillness of Strathoran, and the stranger entered unmolested and unseen. He directed his steps to the chapel, climbed the broken stair, and entered the small unroofed apartment, with its ruined walls, and trailing ivy, and floor of lettered flags, bearing upon them the names of those who slept below—for this was the burial-place of the long-descended Sutherlands of Strathoran. Another uncertain glance of the wan moon directed him to a marble tablet in the wall, by the side of which he stood long in the dreary silence, motionless and still, himself like some dark statue, mocking the dead with empty honor. Hugh Sutherland and Isabel his wife, lay underneath the watcher's feet; and the son to whom they had left so fair a heritage, and who had visited their grave two twelvemonths since, bearing a name of universal honor, and looking forth upon a smiling future, through natural tears that became him well—stood there now, tearless and stern in the thick gloom of night—a houseless, joyless man.

"I have obeyed," said Archibald Sutherland, leaning upon the ruined wall. "I have returned to see my father's house in the hands of an alien to his blood—and now what remains?" His knees were bent upon the stone that covered the dust of father and of mother—his brow pressed to the tablet that chronicled their names; and the ruined man in his extremity, poured out his full heart into the ear of One who heareth always, and never more certainly than when the voice of supplication rises to Him "out of the depths." "Who shall stand before thee if thou markest iniquity? yet is there forgiveness with thee, that thou mayest be feared, and plenteous redemption."

Yes, that remained—omnipotent, over all, in His tender mercy, the God whose plentiful redemption encircles with its arms of divine compassion its every returning prodigal—the loving-kindness that turns no supplicant away. The sympathy most wonderful and strange of all, which "touches"—the heart of the Incarnate God with "a fellow-feeling for our infirmities!"—these remained—greater than all sorrows of the earth.

So with less sternness in his pale face, and less despair in his heart, Archibald Sutherland retraced his steps, and turned to the humble fisher's house far down the Oran, the inhabitants of which had recently come to the district, and knew not either the name or the quality of the stranger whom they had reluctantly agreed to shelter for the night.

He had hovered that same evening in cover of the darkness, in the neighborhood of the Tower—had passed the hospitable walls of Woodsmuir, and looked through the bare trees at Merkland; but drawing back in painful shame, had not dared to enter, or make himself known to any of them all—they all had households, kindred, warm friends about them. He only was alone.

The next night, with his plaid wrapped as closely about him as before, and serving as a disguise, he passed along Oranside in the darkness, turning his steps to the Tower. He could not delay longer—already perhaps in the bitter pain of last night's trial, he had delayed too long, and in passing those wide-spreading fields and plantations, once his own, but in which now the meanest hind dwelling among them had more share than he, he felt that last night's trial might be indefinitely prolonged. He came to the Tower at last, and found it also gay and full of light. The hall-door was open, and within stood a knot of servants. The door of Mrs. Euphan Morison's snug room was ajar, and showed Duncan from Merkland, and Mr. Coulter's grave man-servant sitting comfortably by the fireside, while the Falcon's Craig groom, and Mr. Foreman's lad, and one or two younger attendants, stood among Mrs. Catherine's maid-servants in the hall listening to the music above.

"Jacky, ye monkey, shut that door," cried Mrs. Euphan Morison, "Idle hizzies clavering nonsense, and decent folk like to get their death o' cauld. I wad advise ye to tak hame some o' that horehound-balsam wi' ye, Duncan—it's uncommon guid for hoarseness. I made it with my ain hand."

Jacky darted forward to do her mother's bidding; and Archibald felt the girl's keen eye pierce his disguise in a moment.—She paused, looked at him. "If ye please, will I tell Mrs. Catherine?"

"Yes—but wait, Jacky, let me go up stairs."

Jacky went gravely forward before him, and drawing his plaid more closely over his face, Archibald followed her unobserved.—The girl led him to a small apartment which opened into that well-remembered drawing-room, and without saying a word, left him there. He sat down and waited. Ah! these gay sounds of mirth and music, how bitterly they mock sick hearts. A sort of hope had inspired him, as he felt himself once more in shelter of these stately walls, but now, within hearing of the sounds of pleasure and rejoicing, his heart again sank within him. There was no place for him—homeless and hopeless, there. As he listened, a simple voice began to sing—words chiming strangely in with his changed fortunes.

"Like autumn leaves upon the forest ways, The gentle hours fall soft, the brightest days Fade from our sight. A dimness steals upon the earth and heaven, Blended of gloom and light; Shuts its soft eyelid o'er day's azure levin, And shades with its soft tints the glories of sweet even To sober-toned night.

"From his deep cradle the woods among His russet robes waving free, The Oran with his kindly tongue, Is travelling to the sea. He rushes to the ocean old, In sparkling wave and foam, And out into that trackless wold Bears the kind voice of home. Wayfaring man, far, on the sea Listen how he calls to thee!

"Warm household lights are shining out His rugged channel o'er. Ill plants of malice, and guile, and doubts Ne'er blossom on his shore. There is Peace in her matron's gown and hood. Her footsteps never roam, And Hope is in pleasant neighborhood And strength is strongest at home Thy foot is weary, thy cheek is wan, Come to thy kindred, wayfaring man

"Oran's ringing voice he hears, The great sea waves among, To yon far shore the ripple bears The Oran's kindly tongue. Yet he labors on, and travels far, For years of toil must glide, Before he sees the even star Rise calm on Oranside. Speed thy labor o'er land and sea, Home and kindred are waiting for thee!

"The gentle hours fall soft, the brightest days, Like autumn leaves upon the forest ways, Fade from our sight. And night and day he labors as he can, Far from home's kindly light. His foot is weary, and his cheek is wan, Ah! pray, young hearts, for the sad wayfaring man Laboring this night."

The air was very simple beginning and ending in a low pathetic strain, and with a quicker measure for the intervening verses—but the music was but a soft chiming breath, bearing along the words. Archibald

Sutherland leaned his head upon his hands, the burden floating dizzily through his mind. Alas! for him, beginning his wayfaring so painfully, neither home nor kindred waited. He heard a step approach—a hand gently open the door of communication, and raised his head, a sad calmness possessing him.— Among the gay hearts, divided from him only by that wall, there might be some one, whose prayer of gentle pity, would indeed rise for the wayfaring man.

CHAPTER IX

Anne Ross was seated near Mrs. Catherine's piano when Alice Aytoun took her place at it timidly, and placing a sheet of manuscript music before her, began her song. Anne started in tremulous wonder as it commenced. Most strange to hear these words repeated by a living voice at all—stranger still that they should fall from Alice Aytoun's. With breathless interest she listened as the lines flowed on. The wayfaring man in toil, and danger, and sorrow, hearing in the ripple of the great sea, far away in some strange country, the kindly call of the Oran to home and kindred. Her cheeks grew pale—her lips quivered. How could this be twined into Norman's history?—or was Alice unconsciously murmuring out the low, sad prayer of its conclusion for her father's murderer?

The tears were swelling in Anne's eyes as the song concluded; and Ralph Falconer who stood near had addressed to her some sneering compliment on her sensibility, when Jacky stole behind her chair, and whispered something in her ear. Anne recollected herself instantly, and, approaching Mrs. Catherine, communicated to her Jacky's intelligence. Mrs. Catherine started—rose from her seat—wavered a moment, and then restraining her emotions, sat resolutely down again.

"See, Anne, there is the key of the little room. Take the dyvour there—I will come myself when I can. Tell him that—." Anne turned to obey. "And, child,—bid Euphan Morison have a good fire kindled in the red room, and tell Andrew he is to hold himself ready to wait on Mr. Archibald—and, child—be kindly to the unhappy youth. It behoves me to be stern myself, but there is no such bondage upon you."

When Archibald Sutherland lifted his head it was Anne Ross who stood before him, her eyes shining wet, her face full of sympathetic sorrow. She held out her hand, and advanced towards him.

"Mr. Sutherland—Archibald."

"Anne!" said the broken man. They shook hands; there needed no more speech; perfect and cordial sympathy, of no exaggerated sort, but such as does sometimes, and should always subsist between those who have passed childhood and early youth together, was between them in a moment. There was no story told—no compassion claimed; but, in the pressure of Anne's hand, and the subdued kindness of her look, the full heart felt itself eased, and leaned upon the unexpressed sympathy as with the confidence of nearest kindred. There were no words; but Anne knew how Archibald's spirit was wading like the moon in clouds and darkness; and Archibald felt that Anne, in the confidence of ancient kindness, was ready to hope and believe all things for his final deliverance and welfare.

"You will not go in," said Anne, gently. "There is a large party, and some strangers."

"No—no," said Archibald. "I regret now that I came at all to-night. I would be a strange spectre, disturbing your merrymaking, Anne."

"Merrymaking! With some of us, at least, there is not much of that," said Anne. "Lewis is home, Archibald; you must see him. But now will you come with me to the little room? Mrs. Catherine will come herself immediately."

"To the little room?"

"Yes; the house is full, and all the other apartments are occupied," said Anne; "that is all. Mrs. Catherine has been looking for you, Archibald."

They left the room together, and, to the great wonder of the congregated listeners in the hall, descended the stair, and turned through a dark passage to Mrs. Catherine's place of especial retirement—the little room. Archibald entered, and Anne, leaving him, hastened to Mrs. Euphan Morison's apartment, to convey to her Mrs. Catherine's orders, in immediate execution of which a reluctant maid was hurried up stairs.

And Archibald Sutherland seated himself alone, fearing the interview which Mrs. Catherine made still more important and solemn by ordaining that it should take place there. The firm, dark face of Sholto Douglas looked down upon him from the wall, and fascinated his restless eyes. There seemed a lofty purity of reproof in those fine lineaments, over which the pallor of death had fallen, before Mrs. Catherine's only brother had told out an equal number of years with himself. Sholto Douglas, in his early prime of manhood, laid in a foreign grave, the odor of a stainless name, and strong faith, numbering him among those just, who shall be held in everlasting remembrance. Archibald Sutherland, in the wreck of hope and fortune, and good fame, preserving barely life. Ah! who would not rather have chosen the solitary grave in far Madeira, in which all sin and uncertainty lay dead, and where, above flowery sod, and gray headstone, there blossomed one sublime and stedfast hope, as sure and true as heaven.

Archibald could not bear, what seemed the cold reproving scrutiny of that noble pictured face, and laying his arms upon the table, he bent down his head upon them. He fancied he could hear the music and gay voices still. Anne had left him. Mrs. Catherine lingered in her coming; even in this household, the only one in the cold world around him, in which he thought himself secure of welcome, the ruined man was nothing; bitter thoughts swelled up within his worn and wearied spirit, despair came back like a flood upon his heart; exhausted in health, broken in mind, disgraced in name—what remained for the once joyous heir of Strathoran, but poverty, neglect, and death.

Large gray eyes, made larger by the dew that swelled beneath their lids, were looking on him, as thus he sank further and further, into that horror of great darkness. Mrs. Catherine, whose slow step he had not heard approaching, in the tumult of his own thoughts, stood by him silently; her strong features moved by the contest between severity and tenderness.

"Archibald Sutherland," she said, harshly. The young man started, but did not lift his head. "Archie, my man!" Her large hand was upon his hair, stroking it softly, as if the head it covered had been a child's. He looked up. "You have sinned against your own spirit, and in the sight of God; but you are home in your own country, and under a kindly roof. Archie Sutherland, give me your hand, and let bygones be bygones between us."

There was a silence of some minutes, during which, Mrs. Catherine grasped Archibald's trembling hand in one of her's, and with the other, smoothed down his dark hair, wet as it was, with the cold dew of mental pain. "Archie!" she repeated, "there have many waves passed over your head since I laid my hand upon it last; waves of sorrow and shame, and waves of sin, Archie Sutherland—but yet—be silent, and listen to me—yet I pray, as I prayed when we parted, that the blessing of the God of our fathers may be about you, boy, at this time, and for ever! Look up, and hear me. Let trouble, and toil, and hardship come, as the Lord will; lift up your head in His presence, Archie Sutherland, and plight me your word, that in your further warfare, manfully and honestly, and in the strength of His name, ye will resist sin. I fear no other thing in this earth, be it the sorest pain that ever wrung mortal flesh; but with a deadly fear do I tremble for that! That you will strive against it night and day, that you will give place to it—no, not for an hour—that wherever ye may be, in joy, or in tribulation, in peace, or in strife—ye will remember the One name whereby we can be saved, and resist iniquity, if need be unto blood. Your word, Archie Sutherland, I am waiting for your word."

And solemnly, with lifted hand, and tremulous voice, the word was plighted. "With all the strength of a sad man, honestly, and in truth. Remembering the One name whereby we can be saved, and in the strength of Him who has overcome sin. God succor me!"

The flush faded from his thin cheek, his hand fell. Mrs. Catherine stood still by his side, in the same attitude, her hand lying fondly upon his hair, and there was again an interval of silence. "The angel that redeemed me from all evil, bless the lad. Archie, be of good cheer. Who kens the ways of the Lord? We are tried, but we are not forsaken."

Mrs. Catherine seated herself opposite him, and looked into his face. "You are white and thin, Archie, spent with that weary trouble—and you have been walking upon the damp road in the night air, like an imprudent lad, as you are, and will have wet feet, doubtless. Go up to your room like a good heart, and change them, and then, Archie, my man, we are all friends together. Come in, and see Lewis Ross, and the rest of them, for I have a houseful to-night."

"I am not fit for any company," said the young man. "I should go in among them like a ghost. Mrs. Catherine, I have obeyed you to the letter. Last night, I saw my father's house in the possession of strangers. Last night, I saw that man in my father's seat. I have not shrunk from the full trial, and now there is no probation so hard, no struggle so bitter, but I am willing to embrace it, if I may but have a prospect of redeeming what I have sinfully lost; although it be only to die when all is done, beneath the roof where my fathers have lived and died before me."

A sympathetic light kindled in Mrs. Catherine's eye; but the wasted young man beside her, needed soothing and rest, as she saw, and after her own fashion she comforted him. "Archie, I am in years, and there is no wish so near my heart, as to see your work done before I go hence; but to do your work you must be strong, and to be strong, ye must rest; this is no time to speak of dying. I ken no man in this world, that has a chain to life as strong as you have yourself, Archie Sutherland, if it be the Lord's will, and truly, I have little hope of a man, with a labor before him, turning to death for ease and idleness. I doubt not, there are many years before you yet, blyther than these; but we will have time to speak of that hereafter. Go up to your room, Archie. It will mind ye of your school days, to have Andrew about you again, and come down when you are ready, to the little east room to me. You must even be a good bairn, and do my bidding to-night."

Mrs. Catherine rose. Archibald rose too, in obedience. The strong old lady took the arm of the weak and exhausted young man, and half supporting him, went with him herself to the door of the red-room, where a cheerful fire was shining upon the warm color of curtains and furniture, while Andrew, with his grey hair dressed, and his best livery donned, in honor of the company, stood waiting at the door: the same room, with all its arrangements perfectly unchanged! the same friendly and well-known face, that had been wont to hover about him in kindly attendance in those joyous boyish days! The prodigal had returned home—the despairing man had entered into an atmosphere rich and warm with hope. Archibald threw himself into the old fire-side chair, and hid his face again in his hands, overpowered with a momentary weakness, from whose tears the strength of steadfast resolution and grateful purpose sprang up boldly, rising over bitterness and ruin and grief in sober triumph, the beginning of better days.

But Archibald did not make his appearance in Mrs. Catherine's drawing-room that night. With the shame of his downfall strong upon him, and feeling so bitterly the disruption of all the ties which formerly bound him in kindly neighborhood to these prosperous people, who knew his fall and humiliation alone, and did not know his painful struggles and sore repentance, he shrank from meeting them; and when, having entered the little east-room, he told Mrs. Catherine what pain her kind wish to cheer him would inflict upon him, she did not repeat her commands.

"But I will meet ye half-way, Archie," she said, "Robert Ferguson, your good friend and honorable steward is laboring at this time redding up the tangled odds and ends of your affairs, and it is meet you should see him and render him right thanks for his good service. You ought to have gone to Woodsmuir first. I know not any mortal you are so much indebted to. Go your ways to the library and shut the door—I will send over for Mr. Ferguson. Na—you shall not stir over my door in a damp night till you have won back your strength again—and Mr. Foreman is here, Archie; would you like me to send him down? or are you able to stand it?"

"Quite able," said Archibald, hastily. "Ask Mr. Foreman to come to me, Mrs. Catherine. With all your kindness, I yet cannot rest till I see something definite before me. I have lost too much time already, and Mr. Foreman is an old and kind friend. I do not deserve so many. Let him come to me, if, indeed, he will come—I need counsel sorely."

Mrs. Catherine made a gesture of impatience. "And I am trysted with these young fools, and cannot win down beside you to put in my word. Mr. Foreman will come blythely, Archie—go your ways, and be careful of shutting the door, that you may not be disturbed. Andrew, let Johnnie Halflin ride to Woodsmuir without a moment's delay. If he tarries on the road, it will be at his peril; and give my compliments to Mr. Ferguson—or stay—Archie, write a word yourself."

Established in the library, Archibald wrote a hasty note to Mr. Ferguson, and in a moment after heard Johnnie Halflin, with many arguments, persuading an unwilling pony to face the damp, chill blast, which swept so mournfully through the naked woods, and over the sighing Oran, and at last galloping off on the road to Woodsmuir, the footsteps of his shaggy little steed sounding in unsteady leaps, as it struggled to turn its head from the wind, and regain its comfortable stable.

Various groups in Mrs. Catherine's drawing room were whispering already reasons for her absence.

"I am afraid, Mrs. Catherine is not well," said Mrs. Coulter, sympathetically. "Her face has had a look of trouble all the night."

"Perhaps it is some unpleasant visitor," suggested Mr. Bairnsfather. "I thought she was agitated."

"Mrs. Catherine agitated," cried Walter Foreman, "you might as soon shake the Tower."

"Hold your peace, Sir," said his father. "These young men are constantly speaking of things they don't comprehend. Mrs. Catherine feels much more deeply than you will ever do."

Walter looked up amazed. His father's eyes were uneasily fixed upon the door; his face anxious and full of care.

"Ay," said Mrs. Bairnsfather, shaking her head pathetically, "it has been a great grief to her this downcome of young Strathoran. A fine life he led in Paris, by all accounts; he will surely never come home, to be a burden on Mrs. Catherine."

Mr. Foreman turned round impatiently, as if to answer, but evidently checking with some difficulty an angry reply, looked again towards the door.

"Poor Archibald," said the kindly Mrs. Coulter, "this is not a time for his friends to desert him. Dear me, there is Mr. Ambler persuading Jeanie to sing. Jeanie, my dear, mind what a cold you have got."

"Just, 'Auld Robin Gray,' for the benefit of the seniors," said Mr. Ambler, "the first notes will call Mrs. Catherine back again."

Jeanie Coulter seated herself at the piano, Walter Foreman took his place behind her. The "seniors" prepared to listen—the younger part of the company to whisper and exchange smiles and glances, the long ballad being too much for their patience.

"Do you think it can be young Strathoran who has arrived?" whispered Mrs. Bairnsfather.

Mrs. Coulter nodded impatiently, resenting the interruption of Jeanie's song.

"Not that new fangled nonsense, Jeanie my dear," said Mrs. Catherine, entering. "You ken the tune Lady Anne wrote it for—a right breath to carry forth the story on—not that—as if sick hearts were like to play with a melody, and did not just seek the needful breath of music to send forth their sorrows withal."

"You knew Lady Anne, Mrs. Catherine?" said Jeanie Coulter, playing with the keys, and finding this a proper opportunity for the hesitation and coyness necessary to set off her pretty voice and tasteful singing.

"Ay, I knew Lady Anne—you all ken that; sing your ballad, Jeanie Coulter, and do not keep us waiting. Mr. Foreman, I have a word to say to you."

The word was said. Mr. Foreman in haste, and not without agitation, left the room, and Mrs. Catherine herself stood near the piano listening to the music. Jeanie Coulter did the ballad—than which it seems to us, there is no history of more perfect beauty and pathos in all the stores of our Scottish tongue, rich though it be in such—full justice. The tremulous sad music stole through the room, arresting even Alice, though she was rising then nearly to the climax of her girlish happiness—"I wish I were dead, but I'm no like to dee." What strange avalanche of trouble could ever bring such words as these from Alice Aytoun's lips? It was impossible.

Yet under that same roof was one, whose youthful beginning had been more prosperous than Alice Aytoun's, schooling himself to patience, as again and again the pain of his past transgressions came back upon him like a flood. Agent and factor had both taken their place beside him in the library—the lamp shone upon the somewhat sharp profile of Mr. Foreman, with its deepset acute eyes and deliberative look—upon the healthful, hardy, honest face of Mr. Ferguson, browned by exposure, and instinct with earnest sympathy and kindness—and upon Archibald Sutherland's wan and downcast countenance, with its mark of past sickness, and present melancholy humility; they were discussing his future career.

"I will tell you what I propose for myself, Mr. Archibald," said Mr. Ferguson, "My occupation is gone, as you know, in respect to the estate of Strathoran. Now there is Loelyin and Lochend the entailed lands—you will remember that Alexander Semple is in them, and there are three years of his lease to run; but Semple has little capital and no enterprise, and I think would be glad to get rid of his lease and try a more productive farm. It is poor land."

Archibald looked up vaguely, not seeing what the factor's remarks tended to:

"The land is poor but improvable," continued Mr. Ferguson; "and the farm of Woodsmuir, which I have occupied myself, is in excellent condition. I believe that with capital and perseverance, the value of these entailed lands might be more than doubled, and Mr. Coulter, a practical man of high authority, bears me out."

Archibald shook his head sadly:

"We have no capital, Mr. Ferguson."

"We have thought of that," said Mr. Ferguson; "but your friends—Mrs. Catherine for example—have, and this would be no temporary relief, but a certain benefit."

"I see," said Archibald; "and yet it is impossible. My most kind friends, do not think it is pride—of all things there is none that would become me worse than that; but I am quite unfit for this trial. I question if now, with my mind excited and unsettled as it has been, I could endure the placid routine of a farmer's life anywhere. I have rather been looking forward to unceasing labor of a more engrossing kind, as the only wholesome discipline for me; but here it is impossible—to live within sight of Strathoran, to reap the bitter fruits of my folly day by day, without intermission, upon my own alienated land—it would kill me—I could not do it, I could do anything but that."

The factor had been waiting eagerly, with his hand lifted.—"Certainly not—surely not—we never could think of such a thing, Mr. Archibald. You must hear out my plan. What I propose is, that I, who have some knowledge of agriculture, and a taste for it, should take these farms into my own hand. I have consulted Mr. Coulter, and I will have the full benefit of his advice; and I am confident of Mrs. Catherine's assistance. In such an investment, capital is perfectly secure, and subject to no vicissitudes—very few, at least; and I fully believe, that, carefully and scientifically cultivated, we may quadruple the poor two hundred a year it yields now: so that, in addition to your own success, which I have no doubt is certain, if you throw your whole strength into any profession, there will be, in not very many years, a property of seven or eight hundred a year waiting for you. The original property, Mr. Archibald, with opportunity of adding to it, perhaps, bit by bit, from the rest of the estate—"

Archibald Sutherland extended his hand silently, and grasped his factor's. "My punishment is to be overpowered with undeserved kindness," he said, his voice trembling. "My obligations to you already transcend thanks, Mr. Ferguson, and yet you increase them."

Mr. Ferguson resumed his statement hastily, as if ashamed of the emotion which wet his own eyes, and brought a kindred tremor to his voice. "I have grown grey in the district, Mr. Archibald, and would like ill to leave it now. My whole family were born in Woodsmuir. I have long been a theoretical farmer, you know; and now I will get some of my favorite crotchets put into practice. We shall come into collision Mr. Coulter and I," continued the factor, with a kind of hysterical attempt at a joke, which broke down woefully; "but we will, at least, have a fair field for our respective hobbies; and the prospect of so great an increase, Mr. Archibald, is worth working for."

"Yes, to the worker," said Archibald; "but what justice can there be Mr. Ferguson, in you devoting years to increase my income? The fruit of your improvements is clearly your own—not mine."

"There! there!" said Mr. Foreman, breaking in impatiently.—"The fact is, Ferguson, that you should have just put in your proposal without any preface to make it hazy. Mr. Ferguson takes Alexander Semple's place, at Alexander Semple's rent, Mr. Sutherland—that's his proposal—continues so, till his improvements are fairly and honestly paying, and then remains your tenant at the advanced rent: we will see that he does not offer you too little. As for the capital, that is our concern; I will undertake that."

Archibald Sutherland said some incoherent words of thanks, he did not himself know what—neither did his hearers, as Mr. Ferguson shook his grey eye-lash free of some encumbering moisture, and Mr. Foreman coughed, and cleared his throat. There was a brief pause.

"And for yourself, Mr. Archibald?" said the lawyer.

"For myself, I do not know. I have formed no definite plan. Give me your counsel: I am ready to do anything."

"The bar?" suggested Mr. Foreman.

"Medicine?" ventured the factor.

Archibald shook his head. "I am no longer a youth, and could ill spare years now for study. Do you know what a great work I am pledged to Mr. Foreman? No less than winning back what I have lost, and doing it in Mrs. Catherine's lifetime. You smile. It looks like a sick fancy, does it not?—yet it is a fancy that stirs me in every vein. I must work, gentlemen—I must work; how hardly I do not care; work for mere mercenary gain. I shall not gain honor with my schoolfellow Robert, Mr. Ferguson; that is beyond my reach. I must toil to the utmost of my strength to regain my birthright. I can afford to lose no time."

Mr. Foreman had smiled gravely when Archibald began, but the smile settled down into a look of earnest attention before he concluded. He thought the hope futile, no doubt; but it was a hope: and his was not the hand to snatch it rudely from the grasp of a fallen man.

"Business?" said Mr. Ferguson, half aloud. "He must be embarked in business—but how?"

"Listen to me," said Archibald, becoming stronger, as it seemed, when his own fate came under discussion. "My friends, I must go abroad; I can neither rest nor work well at home—at this time, at least. Let me go alone, as humbly as may be. I will put myself under mercantile training at first, if you think it necessary. My own idea is—I have some poor pride, perhaps, in letting you see that I am not too proud for my fallen fortunes—that I should get a clerk's situation in some commercial house abroad—I do not care where—and work my way upward, as I can. I have no money; and what bare influence I could command, would help me little, I fancy. Let me make this experiment, with no adventitious help of patronage or introduction. If I fail, I will promise to return upon your hands again, trusting that your kindness will counsel the unhappy waif once more; but I hope not to fail. All the details remain to be considered.—When or how I am to endeavor to begin, I have not thought; and for whatever your kindness and better knowledge can suggest, I am in your hands."

Neither of his grave counsellors spoke for some minutes; at last, Mr. Foreman said: "You are right, Mr. Archibald. I thought of that myself, formerly, but imagined foolishly, that you would shrink from trade. Your resolution is proper and wise; but remember—I do not wish to discourage you, but there are only a very few, who rise from the class of clerks into that of merchant princes. We are apt, in these days, to form mercantile romances for ourselves; there are some very wonderful instances, I grant, but they are rare."

"As in all other professions," said Mr. Ferguson, watching the changes of Archibald's face anxiously; "but talent and vigor still more rarely remain in the humblest class. You are wearied, Mr. Archibald; let us adjourn this discussion. We can meet in Portoran in a day or two, if you are able," continued the factor, turning with all the solicitude of a nurse to his late patient, "if you are sure you are able."

And with that agreement, Archibald, indeed thoroughly exhausted and worn out, parted with his kind advisers and retired to his room, where he fell asleep in dreamy peace, and strange unwonted quiet, in the pleasant, ruddy twilight, which the fire made, as it glimmered in its shooting lights, and depths of fantastic shadow, through the familiar room.

The slight excitement of Archibald's arrival over, Anne returned to the company, with Alice Aytoun's song still ringing in her ear. Strange it was, how every passing event seemed to have some link of incoherent connection with Norman's terrible history. The stranger child in Mrs. Melder's cottage; the unconscious Alice; the magic threads were extending themselves in all directions. Anne almost feared to see new faces, to make new friends. Norman's image was growing before her eyes, filling up the whole horizon of that dim future. If she should meet himself! the wandering Cain might, with a strange fascination, such as she had read of, seek his own birthplace, ere he died; the idea was fearful—a constant haunting dread, surrounding her like a mist wherever she went.

The evening wore on, and as the guests began to disperse, Anne, in virtue of her standing in the household, had various parting courtesies to pay; to stand at the hall door, while Mrs. Coulter's carriage was packed with the many members of her family; to see Miss Falconer away, and Mrs. Bairnsfather; and when she returned to look for Lewis, the drawing-room was nearly empty. Lewis was not there, neither was Alice Aytoun. The door communicating with the little east room was ajar, and Anne entered, seeking her brother. The room was dimly lighted with one candle. Who stood at its further end? Lewis Ross and Alice Aytoun, hand in hand. Anne stood silent, on the threshold, in chill, fear and apprehension, her head bent forward, her eyes fixed upon them. Little Alice, drooping, blushing, leaning on her companion. Lewis, triumphant, proud, meeting his sister's gaze with a smiling defiance. Anne stood still, seeing all, and could not speak. In another moment, Alice had glided towards her, thrown her slight arms round her waist, and was clinging to her like a child.

"Anne, be her sister," said Lewis, with unusual emotion. Anne smiled a sickly smile, as in a painful dream, laid her hand unconsciously upon the girl's fair hair, felt Alice start, and shiver at the touch of her cold fingers, and then, hastily disengaging herself, left the room, her very brain reeling, leaving Lewis enraged, and Alice grieved and alarmed, in the very fulness of her joy. It was all over now; the fatal engagement was made, and what remained but to blight the girlish gladness, and pour upon Lewis's startled ears, the knowledge of that fatal crime, which stood like a spectre between his betrothed and him.

CHAPTER X

Lewis Ross and his sister walked home together in silence and alienation. Lewis was sullenly indignant, while Anne, still overpowered by that whirl of agitation, pain and fear, felt grateful for Duncan's officious attendance with his lanthorn, which precluded any conversation of a private kind, between her brother and herself. In her first shock and bewilderment, she knew not what to do—whether to communicate her secret at once, or to delay until she herself knew the terrible story more perfectly. She determined on the latter course, before they reached Merkland, and pained still further by her brother's averted looks, and sullen silence, whispered: "Lewis, forgive me, I knew not what I was doing," as they entered the house. Lewis took no notice, but went angrily into the parlor, in which his mother usually sat. A fit of ill-humor had prevented Mrs. Ross from accompanying them to the Tower—the same cause had afflicted her with headache, and sent her to her room, full two hours before they returned home, and to Anne's satisfaction, there was no family intercourse of any kind that night.

Once safe in the shelter of her own apartment, she sat through the dead hours of that chill January night, laboring to form some plan for her further proceedings. She could not concentrate her mind upon them—shooting off, now here, now there, those floods of distempered thoughts refused that bondage—now called back from a long and vivid picturing of Norman's desolate and hopeless way, and Norman's blighted life—now from recalling in strange caprice the girlish gaiety and sunny future of Alice Aytoun, dwelling upon its bright particulars, as if to exaggerate the gloom that now lowered over the gladness of those youthful days. The host of indefinite and conflicting purposes, which terminated all these discursive wanderings of thought, would not be reconciled. Crowding about her like so many phantoms, they even stifled the voice of her appeal to that One counsellor from whom it was Anne Ross's constant wont to seek wisdom and guidance. Confused words, meaningless and often repeated, swelled up from her heart, constantly—a mere vacant cry of agony—for her mind was wandering all the while, from point to point, in aimless and bewildered speed.

With but the slight difference, that, for an hour or two, these confused thoughts, remaining as active as before, took upon them the yet more fantastic garb of dreams; her mind continued in the same state of excited agitation during the whole night, and it was only when the chill morning began to break, grey and faint, through the dark clouds of the east, that springing from her feverish sleep and unhappy fancies together, Anne girded herself for the work that lay before her. To see Mrs. Catherine, and ascertain beyond doubt that Alice was the daughter of that Aytoun who fell by Norman's hand—that seemed her first step. To learn as fully and clearly as might be the particulars of the tragedy itself, and if possible, to get possession of Norman's letter to her father, which Mrs. Ross had mentioned, and which, with foolish procrastination for which she now blamed herself, Anne had shrunk from seeking. If she had but accomplished these necessary preliminaries, Anne hoped that her mind might acquire more coherence, and that she might be able to resolve what was best to be done, for making known the secret to Alice and Lewis—the two individuals most deeply concerned.

Dressing herself hastily, she left Merkland, and took the path up Oranside, which led to the Tower. Anne was privileged to have admittance at all times, and knew that Mrs. Catherine was, comparatively, an early riser. The path was damp and slippery—the morning coming in, in clinging garments of wet mist, grey, drizzling and disconsolate, with blasts of thin rain, sweeping now and then in her face.

Mrs. Catherine was seated in her small dressing room, which was immediately over "the little room"—and like it looked out upon the bare ascent of the hill behind the Tower. She was dressed, all but the large soft grey shawl which her stately attendant Mrs. Elspeth Henderson was carefully unfolding; and seated in an easy chair by the fireside, was having her usual half-hour's gossip with her "gentlewoman."

"And so you think Anne Ross is looking ill, Elspat," said Mrs. Catherine; "it's my hope you and your wise daughter have no design upon the poor bairn. Mind, I will have no doctoring of my Anne. I believe Euphan Morison is crazy!—my best cow in the deadthraw with her abominations! I will not have it, Elspat, though she is your daughter. My household shall be poisoned with physic at the will of no woman."

"Euphan walks according to her lights, Madam," responded Mrs. Elspat; "but if ye ask my opinion, I would say that Miss Ross needit spiritual physic, and no temporal: the bitter herbs o' repentance and grace, and no camomile and wormwood—though I hold with Euphan doubtless that the last are of service in their place."

"Hold with Euphan—a great authority truly!" said Mrs. Catherine. "Spiritual physic, bitter herbs—ye are all fools together, the whole household and lineage of you! Not that I am saying we are, any of us, above grace and repentance—forbid that such a profane thing should come from my lips, but—Elspat Henderson what are you groaning at?—the bairn Anne is more simple and devout than the whole tribe of you."

Mrs. Elspat Henderson looked meek and injured.

"It would ill become me, Madam, to maintain that anything is, when it's your pleasure to say it is not. Nevertheless, it's my privilege to lift up my testimony to the iniquity of human-kind, all and haill. We are all perverse, yea we have gone out of the way—we have together become unprofitable; there is none—"

"Woman, woman, hold your peace," said Mrs. Catherine, "as if I was like to hold inherent ill of light import—me that have seen its outbreaking, time after time, in lives that the world called pure, and no less in my own. Carry your testimony to your Maker's presence, Elspat Henderson, and mind that ye stand sole there, and cannot glide out of your ain private evil in the cover of a 'we.' And what is your special ill-will at Anne Ross? what is her misdeed the now?"

Mrs. Elspat gave a prolonged sigh.

"That ye should have so puir an opinion of me, as to throw such a blame on your auld and faithful servant. Me, a special ill-will at the young lady! it's my hope I will never be so far left to mysel, frail vessel as I am."

Mrs. Catherine groaned.

"Is it your purpose to drive me out of all patience, Elspat Henderson? Truly, if the three of you are no enough to banish peace from any mortal, I am no judge. What cause of censure have you, then, if I am no to say ill-will against my Anne? What has she done?"

Mrs. Elspat coughed solemnly.

"Miss Ross has been looking uncommon white and thin, Madam, since ever the day that Miss Aytoun came to the Tower; and if ye'll notice yoursel how she looks steadfast at Miss Alice, and syne grows white, as if she would swarf away, you'll see that what I am saying is true, neither less nor mair."

Mrs. Catherine seemed struck, and did not answer immediately. Her attendant approached with the shawl. Mrs. Catherine took it, and wrapped it round her.

"Ay!" she exclaimed at last, "and what does your wisdom make of that?"

"If there is a sore evil under the sun," said Mrs. Elspat, oracularly, "it is envy, and a jealous ill-will at folk better gifted and better likit than oursels. Far be it from me to lay a hard word upon a young lady like Miss Ross, but—"

"Elspat Henderson!" said Mrs. Catherine, angrily, "your learned daughter will be waiting on you for her breakfast. Go your ways down the stair, and, between this time and the morn, look me out the Psalm that gives a righteous reward to him that slanders his neighbor privately. I know well David, honest man, let his pen fall ajee when he wrote it 'him,' and no 'her'—and see that you coin no more scandal out of the ill mists of your own brain to rouse my wrath withal. You may leave the room, Mrs. Elspat Henderson—I have no further need of you."

The cowed attendant withdrew, and Mrs. Catherine seated herself in stately indignation. By-and-by her face grew calmer, graver. The suggestion awakened a new train of thought, and roused anxieties and fears, hitherto, in the pre-occupation of her mind, never dreamed of. Anne Ross's light tap at the door came when she was deeply engaged in these, and Mrs. Catherine rose and opened it with some anger remaining in her face.

"Child!" she exclaimed; "at this time in the morning—through the mist—and with trouble in your face! What is the matter?" Anne entered, and sat down to recover her breath, and re-arrange her thoughts. Mrs. Catherine closed the door carefully, and, resuming her seat, looked in Anne's face and waited.

"There is nothing the matter, Mrs. Catherine," said Anne, smiling faintly; "that is—they are all well in Merkland, and I—I just wanted to consult you—to ask your advice."

"Speak out, child," said Mrs. Catherine. "It is something not common that has brought you here this morning. Tell me what it is. Does it concern Archie?"

"No, no," said Anne. "Something far more—I mean just a little matter connected with ourselves—I should say myself, rather, for neither Mrs. Ross nor Lewis know my errand, Mrs. Catherine—"

"Child, speak out," exhorted her friend.

"You will think it very foolish," said Anne, a sickly ray of hope breaking upon her as the time of certain knowledge drew so near, "I only wanted to ask you about Miss Aytoun's family. I mean—Miss Aytoun—Alice—is her father alive?"

Mrs. Catherine regarded her for a considerable time in silence. Anne felt the long, firm look a death knell to her last hope, and returned it with a strange, callous steadiness, such as comes occasionally in the extremity of trial, imparting to the sufferer a fictitious strength.

"Her father is not alive. Wherefore do you ask me, child?"

The unnatural flicker of hope rose again.

"Where did he die, and how? I beseech you to tell me, Mrs. Catherine!"

"Anne," said Mrs. Catherine, gravely; "for what purpose do you seek to know? Wherefore do you question me so?"

"Where did he die, and when, and how?" repeated Anne.—"Answer me, Mrs. Catherine—do not hesitate—I am prepared."

Mrs. Catherine paused long before she answered.

"The place was a country place—far south from this; the time was seventeen years ago; the way was—" Mrs. Catherine paused again. "To what purpose is this questioning, child? It is a matter that concerns you not."

"The way was—?" repeated Anne, clasping her hand eagerly.

"The way was—he was killed," said Mrs. Catherine, in abrupt haste. "Shot, as men shoot beasts. Anne Ross, I brought the bairn Alison to my house, because she was an innocent bairn that I wanted to do a kindness to, and not because of her parentage."

Anne heard the words, but did not discern their meaning, and sat, in the blind, fainting sickness that possessed her, repeating them to herself, unconsciously.

"Child, child!" said Mrs. Catherine, in alarm. "What ails you? What have you heard? I am meaning, why have you come to me with such a question?"

"One other—only one," said Anne, recollecting herself. "Mrs. Catherine, who was it—who was the murderer?"

Mrs. Catherine made an appealing motion with her hand, and did not answer.

But Anne was perfectly self-possessed again.

"Was it Norman?"

Mrs. Catherine did not speak; it was not necessary. The answer was far too legibly written in the long, steadfast look of grief and sympathy which she fixed upon her companion's face.

And so they sat in silence for some minutes, too deeply moved and engrossed for words. At length Anne started up.

"That is all," she said, hurriedly. "I must go now. I have much to do."

Mrs. Catherine rose also, took her hand, and led her back to her seat.

"You shall not leave my house, child, till I hear more of this. Who was so cruel as to tell you this sorrowful story? and what is it that you have to do?"

Anne sat down again, mechanically.

"Child, ' said Mrs. Catherine; "I have never spoken Norman's name in your hearing, nor suffered it to be spoken. Who has told you a terrible story, which was buried in grief and forgetfulness long ago, when the unhappy lad found his grave under the sea? It is not known in the countryside, for the deed was done far from here, and your father hung back, and took no note, outwardly, of the miserable boy's fate. He was right maybe. I would not have done the like—but that is little matter. Who told you?"

"Found his grave under the sea!" murmured Anne, unconsciously.

"What say ye, child?"

"It was Mrs. Ross," said Anne, "when Miss Aytoun came first to the Tower, she told me that she feared this was his daughter. Oh! Mrs. Catherine, why did you not keep her separate from us? If we had not been brought so much together, this could not have happened."

"Child," said Mrs. Catherine, "there is something on your mind yet, which is not known to me; the story is a woeful story, dark enough to cause sore grief; but it is over and past, and there is some living dread upon you. What has happened?"

Anne looked up—she could not find words to communicate her "living dread"—she only murmured "Lewis."

Mrs. Catherine started. "Lewis? Child what is it ye mean? No that there is anything—No, no, what makes me fear that—there can be no liking between the two."

"There is, there is," said Anne.

Mrs. Catherine rose, and walked through the room uneasily.

"It must be put to an end—immediate—without delay. I brought the bairn here to do her a kindness, no to give her a sore heart. Child, Lewis must not enter my house again till Alison Aytoun is home. She is but a bairn—it can have gone no further than the slight liking of a boy and a girl. Where were my eyes that I did not see the peril? Child, it must end this very day—better the pang of a sudden parting—better that each of them should think they were slighted by the other, than that it should ever come to an explanation between them, and then to the rendering of reasons—it must go no further."

"It is too late," said Anne; "there has already been an explanation between them. Mrs. Catherine, they are engaged."

Mrs. Catherine paced up and down the small apartment with quick steps.

"I am compassed with troubles! no sooner seeing my way out of one, than another opens before me. Anne, my puir bairn, I am a selfish fool to think of my own gray head, when the burden falls the heaviest on your young one. What will we do? there is a purpose in your eye as I can see—tell me what it is."

Anne did not know how to proceed: she could not betray Norman's secret even to Mrs. Catherine.

"I will tell Lewis," she said, "and perhaps, Mrs. Catherine—I do not know what is best to be done with poor Alice, so happy and young as she is—perhaps you will tell her—not all—but something to excuse Lewis."

Mrs. Catherine shook her head.

"It will not do. It will not do. If I excuse Lewis, she will think it is but some passing thing that awhile will wear away.—No, child, no, if the bairn hears anything, she must hear all."

"I will tell Lewis," said Anne; "but I must first learn the whole of this dreadful story more perfectly. I thought of going to old Esther Fleming: she was Norman's nurse, Mrs. Catherine—is she likely to know of this?"

"I mind much of it myself," said Mrs. Catherine, "but you will get it better from Esther Fleming than from any other mortal. I have been taken up with many diverse things, but Norman and her own son were year's bairns, and Norman was the light of Esther Fleming's eyes. Your father made no endeavor to help the miserable young man, child. I know what you would say—there was no time—and it is true—for the deed had not been two days done, when he was on the sea—be thankful, child, that he perished in the sea and did not die a shameful death."

Anne trembled—the consciousness of her secret overpowering her as if it had been guilt. Alas! over the head of the murderer the shameful death impended still.

"Did the family know?" she asked, her mind becoming strangely familiar with the subject: "could they know of Norman's relationship to Lewis?"

"No," said Mrs. Catherine. "When Arthur Aytoun died, his wife was a young thing, feeble in her health, and oppressed with many troubles; for I have heard that he was far from a good man. James Aytoun was but a bairn then, and Alison was not born; besides that, they were strangers in that countryside, as well as Norman—being from the south—and would know little of him but his name. Mrs. Aytoun is a woman of a chastened spirit, child; she knows the unhappy lad has answered for his guilt langsyne before his Maker; and think not that she will keep his name in the mother's heart of her, in any dream of vengeance."

Anne could not answer: her secret lay upon her like a cloud, weighing her down to the very earth.

"I must tell the bairn," continued Mrs. Catherine, as if consulting with herself; "ay, I must tell the bairn, that she may know, without having any sick month of waiting, that there is a bar between Lewis and her that cannot be passed over—that there is a stern and terrible conclusion put to the dreams of their young love.—Child! it is a sore weight to lay upon a spirit innocent of all sorrow."

Anne assented silently.

"And you will have a harder battle with the youth," said Mrs. Catherine. "Child, there are bairns in this generation that would fain inherit the rights and possessions of their fathers, without the ills and the wrongs. Take heed of Lewis, lest he endeavor to hold this black deed lightly. I will not have it. The blood that a Ross spilt must never be joined in near kindred to another Ross. There is a deadly bar between the houses. Forgiveness there may be, full and free—I doubt it not—but union never. Mind, there can be no softening—no forgetting. The spirit that was sent to its account in violence and haste, by Norman's hand, would rise to bar that ill-trysted betrothal. It must end."

Anne rose.

"I will go," she said. "I parted from Lewis last night in anger, because I had no kind word to say to Alice when he bade me be her sister. I must hasten now to learn these terrible details more accurately. Lewis might refuse to believe a story which came so suddenly upon him, and came for such a purpose, if I did not know it all. I must go now."

"You will get it best from Esther," said Mrs. Catherine. "I know she has brooded, in secret, over his sin and his death, since ever his sun set in yon terrible waves of blood-guiltiness. Anne, my bairn!" Mrs. Catherine paused, laid her hand upon Anne's drooping head, and went on, her voice sounding low and solemn. "The Lord uphold and strengthen you for your work; the Lord guide you with the uplifting of His countenance, and give you to walk firm in the midst of tribulation, and not to falter or be weary in the way."

Once out again upon Oranside, Anne felt the oppression of her terrible secret grow upon her to suffocation. "He is alive! he is alive!"—the words came bursting to her lips; she felt tempted, in the strange, almost irresistible, insanity of the moment, to proclaim it aloud, as she hurried along; running sometimes, with a sick feeling of escaping thereby from the phantom that overshadowed her inmost heart. The crime itself seemed to become dimmer, in its far distance. The thought that Norman was alive, laden with his fearful burden of remorse and blood-guiltiness, abiding perchance the shameful death of the murderer, filled her whole being almost to frenzy, and, with its circle of possibilities, curdled her very blood with terror.

Mrs. Ross and Lewis were about sitting down to breakfast, when Anne returned to Merkland, and the domestic horizon was anything but clear. Lewis, forgetful of his last night's sullen petulance, was in high spirits—spirits so high as to aggravate his mother's ill-humor. She grudged that he should have found so much pleasure at the Tower; and, sneering at Mrs. Catherine, whose unquestioned superiority had always galled her, kept up a biting war of inuendo and covert sarcasm.

"A pleasant morning for walking, Miss Ross," she said, as Anne took her seat at the table.

"Why, Anne, have you been out?" exclaimed Lewis. "You have good taste certainly, so far as weather goes. Where do you go to, so early in the morning?"

"Oh, no doubt she has been at the Tower," said Mrs. Ross. "Duncan and May will be going next. We are possessed with a Tower fever. I presume you were making tender inquiries after Mr. Sutherland, Miss Ross? At this time, of course, it is quite sentimental and romantic to entertain a friendship—nay, perhaps, something warmer than friendship—for the interesting unfortunate."

"I might have asked for poor Archibald," said Anne, "if I had thought of him at all; but I did not remember even that he had come home."

"Then you have been at the Tower?"

Anne hesitated. "I did go in to see Mrs. Catherine," she said, falteringly.

Lewis looked up gratefully, and smiled upon her with a smile which said, "I thank you;" before which Anne shrank, and turned away her head.

"I do not know how we shall get on in the ordinary affairs of life," continued Mrs. Ross, "while this Tower madness lasts. I should like to know wherein the fascination lies. One can understand a passing infatuation, in a boy like Lewis; but for you, Anne, who should have some idea of propriety and decorum, to be visiting the house, where you knew that young man had arrived at night, so very early in the morning—I really am amazed; I do not understand it."

Anne blushed painfully: Lewis drew himself up in towering indignation. "Passing infatuation!"—"a boy like Lewis!"

There was a fortunate diversion made, however, by the entrance of May, with letters, and until their meal was ended, there was a cessation of hostilities, though Mrs. Ross still kept up a fugitive fire, hitting right and left, Lewis and Anne alternately. The breakfast over, Lewis rose to leave the room.

"Oh!" exclaimed his mother. "I suppose you are going to the Tower."

"Yes, mother," said Lewis, gravely, "I am going to the Tower; and when I return I shall have something to tell you, which, as it will be of great importance to me, I hope you will receive calmly, and in a more gentle spirit."

He left the room. Mrs. Ross followed him with her eyes in astonishment, and then going to the window, watched him turn up Oranside. Anne sat in terror, lest she should be questioned as to the mystery of Lewis' words, but fortunately, she was not. Mrs. Ross sat down, and took her sewing. Anne had done so before, and the two ladies pursued their work in silence.

The needle trembled in Anne's excited fingers; she felt the acceleration of her pulse, she heard the loud, quick throbbing of her heart. The silence became awful; she fancied Mrs. Ross could hear her fingers stumbling at every stitch. "Mother," she said, looking up at last. "I have a great favor to ask of you."

Mrs. Ross glanced at her impatiently. "Well; what is it?"

"You spoke to me once, of a letter—a letter," continued Anne, growing bolder, as she steadied her voice, "which my unhappy brother, Norman, wrote to my father; you said I might see it some time, mother!"

"Upon my word, girl, I believe you want to drive me mad," exclaimed Mrs. Ross, angrily. "You see me half distracted, with the wilfulness and regardlessness of Lewis, and you bring in your own foolish fancies, and your brother's shameful story, as if I had not enough to vex me without that. Try to come down to ordinary life a little, and do not torment me with your chimeras."

"This is no chimera," said Anne, "nor whim, nor fancy, nor anything of the kind; it is of the gravest importance that I should see that letter. It is not even curiosity, though I need hardly be blamed for feeling deep interest in the history of my brother. For the sake of my father's memory, and for the sake of Lewis, the two bonds between us, give me Norman's letter. I will ask nothing further of you; this I must beg and plead for, this you must give me."

Mrs. Ross stared angrily in her face, resenting, and yet something impressed by the very strange tone of command, which, impelled by the vehemence of her feelings, mingled with Anne's entreaty. At last she rose, and walking quickly to her desk, opened it, and took from an inner drawer a small key, which she threw upon the table.

"There! let me have no further heroics; that is the key of an old bureau of your father's, which you will find up stairs among the lumber. The letter is in some of the drawers. At least, don't let me have any further trouble about it. I yield to you now, only to take away from you the power of tormenting me at another time."

Anne did not pause to note the ungracious manner in which her petition was granted; but laying by her work nervously, she took the key, and hurried upstairs. The old bureau, of dark carved wood, stood dusty and damp in a recess, and Anne had to draw aside boxes of mouldering papers, and articles of broken furniture, before she reached it. The picture stood in her way; she knelt down again, delaying in her very eagerness, now, that the long wished-for letter was within her reach, to look upon the portrait; so bold, and frank, and open, in its flush of manly boyhood. Was that the face of a murderer?

Her fingers trembled so with haste and agitation, that she could scarcely open the many drawers, and examine their contents. In the last of all she found the letter, wrapped in a large sheet of paper, within which was something written, in the tremulous scratchy hand, which Anne knew to be her father's. With Norman's letter before her, she yet paused to read the comment of the dead—a comment which startled her into wild agitation, and still wilder hope.

"To my children, Anne and Lewis Ross:

"I am a dying man, and will never see either of you arrive at years to be trusted with such a secret; but I charge you, when this packet comes to your hands, to give earnest heed to it, as you value the last words of your father. I am standing in the presence of my Lord, with death at my door, a hoary-headed man, bent to the grave with trouble, and I leave to you who come after me, my solemn conviction that Norman Rutherford, your brother, is innocent of the crime laid to his charge. The whole course of his past life is before me, and my eyes are clear with looking upon death face to face. This blood is not upon Norman's hand. Listen to his own words, children; and believe with me that his words are true. A frail and stricken man, I have done nothing to clear him of the imputed guilt; but as a special heritage, I leave this work to you. His blood is in your veins; he is your nearest kindred. Children of my old age, save my son Norman! As you would have a blessing on your own youth and prosperity, remember the desolate exile in his wanderings, and clear his name and fame. My eye is waxing heavy, and my hand weak—it is the beginning of death. Anne, sole child of his mother! Lewis, heir of my name! my charge is upon you. I appeal you to the throne of Him, who, in the fulness of His glory, forgot not this fallen world, but left a heavenly kingdom to save and die for it—if you disregard the last petition my lips will ever utter on this earth. My son Norman is innocent of this blood—clear him of the blot upon his name—bring him back to die peacefully in his own land, and the blessing of the God who binds up the broken-hearted, be about you all, for evermore.

LAWRENCE ROSS."

Anne laid down the letter, her eyes full of grateful tears, almost joyful in their tremulous solemnity. There was sorrow, and labor, and darkness in the way—there was not crime. The blessed belief came into her soul in solemn sunshine—the cloud rolled off her head. A strange invigoration was in every vein. Norman was alive! alive to receive the triumphant acquittal of justice—alive to be saved! She opened his letter, her tears falling thick upon it: other drops had fallen there before—the tears of the old man's agony. She read it.

"Before you see this, they will have told you that I am a murderer. It is not so, father: believe a despairing man, it is not so. Arthur Aytoun has done me wrong: but I would not have put a hair of his head in peril. I would have guarded him with my own life. Wherever he is, be it in joy or misery, he bears me witness, before God, that I am innocent of his blood. Father my heart is like to burst. What can I say to you—my hand is clean. I am innocent!—I am innocent! there is no blood upon my soul. And yet I dare not venture to trust myself to a trial, with every circumstance against me. I have nothing for it but flight. To-night I go further away—I know not where—under cover of the darkness, like a felon and a criminal, as men will call me. It gnaws at my very heart. I would rather have died a thousand times—a cold-blooded, cowardly murderer! Father, father! you will not believe it of your son!

"They would find me guilty if I remained—they could not fail to find me guilty—and the disgrace of a fugitive will be less upon our house and name than the disgrace of a convicted murderer, dying a shameful death. It is like a coward to fly. I am a coward. I do not dare to meet that fatal judgment. I could not bear to hear myself called guilty, with my innocence strong in my heart. I have a suspicion, too—a terrible fear and suspicion—and I must fly. Father, I can say no more, even to you. I am a sinful man before God; but my hand is as pure of blood, as when I stood beside you on Oranside, before death had ever entered Merkland. They know in Heaven—if they can see my unhappy fortunes—my mother, Lawrence, Edward—they know that I am innocent. I do not know what I say. My thoughts are wandering like a sick man's. Father, I am innocent!

"Marion is with me—she is my wife. We have escaped from the sea in peril of our lives—they will tell you I have perished in it—I would I had, but for Marion. Father, you may never hear from me, or of me, again; but again remember, I am innocent—this blood does not stand between God and me. Why this fearful cloud has covered us, He knows who sent it. It may depart yet, in His good time. For this unjust world, farewell, father. We will meet where there are no false accusations—where God himself shall vindicate the right. I become patient—I become trustful. Father, pray—pray that I may live to be cleared of this horror—that the curse may be taken from my name—that I may be acknowledged guiltless.

N. R. R."

Norman Rutherford's sister was kneeling before his portrait—her clasped hands holding her forehead, her eyes raining hot tears, her soul poured out before God. Norman was alive—could be prayed for, hoped for, toiled for. The curse was turned into a blessing. The path was wintry still, and bare, and laborious; but that horrible spectre of blood was gone; and the majestic presence of justice, and the clear rays of hope, were on the way instead. She was able for all labor, all patience, all sorrow in his cause. Norman was innocent.

Anna rose at length, folded the precious letters carefully, placed them in her bosom, and then hastily descended the stair, and set out again for the old nurse's cottage, to learn, according to her original intention, the particulars of this dark history there. The Oran moaned no more, but only murmured plaintively, between his banks, the kindly song of home; and Anne, as she passed under the trees, almost with a light heart, murmured to herself the prayer of Alice Aytoun's song—for the wayfaring man.

CHAPTER XI

Esther Fleming, Norman Rutherford's nurse, lived in a cottage by herself, not far from Merkland. When the first Mrs. Ross's first son was born, Esther had entered her service as "bairns'-maid," had left it again to be married, and after a brief period of two years had returned a youthful widow, with one boy infant of her own, between whose birth and Norman's there was but some brief intervals of weeks. Esther had remained the head of Mrs. Ross's nursery through the vicissitudes of all the succeeding years; had received into her charge infant after infant of Mrs. Ross's family, and with grief, less only than the mother's, had seen the tender blossoms fall one by one into the family grave: but Norman was peculiarly her own—a tie especially tender attached the generous, manly boy, to his foster-mother; and when her own handsome sailor-lad, returned from his first voyage, stood up to measure his height with that of his playmate and comrade, Esther's overflowing eye looked with scarce less partial pride upon Norman Rutherford than upon William Fleming. When Mrs. Ross herself died, the little Anne became the object of Esther's devoted and unceasing care, although her removal from Merkland to the cottage she now occupied took place before the second marriage of Mr. Ross; but even after that event, bitterly as the faithful servant resented it, Esther continued, for her delicate nurseling's sake, to hold her footing in Merkland, and to pay daily visits to her old dominion in the nursery, asserting against all comers, and in face of the new darling, Lewis himself, the rights and privileges of "Miss Anne." But when Anne was still a child, a blight fell upon Esther Fleming; the self-same blight, which brought the gray hairs of Norman Rutherford's father in sorrow to the grave. The old nurse, stronger, or more tenacious of life, had borne her sorrow silently, and marked it more by her utter seclusion from the rustic society round her, than by any other demonstration. She had a little niece living with her, to manage her small domestic concerns, and except through this girl and Anne, Esther had no intercourse with the world— the very brief and quiet world—about her. Her house stood on a high bank of the Oran, with a pathway winding before it; and the grassy descent, dark with old trees and bushes, shelving steeply down behind.

Within, the little dwelling consisted of two apartments, perfectly clean and neat (as is, indeed, much more usual in our Scottish cottage than southern readers give us credit for,) though without any attempt at ornament, except the two or three small profile portraits of children, which hung over the mantlepiece of the outer room, the only existing memorials of the dead sons and daughters of the house of Merkland, which Esther had rescued from their disgrace, in the lumber-room, after Mr. Ross's death.

The nurse herself, in her gown and petticoat of dark print, and white cap bordered with narrow lace, and carefully-kept hood of black velvet, sat sewing by the fire, making shirts for her sailor son, then far away in a man-of-war, toiling upon the sea. Esther was alone, so there was no obstacle in the way of Anne's errand.

"Esther," she said, when she had delayed nervously for some time, in indifferent conversation, "I have come to ask you about a very grave matter, of which I only heard recently. A secret, Esther—you know—"

She paused. Esther looked up gravely in her face, and then, rising, closed the door.

"Mr. Norman?" she asked in a very low voice.

"Yes," said Anne. "You know it all, Esther?"

"God be thanked that has put it in your heart to ask," said the nurse, solemnly. "Yes, Miss Anne, I ken. It has been lying heavy on my heart since ever that cloud fell upon my boy. I have looked to you—I have aye looked to. Ye are like your mother, and will not falter. Oh, Miss Anne! if ye but kent how it has lain upon my heart!"

Anne looked at her inquisitively, uncertain how far her knowledge went, or whether it was safe to speak to her of Norman, as alive.

"Ye are doubtful of me, Miss Anne," said Esther. "I see it in your eye. What of this story do ye ken yoursel? Have ye heard it all?"

Anne faltered.

"I do not know, Esther. I have heard—"

"Let me tell ye what I ken," interrupted the nurse, "and then ye can give me your full trust. I claim nothing less from your mother's bairn. Miss Anne, your brother Norman lies under the reproach of a black crime—the blackest that man can be blotted wi'. Folk think that he is dead, and he is guilty; he is not either the one nor the other. He is a living and an innocent man!"

Anne's whole frame thrilled with joy as the words were said.—Solemn as was the testimony of the dead, and deeply as her hapless brother's self-defence moved her, the words seemed surer and more hopeful when a living voice pronounced them.

"I want you to tell me everything, Esther," she said, eagerly.—"I have Norman's letter, and my father's testimony, but, except these, I have heard little. This morning I was in despair, because I knew that

No man lived, and believed that he was guilty. Now, I can do anything. His innocence is all I care for. Tell me what can be done to prove his innocence—rather, I should say, tell me every circumstance, Esther—tell me all you know."

"I care about his innocence also," said Esther. "Yes, living or dead, I care about that first. But, Miss Anne, ye dinna ken—ye canna fathom how dearly I care about himsel. He was laid in my arms a helpless, greeting bairn, the first day o' his life; wi' my ain hands I put his first mortal claes about him—my boy!—my gallant, mirthful boy! And to think of him spending his best years toiling in a strange country, wi' a dark end hanging ower him, his name cursed, and his lands lost!—and him an innocent man! Oh! I have thought upon it till my heart was like to burst!"

"Why did you not tell me?" said Anne. "We have lost years! Esther, there might have been something done long ago, if you had only told me."

"I curstna," said the nurse. "I was feared to whisper to mysel that he was living, for fear of trouble; but now, Miss Anne, now, ye have your work before ye—and a strange work it is for a young lady. But ye maunna shrink or fail."

"I will not—do not fear me," said Anne. "Only tell me, Esther—tell me everything you know—let us lose no more time."

"It's a lang story," said Esther, "and ye maun let me tell ye my ain way, Miss Anne, as I have thought it ower in my ain spirt, money a time, looking for this day. Maybe, if ye haena patience wi' me, I may mak it no sae clear. It's a lang story, and, to understand it right, ye bid to ken his nature. I maun begin at the beginning."

Anne assented, and Esther went on. "Miss Anne, he was the sweetest bairn that was ever putten into mortal hands for earthly upbringing. I think I can see him before me yet; aye the head o' them a' in their wild plays, and never out o' mischief; but, for a' that, as gentle as a lamb. I used to tell them, when they came in to me wi' torn claes and dirty shoes, and blythe, black faces, that they were the plagues o' my life—eh! Miss Anne, the ill o' thae idle words—they were its very joy and sunshine; my blythe callants!—my bonnie, brave, pleasant bairns!

"For Mr. Norman was alike in age wi' my Willie, and the twa were like brithers; they lay in the same cradle, and were nursed in the same arms—puir, feckless, withered arms, as they are noo!—and I had a conceit that they were like ane an ither, though Mr. Norman was head and shouthers higher than Willie, and had eyes like stars in a frosty nicht, and hair as dark as the clouds; and Willie was blue-e'ed and fair-haired, like his father before him. Ony way, they were like in spirit; the very look of them was heartsome in a house.

"But there was ane thing special, Miss Anne, about your brother; a thought o' pleasure never entered his head; he had a sunshine within himsel that keepit him aye cheery; and the bits o' dawting, and good things, and makings o', that ither bairns fecht for, he heeded not, though I never saw a laddie that liket better the quietest mark of kindliness: only, if there was onything like a privilege or an honor, he would aye have it wared on the rest; no jealous and grudging, like as ye will see some bairns, that are learned to pretend to do the like, and no to be selfish; but with a blythe spark shining in his eye, enjoying the good thing, whatever it was, far mair than if he had gotten it himsel.

"It might be because Mr. Lawrence was aye delicate, and bid to get his ain way; but the maist of it, without doubt, was in the nature. My ain Willie was a kindly callant, as need to be; but I have seen him (who was only a poor man's son, and no equal to the young Laird,) standing out against Mr. Lawrence in his pets, when Mr. Norman gaed way, in his blythe, frank manner, without sae much as a thought about ony pride o' his ain; and I have kent him, money a time, when ony o' them were in the wrang, taking the blame upon himsel.

"Ye will think I am dwelling on thae auld stories ower lang, Miss Anne; but I see them—I think I can see them on Oranside, Mr. Lawrence sitting, white and thin, on the bank, watching them; and my ain twa, my beautiful laddies! as wild in their innocent play as twa foals on a lee; and the cut fingers, and the torn clothes, and the fa's into Oran: waes me! what were a' their bits o' tribulations but just another name for joy?

"Weel, Mr. Lawrence died, as ye ken. If he was petted whiles, it was wi' sickness and suffering—pain that the young spirit could ill bear, and that awfu' cough; but he was a blessed bairn, and departed as calm and pleasant as an angel gaun hame—as truly he was, puir lamb!—out of a world that had held nothing but ill to him; and the other bairns dwined away from the house o' Merkland. Eh! Miss Anne, ane canna read thae sore and sorrowful dispensations! To think that there should be sae mony blythe families round about, wi' no ane wee head lifted out among them, and a' the Mistress's lilies gathered—a' but Mr. Norman; and ye wad have thought the rest had left a portion of their life to him, as that strange lassie, Jacky Morison, was saying to me out of a book of ballants, about three knights—aye as the ane was killed, the spirit and the strength of him entered into the other; but that's a fule story. So, as I was saying, ye might have thought it was so wi' Mr. Norman; for, the mair death there was in the house, the stronger and fuller of life he grew. Ye may think, Miss Anne, how the Mistress's heart was bound up in her one son, growing among tears and troubles, like a strong young tree by the waterside.

"And then she died hersel. He wad be haill eighteen then, maistly a man; and ye wad have thought his heart would burst. For months after that, he used to come in and sit beside me in the nursery, never speaking a word. We were the truest mourners in Merkland, him and me, and maybe it made us like ane anither a' the better.

"It was a dreary year, that first year after your mother died; but there were drearier years to come. The twelvemonth was just out, when it began to be whispered in the countryside that Merkland was courting a new wife. I could have felled the first body that said it to me, and Mr. Norman flew upon Duncan, in the greatest passion I ever saw him in, for dauring to hint at sic a word; but the rumor rose, for a' that (folk said it was because Mr. Norman had been put aside from inheriting Merkland, because he was to take his uncle's name, and sae noo there was nae heir,) till I put it to the Laird my ain sel—ye may think it bauld, Miss Anne, but I had been about the house a' his married life.—That very night—for I wasna likely to bide wi' a strange woman in my mistress's seat—I was sorting my bits of odds and ends to gang away; and looking at you, sleeping in your wee bed, and murning for ye, an innocent lamb, left to the cold mercies of a stepmother, when Mr. Norman came in. I saw, by the white look of him, in a moment, that he had been hurt and wounded to the very heart (and so he was,) for his father had tell't him. Eh! Miss Anne, to think that he could tell the fine, manly, grown-up lad, that nae mortal could help being proud o'; and that was liker being marriet himsel than hearing tell o' his father.

"So he sat down by the fireside and covered his face wi' his hands, and did not say a word to me—only I heard him moaning to himsel, 'O, mother, mother!' Nae wonder—we were wearing our murnings still, and she had been but ae twelvemonth gone.

"So the marriage-day came at last. I had flitted into this house the week afore—and there were mony folk at the wedding, only Mrs. Catherine, and Strathoran's lady, and some more, wouldna come; and when they sought Mr. Norman, he wasna to be found far or near—where think ye he spent that day, Miss Anne? at his mother's grave!

"Ye're wearying on me—it's just because it's a' sae clear in my ain mind—I canna help it; but I am coming to the time noo. Mr. Norman ye ken, had an inheritance o' his ain by the mother's side. Your uncle, Mr. Rutherford, of Redheugh, was a bachelor gentleman, and died three or four years before your mother—and Mr. Norman was his heir. He was to take both the land and the name, and I have heard it was a better property than Merkland, only it was far south by this, on the ither side o' Edinburgh. Mr. Norman was to bide wi' his father till he came of age, and a sore and weary time it was, for this Mrs. Ross couldna bear the sicht of him, and he likit her as ill. I maistly wished for his ain sake that the time was come, though it was a sore thought to me that I was to have the sight o' him, gladdening my auld e'en (I wasna sae auld then either nae mair).

"And at last his one-and-twentieth birthday came, and he gaed away. I did not see him after that for a whole year. The light of my eyes was ta'en from me, Miss Anne—I had little pleasure of my life, for both my boys were away.

"Willie had served out his prenticeship, and was sailing second-mate in a timber ship to the Baltic; but that time he had ta'en a langer voyage, to India and thereaway, and didna came hame till the year was out. The very next day after Willie came, Mr. Norman arrived on a visit at Merkland, and the first body he came to see, after his father, was just my very sel—and what do ye think he had been devising in the kindness of his heart for my Willie? There was a schooner lying at Leith on sale, and Mr. Norman had made an offer for't, for Willie's sake, and no ither, to make him captain; and when they had rested themsells a week at hame, Mr. Norman took Willie away to Leith wi' him to see the ship. Weel, Miss Anne, every thing was bright for baith o' them when they gaed away; but when they got to Leith, and had near settled about the boat, my puir Willie, being maybe ower proud and uplifted about the honor, and the grand prospect, was careless o' himself: and the first word that came to me was, no that he was captain of Mr. Norman's ship, but that he was pressed, and ta'en away to some of the muckle English sea-towns on the east coast, to be a common man afore the mast in a man-o-war."

Esther paused to wipe her eyes with her apron.

"Eh, Miss Anne, thae sore and humbling providences! just when ane thought every thing was prosperous and full of promise to be cast down into the very depths—my heart was sick within me. I had no more spirit for onything, but just gaed about the house like a ghaist, and caredna to spin, as the lass says in the sang. Mr. Norman did his endeavor to free my puir laddie, but it couldna be—and ye may think what a clould fell upon me, dwelling here alane, and my son far away in the dangers o' the war, where, if he were spared, I couldna see him for years.

"Mr. Norman came seldom back to Merkland after that. He liked Mrs. Ross but little at all times, and I think he reproached himsel for no being carefu' enough of Willie, though I never blamed him—no for a moment; but onyway he was altogether pairted from his ain auld hame—no that he forgot us; there was aye the tither bit present coming to me, at New-year's times, and his birth-days and the like; and many fine claes and toys, and things, to yoursel, Miss Anne, that ye didna get the half o'—

"So three years ran out, and ane day when I happened to be up at Merkland, on some errand concerning yoursel, ye came, to me, Miss Anne, wi' a paper in your hand, to let me hear ye read (ye were six years auld then.) So I got the paper—ye had slipped it out o' the lockit book-case in the library, the time your papa was writing a letter, and didna see ye. I mind the very words ye said—because I likit to see the papers—and so I did, to see what word there was about the war, and if there was ony tidings of Willie's ship. Sae I got it, and began to read it, the time Mr. Lewis and you were playing at my fit.

"Eh! Miss Anne: I mind the bits of words that came in upon me now and then, when I was looking at that awful paper, as if I had heard them in a fever. There was the haill story of the murder in't; of how Mr. Norman and Mr. Aytoun had had a bitter quarrel the night before, and parted in anger—and how, the next morning. Mr. Aytoun was found lying dead in a lone place by a waterside—and how a man, gaun to his work, had met Mr. Norman coming, like from the same place, just about the time the deed bid to hae been dune—and there was mair than that still—a gun was found in the wood, and the gun was Mr. Norman's, and when the officers gaed to take him up, he had fled, no man kent whither. My e'en were reeling in my head, but I could read it for a' that—I didna lose a word; and in anither place there was mair news—the murderer, as they daured to ca' him, had been traced into a Holland boat, and there was certain word of it, that it was wrecked, and all on board lost, so he had come, they said, to speedy punishment. I ken not now, how I had strength to do it; but I rose up the moment I was done, and went down into the library mysel'—what cared I at that time, if I had met a' the leddies in the land?—to put it back secretly into the book-case again. Your father was sitting in the library, Miss Anne, a changed man; the white on his face was the white of death, and he was trembling like as with the cauld, and had the darkest woe in his e'e, that I ever looked upon. I put down the paper on the table, and he started, and looked up at me. There was never a word said between us; but we were equal in our terrible sorrow. He kent that, and so did I.

"I know not how I gaed hame that day; it was a bonnie day in June, but I thought that the sky, and the earth, and the trees, were a' black alike, and the running of the Oran was hoarse and loud, like the wild sea that was flowing over my dear, dear bairn. It was before my eyes night and day, sleeping and waking. I kent he couldna have done it out of evil counsel or malice, but he might have done it in passion. The sinking ship, and the storm, and the black sky, and my pleasant laddie in the midst, wi' bluid on his hand, and despair in his soul; oh, Miss Anne!

"A month past in that way. I dauredna face Merkland, and he never came near me, and I thought not there was any hope for Mr. Norman; I never doubted he was dead. In the beginning of July, I got a letter from Willie, telling me his ship was lying in Leith Roads, and I was to come and see him. So I put up a bit bundle, and took some lying siller, and set out upon the road. I wanted to buy some bits of things the puir laddie needed, and so I couldna afford to tak the coach, but walked every step, and a weary road it was. So Willie met me in my cousin's house in the Citadel, and whenever our first meeting was ower, he came after me to the room I was to sleep in, and shut the door, and I saw there was trouble in his face. So I did not doubt he had heard. 'Mother,' he said to me, 'I have news to tell you.'

"'Oh, Willie!' said I. 'I ken, I ken; it has near broken my heart.'

"So Willie went to the door again, and saw it was safe shut, and said he, 'Mother, what do ye ken?'

"'About Mr. Norman, my dear laddie,' said I; 'that he has been left to himself, and done a terrible crime, and died a terrible death. Oh, that we had but kent that he repented; oh, that we had ony token that the Lord had visited his soul.'

"'Mother,' said Willie, very low, 'do ye need me to tell you that he didna do it? Do you no ken that yoursel? O, mother! mother! him that wouldna have harmed the worm at his fit.'

"'Ane disna ken—ane canna tell,' said I; 'he never did it wi' purpose and counsel, Willie; but he may have been beguiled by passion. God send that it hasna been counted to him.'

"'Mother,' said Willie. 'Whisht! mind that a precious life is hinging on't. I have seen Mr. Norman.'

"Miss Anne, I thought I would have fa'en at his feet, for what could I think, but that it was the unquiet spirit my puir laddie had seen.

"'Mother,' said Willie, 'God has saved him out o' the sea, near by a miracle. Mr. Norman is a living man, and an innocent man. The hand that saved him will clear him in its ain guid time; but he bade me tell you. He couldna bear, he said, that folk that had kent him, and likit him weel should think he had done that crime; and he minded me that folk could pray for a living man, and couldna for a dead, and bade me tell you, mother.'

"'O, Willie!' said I, 'wherefore did he flee?—the right would have been proved, if he had but waited for the trial.'

"'I canna tell ye, mother,' said Willie, 'but he said every thing was against him; and it was borne in on my mind, that he knew wha had dune the deed, and that it was ane he likit weel and was willing to suffer for—ye ken his nature—but mind, that was only a fancy o' my ain, for he did not mint a word of it to me.'

"'And where was he, Willie?' said I, 'where was my dear laddie?—was he out of peril?"

"'It was in a town on the Holland coast,' said Willie, 'a bit sma place, less than Portoran. They had travelled there on fit, from the place where the boat was cast away; and Mr. Norman was waiting till there should be some ship sailing from Rotterdam to India. He said to me, mother, that he would never daur write hame again; but if he died he would cause that word should be sent baith to Merkland and you—but as lang as ye didna hear, ye were to mind and pray for him, as a living and sorrowful man, and no to think he was dead.'

"'My laddie!' said I, 'my dear bairn!—oh, that the Lord would bring forth His righteousness as the noonday, and His judgment as the morning light. Ye said they, Willie—was there onybody wi' him?'

"'Yes, mother,' said Willie; 'Mr. Norman was married the nicht before he fled, and there was a young lady with him. She didna belang about Strathoran—I never saw her before, but Mr. Norman said that in the wreck, she was some braver than him, though she was a bit genty, delicate-looking thing. Mr. Norman took me in to see her, and tell't her I was his foster-brother and friend. He is aye like himsel, thinking on pleasuring me, in the midst o' a' his ain trouble—and she gaed me her hand wi' a sorrowful smile, that made me like to greet—and whiles when he was speaking to me, when his grief was like to get the better of him, she put her bit little hand on his arm, and said, "Norman, Norman," and then he aye calmed down again.'

"So that was a' that Willie had to tell, and in little mair than a week after that, his ship sailed again, and when I was on my road hame, I went first of a' to the place where the deed was done. Its on the south side o' the Firth, far down—but I could find out naething there, except that everybody blamed Mr. Norman, and naebody would believe but what he was the murderer.

"And since then, Miss Anne—it's seventeen years past in the last July—I have been a bereaved woman, for Willie never came hame but ance, when the war was ended, and that was just for a while, for he had pleased his captain unco weel, and was made gunner in the ship, and he had got used wi' their life, and liked it, so he just gaed back. He said to me, I mind, that he might aye be in the way of hearing tidings of Mr. Norman, and would come hame without delay if there was ony guid word. But word, guid or bad, there has been nane since that time, Miss Anne; a weary time it has been to me—but your brother is a living man, and the work is not too late."

"What can be done?" said Anne; "what can be done?"

She felt an impulse to rise and hurry to the work at once. She felt it a sin to lose a moment. Yet all the difficulties rose up before her. What steps to take—what to do!

"Miss Anne," said Esther; "I have pondered it, and ower again pondered it in my ain mind since I came hame frae that weary journey, and often I have been on the point of gaun away back again, to see if I could hear onything mair. But what I would bid ye do, would be to gang, or to get some of thae keen writer chiels to gang, cannily, without letting on what they want, to do their endeavor to find out if onybody else in that countryside had an ill-will at Mr. Aytoun: he was a wild man, I heard, and nae doubt had enemies—and if ony other man had been seen leaving the wood that awful morning bye Mr. Norman. There's been a lang time lost, but I've thought often, it might maybe put the real sinner aff his guard, and so he micht be easier found. Miss Anne, that is the way, sae far as I can see. Ye maun try and find the true man that did it, living or dead."

"And bring disgrace and ruin into some other peaceful family, Esther," said Anne, sadly. "It is a terrible alternative!"

"Miss Anne," said Esther, "my dear laddie Norman maun be saved, if I should gang away mysel. I aye waited for you. I had no thought ye wad falter. The work is a sore and painful work, but if ye will not do it, that have better power, I will try myself."

"I had no thought of faltering, Esther," said Anne. "I only said it was a very sad and terrible alternative, and so it is—if William was correct—if we are to endeavor to prove the guilt of one whom Norman was willing to sacrifice name and fame for, it is only so much the more painful. Yet I do not falter—you say truly, Norman must be saved—if it is within human power to clear his name, he shall be saved. But, oh! for guidance—for wisdom!"

When Anne left the house, Esther accompanied her to the door, earnestly urging upon her the necessity of losing no time. To lose no time!—no, surely; when, for all Alice Aytoun's sunny lifetime, Norman had been an outcast and an exile.

And the "Marion!"—who was this who had not deserted him in the midnight of his calamity? this who had been bolder amidst the perils of the wreck than he, and who had gone with him to the unknown far country, the outcast's wife? Anne's imagination no longer pictured him alone, abroad beneath sweeping blast and tempest. A calmer air stole over the picture. It might be from some humble toiling home—not bright, yet with a chastened sunshine of hope and patience about it still—that the tidings of restored honor and fortune should call the exile, and the exile's household, rejoicing to their own land.

CHAPTER XII

Lewis Ross found but a cold welcome at the Tower from its aged mistress. Why she addressed him with so much reserve, and without even the familiar harshness of her usual manner, Lewis could not understand, and it roused his indignation mightily. He, an independent man, a landed proprietor of influence, a travelled, educated gentleman, to be over-borne by the caprices and prejudices of a set of old wcmen! His dignity was hurt, his petulant pride roused. He certainly was conscious of doing simple Alice Aytoun some considerable honor, and did not fancy there was anything unnatural in his mother thinking that he might have done better—but to control his liberty—to think that by all this coldness and discouragement, they could change the current of his inclination and affections—it was quite too much. Lewis did not feel by any means inclined to submit to it. He felt, too, that Archibald Sutherland shrank from his not very delicate questionings, and that, beyond all doubt, he himself, Lewis Ross, of Merkland, important person as he was, was decidedly de trop in the Tower.

Even Alice felt it, as she sat in her corner by the window, that delicate embroidery, which she wished to finish for a cap to Mrs. Catherine, before she returned home, trembling in her small fingers, and her heart beating loud and unsteadily. Mrs. Catherine had been so tender to herself this morning, almost as if she knew—it was so strange that she should be cold to Lewis. Mrs. Catherine left the room for a moment: Lewis approached the window, and whispered a petition, that she would meet him at "the little gate." Alice did not say no. "Immediately," whispered Lewis. "I have a great deal to say to you."

Alice laid down her embroidery, and leaving the room, stole tremulously up stairs, to put on her bonnet and shawl, and steal tremulously down again, and out to her first tryste. The little gate stood on a shady by-way, or "loaning," which ran by Oranside through the grounds of Strathoran and the Tower. Lewis joined her immediately. He had much to say to her—much that was very pleasant to hear, if it was not very wise, nor even very connected and relevant, for Lewis, spite of his boyish pride and self importance, felt truly and deeply, so far as little Alice was concerned, and had not escaped the ameliorating effect of that influence, which, according to the gay old epicurean of our Scottish ballad-writers, "gives one an air, and even improves the mind."—The youthful couple wandered through the loaning, unconscious in their own dreamy happiness of the chill wind that swept through its high bare hedges, till nearly an hour had passed. But Alice suddenly saw, through the gap in the hedge, Miss Falconer riding quickly to the Tower; she came, by appointment, to bid Alice good-by, and so that most pleasant ramble must, of necessity, be terminated. Alice accompanied Lewis a little further down the lane, lest Marjory's quick eye should discover him, and then they parted.

She was to leave the Tower in a week; but too pleasantly absorbed to think even of that, Alice went lightly along the dim loaning, with its high rustling hedges, and borders of wet herbage. Only one little grief lay within the glad heart, which began to throb now with deeper happiness—Anne; why would not Lewis Ross's sister acknowledge, last night her agitated, shame-faced, simple embrace? It was the only way which Alice could think of, for intimating to Anne the connexion now formed between them; and she trembled again, to remember the cold hand that had been laid upon her head, the look of sharp silent pain, that had fallen upon Lewis and herself as they stood together, in the first confidence of their betrothal—Anne, who had always been so kind and gentle to her! It made Alice uneasy, as she went dreamily forward, until brighter imaginations came to the rescue, and Anne's neglect sank into the background, in presence of that more immediate sunshine, the warmer devotion of Lewis.

Loud gay voices startled her, when she had nearly reached the little gate, and looking up, she saw a couple of gentlemen approaching, whom she immediately knew to belong to Lord Gillravidge's not very orderly household at Strathoran. The aforesaid little gate was the boundary of Mrs. Catherine's property, so Alice was then in the grounds of Strathoran—the gentlemen were returning home. Alice proceeded quickly, eager to pass them, for their loud tone startled her, and she was near enough to hear a rude compliment aimed at herself, which sent the womanly blood to her cheek in indignation. They met at last, and suddenly extending their arms, the strangers barred her passage. Little Alice's heart beat like a frightened bird. She ran to each side of the road, only to shrink back again from the rude hands extended towards her; she looked back to see if there was any chance in flight, she lifted her simple face imploringly to them, and said; "Pray, let me pass; pray, gentlemen, let me pass." They laughed at her; poor little Alice was in despair.

One of the strangers was the "hairy fule," who had visited Mrs. Catherine. Jacky's expressive description of him: "A man, dressed like a gentleman," was emphatically correct. The other was a simple, foolish, fair-haired lad, who, besides some boyish admiration of the pretty girl, thought this interruption of her progress a pleasant frolic, and good fun. There was no other way of entering the precincts of the Tower, except by the gap in the hedge, which the timid Alice did not dare to venture on, and so she renewed her prayer. "Pray, let me go on; pray, gentlemen, let me pass."

A crash of the boughs behind her, made Alice turn her head.—Marjory Falconer, riding-whip in hand, came springing through the gap. "What is the matter, Alice?" cried Miss Falconer; "who obstructs you? Gentlemen, be so good as give way."

The gentlemen laughed. The house of Falconer, like the house of Seton in old days, was of prompt ire, and its sole daughter did it no discredit. "This is great impertinence," exclaimed Marjory; "pass immediately, or—" she gave an emphatic flourish of her whip.

A louder laugh than before bade her defiance; in another moment an unhesitating cut of the ready whip made the younger of the two spring aside. Alice flew past, and Marjory lingered for an instant to sweep a few short, sharp lashes over the amazed Fitzherbert, whose strange grimace of rage sent his young comrade into a fit of laughter, and earned for Marjory a full forgiveness of his own individual stroke. "There!" cried Marjory Falconer, as she closed the gate behind her, her face shining with mingled mirth and anger. "You can boast that you have had the honor of being horse-whipped by a lady."

Little Alice was running on, in a great tremor, to the Tower.—"What is the matter?" said her deliverer, laughing, as she overtook her. "What a trembling, frightened bird you are, little Alice Aytoun. Why, we have had an adventure: only, to be correct, it should have been Lewis Ross who delivered you, and not I: is it so? Ah, I am afraid he has been doing damage here, this same Lewis Ross. It is a great shame—these men monopolize everything; one cannot even get a nice little girl kept to oneself."

Alice drew herself up. It was not quite proper that she, the head elect of an important house like Merkland, with a shadow of matronly dignity upon her fair brow already, should be spoken of as a little girl. "I was so glad you came, Miss Falconer. It was very foolish, perhaps; but they frightened me."

"And you had no whip, even if you had been bold enough to use it," said Miss Falconer, laughing, as she gathered up the train of her riding-habit, which had escaped from her hand, and bore sundry marks (no uncommon thing, however) of its contact with the damp path. "You may be thankful it was my indecorous, unfeminine self, and not any of the proprieties. Suppose it had been Jeannie Coulter—why, they would have caught you both."

"But Miss Coulter is a very nice girl; is she not?" said Alice.

"Oh! exceedingly—as nice a girl as could be; and will be as good-looking, and proper, and sensible a Mrs. Walter Foreman as it will be possible to find in the country; as proper, and not quite so good-looking, and more sensible, than you will be, when you are Mrs. Lewis Ross; for she has come to years of discretion, you know, and you are only a little girl."

Alice did not like all this. "I wonder at you, Miss Falconer! I am sure it is far better to be what you call proper than—" Alice hesitated; "I mean, no one thinks Mrs. Catherine, and Mrs. Coulter, and Miss Ross weak, because they are always like what ladies should be."

Miss Falconer laughed. "Well done, my little Mentor; but, for all that, confess that I was of more service to-day, with my good stout arm, than if I had been always like what ladies should be. Miss Lumsden is staying with me at the Craig: I had a bold purpose of getting my poor mother's old phæton hunted up, and driving her over to see you; but we cannot compass a vehicle, we Falconers, so I had to give it up. It is just as well. Miss Lumsden (she's John Lumsden's sister, of Portoran,) would have been shocked. I shall take your advice, little Miss Aytoun; I shall abstain from shocking people unnecessarily, after this, when I can help it."

This was better: the little matron elect was pleased to have her advice taken, and so ventured further. "And, Miss Falconer, don't be angry—wouldn't it be better not to speak so? I don't like—I mean Anne Ross does not like—she says it makes foolish people laugh, and be impertinent."

Miss Falconer's face became crimson. Miss Falconer drew up her tall, handsome figure, to its full height, and looked haughty for a moment. Alice was afraid.

"There! that will do. You will be able to give gentle reproofs, by-and-by, beautifully: only you must not experiment on me much, you know, lest I should grow angry. No, no; do not lift up those blue eyes of yours so pitifully. I am not angry now—but I am sometimes, and I should not like you to see me so."

The straightforward little Alice looked up in wonder, fancying that the blunt, strong, unschooled mind beside her, might be in the habit of giving way to ungovernable and wild fits of passion, such as she had read of; it was all a mistake. Marjory Falconer was by no means so rude and unfeminine as she gave herself credit for being, and had bitter compunctions of outraged delicacy sometimes, after those masculine speeches, which revenged her womanhood completely. But the little world of Strathoran did not know that—did not know either how the strong and healthful spirit of the motherless, ill-educated girl was forcing itself through a rough process of development, and, like other strong plants, was rank and wild in its growth, and needed vigorous pruning—pruning which it would not fail, by-and-by, to manage for itself, with an unhesitating hand.

So the youthful people of Strathoran laughed, and the elders hung back, and called her improper and unfeminine; and thus the original evil was increased by the grievance of which she herself complained;

she was left to the company of men—men, moreover, of that rude, uncultured, sportsman class, her own superiority over whom she felt bitterly, and asserted with characteristic vehemence.

Alice Aytoun saw, when her visitor was gone, still more visibly than she had done in the morning, that Mrs. Catherine was sad.—She could not help observing the long, wistful looks bestowed upon herself—the hundred little indulgences which Mrs. Catherine gave her that day, as she would have given them to a sick child; and Alice wondered. These steadfast, compassionate looks became painful at last, and there was so great a chill of gravity and sadness about the stranger, Archibald Sutherland, that Alice, carried that tremulous happiness of hers—so much deeper, and yet so much less exuberant than it had been one little month ago—into her own pretty room.

Bessie sat there sewing, and disconsolate. Johnnie Halflin had protested vehemently last night that "the Tower wadna be like itsel when she gaed away." The Falcon's Craig groom had particularly distinguished little Bessie by his notice. Mr. Foreman's lad from Portoran had bidden her "be sure and come soon back again," when he shook hands with her. Jacky, with her eldritch voice, had attempted to sing 'Bessie Bell' in her honor—and to leave it all! So little Bessie sat sentimental and despondent in the room, with some vision of breaking hearts, and never being happy again, while her youthful mistress sat down by the window, and looked over to Merkland.

Ah! that breadth of hazy air which hovered between the house of Merkland and Alice Aytoun's chamber window, how full of beautiful shapes it was—and how instinct with gladness! Mrs. Catherine dined at four—never later, except on some very great and solemn occasion; and when dinner was over that day, and the darkness of the long January night had begun, Mrs. Catherine took her youthful kinswoman by the arm, and led her away from the dining-room without speaking. They did not go up stairs; they went away through that dim passage, and stopped at the door of the little room. Alice was terrified. Mrs. Catherine unlocked the door, drew the girl in with her, and closed it again in silence. Alice's heart began to beat loud, in awe and terror. What strange discipline was this?

There was a fire burning brightly; the waning gloaming without gave the whins, that almost touched the window, a ghostly look. The gray crag above seemed to be looking in with a pale, withered, inquisitive face. Mrs. Catherine seated herself on one of the chairs and bade Alice take the other. The firelight fell warm and bright upon that fine dark portrait on the opposite wall. There was a lamp upon the table, but it was not lighted. Alice sat trembling, silent, apprehensive. What could Mrs. Catherine have to tell her?

"Alison," said Mrs. Catherine, "do you see that picture?"

"Yes," said Alice, timidly.

The light was hovering about it, shooting now a spark of radiance into the eye, and now moving in a strange, fantastic smile upon the lip. Alice had heard from some of the visitors at the Tower of Mrs. Catherine's brother, and knew that this was his portrait.

"Ye ken who it is?—my one brother, Sholto Douglas," said Mrs. Catherine. "Look at him well. Do you see how strong, and full of health, and strength, and youth that face is, Alison? Look at him well."

Alice looked again wonderingly at the fine face of Sholto Douglas. To her, as to Archibald Sutherland, it looked loftily calm and pure, removed far above all the changeful hopes and fears of this "pleasing, anxious being."

"Alison," said Mrs. Catherine, "I want to tell you the history of Sholto Douglas. Sit quiet, and do not tremble, but listen to me."

Alice tried not to tremble—she could scarcely help it. The ghostly inquisitive crag, behind which she could fancy some malicious elf watching them—the dark whins pressing close to the window—the dreary sough of the wind as it swept through the bare trees without, and the long passages within, moaning so eerie and spirit-like—the calm, unmoved face looking down from the wall—the comparative gloom of this sacred and mysterious apartment—she could not repress the involuntary thrill of fear and wonder.

"Sholto Douglas was my one brother—we were the sole children of our name," said Mrs. Catherine, her utterance so slow and marked the while, that it was easy to recognise this as the history of her great sorrow, "and I cannot tell you how dear we were to one another. You are a bairn, yourself, of too gentle and quiet a spirit. You cannot know the loves and griefs of harsher natures.

"We were never separate a day; we were bairns; we grew up into youth; we passed to manhood and to womanhood hand in hand. In his earliest flush of strength and manliness, Sholto was arrested on the way. I am a woman now laden with years, and drawing near to the grave, but, bairn, there is no earthly motive that would rouse me to any work or labor like the remembrance of my brother Sholto, that I left lying in foreign earth, thirty years ago.

"That is not the matter I have to speak of first. When Sholto Douglas was in the strength of his youthful manhood he was trysted in solemn betrothal, whereof I myself was a witness, to Isabel Balfour, the mother of the young man who came to my house last night. She was a gentle, pleasant, gladsome girl, like your own self, Alison Aytoun. I liked her well before for her own sake, and I liked her dearly then for Sholto's. The day was set for the bridal—the whole kindred were stirred to do them honor—there was nothing in their way, but joy, and blessings, and prosperity, as we thought in our vain hope. Alison! between them there was the stern and sore shadow of death, and they knew it not!

"A week before his bridal day, Sholto came home from Edinburgh a stricken man. I read it in the doctor's face that came to see him first. I saw it in the blood they took from him, till he was worn and wasted to a shadow. The burning heat of his inflammation was on him the day that should have been his bridal day—and when he rose from that bed it was only to sink into the terrible beauty of decline—with all its dreams of health, and wild hopes, and sick delusions. Be thankful, bairn, that no such weird is laid upon you.

"I saw him dying before me day by day. Into my heart there had never mortal man entered but Sholto, my one brother; and in his prime of youth, with hopes thick about his brow like the clusters of his hair, was the Lord parting him from me. I could not hope—when Isabel leant upon his chair, and looked into his face—his cheek with its bright color, and his glorious e'en—and smiled and rejoiced, and said he would be well, I turned from her, my heart within me sick unto death. I knew he was a doomed man—I saw there was no hope.

"They said at last that the air of some sunnier country would heal him of his trouble, and I prepared for the journey; anxiously I pleaded with Isabel to go with us, that he might have the comfort of her presence. Her kindred would not let her—she thought it not needful herself, neither did he: they would meet again, he said, so soon in health and gladness. I turned away from him—my heart was bursting. I kent they would never meet again—I kent that I took him away to die.

"Alison, I saw the parting of the two. I saw the sick hope in Isabel Balfour's face, and the wan courage in Sholto's—their hearts misgave them at that moment. There is a shadow of fear upon all partings, and it was deepened upon theirs. As for me, my sky could not well be darker—it was not fear with me, but a deadly knowledge. I kent they would never meet again.

"And so I went away with him—guarding the young man that had been so strong and healthful, from every blast of wind, as ye would guard a sick bairn. I went with him to Italy—to France—syne when he got no stronger—I took him away to that sunny island in the sea, where so many are sent to die. His doom was upon him—the light was in his eye more glorious than ever, the hectic was burning on his cheek. What was the soft air and the beautiful days, in comparison with the might of death. He died. I saw him laid in the cold earth of a foreign country, far away from the grave of his fathers, and turned in my desolation to come back to my own country, my lane.

"Alison! you do not ken the blackness of darkness, the shadow of that terrible wing of death. Think of it—think of my desolate journey—think of my first parting with my one brother. Could ye have borne a woe like that?"

Alice was weeping—she had forgot herself and Lewis for the moment. Her gentle heart could not fathom the stern depths of suffering, which still swelled in Mrs. Catherine's larger spirit, but she recognized the sovereignty of grief, and answered with her tears:

"And there was the bride to come home to—the desolate bride, that had been dreaming vain dreams of pleasantness and hope to come. A year before you would have thought that if ever there were two fated to a bountiful and gladsome lot, it was Sholto Douglas and his trysted bride. Now, she was stricken down in her first agony, and he was lying in his stranger grave.

"Know you, Alison, that there are woes like that wherever there are living men?—that there is some shadow on every lot, how fair soever, may be its beginning?—that even the like of you, in your youth and smiles, have a weird to watch and weep through, every one of you for her own self, and not another?"

Alice looked up—the tears stealing over her cheeks, the "hysterica passio" swelling up in its "climbing sorrow" in her tightened breast. Her blue eyes looked fearfully and anxiously in Mrs. Catherine's face. This most sad history, Alice felt, was the preface of some personal evil to herself, some misfortune to Lewis. She could not speak—she only looked imploringly in sad fear and wonder into the face of her kinswoman.

"My poor bairn!" said Mrs. Catherine, "you can think how Isabel mourned in her dark solitude? ye can feel for Isabel?"

Alice started up, all her gay hopes and girlish happiness floating away before that blast, as such light things will float, and threw herself unconsciously at Mrs. Catherine's feet, kneeling there in incoherent grief and terror, and burying her fair head in the lap of her kinswoman: "What is it—what is it? I will bear it—tell me what it is."

Mrs. Catherine's hand lay upon her fair hair in grave kindness. Mrs. Catherine bent down. "Alison! wherefore did ye not tell me of this unhappy tryste, that has been made between Lewis Ross and you?"

Alice could not look up; trembling through all her slight figure, she waited for the next words.

"My bairn! my poor fatherless bairn! if there was but any weight on my gray head that could keep off this sore stroke from your's! It is your appointed weird; ye must be strong, and listen to me. In the fulness of their joy and hope, it pleased the Lord to sunder for ever, in this world, the two I have told you of. Alison! there lies as deadly a bar between Lewis Ross and you; a bar that can never be passed, or lifted away in this life. You may hear of his welfare and prosperity, and he of yours; but in this world you must be strangers. It cannot last a day, this link between you; you cannot go a step further in this perilous road, Alison!"

One great convulsive throb had shaken the slender frame that leant upon Mrs. Catherine's knee. There was a moment's pause, and then Alice rose, her tears dashed away, yet still noiselessly welling out, and a momentary flush of womanly pride inspiring her girlish figure. "He might have told me himself," she exclaimed, passionately. "He need not have been afraid; I—I am not so foolish—I can bear it—my heart will not break; he had no right to think—he might have told me himself!"

Mrs. Catherine rose, and put her arm round her. The girl turned away, and endeavored to release herself; endeavoring vainly also to hide the large hot tears, that, spite of pride and resentment, were falling passionately again.

"Alison," said Mrs. Catherine, "the youth did not ken himself. I cannot deny him justice, though I have little wish that you should think of him more. He did not know himself. It will fall as heavily on him as it does on you."

Alice endeavored again to free herself, her tears flowing more gently, and the weight and oppression at once lifted off her youthful heart. So long as change did not come upon either herself or Lewis, what were external obstacles to them, in their triumphant hope and affection? But injured pride, and outraged feelings, made her reject Mrs. Catherine's offered kindness. Why should she interpose between these two?

"Alison," said Mrs. Catherine, "listen to me. If Lewis's heart were brimming full with the greatest love that ever was in the heart of mortal man, and if you yourself were clinging to him as never woman clung before, yet must ye part: there is no hope—no choice. Before ever you were born, there was a deadly bar laid between Lewis Ross and you. It cannot be passed: there is no hand in this world that can lift it away: it is as unchangeable as death. Bairn, I am speaking to you most sorrowfully. I would not, for all my land, have laid this burden on your young head, if there had been either help or choice: there is none. You must be parted. Alison, look at me."

Alison looked wistfully through her tears at the strongly-marked stern face, now so strangely moved and melted. She saw the steadfast, sorrowful, compassionate look, in which there was no hope; and, yielding to the pressure of the encircling arm, leaned her head upon Mrs. Catherine's shoulder, and nestled into her breast like a grieved child.

By-and-by, they had returned to their original positions. Mrs. Catherine seated herself in her chair again, and Alice glided down passively, and lay like a broken lily, with her head hidden in Mrs. Catherine's lap.

She was stunned and overpowered. The gentle heart lay in a kind of stupor, a dead and vacant sleep; she hardly felt it beat. The hope, and shame, and anger, the very wonder and grief, seemed gone; yet in her crushed apathy, she listened—the faintest word, uttered near, would not have been lost on the ears so nervously awake to every sound. She was waiting for further confirmation of the strange fate pronounced upon her.

"Are you content?" said Mrs. Catherine, lifting the fair head tenderly in her hand—"are you content to believe me, my poor bairn, and to give up the gladness of your youth? Speak to me, Alison. I have maybe been harsher than I should be with your gentle nature, and I am asking you to make a sore sacrifice. For the sake of your kindly mother, Alice; for the sake of your honorable and upright brother James: for the memory's sake of your dead father, whom you never saw, I ask you to give up this stranger lad. He was nothing to you three months ago. They have nourished you, and cherished you, all the days of your life. Believe me, Alison, my bairn, that what I have told you is true; and, for their sake, give up this Lewis Ross. The bar between you is deadly and unchangeable: you cannot pass it over, were you to wait a lifetime."

Alice lifted her wan cheek from Mrs. Catherine's knee, and looked up with sad, beseeching eyes. "What is it? Tell me what it is?"

"It might do you ill, but it could not do you good," said Mrs. Catherine. "Take my word, Alison, and give me your promise. It is a thing that cannot change—that nothing in this world can make amends for. Alison, it is your weird—it has been laid on you, to prove what strength you have. You must make the sacrifice, hard though it be."

"I have not any strength," murmured poor little Alice, in her plaintive, complaining voice: "I am not strong, and there is no one with me. Mrs. Catherine, what is it? Tell me what it is?"

"Bairn," said Mrs. Catherine, "you would need to be strong to listen to the story, and I have withheld it to spare you. You are but a frail, young, silly thing, to have such troubles shadowing you; but it may be most merciful, in the end, to let you ken it all. Listen to me." Mrs. Catherine paused for a moment, and then resumed: "You have heard tell of your father, and how he died a violent death? Alison Aytoun, did you ever hear who it was that killed him?"

Alice shivered, and glanced up in trembling wonder. Mrs. Catherine went on: "The name of him was Norman Rutherford. He was a young man, as gallant and as generous as ever breathed mortal breath. Why he was left to himself in so dreadful a way, I cannot tell. It will never be known on this earth. Alison Aytoun, are you hearing me? Norman Rutherford, your father's murderer, was the nearest kindred of Lewis Ross; he was his brother!"

A long, low cry of pain, involuntary and unconscious, came from Alice Aytoun's lips. She turned from Mrs. Catherine's lap, and covered her face with her hands. There was nothing more to say or to hope; and the mist and film of her first sorrow blinded and stilled the girlish heart, which beat so gay and high when that dull morning rose.

By-and-by, she had wandered up stairs, and was in her own room alone. The room was dim, and cheerless, and cold, she thought; and Alice laid herself down upon her bed, and hid her sad, white face in the pillow, and silently wept. The girlish light heart sank down under its sudden burthen, without another struggle. "I am not strong," murmured little Alice; "and there is no one with me."

There was no one with her. Never before had any misfortune come to her youthful knowledge, which could not be shared. Now the shrinking, delicate spirit, half child, half woman, had entered into the very depths of a woe which must be borne alone. The dull, leaden darkness gathered round her; the tears flowed over her white cheek in a continuous stream; and into the dim, disconsolate air the plaintive young voice sounded sadly, instinctively calling on its mother's name. Alice was alone!

CHAPTER XIII

When Anne entered Merkland after her visit to the nurse's cottage, and was proceeding, as usual to her own room, she was stopped by Duncan.

"Miss Anne," said Duncan, significantly, "Merkland is in the parlor."

"Well, Duncan," said Anne, "what of that? Does Lewis want me?"

"Na, I'm no saying that," said the cautious Duncan; "but I just thought within mysel that maybe ye were wanting to see the Laird; and he's in the parlor, and so's the mistress. Mr. Lewis has been hame this half-hour."

Anne comprehended. The clouds of the morning had broken into a storm, and Duncan, with whom "Mr. Lewis," partly as a child of his own training, and partly as the Laird of Merkland, was a person of the very highest importance, and not to be teased and incommoded by "a wheen woman," desired her interposition to receive the tempest upon her own head, and avert it from Lewis, as was the general wont, when Anne made her appearance in the midst of any quarrel between the mother and son.

"I will return immediately, Duncan," she said, as she ran up stairs to take off her cloak and bonnet.

Duncan turned away satisfied.

"A wheen, silly, fuils o' women, as they are a', the haill sect o' them," he soliloquized, fretfully; "wearing the very life and pith out o'the lad, wi' their angers, and their makings o'. First the one and then the other. Ane would need lang tack o' patience that ventured to yoke wi' them, frae Job himsel, honest man, doun to Peter Hislop, the stock farmer at Wentrup Head. 'Deed, and the twa are in no manner unlike, when ane has a talent for similarities. They were baith rich in cattle, and had a jaud of a wife to the piece o' them. Clavering, ill-tongued randies, wearing out the lives of peaceable men."

When Anne entered the room, she found Lewis pacing back and forward in it, in haste and anger, while Mrs. Ross sat leaning back in her chair with the air of a besieger, who has thrown his last bomb, and waits to see its effect.

"I cannot believe it,—I will not believe it!" exclaimed Lewis, as Anne entered. "If it had been so, I should have heard it before. Oh! I know you could not have kept this pleasure from me so long, mother! and I declare to you that this stratagem—I say this unworthy stratagem—only strengthens my determination. Anne," continued Lewis, perceiving her as he turned, in his hasty progress from one end of the room to the other, "you have heard this story—this phantom of Norman—the murderer, as he is called—which my kind mother has conjured up to frighten me. Join with me in telling her it is not true—that we are not to be deceived—that we do not believe this!"

Mrs. Ross endeavored to toss her head as contemptuously as was her wont—it would not do; the motion was spasmodic. She was reaping the fruit of her own training, and the ingratitude and rude anger of her only son, from whom, indeed, she did not deserve this, stung her to the heart.

"Lewis," said Anne, "you are behaving very unjustly to your mother. Be calm, and do not give way to anger so unseemly."

"Oh! do not interrupt him," said Mrs. Ross, "let him go on; it is pleasant to insult his mother."

Lewis turned from her angrily.

"This is not a time for any absurd punctilio, Anne. Let me hear you say this is not true—this story—this scheme. I will not submit to it. Am I a boy, I wonder, that I am to be frightened by such a—"

Mrs. Ross rose. The darling son—the only child—to turn on his mother thus!

"Lewis!" she said, her features twitching, her voice husky. "Beware!"

"Lewis!" said Anne; "I cannot bear this either; it is mere madness; sit down quietly and listen. Mother, I beg of you to sit down; forgive him this; he does not know—he cannot comprehend. Lewis, when your mother told you this very terrible story, she believed it true."

Mrs. Ross had been regarding Anne, whose support she deserved as little as she did the insults of her son, with a face in which wonder and shame were strangely blended. Now she darted up a sharp, keen glance.

"Believed it true! This from you, Anne Ross—this from you!"

"Bear with me, mother," exclaimed Anne; "and you, Lewis, be still and hear me. I believe with my whole heart that our brother, Norman Rutherford, is innocent of this terrible deed; but, in the judgment of the world, he is condemned long years ago. Every one thinks him guilty. Not your mother only, but Mrs. Catherine, and all who know the story, except myself and one other. Lewis, I do not say how unbecoming and unnatural this passion is, but your mother has only told you, what I have been eager to tell you through all these anxious months. So far as common belief goes, you have heard rightly."

"But it is not true," said Lewis, doggedly, throwing himself into a chair; "you admit it is not true. A scheme—a—"

"Mother, leave this to me," cried Anne, trembling as she saw the contortion of Mrs. Ross's face. "It is no scheme, Lewis. You do us cruel wrong in using such a word. It is true in every particular, but in the one which has given it all its bitterness to me. It is not true that Norman is guilty. It is true, that for seventeen years—for all Alice Aytoun's sunny lifetime—he has been expiating, in a foreign country, the crime of another man. Do not sneer, mother; I cannot bear it. Do not turn away Lewis; I will not be disbelieved. My brother Norman is innocent; the two hearts that knew him, and loved him best, have put their seal upon his truth, one bearing witness in the clearsightedness of nearly approaching death, the other cherishing it in her inmost heart as the one hope of her waning years. Lewis, here is your father's latest words and testimony. Read it, and believe that it is true."

"What is true?" exclaimed Lewis, starting up, without, however, taking the letters which Anne held out to him. "What is the meaning of all this, Anne? My mother tells me first, that this Norman killed the father of Alice Aytoun, and then you come in, and tell me all the story is true, and yet that Norman is innocent; what do you mean? I am not to be treated as a schoolboy. I shall not submit to these mysteries; tell me plainly what you mean."

Anne looked anxiously at Mrs. Ross. "Have you told him all? Does he know all, mother?"

"I don't understand you, Anne," said Mrs. Ross, sullenly.

Anne stood between them, baited by both, her patience nearly breaking down. "Does he know all?" she repeated; "does he know that Norman is alive? Lewis, have you heard that?"

Lewis walked through the room hastily, and did not answer. He had heard it—it was clear; and Anne fancied that, like herself, the thousand apprehensions connected with that secret were overwhelming Lewis, that grief and fear for their unhappy brother were swelling up in his heart, too great for speech.

"Lewis," she continued, "you ask me what I mean—I will tell you. This morning, and for many a sorrowful and dreary morning before this, I knew the history of Norman, as you know it now. I knew that the stain of a great crime was upon his name. I believed that Alice Aytoun's father had fallen by his hand. I knew that justice had set its terrible mark upon him, and that the world thought him already dead; yet, all the while, I knew he was alive, still wandering, Cain-like, with his guilt and his condemnation upon his head. Lewis! since Alice Aytoun came to the Tower, this has haunted me night and day, waking and sleeping; it has tinged my every thought and every dream; it has never left my mind for an hour. You thought I wished to put obstacles between Alice Aytoun and you; you were right, I did so. I endeavored in every possible way to keep you separate. I schemed as I never schemed before; you know now the reason. I wanted to preserve you both; to save her young heart from this cloud, and to keep you even from knowing it, because it was your mother's wish you should not know. Our plans are not the best, and Providence has mercifully baulked mine. Lewis, with you I am sure, as with me, the one circumstance in Norman's calamity that makes it bitter, is the crime. What happened last night, driving me, as it did, almost to absolute despair, drove me also to exertion. And this morning, I found these precious letters—look at them, Lewis—which clear Norman, and which leave to us my father's dying charge, to redeem the fame of his unjustly accused son. Lewis, take the letters; they are addressed to you no less than to me, and if we but discharge our trust faithfully, all will be well."

Something moved by Anne's earnestness, Lewis took the letters, and sat down to examine them. Anne threw herself, exhausted, into a chair; the mental excitement of the morning, and its sudden transition from despair to hope, had worn her out. Mrs. Ross glanced from the one to the other angrily, and cast keen glances at the yellow tear-blotted letters in her son's hand. He had laid down his father's cover, and was reading with kindred keenness, Norman's incoherent self-defence. The young man's sharp, cold scrutiny, was little like that of one, whose present happiness depended upon the truth of this; his steady hand, and business-like demeanor, revealed no deeper interest in that cry of agony, than if its writer had been the merest stranger, and not a much-suffering brother. Anne watched him also, with compressed lips, and anxious eyes; she thought his indifference firmness, or tried to think so, though very differently, she knew, that utterance of Norman's distress had entered into her own heart.

He finished the letters; but there came no exclamation of hope or thanksgiving from the steady lip of Lewis. He folded them up carefully, and laid them on the table. Anne waited in breathless anxiety. "Well," he said, coldly, "and what do you think you can make of these?"

"Lewis!" exclaimed Anne.

"Ah! I thought you would be disappointed. It's not at all wonderful that you should think these letters could do a mighty deal of themselves, for you've no experience, you know nothing of the world; and yet, I thought you had better sense, Anne. They're not worth a rush."

Anne looked at him in amazement; she would not understand his meaning.

"They prove nothing—nothing in this world," said Lewis, with some impatience. "An incoherent attempt to deny a crime, which nobody could suppose he would like to acknowledge, and simply my father's belief, that what his son said was true, to support it; it is quite nonsense, Anne; nothing could be founded upon such things."

"Yes; I hope you will see the folly of that romantic stuff," said Mrs. Ross; "a man sacrificing himself entirely, rather than venture to stand a trial! Depend upon it, Anne Ross, your brother Norman had his senses better about him than you; he fled, because he knew that his only chance of escape was in flight, you may take my word for that. And now that you are satisfied, Lewis; now that you have received the testimony of some one you can credit, that your mother has not told you a lie; you will not hesitate, I trust, to take the only honorable step that remains for you, and immediately give up your very foolish engagement with this girl."

Lewis looked up indignantly.

"I am old enough certainly to manage that for myself. I shall make my own decision."

Mrs. Ross rose, lowering in sullen anger, and left the room; and Anne, pale and excited, rose to claim her letters. The youth's heart was moved within Lewis Ross at last, in spite of all his premature prudence, and worldly wisdom; he met his sister's inquisitive, searching look, with his own face more subdued and milder.

"Well, Anne?"

Anne lifted the letters.

"Is it possible, Lewis—is it possible, that you can have read these, and remain unconvinced? Has my father's charge no weight with you? Has Norman's distress no power? I cannot believe it—you feel as I do, Lewis, that Norman is not guilty."

"I don't know, Anne—I can't see it," said Lewis, leaning his head on his hand. "Here is every chance against him—every circumstance, and nothing in his favor but these two incoherent rambling letters. He was an excitable nervous person himself, and my father was an old man, almost in his dotage. I have my mother's authority for saying so—and what is their mere assertion against all the evidence?"

"What evidence, Lewis?"

"Oh, I have seen it all!" said Lewis, waving his hand: "my mother had the papers ready for me when I came in; she has hoarded them up, I fancy, to let me have the pleasure. If you had not said it, Anne, I should never have believed that the Norman Rutherford she told me of was any brother of ours; but since he is—the evidence it seems to me is irresistible. No, I can't say these letters convince me. It may be all very well to maintain a friend's innocence to the world, but between ourselves, you know, I see nothing in them."

Anne turned from him impatiently.

"Well!" exclaimed Lewis, "upon my word you bait and badger a man till he does not know his own mind. What would you have me do, Anne? Shall I go away and labor to find this Norman, and beg him to take Merkland off my hands, and permit me to remain his very humble servant? What do you mean? what would you have me do?"

"I would have you do the duty of a son and a brother," said Anne; "and if you will not do it, I warn you, Lewis, that I take this work upon myself, however unsuitable it may be for a woman. You have a special stake in it, Lewis—you must see that, till this mystery is cleared, Alice Aytoun is unapproachable to you; the brother of her father's accused murderer can be nothing to her, but a stranger whom she must shrink from and avoid. I know how this will crush poor Alice, but she is far too gentle and good a girl to go to any passionate extreme. You would speak of prejudice, and revenge, and arbitrary custom, Lewis: it is nonsense to say that; but were it only custom and prejudice, Alice will be ruled by it. She will not see you again."

"Will she not?" exclaimed Lewis, triumphantly, "we shall soon see. I don't mean to do anything tragical or high-flown, Anne, there's an end of it. Thanks to the difference of name, Alice knows nothing of this, and I do not see the remotest occasion for her ever knowing. I shan't tell her certainly. I intend to write to her mother to-day—you need not look horrified—this shall not keep me back an hour. Why should it? I had no hand in her father's murder; and as for Norman, I am very sorry, but I cannot help him in any way. If he has not deserved this by his guilt, he has by his folly; and it's not to be expected, I fancy, that I should entirely sacrifice myself for the sake of a half-brother whom I never saw—more particularly as the chances are, that the sacrifice would do him no good, and only waste my time, and make me unhappy."

"And have you no fear of Mrs. Aytoun and her son?" inquired Anne, in a low voice.

"No; the difference of name is very fortunate—how should any one suppose that a Rutherford in the east was the brother of a Ross in the north? Besides, if they had any suspicion, I hope they are sufficiently anxious about Alice and her happiness, to keep it to themselves. We are not in the age of feuds now, sister Anne: don't trouble yourself about it."

"If we are past feuds, we are not past nature," said Anne, hastily. "Lewis, I saw Mrs. Catherine this morning. I could not rest till I had ascertained whether there was any hope, that Alice was not this man's child. Mrs. Catherine knew the reason of my inquiries and agitation, and exclaimed immediately that you must not see Alice again; before this time Alice knows all, and however you might hope to weaken the impression it will make upon her—and you could not succeed even in that, for Alice with all her gentleness would do nothing so abhorrent to natural feeling and universal opinion, were her heart to break—you know very well that it would be folly to attempt moving Mrs. Catherine.—She will not permit your engagement to continue, Lewis—you may be sure of that."

Lewis burst forth into indignant exclamations: "Who dared to interfere between Alice and him? who would venture, for a crime done before her birth, to hinder their happiness?"

"Lewis," said Anne, "this is quite useless. I do not want to interfere between Alice and you. I believe the great obstacle is removed, and that with but proper exertion on your own part, you may at once secure your purpose, and deliver our poor Norman; but, as for daring and venturing, would Mrs. Catherine hesitate, think you? would Alice Aytoun's brother be afraid? Lewis, you are mistaken: it may break poor Alice's girlish heart—far too young for such a weight—but it will not make her rebelious; it will lead her to no unwomanly extreme: she will submit!"

Lewis was for a time passionate and loud, inveighing against them all for keeping him in ignorance, blaming Anne for telling Mrs. Catherine, and indulging in a thousand extravagances. Anne stood calmly beside him, and bore it all, too deeply bent on her own object to heed these effusions of passion.

"And supposing it possible," exclaimed Lewis, sitting down again, after his passion had nearly exhausted itself—"supposing it possible to prove Norman innocent, what then? I don't see how my position is at all bettered. What will I have to offer Alice? Some poor thousand pounds, perhaps, that may be doled out to me as the younger brother's portion—no house, no certain means of living. I suppose you would have me get a school in Portoran, or apply for a situation in the Bank, or go into a writer's office in Edinburgh," continued Lewis, bitterly, "and think I was anticipating love in a cottage, when I spoke of Alice Aytoun!"

Anne could have said much—could have begged and prayed him to believe that the landless Lewis Ross, who had saved his brother, would be a nobler man by far than the Laird of Merkland, who had left his nearest relative to languish out dishonored days in a strange country, uncared for and unsuccored: but she began to know better the material she had to work upon.

"Norman has his own land, Lewis," she said. "Had he remained at home, and had all been well with him, you still would have inherited Merkland. I know that certainly."

"Is it so?" said Lewis, eagerly. "If it is legally so—if the estate is settled on me to the exclusion of Norman, of course that puts the matter in quite a different aspect. And so you think he is innocent?"

Lewis took the letters in his hand again.

"I do not think he is innocent, Lewis," said Anne. "I may take your licence of strong speaking, in respect to this. I never had a doubt—never a fear. I felt that he was innocent. The joy was almost too much for me this morning. Lewis, do not think at all—open your heart to feel the agony of Norman's, and you will know that he is not guilty!"

"Sit down, Anne," said Lewis, more gently. "I want to look at these letters again."

Anne sat down. Lewis opened the papers and read them over carefully once more. He did not say any thing when he had finished, but remained for some time in silence. Their own internal force of truthfulness did not carry conviction to the cold, logical understanding of Lewis; he did not let his own heart have any influence in the judgment: he thought of legal evidence, not of moral certainty.

"And what would you advise should be done?" he said at length, as he met Anne's eye.

Anne repeated to him all the further particulars which she had learned from Esther Fleming, together with the nurse's suspicion that Norman knew who was the murderer, and was content thus far to suffer in his stead. Lewis's interest was excited by the idea of discovering the true criminal, but flagged again when Anne told him how bootless Esther's inquiries had been, and how widely spread was the conviction of Norman's guilt—and again he repeated, almost listlessly: "What would you have me do?"

"I would have you go to this place yourself immediately, Lewis," said Anne. "I would have you set out at once without the loss of any more time, and yourself go among the people.—You will find many of them, no doubt, who remember the story—it is not of a kind to be forgotten. Act upon Esther's suggestion—endeavor to find the real criminal—go over the whole neighborhood—spare no labor—no trouble. It may be a work demanding much time and much patience. Never mind that, the result is worth the toil of a lifetime, and you, Lewis, you have a special stake in it—there is a definite reward for you."

But the work, albeit he had a special stake in it, looked very different in the eyes of Lewis. He did not answer for some time, and then said: "It's entirely out of the question to go myself. I could not do it. I have neither time nor patience to expend so, but I'll tell you what I'll do, Anne—I'll write to Robert Ferguson—I saw him this morning leaving Woodsmuir to return to Edinburgh; he is a cool, shrewd, lawyer-like lad. I'll trust it to him."

"But think of the danger to Norman in making this secret known," exclaimed Anne.

"We need not tell him that," said Lewis, "there is no occasion whatever for trusting him with that. He can have some hint of what has occurred lately, and that it is a matter of some importance to us. I will write to him to-day. Does that satisfy you, Anne?"

There was no choice; she was compelled to be satisfied with it. The lawyer, no doubt, might manage it best, yet Anne had an instinctive confidence, in a search which should be guided, not by business-like acuteness alone, but by the loving energy of a heart which yearned over the outcast Norman, the desolate exiled brother. And Lewis spoke so coldly, "of some importance"—how the strange limitation chilled her heart.

"And I want you to do something for me in return, Anne," said Lewis, looking at his watch. "After dinner, come up with me to the Tower, and tell your story to Mrs. Catherine and Alice, your own way. You can do it better than I could, for you have more faith in it than I—altogether," he continued, rising, with a laugh: "You are more a believing person than I am, I fancy, Anne—no doubt it is quite natural—you women receive whatever's presented to you—it's all very right that you should—but something more is required of us."

Alas! poor Lewis! He did not know how incomparably higher that faculty of belief was than his meagre and poor calculations; nor could comprehend the instant and intuitive apprehension, which darted to its true conclusion at once, and left him weighing his sands of legal evidence so very far behind.

The evening was gusty, wild and melancholy, one of those nights that make the fireside lights look doubly cheerful; and just as little Alice Aytoun crept disconsolately up stairs in the darkness, Lewis and Anne left Merkland for the Tower. They had not much conversation on the way, for Anne was busied, chalking out a plan of procedure for herself, should Robert Ferguson's mission fail, and Lewis had lighter fancies, unwillingly obscured by some tinge of the truths he had learned that day, to keep him silent. There were no lights in the accustomed windows when they reached the Tower. Mrs. Catherine's own sitting-room was dark, and from the windows of the dining-parlor, there came only the red glimmer of firelight. Archibald Sutherland sat there alone, as Mrs. Catherine and Alice had left him, and had been too deeply engaged with his own thoughts to heed the gathering darkness.

"Mr. Archibald is in the dining-parlor," said Jacky, opening the door, as she spoke, to admit Lewis, and gliding back instantly to Anne's side. With natural delicacy, the servants had followed Mr. Ferguson's example, and when they could no longer call the broken man "Strathoran," returned to the kindly name of his boyhood.

"And if ye please, Miss Anne," continued Jacky, looking up wistfully into Anne's face. "Mrs. Catherine is in the little room."

Anne hesitated—Jacky's keen eyes were fixed upon her anxiously. "May I go in, I wonder, Jacky?"

"If ye please, Miss Anne—" began the girl.

"What, Jacky?"

"Miss Alice is no weel—I saw her gaun up to her ain room, slow and heavy. Mostly ye canna hear her foot, it's like a spirit's—the night it was dragging slow and sad-like, and I heard her say—"

Jacky paused.

"What did you hear her say?"

"It was in her ain room—I wasna listening, Miss Anne, I just heard it—she said 'there is no one with me'—low, low—like as if she was in grief. Miss Anne, will ye go up to Miss Alice? There was naebody near her but me, and she wasna wanting me. Will ye go, Miss Anne?"

Jacky's keen eyes was softened with an involuntary tear.

"I must see Mrs. Catherine first," said Anne, passing on hurriedly to the little room. Jacky seated herself in the window-seat near the library-door, in meditative solitude; the strange, chivalrous girl's heart within her beating high with plans of help and aid to that gentle, weeping Alice, whom all the stronger spirits round her seemed instinctively to join in warding evil and trouble from.

The door of the little room was at once opened to Anne, and she found Mrs. Catherine within, the trace of a tear even visible upon her sterner cheek.

"The poor bairn, child!" she exclaimed. "The poor, bit, silly, gentle thing! I could almost have seen yourself suffering, sooner than her. If stronger folk feel it even more painfully, there is aye a kind of struggle with their sorrow; but yonder, there was no strength to make resistance, child. The trouble sank down, like a stone, to the bottom of the bairn's heart. I cannot get away from my eye the bit, wan, unresisting, hopeless look of her."

"Mrs. Catherine!" exclaimed Anne, "I must go to her instantly. I bring hope. Do not look at me in anger. I am speaking words of truth and soberness: the matter does not stand as you think—as I thought this morning. Mrs. Catherine, Norman is innocent."

Mrs. Catherine made an emphatic motion with her hand, as if commanding Anne to go on; and waited breathlessly.

"Mrs, Catherine, I have his own words to build upon. I have the recorded conviction of my father. Do you think they could be deceived, to whom he was dearest upon earth? My father, Esther, Marion his wife, who went with him, they all believed him innocent—the last, by sharing his fate. You could not but believe his own words. He did not do it, Mrs. Catherine. He is innocent."

Mrs. Catherine laid her hands upon Anne's shoulders, and gazed with earnest scrutiny into her face.

"His own words—sharing his fate—what does the bairn mean? Child, I thought there was some other terror upon your mind, this morning, that ye did not tell me. Is Norman Rutherford alive?"

"Mrs. Catherine, his secret is safe with you," said Anne, drawing the letters from her bosom. "Norman is alive, unjustly condemned, and innocent. We must prove that first: but take these, and let me go to Alice."

"Sit down upon that seat, and wait," said Mrs. Catherine, peremptorily. "I must see the ground of your hope myself, before ye sicken the silly bairn with what may be but a false sunshine. Give me the papers, child."

The lamp was speedily lighted, and Mrs. Catherine seated herself to examine them. How different was the keen interest inspiring the strong face which bent over them, the eyes that traced their incoherent lines so rapidly, from the cold examination of Lewis. How different the conclusion.

"The Lord be thanked!" burst from Mrs. Catherine's lips, as she came to the end of Norman's letter. "The Lord, in His infinite tenderness, be thanked for the comfort. Gowan, what are ye lingering for? Go to the bairn, and give her the good news. It is meet that I should be alone. Hear ye, child, go to the bairn."

Anne needed no urging—she left the room instantly, and hurried up stairs.

Alice's gay bower was dark—the fire burning dull and low: the very flowers drooping like their mistress. Anne passed through the opened door hastily, to the still darker and chiller bed-chamber within, where she could see the girl's slight figure lying on the bed. Alice was roused by the approaching footsteps, and said, as Anne drew near her:

"Not now, Bessie; leave me, I do not want you now."

Anne advanced, and gently drew the hidden cheek from the wet pillow.

"It is not Bessie," she said: "it is I, Alice, Anne Ross, your sister."

Alice raised her head.

"My sister! Ah! you do not know."

Her hair was thrown back in a momentary attempt at pride, and then Alice hid her face again in her hands. It was as Mrs. Catherine said; the gentle little heart could offer no resistance to this dull, dead weight of sorrow.

"I do know, Alice!" said Anne. "Look up now, and do not weep. Lewis is waiting to see you. Mrs. Catherine knows he is here—Alice!"

"Is it not true?" whispered Alice; "is it not true? You would not call me Alice if it were true. Oh! Miss Ross, tell me."

"It is not true; we have found out that we were wrong," said Anne, soothingly. "Rise, now, and let me be your maid instead of Bessie, and you shall hear it all when you are able."

Alice had half risen, and was already clinging to Anne like a child.

"Tell me now; I am able. Oh! Miss Ross, why did Mrs. Catherine tell me that? why did you let her? I could not bear it. If it were to come back again I should die—I know I should die!"

Anne smiled sadly. And yet it might have been so; the gentle and weak may droop their heads like flowers, and die; the stronger must live on, bearing undying griefs through long lifetimes: it is so appointed. Very sad was this plaintive, murmuring sorrow from lips so young. Sadder still was the conscious life of that other more perfect woman of the ballad: "I wish I was dead, but I'm no like to dee."

Jacky was hovering not far off with lights, and Anna lifted her little patient tenderly, put her dress in order, and led her down to the cheerful fireside of Mrs. Catherine's inner drawing-room, where Lewis joined her by-and-bye, and from the warm and hopeful air of which, glad lights went flashing back again over the fair horizon of Alice Aytoun's life.

"Child," said Mrs. Catherine, as they parted, "I perceive it will be a hard work and a sore; but let me see you fainting, if you daur! Make no scruple to ask whatsoever aid is needful from me—ye ken that. You cannot see the truthfulness of it, child, as I do, that ken the lad. Be of good cheer, and never doubt that the Lord will bring light out of this great darkness in his own time."

CHAPTER XIV

Within a week after these agitating events, Archibald Sutherland, in company with the anxious and attentive factor, rode into Portoran, to meet the third individual of their council, Mr. Foreman, and engage in a final consultation. During the days which had intervened since Archibald's return, there had already been much discussion and deliberation between the two good men, who took an interest so kindly in his changed fortunes. Mr. Ferguson, who had a distant kinsman, the most inaccessible and hypochondriacal of nabobs, and under whose ken had passed various bilious, overgrown fortunes accumulated in the golden East, gave his voice for India. Mr. Foreman, whose brother had grown comfortably rich, on the shores of that river "Plate," whose very name in mercantile mouths, seems to savor so pleasantly of golden harvests, spoke strongly in favor of South America. Mr. Foreman had been consulting with his minister, of whose business head, and clear judgment, the good lawyer was becomingly proud, and slightly given to boast himself; and it happened that, at that very time, Mr. Lumsden had heard from his brother, the clever manager and future junior partner of Messrs. Sutor and Sinclair's, great commercial house in Glasgow, that Mr. Sinclair, the partner in Buenos Ayres, was in urgent want of an intelligent and well-educated clerk, and had written to his partner and manager, desiring them, either to send one of the young men in their Glasgow office, or to employ one of higher qualifications, if need were, and send him out without delay. Now it happened, wrote Mr. Lumsden's brother, that the house of Sutor and Sinclair had divers other branches, in different parts of the world, and their clerks of experience having been drafted, one by one, to these, they were now left with none of sufficient age, or acquirements, to suit the fastidious Mr. Sinclair, whose letter had conveyed a delicate hint, that if it were possible, he should desire a young man of some culture and breeding to fill the vacant post. Mr. Lumsden's brother further explained, that this was a quiet stroke at the less polished Mr. Sutor, who had previously sent a clerkship, in the shape of a great hearty, joyous, enterprising cub, of true Glasgow manufacture and proportions, born to make a fortune, but unfortunately, not born either to be or look anything beyond the honest, genial, persevering, money-making man he already was. Mr. Sinclair's health was delicate; his mind, considering that he was a clever and very successful merchant, pre-eminently so; and the choice of his confidential clerk, puzzled Mr. George Lumsden and his principal sadly.

Mr. Foreman, on hearing of this, had written without delay to his minister's brother, desiring to know whether poor Archibald—the ruined laird—might have any chance of suiting so peculiar a situation. His name, Mr. Foreman wrote somewhat proudly, was a sufficient voucher for his personal acquirements; he had been unfortunate, but the youthful madness which occasioned these misfortunes had been bitterly repented of, and there was little doubt that his ability, and earnest endeavor to redeem his lost ground, would carry him to the head of whatever he attempted. When Mr. Ferguson and Archibald entered Mr. Foreman's private room, they found him waiting in nervous expectation for an answer to this letter. He knew the mail had come in; he had dispatched a messenger to the post-office half an hour ago, and was fuming now over the vexatious delay. In the meantime, however, he managed to explain the matter to his visitors.

"From all that I can hear, Mr. Archibald, is just the thing for you—without office drudging, and with a man who could understand and sympathize with your feelings. I do think we have been fortunate in hearing of it."

Archibald shook his head. "You are too ambitious for me, Mr. Foreman. I would rather—it may be a sort of pride, perhaps, though pride sits ill on me—I would, indeed, rather not have my feelings sympathized with by strangers. I should prefer no manner of distinction.

"Well, well!" said Mr. Foreman, "neither there will be; only the situation is a superior one, and you would have in it the best possible opening."

"Don't think me ungrateful," said Archibald. "I shall be very glad of it, if you think me at all likely to have the necessary qualifications. But in business, you know, I want experience entirely. I almost want even elementary knowledge."

"No fear of that," said Mr. Ferguson, "a good head and clear mind soon master the details of business—but India!"

"Ah! has the little wretch come back at last?" cried Mr. Foreman, darting into the outer office, and seizing upon his messenger, who, lingering only to watch the progress of one most interesting game at "bools," which came to a crisis just as he was passing, had returned from the post-office with his load of letters. These were examined in a moment; one bearing the square Glasgow post-mark selected, the others tossed over in an indiscriminate heap to Walter, and Mr. Foreman, opening his letter hurriedly, re-entered the room reading it. It was decidedly favorable. Much of sympathy and compassion for the young man shipwrecked so early, much of regret for the downfall of an old house (for Mr. Lumsden was a north countryman, and knew the Sutherland family by name) were in it; but these Mr. Foreman kept to himself. The prudent manager of Messrs. Sutor and Sinclair's Glasgow house, was rather dubious, as to a young man, who had managed to ruin himself at five-and-twenty, being quite a suitable person for a merchant's trusted and confidential clerk; but proposed that Mr. Sutherland should come, for a month or two, to the Glasgow counting-house, to acquire a knowledge of the business, and enable them to form a better judgment of him, on personal knowledge. Mr. Lumsden's words were quite kind, and perfectly respectful, yet Mr. Foreman delicately softened them as he read, and when he had concluded, looked triumphantly from Archibald to Mr. Ferguson.

"Well, gentlemen; what do you say?"

The factor gave in his adhesion; his own vague hope from India could not stand before a definite proposal like this. "It looks well, Mr. Archibald; upon my word, I do think it looks well."

"It is quite above my expectations," said Archibald. "I am perfectly ready to enter upon my probation at once—without delay. I accept your friend's offer without the least hesitation, Mr. Foreman; write him, I beg, and tell him so, and let the time be fixed for the commencement of my apprenticeship—and then, if I satisfy my new employers—then, for the shores of that luxurious Spain in the west, and such prosperity as Providence shall send me there. Nay, nay; you look sorrowfully at me, as if I mocked myself; I do not—my second beginning is more hopeful than my first. I will do no dishonor—I trust—I hope I shall do no further dishonor to your kindness, or my father's name: only let us have it settled upon, and begun as early as possible, Mr. Foreman. I have no time to lose."

"I am glad! I am delighted!" exclaimed the honest lawyer, "to see you take it so well. If the first disagreeables were but over!"

"Never mind the first disagreeables, Mr. Foreman," said Archibald, cheerfully. "I shall be the better of difficulties to begin with—if I only were begun."

"We will not linger about that," said Mr. Foreman, catching the contagion of his client's cheerfulness, which, to tell the truth, was more in seeming than reality. "I shall write to Mr. Lumsden at once."

Other arrangements had to be made before they left Portoran—the transfer of Alexander Semple's lease to Mr. Ferguson being the principal matter which occupied them. Semple was a soft, spiritless man, of indolent temper; and no enterprise, and the bleak, unprofitable acres were certain to remain as unprofitable and bleak as ever during his occupancy. Already many times Mr. Coulter had sighed over them, and poured into the ears of their listless tenant vain hints, and unheeded remonstrances. Mr.

Coulter was most pleasantly busied now devising the means for their fertilization, and, in company with Mr. Ferguson, had already taken various very long, wearisome, and delightful walks, partly from a neighborly regard for the interests of the broken man, and partly from his own entire devotion to his respectable and most important science, advising with the new farmer as to the various profitable and laborious processes necessary for these unpromising and barren fields. The rental Archibald Sutherland insisted should remain in the factor's hands, or in Mr. Foreman's hands, or in the Portoran branch of the British Linen Company's Bank, if his zealous friends insisted on that, his own resolution being to spend nothing beyond the income he worked for, however small that might be at first. His own tastes had always been simple, and money the mere bits of gold and scraps of paper—had become precious in his eyes. There was little fear either that he should ever be a worshipper of the golden calf—the unrighteous Mammon. But Strathoran—his home—his birth-place—the house of his fathers!

He saw its turrets rising from among the trees as he turned his horse's head from the pleasant threshold of Woodsmuir, to which he now paid his first visit. These fair slopes and hollows, the brown moor running far northward, the gray hills in the distance, with the red glory of the frosty January sunlight on their bare, uncovered heads. What were they now to him? What? Dearer, more precious than ever; the aim to which he looked forward through a dim vista of hard-working years; a prize to be won; a goal to be attained; a treasure to be brought by his own toil! Was there no sickening of the heart, as the young man, born and nurtured in that proud old house of Strathoran, the heir of all its inherited honors, looked forward to the lifetime of toil that lay before him, obscure, ignoble, unceasing? The office in Glasgow where he should be put on trial, and have the strange new experience of unknown masters, on whose favor depended all his prospects; the still more dim and unknown counting-house of Buenos Ayres, with its exile and estrangement from home-looks and language. Was not his heart sickening within him? No! Who that has felt his pulses quicken, and his heart beat, at the anticipation of a clear and honorable future, filled only with unencumbered labor, a healthful frame, a sound mind, and a great aim in view, could ask that question? Sickness, deadly and painful, overpowered Archibald Sutherland's heart when he looked behind; that wild lee-shore of weakness, those fierce rocks of temptation and passion upon which his fortune and his honor had made disastrous shipwreck. These are the things to sicken hearts and crush them, not the bracing chill air that swept the path to which he began to bind his breast. The hill was steep, the way long, rough, laborious. What matter? There was hope, and mental health, and moral safety in his toils; a definite aim at its summit; an All-guiding Providence, giving strength to the toiler, and promising a blessing upon every righteous effort, to uphold and bear him on.

The cloud that had passed over that little, blue-eyed, gentle girl at the Tower—the new interest which occupied the mind of Mrs. Catherine, were known to Archibald in some degree, and interested him deeply. But the great secret—that Norman lived yet to be toiled, and hoped, and prayed for—was not communicated to either Archibald or Alice. They knew only that their friends believed him unjustly accused, and intended to labor for proof of that—proof which might be difficult enough to find, after the lapse of so many years—but the fact of the engagement between Lewis and Alice, was quite sufficient to account for the suddenly awakened anxiety concerning Norman's innocence.

The first week of the new year was past: the next day little Alice was to return home. They were all sitting in Mrs. Catherine's inner drawing-room, about her cheerful tea-table—Mrs. Catherine herself, Alice, Anne, Archibald, and Lewis. The spirits of the young people had risen; they were all hopeful, courageous, and conversing with that intimate and familiar kindliness which unites so much more closely and tenderly on the eve of a parting than at any other time. Alice was to sing to them—to sing as Anne and Archibald begged—that song of the 'Oran' which had moved them so deeply on the night of the new year. The sweet young voice had grown more expressive since that time; the gentle, youthful spirit had passed through greater vicissitudes in that week than in all its previous bright lifetime, and, therefore, the song was better rendered—its tinge of sadness—its warm breath of hope—

"Ah, pray, young hearts, for the sad wayfaring man!"

Anne met Archibald's eyes with a supplicating glance in them as the melody ended. Her own were wet with sympathetic tears. Yes, for him who must count so many years of toil before he could see the evening star rise calm on the home-waves of Oran, she echoed the prayer, but more deeply, and with a thrill of still devouter earnestness, for that exiled brother who already had borne the burden of the long laborious day, so far from home and all its comforts, so far from hope and honor.

Alice sang again, a pretty little pastoral song of the district, which was a favorite with Lewis. He was leaning over her chair, and Anne, approaching Mrs. Catherine, took the opportunity of asking her about this ballad—whether it really had any connexion with Norman, or was but linked to him, by her own fancy.

"It is Norman's song," said Mrs. Catherine. "Ye know, child, that I like ballads that have the breath of life in them. Langsyne, Norman left that with me; the author of it was some student lad about Redheugh, that he liked well, and it has lain bye me ever since. I desired the bairn Alison to learn it. I am an auld fuil to heed such bairnly things, child; but it pleased me to hear her father's daughter singing that. There was a kind of forgiveness and peace in it to the memory of the unhappy callant.—It was a foolish fancy, was it not, for an auld wife? But silence! let us hear her."

And so, next morning, little Alice, very sadly, and with many tears, went away; Lewis and Anne accompanying her to Portoran. Alice wore a little ring of betrothal upon her slender finger, and carried with her a letter from Mrs. Catherine, stating all the circumstances of her engagement, and their conviction that they could prove to Mrs. Aytoun's satisfaction the innocence of Norman. It had been thought best that Lewis should not write himself, until Mrs. Catherine had explained his peculiar position to the mother and brother of Alice; and they had arranged that he should follow her, very shortly, to Edinburgh, to present himself to her family, and urge his suit in person.

Very sad also was the leave-taking of Bessie and her friends at the Tower. Johnnie Halflin had bought a pretty little silk handkerchief for her, which Bessie, in simple fidelity, vowed never to part with. Jacky had bestowed a book, and some very beautiful moss, from a gray, old tombstone in the graveyard on Oranside, which, tradition said, covered the last resting-place of the heroine of an old, pathetic ballad, current in the countryside. Bessie let the book slide thanklessly to the bottom of her little "kist," and was sadly at a loss what to do with the moss, which however, was finally thrust into the same repository. Poor Jacky had chosen her parting presents unhappily.

And at last, they were away. The frost had broken, through the night, and it was another of those dull, drizzling, melancholy winter days. Lewis placed Alice, carefully wrapped up, and protected from the cold, in the corner of the same coach in which she had seen him first. Little Bessie was seated by her side, and leaving the Tower and all its pleasant neighborhood lying dark behind her, Alice Aytoun was whirled away home.

It cost her no inconsiderable amount of exertion and self-denial to have the tears and sadness sufficiently overcome to meet her mother's greeting as she wished to do. But Alice schooled herself bravely, like a little hero, and conquered. They were home, in the old familiar room, by the well-known fireside. Mrs. Aytoun was smiling, as she had not smiled before since Alice went away. James was half-ashamed of being so unusually joyous. They had all her news to hear, all her three months' history over again, in spite of the long recording letters.

"And what is this?" said Mrs. Aytoun, taking her daughter's small white hand, upon which glittered the little token ring. "Is this another of those delicate gifts of Mrs. Catherine's?"

Little Alice could not answer; the blood flushed over her face and neck. She stammered and trembled. Mrs. Aytoun looked at her, in alarm and wonder.

"Read this letter, mother," whispered Alice, at last, putting Mrs. Catherine's letter into her mother's hands, and sinking upon a stool at her feet. "It will tell you all."

James had left the room, a minute before. Mrs. Aytoun, somewhat agitated, opened the letter, and Alice laid her head upon her mother's knee, and hid it in the folds of her dress. Mrs. Aytoun read:

"I herewith send back to you, kinswoman, your pleasant bairn, who has been a great comfort and solace to me, though my old house was maybe too dark a cage for a singing bird like her. I am by no means confident either whether I will ever undertake the charge of any such dangerous gear again; for in the ordinary course of nature, the bit gay spirit and bonnie face of her have been making mischief in Strathoran; and besides having my door besieged by all manner of youthful company, there is one lad, who, I am feared, has crossed my threshold too often, maybe, for your good pleasure.

"The lad is Lewis Ross, of Merkland, a gallant of good outward appearance and competent estate, with no evil condition that I can specially note about him, except having arrived at that full period of years, when it is the fashion of young men to give themselves credit for more wisdom than any other mortal person can see. In other things, so far as I can judge, the two are well enough matched: for Lewis is the representative of a family long settled in the countryside, and has his lands free of any burden or encumbrance, besides being in all matters of this world a prudent, sensible, and managing lad.

"I would have put in a reservation, however, till your pleasure was known, but doubtless the deliberate ways of age differ from the swift proceedings of youth; and the two had plunged themselves beyond power of redemption, before I had any inkling of the matter. I see no good way of stopping it now, and I think you may trust your Burd Alice in the hands of Lewis Ross, without fear.

"And now, kinswoman, there comes a graver and darker matter into the consideration. I will not ask you if ye mind the beginning of your widowhood. It is pain and grief to me to say a word that may bring that terrible season back to ye, even in the remembrance; only it has so happened, in the wonderful course of Providence, that it should have an unhappy connection with the troth-plighting of these two bairns. Kinswoman you are younger than me, and have seen less of this world's miseries, though your own trials have not been light. But what think you of a young man, in the bloom of his years and his hopes, with a pleasant heritage and a fair name, suddenly covered with the shame and dishonor of a great crime—threatened with a shameful death—exposed to the hatred of all men, that bore the love of God and their neighbors in honest hearts,—and him innocent withal? What think you of a lad—generous, upright, honorable—as true and single-minded a youth as the eye of day ever looked upon, suddenly plunged into a horror of darkness like this—knowing himself everywhere condemned, yet, in his true and honest heart, knowing himself guiltless? I say, what think you of this? Was there ever a darker or more terrible doom, in this world of ills and mysteries?

"I knew him—kinswoman, from his birth-year to the time of his blight, I knew this unhappy heart: the truthfulness of him—the honoring of others above himself, that was inherent in his simple, manly nature—the strength of gentleness and patience, that might have been crowning an old and wise head, instead of being yoked with the impetuous spirit of youth! All this I knew; and yet, painfully and slowly, I also was permitted to believe that his pure hand had blood upon it—that he had done this crime.

"My eyes are opened. I am humbled to the ground in my rejoicing, that I should have dared, even in my own secret spirit, to malign the gracious nature I knew so well. Kinswoman, the violent death of your husband, by whom or wherefore done I know not, brought this sore doom undeserved upon Norman Rutherford. The bridal tryst of your pleasant bairn Alice, will clear his dishonored name again.

"You think he killed your husband. I am not given to hasty judgment, nor am I easily misguided. He did not do it; and when I tell you that your bairn Alison is plighted to a near kinsman of Norman Rutherford's, I lay my charge upon you not to let your heart sink within you, or suffer the bairn's bit gentle spirit to be broken again. I pledge you my word, that they will seek no further consent from you, till Norman's righteousness is clear to your eyes as the morning light. There are two urgent reasons pressing them—I am meaning Lewis Ross, and his sister, my own Anne,—on this work; the winning of your pleasant bairn and the clearing of their brother's lost fame and honor.

"For he is their brother, their nearest kin. Again, I charge you, think of this terrible doom laid upon a gallant of as clear and lofty a spirit as ever was in mortal knowledge; and let the mother's heart within you have compassion on his name. Shut not your mind against the proof—it may be hard to gather—and take time and patience; but if mortal hands can compass it, it shall be laid before you soon or syne.

"Lewis Ross (trusting you will receive him) will shortly tell you of this himself, with his own lips; and having maybe some right of counsel, in virtue of my years, and of our kindred, it is my prayer that you put no discouragement in this way.

"Be content to wait till the proof is brought to you; and break not the gentle spirit of the bairn, by crossing her in the first tenderness of her youth.

CATHERINE DOUGLAS."

Mrs. Aytoun was greatly agitated. James had entered the room, and stood in silent astonishment, as he looked at Alice clinging to her mother's knee, and the letter trembling in Mrs. Aytoun's hand. "Mother—Alice—what has happened? What is the matter?"

Mrs. Aytoun handed the letter to him in silence, and, lifting her daughter up, drew her close to her breast: "My Alice! my poor, simple bairn! why did I let you away from me?"

The girl clung to her mother, terrified, ashamed, and dizzy.—She trembled to hear some fatal sentence, parting her for ever from Lewis. She fancied she could never lift up her blushing face again, to speak of him, even if that terror were withdrawn: she could only lean on that kind breast, and cling, as is the nature of such gentle, dependent spirits. Anne Ross's words were true.—Had Mrs. Aytoun but said that she must never see Lewis again, poor little Alice would have submitted without a struggle, and would have been right; she was safe in that wise guidance—she was not safe in her own.

But Mrs. Aytoun's motherly lips gave forth no such arbitrary mandate. She rose, still holding Alice within her arm. "James," she said, "that letter is a most important one: read it carefully.—We will join you again by-and-by."

And leading and supporting her drooping daughter, Mrs. Aytoun went to her own room, and, seating herself there, began to question Alice.

And then the whole stream came flowing forth, hesitating and broken; how Lewis had travelled with her, and had been constantly at her side, ever since that momentous journey; how Anne had been her patient, kind, indulgent friend; how at last, upon that eventful New year's night, Lewis and herself had been alone together—and then—and then—there followed some incoherent words, which Mrs. Aytoun could comprehend the purport of; how Anne came in, looking so chill and pale, and horror-stricken; how Mrs. Catherine next day took her into the little room, and almost broke the gentle heart that was beating so high now, with anxiety and suspense; how Anne returned at night with voice as tender and hand as gentle as her mother's telling her that Norman was innocent; and then, how glad and happy they had all been together again—and then—if her mother could only see him—if she could only see Anne—they could tell her so much better!

Mrs. Aytoun was still anxious and pale, but her tremor of agitation was quieted.

"She must be a very kind, good girl, this Anne, Alice."

Alice breathed more freely—if her mother had been very angry, was her simple reasoning, she would not have spoken so.

"She is very good—very kind, mother—like you, gentler than Mrs. Catherine; but she is not a girl, she is older than—than Lewis."

Mrs. Aytoun smiled.

"How old is Lewis?"

The simple little heart began to beat with troubled joy.

"He is twenty-one, mother. It was his birthday just a week after I went to the Tower."

Mrs. Aytoun did not speak for some time.

"Alice," she said at last, "I must see this Lewis, and consult with James, before I make any decision—in the meantime you will be very patient, will you not?"

"Oh, yes, yes—I do not care how long—only—if you saw him, mother, if you just saw him, I know how you would like him!"

"Would I?" said Mrs. Aytoun, smiling: "well, we shall see; but now dry your eyes, and let us go back to James again."

They returned to the parlor. James sat at the table, the letter lying before him, and his face exceedingly grave. He was very much disturbed and troubled. He did not well see what to do.

For some time there was little conversation between them—the mother and son consulted together with their grave looks. Little Alice, again sadly cast down, sat silent by the fireside. At last her brother addressed her with a sort of timidity, blushing almost as she did herself, when he mentioned the name.

"Alice, when does Mr. Ross come to Edinburgh?"

Mr. Ross! so cold it sounded and icy—would not Lewis be his brother?

"In a fortnight," murmured Alice.

"A fortnight! then, mother, I think my best plan is to go down to Strathoran myself and make inquiries. In a matter which involves two such important things as the happiness of Alice, and the honor of our family, there is no time for delay. I shall start to-morrow."

"Can you spare the time?" said his mother—while Alice looked up half-glad, half-sorrowful—it might keep Lewis from coming to Edinburgh—at the same time, James was so sure to be convinced by Lewis's irresistible eloquence, and the gentler might of Anne.

"I must spare it, mother," was the answer, "my ordinary business is not so important as this. What do you think—am I right?"

"Perfectly right, James," said his mother, promptly, "I was about to advise this myself; and if you find anything satisfactory to report, you can bid this Lewis still come. I shall want to see who it is, who has superseded me in my little daughter's heart."

"Oh, no, mother—no, no," cried Alice, imploringly. "Do not say that."

James Aytoun rose and laid his hand caressingly upon his little sister's fair hair. She had been a child when he was rising into manhood. He thought her a child still—and with the grave difficulties of this, very unexpected problem, which they had to solve, there mingled a half-mirthful, half-sad, sort of incredulous wonder. Little Alice had done a very important piece of business independently and alone. Little Alice had the sober glory of matronhood hanging over her fair, girlish forehead. Little Alice was engaged!

CHAPTER XV

Several days before Alice left the Tower, Lewis had written to Robert Ferguson, the youthful Edinburgh advocate, of whose very early call to the bar his father was so justly and pleasantly proud, telling him all they knew and guessed of Norman's history, except the one circumstance of his escape from the shipwreck; and explaining, in some slight degree, the immediate reason of their anxiety to clear their brother's name from the foul blot that lay upon it. Very shortly after Alice Aytoun's departure, an answer came to the letter of Lewis.

With quick interest, partly in that it was one of the first cases in which his legal wisdom had been consulted, and partly from the kindly feeling of neighborhood, which is so warm in Scotland, the young lawyer embraced the search, and promised to go down instantly to the parish in which the deed was done, or even to engage the assistance of an acute writer, of experience in his craft, if Lewis thought that desirable. Mr. Robert, however, with a young man's abundant confidence in his own power, fancied that he could accomplish the work quite as well alone. "He would go down quietly to the village," he said, "taking care to do nothing which might put the true criminal, if he still lived, upon his guard; and as soon as he had procured any information, would report it to Lewis."

The letter was satisfactory—the warm readiness of belief in Norman's innocence pleased Anne. In such a matter, however strong one's own faith may be, it is a great satisfaction to hear it echoed by other minds.

In the afternoon of that day, Anne went, by appointment, to the Tower, to communicate Robert's opinion to Mrs. Catherine.—She made a circuit by the mill, to see Lilie; for Mrs. Catherine and Archibald, she knew, had business in Portoran, and would not return early. It was a clear, bright, mild day, with a spring haze of subdued sunshine about it, reminding one, pleasantly, that the year "was on the turn." Lilie was not at home.

"And I wish ye would speak to that outre lassie, Jacky Morison, Miss Anne," said Lilie's careful guardian. "She had the bairn away this morning, and trails her about to a' kinds of out o' the way places; in the wood, and on the hills; and I'm not sure in my ain mind, that it's right to let the bairn wi' the like o' her."

"Jacky is sure to be very careful," said Anne.

"Na, it's no sae muckle for that," said Mrs. Melder; "though I have a cauld tremble whiles when I think o' the water. Jacky's no oncarefu. It's a great charge being answerable for a stranger bairn, Miss Anne; but Lilie's learning (it's just a pleasure to see how fast she wins on) a' manner o' nonsense verses; and has her bit head fu' of stories o' knights and fairies, and I kenna a' what. It's Jacky's doing and no ither. I am at times whiles far frae easy in my mind about it."

"No fear," said Anne, smiling. "Jacky will do Lilie no harm, Mrs. Melder."

"To be sure," said Mrs. Melder, thoughtfully, "she's no an ill scholar, to be sic a strange lassie; and has been lookit weel after at the Tower. She was here the other day, when the minister was in—that's Mr. Lumsden—he had a diet[1] in my house, Miss Anne—and it wad have dune ye gude to have heard her at the questions. No a slip; and as easy in the petitions as in man's chief end. They say," continued Mrs. Melder, somewhat overpowered, "that she can say the hundred and nineteenth psalm a' out, without missing a word."

[1] A diet of examination. One of the periodical visits made by Scottish clergymen in former times, during which the household, and especially its younger members, were examined on the "Shorter Catechism," the universal text-book of Scottish Theology.

Leaving the miller's kindly wife a good deal reassured by these signs of Jacky's orthodoxy, Anne proceeded towards the Tower. The highroad was circuitous, and long; and the direct and universally-used path ran along the northern bank of the river, through the grounds of Strathoran. The little green gate, near which Alice had met Mr. Fitzherbert, was at the opposite extremity of this by-way, where it entered the precincts of the Tower.—As she drew near the stile, at which the narrow path was admitted into the possessions of the fallen house of Sutherland, Anne heard voices before her. One of them, whose loud tone was evidently full of anger and excitement, she recognised at once as Marjory Falconer's; and having heard of her former adventure with Mr. Fitzherbert, and gallant defence of little Alice, Anne hurried forward, fearing that her friend's prompt ire, and impetuous disposition, had involved her in some new scrape. It was evident that Marjory had some intention, in raising her voice so high. Anne could hear its clear tone, and indignant modulation, before she came in sight of the speaker.

He would venture to take the airs of a chieftain upon him—he, an English interloper, a mushroom lord! "Pull away the branches, George: never mind, let them indict you for trespass if they dare."

Anne had quickened her pace, and was now close to the stile. Miss Falconer, her face flushed, her strong, tall, handsome figure swelling stronger and taller than ever, as she pulled, with an arm not destitute of force, one great branch which had been placed with many others, across the stile, barring the passage, stood with her head turned towards Strathoran, too much engrossed to notice Anne's approach. The Falcon's Craig groom was laboring with all his might to clear away the other obstructions, his broad face illuminated with fun, and hot with exertion, enjoying it with his whole heart. Miss Falconer went on:

"A pretty person to shut us out of our own country—to eject our cottars—honester men a hundredfold than himself; a chief forsooth! does he think himself a chief? I would like to see the clan of Gillravidge. Pull away these barriers, George; if Mrs. Catherine does not try conclusions with him, I do not know her."

"Marjory," said Anne, "what are you doing?—what is the matter now?"

"Anne Ross, is that you?—the matter!—why, look here—here is matter enough to make any one angry—our road, that belonged to us and our ancestors before this man's race or name had ever been heard of—look at it, how he has blocked it up—look at this 'notice to trespassers'—'to be prosecuted with the utmost rigor of the law'—very well, let them prosecute!" continued Marjory, raising her voice, and sending a flashing, keen glance towards a corner of the adjoining plantation, "let them prosecute by all means—in five minutes more, they shall have some trespassers. These paltry little tyrants—these upstart Englishmen, daring, in a lowland country, and on poor Archibald Sutherland's lands, to do what a highland chief would not venture on, on his own hills!"

"It must be some mistake, Marjory," said Anne, "it is impossible any one could do this with the intention of insulting the whole countryside. It must be a mistake."

"Mistake, indeed!—throw it into the Oran, George, throw it over the water," cried Miss Falconer, as the groom raised in his arms an immense piece of wood, the last barrier to the passage. "We shall see that by-and-by—come, Anne."

Marjory mounted the style, and sprang down in the Strathoran grounds on the other side. "Come, Anne, come."

"Had we not better go the other way?" said Anne. "It is but subjecting ourselves to impertinence, Marjory. Nay, do not look contemptuous. I am not afraid of accompanying you, but I do think that Lewis and Ralph might manage this better than we can."

Marjory threw back her head with an indignant, impatient motion. "Don't be a fool, Anne. Come, I am going to the Tower. Lewis and Ralph indeed!"

"Well," said Anne, "if they could not do it better, it would be at least more suitable. We shall only expose ourselves to impertinence, Marjory. Let us go round the other way."

"Very well," said Miss Falconer, turning away; "I will go alone."

Anne crossed the stile. It was annoying to be forced into any altercation, such as was almost sure to ensue upon their meeting any of the dependents of Lord Gillravidge; at the same time, she could not suffer Marjory to go alone. George lifted a large, empty basket, and followed them, his hot, merry face shining like a beacon as he passed beneath the bare and rustling boughs.

Miss Falconer, with the large basket full, had been visiting a widow, whose only son had met with a severe accident, while engaged in his ordinary labor. The widow had some claim on the household of Falcon's Craig—some one of those most pleasant and beneficial links of mutual good-will and service which unite country neighborhoods so healthfully, subsisted between the poor family and the great one, and as, on any grand occasion at Falcon's Craig, the brisk services of Tibbie Hewit, the hapless young mason's mother, would have been rendered heartily and at once, so the accident was no sooner reported to Miss Falconer, then she set out with her share of the mutual kindliness. We cannot tell what was in the basket, but Tibbie Hewit's "press" was very much better filled when it went away empty, than when Miss Falconer entered her cottage.

"What a pity I have not my whip," said Marjory, as, drawing Anne's arm within her own, they passed on together. "You should have seen that cowardly fellow who stopped little Alice! what a grimace he made when he felt the lash about his shoulders! I say, Anne,"—Miss Falconer's voice sank lower—"did you see them hiding in the wood?"

"Who, Marjory?"

"Oh! that ape with the hair about his face, and some more of them. I should not have pulled down their barricade, I dare say, if I had not seen them. But you do not think I would retreat for them?"

"I do think, indeed," said Anne, looking hastily round, "that retreat would be by far our most dignified plan. Suppose they come down to us, Marjory, and we, who call ourselves gentlewomen, get involved in a squabble with a set of impertinent young men. I do think we are subjecting ourselves to quite unnecessary humiliation."

A violent flush covered Marjory Falconer's face—one of those overpowering rebounds of the strained delicacy and womanliness which revenged her escapades so painfully—the burning color might have furnished a hundred fluttering blushes for little Alice Atoun. But still she had no idea of yielding.

"Perhaps you are right, Anne. I did not think of that; but at least we must go on now. And think what an insult it is!—to all of us—to the whole country. We cannot suffer it, you know. Mrs. Catherine, I am sure, will take steps immediately."

"Very likely," said Anne.

Anne was revolving the possibility of crossing the Oran by the stepping-stones, which were about a quarter of a mile along, and so escaping the collision she dreaded.

"There, you see!" exclaimed Marjory, triumphantly; "there is a proof of the way we are dealt with, the indignities they put upon women! Neither Lewis nor Ralph would have the public spirit to resist such a thing as this. Oh! I can answer for Ralph, and I know Lewis would not. But one can be quite sure of Mrs. Catherine—one is never disappointed in her. Yet you will hear silly boys sneer at her, and think her estate would be better in their feeble hands, than in her own strong ones. I ask you, what do you think of that, Anne Ross—can you see no injustice there?"

"Injustice?" said Anne, laughing. "No, indeed, only a great, deal of foolishness and nonsense; both on the part of the silly boys, and—I beg your pardon, Marjory—on yours, for taking the trouble of repeating what they say."

"Oh, very well!" said Miss Falconer, coloring still more violently, yet, with characteristic obstinacy plunging on in the expression of her pet opinions. "Yes! I know you think me very unwomanly; you pretend to be proper, Anne Ross—to set that sweet confection of gentleness, and mildness, and dependence, which people call a perfect woman, up as your model; but it's all a cheat, I tell you! You ought to try to be weak and pretty, and instead of that, you are only grave and sensible. You ought to be clinging to Lewis, as sweet and timid as possible; instead of that, you are very independent, and not much given, I fancy, to consulting your younger brother. You're not true, Anne Ross; you think with me, and are only quiet to cover it."

"Hush!" said Anne; "do not be so very profane, Marjory.—Do you remember how the Apostle describes it; those words that charm one's ear like music, 'the ornament of a meek and quiet spirit.' Are not the very sounds beautiful? Mildness and gentleness are exceeding good things; but I do not set any sweet confection before me, for my model. Marjory! do you remember those other beautiful words; 'Strength and honor are her clothing; she opens her mouth with wisdom, and in her lips is the law of kindness?' There is nothing weak about that, and yet that seems to me a perfectly womanly woman."

Marjory Falconer did not answer.

"But I feel quite sure," said Anne, smiling, "that when she opened her mouth with wisdom, she never said a word about the rights of women; and that when her husband went out to the gate, to sit among the elders, she did not think her own position, sitting among her maidens, a whit less dignified and important than his, or envied him in any way indeed. When you are tempted Marjory with this favorite heresy of yours, read that beautiful poem—there is not a morsel of confectionery about it; you can see the woman, whose household was clad in scarlet, and whose children rose up and called her blessed, and know her a living person, as truly as you know yourself. You call me quiet, Marjory; I intend to be demonstrative to-day, at least, and I do utterly contemn and abominate all that rubbish of rights of women, and woman's mission, and woman's influence, and all the rest of it; I never hear these cant words, but I blush for them," and Anne did blush, deeply as she spoke; "we are one half of the world— we have our work to do, like the other half—let us do our work as honorably and wisely as we can, but for pity's sake, do not let us make this mighty bustle and noise about it. We have our own strength, and honor, and dignity—no one disputes it; but dignity, and strength and honor, Marjory, are things to live in us, not to be talked about; only do not let us be so thoroughly self-conscious—no one gains respect by claiming it. There! you are very much astonished and horror-stricken at my burst. I cannot help it."

"Very well! very well!" exclaimed Miss Falconer, clapping her hands. "Utterly contemn and abominate! Hear, hear, hear! who could have believed it of quiet Anne Ross?"

Anne laughed. "Quiet Anne Ross is about to dare something further, Marjory. See; when did you cross the stepping-stones?"

They had reached them; three or four large, smooth stones, lay across the stream, at a point where it narrowed; the middle one was a great block of native marble, which had been there, firm in its centre, since ever the brown Oran was a living river. The passage was by no means perilous, except for people to whom a wet shoe was a great evil. It is not commonly so with youthful people in the country; it was a matter of the most perfect unconcern to Marjory Falconer.

"When did I cross the stepping-stones? Not for a good twelvemonth. I challenge you, Anne; if we should stumble, there is no one to see us but George. Come along."

And Marjory, in the close-fitting, dark-cloth pelisse, which her old maid at Falcon's Craig congratulated herself "could take no scather," leaped lightly from stone to stone, across the placid, clear, brown water. Anne, rejoicing in the success of her scheme, followed. So did George, somewhat disappointed, at losing the expected fun, of a rencontre with "some o' the feckless dandy chaps at Strathoran," and the demolition of the barricade at the other end of the way.

They had to make a considerable circuit before they reached the road; but Anne endured that joyfully, when she saw through the trees the hirsute Mr. Fitzherbert, and some of his companions, assembled about the second stile—Marjory saw them too—the deep blush of shame returned to her cheek in overpowering pain: she did not say anything, but did not feel the less for that. Did Anne, indeed, need to scheme, for the preservation of her dignity?

Little Lilie came running forth from Mrs. Euphan Morison's room, to meet them, as they crossed the bridge. Lilie had wonderful stories to tell of her long rambles with Jacky. The delicate moss on the tomb of the legendary maiden in the graveyard of Oranside, received more admiration from the child's quick sense of beauty, than it could elicit from the common-place mind of Bessie; for Lilie thought the graveyard was "an awfu' still place—nae sound but the water rinning, slow—slow; and the branches gaun wave wave; and the leaves on the wind's feet, like the bonnie shoon the fairies wear; and a' the folk lying quiet in their graves."

They were lingering without—the air was so very mild and balmy, as if some summer angel had broken the spell of winter for one day. Marjory leant against a tree; her clear, good face, more thoughtful than usual. Anne had seated herself on a stone seat, beside the threshold, and was bending over Lilie, and her handful of moss; while Jacky, like a brown elf, as she was called, hovered in the rear. Mrs. Catherine had not yet returned from Portoran.

"If ye please will ye go in?" asked Jacky.

"No, let us stay here, Anne," said Miss Falconer. "Jacky, how did Mrs. Catherine go?"

"If ye please, she's in the phaeton," said Jacky.

"In the phaeton? oh!" exclaimed Miss Falconer, in a tone of disappointment; "and those steady wretches of ponies—there is no chance of anything happening to them—there is no hope of them running away."

"Hope, Marjory?" said Anne.

"Yes, hope! If Mrs. Catherine could only be caught in that shut-up by-way herself. Anne, I would give anything, just to find her in it."

"Here she comes," said Anne, as the comfortable brown equipage, and its brisk ponies, came smartly up towards the door, driven by Archibald Sutherland. "Ask her to walk to the little gate with you, Marjory—she will do it. But be careful not to speak of it before Archibald."

"Thank you for the caution," said Miss Falconer, in an undertone. "I wont; but I had forgotten—"

The vehicle drew up. Mrs. Catherine alighted, and, at Marjory's request, turned with her to the little gate, from the shady dim lane beyond which the barricaded stile was visible, which shut passengers out from the sacred enclosure of Strathoran.

Archibald sat down on the stone seat at the threshold, by Anne's side. Lilie was very talkative—she had seen the little ruined chapel on Oranside for the first time that day.

"There's grass upon the steps," said Lilie, "and they're broken—and then up high it's a gray, but the branches, and they're like the lang arms of the brown spirits on the muir that Jacky kens about. Ye would think they had hands waving—"

Anne patted the child's head, bidding her describe this at another time: but Lilie was i' the vein.

"And upon the wall there's something white, printed in letters like a book—and down below, Oh, ye dinna ken what I found!—Jacky's got it. It was a wee, wee blue flower, growing in a corner, where it could see naithing but the sky. Would that be the way it was blue?"

Anne could give no satisfactory answer, and Lilie went on.

"Jacky was to keep it for me, but I'll give it to you, because it's pretty,—like the Oran, in the gloaming, when the sky's shining in the water. There's no flower but it—no—" said Lilie, comprehending in one vast glance the whole wide sweep of hill and valley round her—infinite as it seemed to the child's eyes; "no in the world—only it, and folk were sleeping below it. Jacky says the angels plant them—is that true? wait till I get it."

The child darted away, and returned in a moment, bringing a small, wild, blue violet, one of those little, shapeless flowers, whose minute, dark leaves have so exquisite a fragrance. Anne took it from her, smiling, and repeating: "It will return in spring," offered it to Archibald. He received it with some emotion.—This sole flower in the world, as Lilie said, brought to him from the grave of father and of mother—the only spot of earth in Strathoran where he was not a stranger. He accepted the emblem, fragrant of their memories, as it seemed, fragrant of hope and life in the dreary winter-time, and, with its promise breathing from its leaves: "It will return in spring!"

They were both silent and thoughtful: Archibald absorbed with these remembrances and anticipations, while Anne, sympathizing fully with him, was yet half inclined to blame herself for her involuntary exhilaration. The weight was lifted off Anne's heart. It was no longer a dread and horror, that secret life of Norman's but a thing to be rejoiced in, and to draw brightest encouragement from—a very star of hope.

The sound of wheels upon the road recalled her thoughts. Mrs. Catherine's ponies had been led away by Johnnie Halflin. It was a shabby inn-gig, driven by one of the hangers-on of the 'Sutherland Arms,' in Portoran, which now drove up, and took the phaeton's place. A young man, with a pleasant, manly face, alighted, and, looking at Anne and Archibald dubiously, stood hesitating before them, and, at last, with some embarrassment, asked for Mrs. Catherine.

Jacky darted forward to show him in, and, in a few minutes, reappeared, breathless, with the stranger's card in her hand.—Archibald had gone in—Anne had risen, and stood looking towards the little gate, waiting for Mrs. Catherine and Miss Falconer.

"Oh! if ye please, Miss Anne—" exclaimed Jacky.

"Well, Jacky, what is it?"

Jacky held up the card—"Mr. James Aytoun." "If ye please, Miss Anne, I think it'll be Miss Alice's brother."

Anne hastened forward to tell Mrs. Catherine, somewhat disturbed by the information. She feared for Lewis. Lewis was not so confident in the truth of these letters as she, and might, betray his doubt to Alice Aytoun's brother, a lawyer, skilled in discerning those signs of truth in the telling of a story, which Lewis would lack in his narrative.

Jacky stole back to the library: the fire was getting low, she persuaded herself, and while she improved it, she could steal long glances at the stranger, and decide that he was "like Miss Alice, only no half so bonnie." When the mending of the fire was complete, she slid into a corner, and began to restore various misplaced books. James watched her for a minute or two with some amusement. Alice had spoken of this dark, singular, elfin girl. She lingered so long that he forgot her. At last a voice alarmed him, close at his ear.

"If ye please—"

He looked up—Jacky was emboldened.

"If ye please—Miss Alice—"

"What about Miss Alice?" asked James, kindly.

"Just, is she quite well, Sir?" said Jacky, abashed.

"Quite well, I am much obliged to you," said James.

Jacky hovered still. Somewhat startled James Aytoun would have been, had he divined the eager question hanging upon her very lips:

"Oh, if ye please, will they no let her be married on Mr. Lewis?" but Jacky restrained her interest in Alice Aytoun's fortunes, sufficiently to say: "Mrs. Catherine is coming, Sir!" and to glide out of the room.

"James Aytoun!" exclaimed Mrs. Catherine, as Anne interrupted the indignant declamation of Marjory Falconer, to inform her of the stranger's arrival. "Ay! that is like a man; I am pleased with that. The lad must have, both sense and spirit.—Send down to Merkland for Lewis without delay, child, and come in with me to the library; the lad's business is with you, more than me. I like the spirit of him; there has been no milk-and-water drither, or lingering here. Come away."

They entered the house. "Marjory Falconer," said Mrs. Catherine, "go up the stair, and wait till we come to you. Say nothing of yon to Archie; but, be you sure, I will stand no such thing from the hands of the evil pack of them—hounds!"

Marjory obeyed; and Mrs. Catherine and Anne entered the library. The young man and the old lady exchanged looks of mutual respect. James Aytoun's prompt attention to this important matter, brought the full sunshine of Mrs. Catherine's favor upon him. She received him after her kindest fashion.

"You are welcome to my house, James Aytoun; and it pleases me, that I can call a lad who give such prompt heed to the honor of this house kinsman. Are you wearied with your journey? or would you rather speak of the matter that brought you here at once?"

"Certainly," said James, smiling in spite of himself, at this abrupt introduction of the subject, "I should much rather ascertain how this important matter stands, at once. Your letter surprised us very greatly, Mrs. Catherine; you will imagine that—and of course I feel it of the utmost consequence that I should lose no time in making myself acquainted with the particulars."

"Wise and right," said Mrs. Catherine, approvingly, "and spoken like a forecasting and right-minded man. Sit down upon your seat, James Aytoun, and you shall hear the story."

James seated himself.

"Perhaps it would be well that I saw Mr. Ross?"

"I have sent for Lewis," said Mrs. Catherine. "He will be here as soon as he is needed. This is his sister, Miss Ross, of Merkland. Anne, you are of more present use than Lewis—you will stay with us."

They gathered round the table in silence. James Aytoun felt nervous and embarrassed—he did not know how to begin. Mrs. Catherine saved him from his difficulty.

"James Aytoun, it would be putting a slight upon the manly and straightforward purpose that brought you here, if we were going about the bush in this matter, and did not speak clearly.—Your father was murdered—shot by a coward hand behind him. The whole world has laid the act upon Norman Rutherford. I have believed the same myself for eighteen years. Listen to me! I am not given to change, nor am I like to alter my judgment lightly; but now I declare to you, James Aytoun, that, far more clearly than ever I held his guilt, do I believe, and am sure, that Norman Rutherford was not the man."

James was uneasy under the gaze of those large, keen eyes, and did not wish either to meet the earnest look of Anne Ross, who seemed to be watching so eagerly for his opinion.

"I shall be most happy, Mrs. Catherine," he said, "to find that you have proof—that Mr. Ross has proof—sufficient for the establishment of this. I have certainly no feelings of revenge; but the crime which deprived Alice and myself of a father must of necessity keep the two families apart. I could not consent to any further intercouse between Mr. Ross and my sister on any other terms than those you mention. But the evidence is fearfully strong, Mrs. Catherine. Since my mother received your letter, I have examined it again thoroughly, and so far as circumstantial evidence can go, it is most clear and overwhelming. I shall be most happy to be convinced that the world has judged erroneously; but you will excuse me for receiving it with caution; if this unhappy young man—I beg your pardon, Miss Ross—had been brought before any court in Scotland, with the evidence, he must infallibly have been found guilty."

"Anne," said Mrs. Catherine, "you have the letters."

Anne drew them from her breast—she had a feeling of insecurity when they were not in her own immediate possession.

"Had we not better wait till Lewis comes?"

"No," said Mrs. Catherine. "What Lewis cares for, is the winning of the bairn Alice—what you care for, first and most specially, is the clearing of your brother's disgraced name. Norman is safest in your hands, Anne. Read the letters."

"Mr. Aytoun," said Anne, with nervous firmness, "we have no systematic proof to lay before you. Anything which can directly meet and overcome the evidence of which you speak, remains still to be gathered—and it is possible, that this, on which we build our hopes, may seem but a very feeble foundation to you. In law, I suppose, it could have no weight for a moment: but yet to those who knew my brother Norman, and were acquainted with his peculiar temperament and nature, it carries absolute conviction.—I scarcely hope that it can have the same power of convincing you—but I pray you to receive as certainly true, before I read this, the judgment which all his friends pronounced upon my unhappy brother, before this dishonor came upon him. They call him the most truthful and generous of men: they distinguish him for these two qualities above all his compeers. Mrs. Catherine, I speak truly?"

"Truthful as the course of nature itself, which the Almighty keeps from varying. Generous as the sun that He hath set to shine upon the just and the unjust. Do not linger, Anne: read Norman's letter."

Anne lifted the letter, and glanced up at James before she began to read—his eyes were fixed upon her, his face was full of grave anxiety—convinced or unconvinced, she was sure at least of an attentive listener. She began to read—her voice trembling at first, as the quick throbbings of her heart almost choked it, but becoming hysterically strong, as she went on; her mind agitated as Norman's was when he wrote that letter, eager like him, by what repetitions or incoherent words soever, that were strongest and most suitable for the urgent purpose, to throw off the terrible accusation under which he lay: it was like no second party reading an old letter; it was the very voice and cry of one pleading for life—for more than life—for lost good fame and honor.

James Aytoun's eyes were steadily fixed upon her; and as she closed the letter, her whole frame vibrating, he drew a long breath—that most grateful of all sounds to the ears of a speaker who desires to move and impress his audience. Anne looked up eagerly and anxious. He had covered his face with his hand. Neither of them spoke; until, at last, James raised his head:

"May I see that letter, Miss Ross? Can you give it me?"

Anne had omitted the sentence in which Norman mentioned his escape. She folded it in, and handed him the letter. He read it again carefully, and yet again. Besides the earnest agony of its words, there was a mute eloquence about that yellow, timeworn paper. Blisters of tears were on it: tears of terrible grief—tears of tremulous hope. Its very characters, abrupt and broken as they were, spoke as with a living voice. Nothing false—nothing feigned, could be in the desperate energy of that wild cry, the burden of Norman's self-defence: "I am innocent! I am innocent!"

"Miss Ross," said James Aytoun, "there never was man convicted from clearer evidence than that which has persuaded the world of your brother's guilt. I cannot comprehend it—my faith is shaken. I confess to you, that I feel this letter to be true—that I can no longer think of him as the murderer."

Anne tried to smile—she could not. A stranger—a man prejudiced against Norman—the son of the dead. The tears came over her cheeks in a burst of joy. She thought it the voice of universal acquittal: she forgot all the difficulties that remained—Norman was saved.

The library-door opened, and Lewis entered. Mrs. Catherine rose, and presented him to James: the two young men shook hands with an involuntary cordiality, at which they were themselves astonished. Anne was conquering herself again; but joy seemed so much more difficult to keep in bounds, and restrain, than sorrow was. She had little experience of the first—much of the other. She started up, and laid her hand on Lewis's arm.

"Lewis, Lewis! the way is clearing before us. Mr. Aytoun gives us his support. Mr. Aytoun thinks him innocent!"

CHAPTER XVI

Lewis Ross was undergoing a process of amelioration. From his earliest days he had been taught to consider himself the person of greatest importance in Merkland; and the pernicious belief had evolved itself in a very strong and deeply-rooted selfishness, to which the final touch and consummation had been given by his foreign travel. Thrown then, with his natural abilities, always very quick and sharp, if not of the highest order, upon the noisy current of the world, with no other occupation than to take care of himself—to attend to his own comforts—to scheme and deliberate for his own enjoyments, the self-important boy had unconsciously risen into a selfish man, having no idea that a supreme regard for his own well-being and comfort was not the most reasonable and proper centre, round which his cares and hopes could revolve.

He returned home. The home routine was going on as before. The servants, his mother, Anne, all did homage to the superior importance of Lewis. He received it as his due. These were but satellites; he, himself, was the planet of their brief horizon. Little Alice helped the delusion on; her simple heart yielded with so little resistance to his fascinations.

All at once the dream was rudely broken. Anne, his quiet, serviceable sister, he suddenly found to be absorbed by the concerns of this unknown Norman, whose very name was strange to him. His own little Alice must consider the pleasure of her mother and brother before his. Lewis was suddenly stopped short in his career of complacent selfishness. The people round him were ready to risk all things for each other. Mrs. Catherine's wealth and lands were nothing to her, as she said, in comparison with the welfare of Archibald Sutherland, who had no nearer claim upon her than that of being the son of her friend. Anne's whole soul was engrossed with anxiety for the deliverance of Norman: her own self did not cost her a thought. Mr. Ferguson and Mr. Foreman were spending time and labor heartily in the service of the broken laird, who could make them no return: and worst of all, they expected that Lewis also should join in that Quixotry, as a necessary and unavoidable duty, without even thinking that by so doing he would deserve any particular praise. In the fastnesses of his self-content, Lewis was shaken.

Then came James Aytoun, the stranger, to whom this Norman, whose very name inspired Anne, was, and could be nothing, except, indeed, a detested criminal—the supposed murderer of his father. He came, he saw: and lo! he was deeper into the heart of the struggle than Lewis had ever been: believing Norman's innocence—declaring his intention of joining Robert Ferguson immediately, and assisting in his investigations; consulting with Anne in frank confidence, and with a far more genuine sympathy than had ever been awakened in the colder heart of Lewis.

The young Laird of Merkland was overpowered: the contagion of James Aytoun's hearty, manly feeling, of his ready and quick belief, smote Lewis with a sense of his own unenviable singularity. The cloak of self he had been wrapped in began to loosen, and drop away; he began to realise the sad lot of his exiled brother, continually waiting for the kind search, and acquitting justice, which should bring him home again; and growing sick with deferred and fainting hope, as year after year went by, and there came no kindly token over the sea. The letter, instinct now with the breath of earnest belief, which had carried it into those other hearts, began to operate upon Lewis. He sat down between James Aytoun and Anne; he took a part in their consultations; he forgot himself, in thinking of Norman. The divine rod had stricken the desert rock once more, and the freshness of new life—a life for others—a life for the world, dawned upon Lewis Ross.

Anne and James were already conversing like intimate friends. Lewis, with his natural frankness, was soon as deep in the subject as they. Anne's face brightened as she looked upon him. Mrs. Catherine sent him now and then a word of kindly harshness, more affectionately than was her wont. Their plans were being laid.

"And I would ask of you, James Aytoun," said Mrs. Catherine, "for what reason that ill-favored buckie of a gig is standing at my door? and what business the cripple helper from the Portoran inn has among my servants? I must take order with this."

"The man is waiting for me," said James. "I must return home to-morrow, Mrs. Catherine—and the day is waning. I must get into Portoran soon."

"You must not think," said Mrs. Catherine, "of crossing my threshold this night again. Hold your peace, young man: there is no voice lifted under this roof with authority but mine, and I will not have it. Jacky!" Jacky made her appearance at the door—"let the man that drove Mr. Aytoun up, get his dinner, and then tell your mother he is not to wait—Mr. Aytoun does not return to-night. And now, young folk, are you nearly through with your consulting? I have a visitor waiting for me up the stair."

"You decide to go with me to-morrow, Mr. Ross?" said James.

"Yes, certainly," said Lewis. "I will not do much good I dare say; but I shall, at least, be on the spot."

"You are done, are you?" said Mrs. Catherine. "James Aytoun I have another matter to speak to you about. Has a stranger in the country—the purchaser of an old estate—any shadow of a right to shut up a road which has been the property of the folk of this parish of Strathoran, since beyond the memory of man?"

"No," said James, "no proprietor has—of however long standing he may be."

"Not myself say you?" said Mrs. Catherine, "that is another thing, James Aytoun. My house has held this land for many generations. I have a right of service from the people; but an upstart—a laird by purchase, by purchase, said I?—by cheatry and secret theftdom, nothing better! There is a creature of this kind upon the lands of Strathoran, and the way by the waterside is blocked up this day—a kirk road! a by-way as old as the tenure of my lands!—the cattle never did a worse thing for their own peacefulness. The road shall return to the folk it rightfully belongs to, if I should have the whole reprobate pack of them before the Court of Session!"

"Who is the proprietor?" said James.

"Lord Gillravidge," answered Lewis.

"Lord Gillravidge? Hold your peace, Lewis Ross, when folk are not speaking to you, as one of your years should. The house of Strathoran has been a sinful house, James Aytoun, and Providence has sent upon it a plague of frogs, as was sent upon Egypt in the time of Israel's captivity—puddocks that have the gift of venom over and above the native slime of them. The proprietor is Archibald Sutherland, who is dwelling in my house at this moment; but the lad has let his possessions slip through his fingers, and the vermin are in them. I would take the law with me. What should be my first step, James Aytoun, for the recovery of the road?"

"Throw down the barricade," said Lewis.

"Lewis Ross, I have told you to hold your peace—though I will not say but what there are glimmerings of discernment breaking through the shell; tell Alice from me, James Aytoun, that the youth, if he were once through this season of vanity, gives promise of more judgment than I looked for at his hands. It is not my wont to wait for other folk's bidding, Lewis—the barricade is down before now; but what order is it right that I should take, if the cattle put it up again?"

"Had you not better try a remonstrance, Mrs. Catherine," said James. "It may have been done in ignorance."

"Remonstrance! a bonnie story that I should condescend to remonstrate with the hounds. Where are you going, Anne? Did I not bid ye remain with us?"

"You forget that Marjory is up stairs, Mrs. Catherine," said Anne.

"I forget no such thing—the bairns are mad! counselling me with their wisdom in my own house—and that minds me that I am forgetting the comfort of the stranger like a self-seeking old wife as I am. James Aytoun, I will let you see your room—and you, bairns, remain where you are, and dine with him. You are like to be near kindred—it is right you should be friends."

Mrs. Catherine led James Aytoun away, and Anne and Lewis joined Marjory in the drawing-room, where, the fumes of her indignation scarcely over, she had been firmly shutting her lips for the last hour, lest some hint of the shut-up by-way should escape them, to pain the landless Archibald.

They spent the evening pleasantly together. James Aytoun was fresh from that peculiar society of Edinburgh, whose intellectual progress is the pulse of Scotland, healthful, strong, and bold, as its beatings have been for these past centuries. His own compeers and companions were the rising generation—lawyers, physicians, clergymen, literati, whom the course of some score years would find in the highest places there. The intellectual life and activity which breathed out from his very conversation, stimulated Lewis. These pursuits of science and literature—those professional matters even, to the consideration of which intellect so elevated and acute was devoted, gave the country laird a new idea of the pleasure and dignity of life. Labor—healthful, vigorous, energetic, manly labor—not vacant ease of frivolous enjoyment, was the thing esteemed in that lettered community of beautiful Edinburgh, the names of whose toiling, daring, chivalrous, intellectual workmen, would be household words to the next wave of Scottish population—would have risen into the mental firmament ere then, stars for a world to see.

It was a particularly happy thing for Lewis at this especial time, his encounter with James Aytoun; the unselfish breadth of his good mind and heart, the generous start to exertion, the clear health and readiness of all his well cultured faculties, and his frank and instinctive energy, carried with them all the better part of Lewis Ross's nature. Their visitor, with his intelligent conversation, and well-cultivated mind, pleased and made friends of them all; but conferred especial benefit and invigoration upon Lewis.

The next day they left the Tower together. Lewis, with his old self-confidence, believing himself sure to help on the search mightily by his presence; but yet so much more earnest and unselfish in his desire to see the truth established, that Anne's heart rejoiced within her. Mrs. Ross was sulkily reconciling herself to the obvious necessity. She was by no means interested in the result of the investigation, and was inclined to hope that it would be unsuccessful, and that Lewis might be released from his engagement, yet, nevertheless, prepared herself, with much sullenness and ill-humor, for "the worst."

Anne accompanied Lewis, in the morning, to the Tower, to bid James good-by, and charge him with various kindly messages, and some little tokens of sisterly good-will for Alice. At Mrs. Catherine's desire she remained. Mrs. Catherine had already despatched Andrew with the following missive to Strathoran:

"Mrs. Catherine Douglas, of the Tower, desires that Lord Gillravidge will explain to her, at his earliest leisure, his motive for shutting up the by-way upon Oranside—a thing both unreasonable and unlawful, and which she has no thought of submitting to for a day. The path belongs to the people of the parish, who had dwelt upon the land for centuries, before ever it passed into Lord Gillravidge's tenantcy. Mrs. Catherine Douglas desires Lord Gillravidge to know that he has done what is contrary to the law of the land, and expects to have an immediate reason rendered to her, for the insult and hardship inflicted upon her people and parish, by the closing of a known kirk road, and public way."

Mrs. Catherine and her household were busied in preparation for Archibald's departure. Mrs. Catherine herself was hemming with a very fine needle, and almost invisible thread, breadths of transparent cambric, for the shirts which her three generations of domestics, Mrs. Elspat Henderson, Mrs. Euphan Morison, and Jacky, were occupied in making.

"And child," said Mrs. Catherine, "I like not idle greives. If you are not pleased with Jacky's stitching, take the other breast yourself—there is plenty to hold you all busy. I have no brood of young folk, sitting with their hands before them. What did you get clear eyesight and quick fingers for?"

Anne took the work—into no unknown or "'prentice hand," would it have been confided. Mrs. Catherine's "white seam" was elaborated into a positive work of art. Within her strong spirit, and covered by her harsh speech, there lay so much of that singular delicacy, which could endure nothing coarse or unsuitable, that the smallest household matters came within its operation. Mrs. Catherine had little faith in the existence of fine taste or delicate perceptions, in conjunction with a coarse or disorderly "seam." Would modern young ladies think her judgment correct?

"Archie is in Portoran," said Mrs. Catherine, after a little time had elapsed, during which the fine work and cheerful conversation proceeded in brisk and pleasant unison. "There are still some matters to be settled with Mr. Foreman, and he expects the letter the day that will fix his going to Glasgow. We are nothing less than a bundle of contradictions, child, we unsatisfied human folk. It was my own special desire and wish that the lad should verily plunge himself into some labor for the redemption of his land; now I have a drither at letting him go away to a mere, hard money-getting work, where little of either heart or head is needed."

"Little heart, perhaps," said Anne; "but, at least, the head must be very necessary, Mrs. Catherine."

"You do not know," answered Mrs. Catherine. "Head! I tell you, child, I have seen divers in my youth who had gathered great fortunes by trade, and yet were vaporing, empty-headed, purse-proud fuils; beginning by running errands, and sweeping shops, and the like, and ending by making bairnly fuils of themselves, to the laughter of the vain and thoughtless, and to the shame of right-minded folk. We have other imaginations of merchantmen, child; we give them a state and circumstance that the men are as innocent of, as Johnnie Halflin out there. We think of the old days when merchants were princes, and of them that stood afar off, and wailed for Babylon. There are some such, doubtless, now, but it is not always the best that are the most fortunate. And to think of Archie living for years among folk to whom the paltry siller is the sole god and good in this world or the next. Maybe, child—maybe in the rebound of his carelessness, getting to like the yellow dirt himself for its own sake!"

"No fear," said Anne. "Archibald is able to stand the probation in every way, I trust, Mrs. Catherine; and it is but a means—it is not an end."

"Ay," said Mrs. Catherine. "The youth has a great stake.—He is a changed man, child, so far as we may form a judgment. Wherefore should I ever have doubted it? As if true prayers could lie unanswered before the Throne for ever!"

Jacky opened the door.

"If ye please—"

"What you elf? Can you no speak out?"

"It's—it's the man—the stranger"—Jacky remembered her former description of him, but scorned to repeat herself; "that came to the Tower with Mr. Foreman. If ye please, will I bring him in?"

"The jackal—the fuil that does Lord Gillravidge's errands," said Mrs. Catherine. "I am lothe that the feet of an unclean animal should come within this room, but what can I do, child? The library is Archie's especial room, and if he comes in, I would like ill that he saw any of this evil crew."

"He had better come here," said Anne.

Mrs. Catherine made a motion of disgust.

"Hear you, you imp! Is he alone?"

"There's a gentleman with him," said Jacky. "No a grown-up man—just young like—but he's a gentleman."

"Bring them up here."

Jacky disappeared, and, in a moment after, ushered Mr. Fitzherbert, and the good-humored, fair-haired lad, who had been with him when Alice Aytoun was intercepted on the way, into the room. Mrs. Catherine's note had been the subject of considerable mirth at Strathoran. The Honorable Giles Sympelton, in particular, had been exceedingly amused at the idea of the old lady "showing fight," and had proposed and urged, something against Fitzherbert's will, this present expedition. Mr. Fitzherbert was elaborately polite and high-bred. The young man was in high spirits, overflowing with suppressed laughter, and anticipating capital fun.

Mrs. Catherine rose, drew up her stately figure, and remained standing. Mr. Fitzherbert bowed with agreeable condescension. The Honorable Giles was startled out of his laughter.—That strong, vigorous, stately old lady was not a person to be trifled with.

"Lord Gillravidge, Madam," began Mr. Fitzherbert, "received your communication, and would have been most happy to have made your acquaintance personally, had it not been for the misfortune of a previous engagement. He has requested me to represent him—quite unworthy, certainly—but, having the honor to be acquainted with his sentiments, shall be glad to give any explanation that you desire."

"I require no explanation from Lord Gillravidge," said Mrs. Catherine, "except of his purpose concerning this unlawful deed he has done. Will he give it up of his own will, or will he be forced to do it? That is all I desire to know of Lord Gillravidge."

Mr Fitzherbert seated himself unbidden.

"Beg you will permit me to make a brief explanation. Lord Gillravidge has the tenderest regard for feelings—indulgent even to a little natural prejudice—means everything to be done in the most friendly manner. I assure you, Madam, I can explain everything with the greatest ease."

The Honorable Giles was still standing. The lad began to have some perception that this was not a place for boyish mirth or derision. Anne silently invited him to be seated.

Mrs. Catherine grew still more stately and erect. She would not condescend to be angry.

"I desire no explanations at Lord Gillravidge's hands. Will he throw the by-way open, or will he not?"

Mr. Fitzherbert smiled insinuatingly.

"Your kind indulgence, Madam—but for a moment. I shall take care not to exhaust your patience, knowing that ladies are not distinguished for patience, a good quality though—I beg your pardon, Madam. I am sorry to see I keep you standing."

"Be not troubled, Sir," said Mrs. Catherine, with bitter contempt; "but make yourself sure that a whole tribe like you would keep me in no position that did not please myself."

"Sorry to have the misfortune of displeasing you, Madam," said the imperturbable Fitzherbert. "Had not the least intention of offence, I assure you—return to the subject. Lord Gillravidge, Madam, is actuated by the best feelings—the utmost desire to be on friendly terms. He only needs to be known to be appreciated. An excellent neighbor, a warm friend—altogether, a remarkable person, is my friend, Lord Gillravidge."

"Fitz, Fitz!" whispered his young companion, reprovingly.

Mrs. Catherine turned round, and looked at the lad with grave concern, and some interest.

"His Lordship is willing to be perfectly tolerant," continued Mr. Fitzherbert; "to give way to prejudices, and make allowance for angry feelings—and of course he expects to be as well used in return. 'Do unto others,'—it is natural that he should look for the same in return."

Mrs. Catherine waved her hand.

"A lady of refined tastes, such as I have the honor of addressing, must perfectly understand the peculiar feelings and excessive delicacy and retirement of my accomplished friend. Feels himself quite wounded by vulgar intrusion—shrinks, above all things, from public notice—extremely susceptible by nature, and of the most delicate constitution."

Mrs. Catherine stamped her foot impatiently.

"Is it the Comus of yon crew of transformed cattle that the man ventures to profane such words upon?"

"Sorry to be so misapprehended," said Mr. Fitzherbert, with an assumption of dignity. "Mere false reports, and vulgar misunderstanding of elegant leisure, and refined amusements—perfectly unfounded, I assure you, Madam. Lord Gillravidge should be judged by his peers, not by a set of barbarous rustics."

"Be silent, Sir," said Mrs. Catherine. "I understand well the people of this parish should be judged by their peers, and that is another race than yours. Beware how you lay ill names, in my presence, upon the natives of this soil!"

"Beg pardon, Madam, I am unfortunate in my subjects—had no idea you were specially interested in illiterate peasants. I beg you yourself will do his Lordship the honor of considering his position. I know him so intimately, that I can speak with confidence of his excessive delicacy and nervous refinement of constitution—quite remarkable, I assure you."

"And what is all this to me?" exclaimed Mrs. Catherine. "Think you I care the value of a straw for the nerves of your lordling? Will he persist in this folly, or will he not? His constitution may be either iron or glass, besides, for any concern I have in the matter."

"Your patience, Madam," said the smiling Fitzherbert, "I mention these characteristics in explanation. My lord is a stranger, not acquainted with the superior character of the natives of this soil. A most distinguished peasantry, moral and intelligent—but vulgar nevertheless, and intruding on his privacy. There is some natural hauteur perhaps—what might be expected from an English nobleman of high family, accustomed to all the privileges of exalted rank, and shrinking from undue familiarity. He really cannot bear intrusion, and therefore shut up the by-way—positively compelled by his delicate feelings— trains of rustics passing through his private grounds! His Lordship could not permit it."

Mrs. Catherine could bear this no longer—she was walking through the room in towering wrath and indignation.

"An English nobleman! an English cheat and sharper! enjoying his ill-gotten gains under a roof, that I marvel does not fall upon the reprobate cattle he has gathered below it. Vulgar intrusion! the passing-by of honorable men and women, that would not change the honest name of their birth, for the disgrace of his wealth and his sin. His private grounds! and who, if it were not the master-spirit of all iniquity, procured that the fair lands of Strathoran should ever brook him as their lord? You, your very self, pitiful animal as you are, the hired servant of this prosperous iniquity, doing its evil bidding, are scarce so abhorrent to decent folk as the master of you; the malignant tempting spirit, that led an innocent youth into the mire of sin and folly, that he might rob him of his inheritance; and now, can venture here, in the very face of me, who know his villanies, to set up for a man of delicate frame and tender mind, shrinking from the lawful passers-by of a peaceable parish; folk of lineage and blood, if that were all, an hundred- fold better than himself!"

Vehemently, and inspired with indignation, Mrs. Catherine spoke, the floor thrilling beneath her hasty steps.

"Fitz," whispered the astonished lad, "the old lady has the best of it—she's right."

Fitzherbert assumed an air of offended innocence. "Really, Madam, after this language—I am amazed— astonished!"—

"And who, think ye, in this house or country is concerned, that you should be astonished or amazed?" interrupted Mrs. Catherine; "or what are you, that I should hold parley with your like, and profane the air of my dwelling with your master's unclean name? Answer me my demand with as much truthfulness as is in you, and begone from my house. I will have the breath of no such vermin near me."

"Upon my word!" exclaimed the astounded Fitzherbert, "this is perfectly unparalleled; if a gentleman were using such language to me—"

"You would fight him," said Mrs. Catherine, disdainfully. "Ay! presuming that he was inclined so to demean himself, and was not content with laying his whip about your shoulders, as Marjory Falconer did."

Fitzherbert started up, enraged. "I can hold no communication with a person who delights in insulting me. You shall rue this, Madam, you shall rue this!"

"Fitz," said the Honorable Giles, interposing as he passed to the door, "Gillravidge will be angry; you have not arranged this."

"And with your permission," added Mrs. Catherine, "I say you do not leave this house till my question is answered."

Poor Fitzherbert could not afford to incur the anger of Lord Gillravidge. He was compelled to content himself with many humiliations, and this among the rest.

"Madam!, in consideration of my friend's business, I overlook these personalities. Lord Gillravidge is, as I have said, a man of ancient family, and high breeding, belonging to a most exclusive aristocratic circle, and will not have his privacy broken. His Lordship hoped to be understood—the peculiar feeling of high birth, and necessity for retirement—and must continue to trust that a lady, herself of some station, will offer no opposition."

"Ancient family!" exclaimed Mrs. Catherine. "Does your English lordling, whose name no man ever heard tell of, till he came to take possession of his prey, dare to say that to me, who can trace my lineage, without break or blot, back to the dark gray man! Tell the reprobate master of you, that my house was set down upon this land, before ever the rank soil and unwholesome heat of cities had brought forth the first ancestor of your evil brood. Tell him, that this people is my people, and that his good blood is a mean fraud, if he does not honor the honorable folk native to a free land. Further, I will spare neither time nor siller to recover them their right; either he will throw open the road this very day, or he will suffer the immediate judgment of the law—I leave him his choice; and now, the need for bearing the sight of you is over, carry my message, and depart from my house."

Fitzherbert did not linger. Young Sympelton rose to follow him.

"Sir," said Mrs. Catherine, "you are young to be in such evil hands. Tarry a moment, I would speak further to you."

The lad hesitated. Fitzherbert was already descending the stair.

"Sit down," said Mrs. Catherine. "I have something to say to you."

The lad obeyed.

"Have you been long in the keeping of these vile cattle? I am meaning, have you been long in the unwholesome neighborhood of that man?"

The Honorable Giles laughed; tried to be very frank, and at his ease, and answered that he had been a month at Strathoran.

"Dwelling night and day under the shadow of uncleanness and all iniquity. Young man, to whom do you belong? Has nobody charge of you?"

To which the Honorable Giles responded, somewhat offended, that he was quite able to take care of himself.

"Are you?" said Mrs. Catherine; "you are the first of your years that I ever knew capable of doing so. Have you father or mother living?"

"My father is: he's in France," said young Sympelton: "my mother is dead."

"Ay, it is even as I thought. Poor motherless lad, trusted in such company. Is your father in his senses, that he perils you thus?"

"In his senses! what do you mean?" exclaimed the Honorable Giles.

"I will tell you, what I mean. You have a youthful face, that looks as if it did not know vice yet, for its own hand. If I tell you there is a deadly plague in that house, will you believe me, and flee from it?"

The youth looked at her in amazement.

"I tell you, young man, there is a mortal malady in that house of Strathoran; a sickness that will kill more than your life; that will strip you of good fame and honor, or ever you have entered the world; and make you a bankrupt, ruined, disgraced man, when you should be but a fresh, youthful, ingenuous man. Mind what I am saying; there are serpents yonder, deadlier than the snakes of India. Do not sleep under that roof another night. Go home to your father, and tell him henceforward to keep an eye on your wanderings himself, and no trust you, a precious laddie, as ye no doubt are to him, to the warning of a stranger."

The young man laughed; he did not know how to understand this, though the kindness of the strange, stern old lady, moved as much as it astonished him.

"Oh! that's because you've quarrelled with Gillravidge."

"I quarrel with no vermin," said Mrs. Catherine. "If I cannot cast the plague out of a land, I warn the healthful and innocent from its borders. Young man! I know not so much as your name; but six or seven years ago, a youth, very dear to me, was as you are, blythe, happy, full of promise, well endowed, and honored. The reptile brood you are among got their meshes over him—corrupted his young mind, broke his blythe spirit, devoured his substance, defrauded him of his land, and then left him—a sinful, broken man, to struggle with his bitter repentance and misery as he best could. Beware, young man—beware of your youth—beware of the gladness that must depart for evermore, if you once taste of that cup of vice. You have a terrible stake in it; for the sake of all that you have, or can gain in this world and the next, come out of that sinful house. I will give you the shelter of mine if ye desire it. I cannot see a young man like what ye are, or seem, lost to all honest uses, and not put forth my hand."

Young Sympelton rose—he lingered—hesitated—there was dew under his eyelids; he was ashamed that any one could have moved him so—him, a man!

Fitzherbert thrust in his head at the door—laughed derisively.

"Ah, a young penitent—very interesting—old lady preaching at him."

The youth dashed out and ran down the stair.

They saw him immediately after, arm-in-arm with the tempter, returning to Strathoran.

"Anne, dear child," said Mrs. Catherine, "the look of that youth's face has made my heart sore. I have warned him—I can help him in no other way. The Lord requite the reprobate race that are leading young spirits to destruction."

CHAPTER XVII

Mr. George Lumsden, the manager of Messrs. Sutor and Sinclair's Glasgow house, was desirous that Mr. Sutherland should enter immediately on his probation. So said the letter which Mr. Foreman read to Archibald, while Mrs. Catherine was receiving at the Tower the emissaries from Strathoran. The good lawyer was in high spirits at the successful issue of his negotiations. Archibald was satisfied that his work was now so near a beginning. Mr. Ferguson acquiesced with a sigh. There were no further obstacles in the way. Next morning, it was arranged, Archibald should leave Portoran.

He rode home to the Tower in a slight excitement of mingled regret and hopefulness. He was sadly wanting in that placid equanimity whose calm is not disturbed by change. He felt these variations of the firmament of his fortune, as the sea feels the wind, answering no less swiftly to the curl of the lightest breeze, than to the sweep of the gale which chronicles its progress in stories of shipwreck and death. He felt it a very momentous thing, this second beginning of his course. Formerly, he had left his native district with every adventitious help—favored of fortune, rich in friends—yet had returned a ruined, solitary man. Now he went forth with every favoring circumstance withdrawn—his own strength and the help of Providence—no other aid to trust to—how, or in what sort, should he make his second return?

Mrs. Catherine's preparations were not quite completed: one half of the abundant outfit which she was preparing for her adventurer, would need to be sent after him to Glasgow. By earliest daybreak the next morning, Mrs. Euphan Morison herself began to make ready the heap of delicate and snowy linen, the making of which had occupied their time of late. At eleven Archibald was to set out.

He had time that morning to visit Merkland, to take leave of Mrs. Ross, and with much silent sorrow, and an indefinite understanding which expressed itself in no words, to bid farewell to Anne. Both of them were immersed in other cares and occupations. A solitary and long warfare lay before Archibald. Concerning matters private to themselves, both were heroically silent. They parted, each knowing the strong, honorable, true heart that was within the other—each aware of the other's entire and full sympathy—in grave faith, fortitude, patience; and with a silent regret, that spoke more powerfully than words.

Mrs. Catherine was in the little room; she had spent most of the morning there. She had provided Archibald with all temporal necessities—she was pleading now, before God, for that other, and yet more needful spiritual providing, which should keep him blameless, in the warfare of an evil world. No vain repetitions were there in that speechless agony of supplication: the strong spirit, with its mighty grasp of faith, was wrestling for a blessing—for prosperity and success, if it should please the Giver of all Good; but, above all earthly success and prosperity, for purity and deliverance from sin. Half an hour before the time of his departure, the young man joined her.

"Archie," said Mrs. Catherine, "I desired to say my last words to you here: you mind your return to my house—you mind your covenant with me, before God, and within the shadow of Sholto Douglas, my one brother, whom, if it had not been otherwise ordained, you might have drawn your name and blood from—Archie Sutherland, you mind your covenant?"

"I do."

"In whatever circumstances the Lord may place you—in peril, in toil, in striving with the world harder than that, in ease, and peace, and prosperity, if it be His will to give you these: with a single eye, and an honest heart, and in the strength of Him that saved you, you will resist sin. Archie Sutherland, you hold by your covenant? you plight me your word again?"

"Most earnestly—most truthfully. You trust me, Mrs. Catherine?"

"I trust you, Archie. The Lord uphold and strengthen you in your goings-out, and in your comings-in!" There was a pause.—"And have you gotten everything right, Archie? are you sure there is nothing wanting that you will need, or that I can get for ye?"

"Nothing," said Archibald. "You are only too lavish in your kindness, Mrs. Catherine; you forget that I am but a poor adventurer now."

"Hush!" said Mrs. Catherine. "Kindness is not a word to be between your mother's son and me. Ay, Archie, you are an adventurer; mind it is no common errand you are going forth upon. To the like of you, hope is the natural breath and common air—the hopes of age are solemn ventures, our last and weightiest—when they fail, there is no new upspringing in the pithless soil that many hopes have withered and died upon, like September leaves. Archie, the last great hope of an aged woman is embarked in your labor. See—look where my first sun set—the darkness of its sinking is not out of my heart yet. You might have been of my own blood, boy; you might have borne the name of Sholto Douglas! Now the last of them all is on your head.—Archie Sutherland, be mindful of it; let me see you honorably home in your own land, before I go to another country."

Archibald answered her almost incoherently: "If it was within the power of man—if any toil could accomplish it—"

The phæton was at the door; Andrew and Johnnie Halflin were placing the traveller's trunks upon it, while Mrs. Euphan Morison, portly and broad, stood in the doorway superintending. The hour drew very near.

"And there is yet another thing," said Mrs. Catherine.—"Archie, it happens whiles that prosperity is not in the power of man—if toil cannot accomplish it—if the blessing that maketh rich, comes not upon your labor, I charge you to spend no time in vain repinings, nor to be cast down beyond measure: mind at all times that my house is open to you—that if you have no other shelter in the wide world, under this roof there constantly remains for you a home. I say, mind this, Archie, as the last charge I lay upon you. If you are like to be overcome in your striving, come home; if your heart grows faint within you, and you find only weariness in your plans of merchandize instead of fortune, come home—you can come at no time when you will not be dearly welcome. Mind, Archie Sutherland, I say to you, mind! that let the world smile upon you or frown upon you as it lists, you have a home to come to—a household blythe to welcome you!"

The time had come at last. The hope of return in his heart bowed down under the heaviness of his farewell, Archibald seated himself in the vehicle, and seizing the reins, drove hastily away, not trusting himself to look back again. When he had reached the high road he paused once more, to answer the mute farewell waved to him from within the enclosure of Merkland, and then turned resolutely away—away from genial home, warm friends, affection, sympathy, to cold toil and friendless labor, an uncongenial atmosphere, a strange country. His heart swelled within him—his breast tightened—his eyes overflowed. Years must pass, with all their unknown vicissitudes, before he looked again upon those familiar faces—before he saw his own country again lie beautiful and calm beneath the sun. He quickened his pace, keeping time with the rapid current of his thoughts. For home—for friends—for country—all his labor, all his endurance, would be for these: was it for him to repine, or murmur, with his work and his reward before him? The remembrance stirred his spirit like a trumpet, and the home voice of the Oran stole in upon his thoughts chiming so hopefully and brave:

"Speed thy labor o'er land and sea, Home and kindred are waiting for thee!"

The remainder of the month passed quietly away; the little world of Strathoran was unusually still. Jeanie and Ada Mina Coulter began to weary for the marriage, which rumor said would shortly bring a very youthful, blue-eyed bride to Merkland, and for the festivities and party-givings consequent thereupon. Miss Falconer was unusually quiet. Walter Foreman, John Coulter and their set, had scarcely any new feats or new speeches of Marjory's to make mirthful comments on. She was becoming intimate with a sober, stout, cheerful, elderly lady, who wore one unvarying dress of black silk, and was Mr. Lumsden's (of Portoran) unmarried elder sister. Miss Lumsden had taken a decided liking for the strange, wild, eccentric girl, whose exploits kept all the parish amused; and had resided one whole fortnight in the immediate vicinity of the Falcon's Craig stables and kennel, in order to assist and counsel her young friend in the onerous duties of housekeeping. To Miss Lumsden's honor be it spoken, she returned to the orderly and quiet Manse, more stanchly Miss Falconer's friend than ever, and that in spite of the very decided hand with which Marjory held the reins of government at Falcon's Craig, barely admitting counsel, and by no means tolerating assistance.

Mr. Foreman, to the great amazement of Lord Gillravidge and his friends, had served upon them sundry mystic papers, interdicting them from their obstruction of the by-way. Lord Gillravidge resisted, and the case was to be tried before the Court of Session.

Mrs. Catherine's stately quietude was broken by the successive charges of this legal war; the old lady entered into it keenly, anathematizing with no lack of vehemence the "hounds" who were usurping the possession of the dignified house of Strathoran.—The more than ordinary stillness of the district brought out the excesses of Lord Gillravidge's household in prominent and bold relief. The country people told sad tales of these—exaggerated no doubt by their own simple habits, and by their thorough dislike to the new-comer; but still possessing some foundation of truth.

Lewis Ross, with James Aytoun and Robert Ferguson, were hard at work in the fair parish on the south bank of "the Firth," where stood the desolate mansion of Redheugh, and where Arthur Aytoun met his fate. Lewis and James were resident in the village inn, Robert had his quarters in a comfortable farm-house at some distance from them. They were pursuing their inquiry with all diligence. In Lewis's letters to Anne, were recorded the long walks they took, the long conversations in peasant houses, to which they were compelled to submit, in return for the scraps of information gathered, the immense quantity of country gossip, with which the history was interlarded, and the very slow progress they made in their search. Many of the elder cottagers of the district, remembered "young Redheugh" well, and spoke of his character, Lewis said, as Esther Fleming and Mrs. Catherine had done; but, though there was much affectionate respect for his youthful goodness, and much pity for his terrible fate, there was no doubt of his guilt among them, and they concluded their history of him, with an "Eh, Sirs! but mortal flesh is weak when it's left to itsel; to think o' sae mony guid gifts coming to sic an end!" Lewis did not know well what to do; he could see no hope.

Early in February they returned to Edinburgh from whence came the following letter to his anxious sister:

"My dear Anne,

"We have at last abandoned the search in despair—there is nothing to be made of it—I thought so before we began. We have awakened the attention of the district, and will, I fear, have to pay the penalty in some newspaper paragraphs resuscitating the whole story, which is disagreeable enough certainly—otherwise we have done nothing.

"I told you that we had, the other day, called at the cottage of the man, who was the first to discover Mr. Aytoun after the murder. This man was an important witness. He had been employed about Redheugh, and was a spectator of the quarrel between Aytoun and Norman. It had reference to a young lady, between whom and Norman there was a rumored engagement; whether Aytoun knew this, or not, I cannot tell, but he spoke disparagingly of the girl, who was of inferior rank. Norman resented the slighting words with the utmost vehemence and passion; so much so, that the man feared some immediate collision between them. This was prevented, however, by some chance interposition, which he does not very clearly recollect. Norman was called away, and Mr. Aytoun returned home.

"It was his daily custom to walk in this wood, though one would fancy from the character they give him, that he was by no means of a contemplative kind. He seems rather to have been one of those cool men, who take prudent means to recover themselves from the dissipation of one night, in order that they may be fit for the dissipation of the next. So it was his habit to walk in this wood early in the morning, and Norman knew it. Our informant was something of an artist, Anne. You should have heard his homely description of the stillness and beauty of the wood, as he went through it, returning from his morning's work, to breakfast; 'the sun was shining as clear as if there was naething below that dauredna be seen, or needit to shrink from the sight of man; and the innocent water running blythe beneath the trees, and the sky spreading calm aboon a', as if violence had never been dune in sicht of its blue e'e;' heightening the serenity of his background by all those delicate touches, that the terrible discovery he was about to make might stand out in bolder relief. You will say I treat this with indifference, Anne, but indeed, you are mistaken. I know Norman better, and am more interested in his fate now, (not to speak of my own individual interest in the result) than when I left Merkland.'

"To resume the story. Our informant going carelessly forward through the wood, came suddenly upon the body of the murdered man, which had fallen, breaking down the low bushes and brushwood upon the waterside. I need not tell you his horror, nor how he describes it. He procured assistance immediately, and conveyed the body home, and afterwards returned to ascertain whether there were any traces visible of the murderer. He says, he never doubted for a moment—the last night's quarrel and estrangement, the cold sneers of Aytoun, and Norman's passionate vehemence, left him, as he thought, no room for doubt. His strong suspicion became absolute certainty, when on returning, he found, lying below some thick underwood, a light fowling-piece, bearing Norman's initials and arms. His story differs in no point from the evidence given by him at the time, and there mingles with it a compassion and regret for Norman, which make its truthfulness still more apparent. When I ventured to suggest, that in spite of all these condemnatory circumstances, the criminal might still be another person, he shook his head. 'I wad gie twa and a plack, Sir, to ony man that could prove that to me; na, bluid winna hide. If ony man living had spilt it, it wad have been brought hame to him before now.' To such a statement one could make no answer. I confess, I left him utterly hopeless; what can we do further?

"The other man, who met Norman upon that fatal morning, leaving the wood, is dead; but his widow lives, and remembers her husband's story perfectly. Norman, the widow says, was smiling and cheerful, humming a tune, and apparently in high spirits, and stopped on his way to greet her husband kindly, as was his wont; for she, too, testifies to the uniform goodness and gentleness of "young Redheugh." It was a mystery to her husband, she says, to the last day of his life, how a man, newly come from such a deed, with the blood of a fellow creature and a friend warm on his hand, should have smiles on his face, and kindness on his tongue, to an indifferent passer-by.

"I cannot understand it either, Anne. It is the one thing, above all others, which staggers me. A calculating, cool, reasoning man, who even, at such a time, could think of the chances of a favorable evidence, might have been supposed capable of this—even then, I fancy there is hardly anything of the kind on record. But an impulsive, generous, sensitive man, such as universal testimony concurs in representing Norman—one cannot comprehend it. If the gaiety had been forced, the man must have observed it—it would have been an additional evidence of his guilt—but it was not so. The favorite tune—the elastic, joyous manner—the frank greeting! I cannot reconcile these with the idea of his guilt. If it had not been for this one very indistinct and impalpable piece of evidence, which, like his own letter, may influence the mind, but can have no legal force as proof, I should at once have given up the search, and taken refuge in the certainty of his guilt.

"All inquiries as to any other suspected party have proved entirely fruitless. Every circumstance had pointed so clearly to Norman, that, as I think, anything inculpating another, must have faded from the memories of the people as quite unimportant.

"James Aytoun looks very grave: he does not say much, and I cannot guess his opinion. He has been very zealous and active in the search, and has conducted it, as it seems to me, with great prudence and wisdom. I think he is very much disappointed. I even think that he still retains a lingering conviction of Norman's innocence, and is, like myself, bewildered and uncertain what step to take, or what to do.

"From Mrs. Aytoun I have received just such a reception as you might have expected from the mother of James and Alice. Tremulously kind, almost tender to me for her daughter's sake, yet often lost in long reveries of silent sorrow. No doubt this search, recalling all the circumstances of her widowhood to Mrs. Aytoun's mind, has cost her much pain. I think, however, that, to speak modestly, they don't altogether dislike me. So far as worldly matters go, we, you know, hold our heads higher than they do, and I cannot help hoping that people so sensible and friendly as James Aytoun and his mother, will not, in the spirit of a darker age, allow this old and forgotten crime to hinder the happiness of their gentle Alice. I have improved my time sufficiently, I trust, to ensure that that same happiness is not very safe, if I am denied a share in it. I intend, to-morrow, to have an explanation with them, and ascertain definitely what are our future prospects. I need not say how gentle, and sympathizing, and affectionate—how entirely like herself, in short, our little Alice is.

"I have not much fear of the eclaircissement to-morrow. They will, very likely, impose some probation upon us. We are both young enough to tolerate that—but that they can steadily refuse their consent to a connection (as I flatter myself) so proper and suitable, an advantageous settlement for Alice, which will secure alike her happiness and her external comfort, I cannot believe. I shall, likely, return some time this week. Let Duncan meet me in Portoran on Friday. If I do not come, it does not matter much—the old man will be the better for the drive.

"LEWIS ROSS."

Beside the letter of Lewis was another, the handwriting of which Anne did not know. She had few correspondents, and opened it wonderingly. It was from James Aytoun.

"My dear Miss Ross,

"Your brother will have informed you of our failure. So far as I can at present see, we have used every possible means, and the only result is, a strengthening of the former evidence, and a more clear establishment of Mr. Rutherford's apparent guilt. For my sister's sake I began this, deeply anxious for a favorable issue. I feel only more anxious now, when I know, and have a personal interest in the nearest relatives of this unhappy young man, whom men call my father's murderer. I cannot comprehend it. In this very clear and satisfactory evidence, I am entirely bewildered and confused. Everything I have gathered in my search has confirmed and strengthened the circumstances against him; and yet, by some strange perversity, everything I have heard has increased my conviction of his innocence.

"I write thus to you, because I feel that you are even more deeply interested in this than your brother. With my friend Lewis it is a secondary matter, and I am rather pleased that it should be. So that we are sufficiently satisfied not to withhold our consent to his engagement with Alice, he has no very engrossing interest in the matter; but with you—if I am wrong you will pardon me—it seems more deeply momentous and important. I also feel very greatly interested in it. If it were but in a professional point of view, it would claim my utmost attention.

"The evidence is very clear and full. Were it brought before any jury, there could not be the slightest doubt of the result.—But, with all the tales of generosity and kindness which yet make your brother's memory fragrant in the district, and with his own very moving self-defence still further to counteract it, I have no hesitation in saying to you that this mass of evidence makes no impression upon my mind, but the very uneasy and painful one of doubt and apprehension. There is no certainty in it. All these things might have remained as they are, and yet your brother's innocence be triumphantly vindicated—if, indeed, it had not been for that last fatal step of his flight. Is he now, truly, beyond the reach of either acquittal or condemnation?—does there remain only his name to vindicate?

"In the meantime there cannot be any nearer connexion between our family and yours. I regret it deeply—but it is impossible to forget that the murdered man is my father, and that while so much as a doubt remains, we must not dishonor the memory of the dead. You will understand and feel for us, I am sure. For my mother, especially, I must beg your sympathy: this matter has most painfully revived the bitterest time of her life; and while, like myself, her feelings—both for Alice's sake, and his own—are all enlisted in favor of your brother, she feels, with me, that until we have some more satisfactory proof, nearer connexion is impossible.

"You will forgive me, if I speak harshly. I feel that you will understand the necessity more calmly than I should wish Lewis to do; and I am confidant that we can trust in your kind co-operation. In the meantime, I shall keep my eye on the district, and let no opportunity of throwing light upon this dark matter pass me. May I also beg your confidence? If there is any further particular of importance, trust me with it. So far as my ability goes, I shall leave no stone unturned; and will, I assure you, betray no confidence with which you may honor me.

"Believe me, my dear Miss Ross, "Very sincerely yours.

"JAMES AYTOUN."

Anne was uneasy and perplexed: this sensible, generous, thoughtful James Aytoun, suspected her secret, and claimed to be trusted with it. Could she withhold it from him? And then, this fallen edifice of hope, with all the sickness of its indefinite deferring—what could be done, indeed? It seemed foolish—it seemed mere madness, the burning desire that rose within her, to hurry to the place herself, and see if the eager eyes of anxiety and sisterly yearning could discover nothing. Alas! were not James Aytoun's eyes eager also? was not his mind trained and practised? It did not matter—Anne felt it impossible to stand still—to wait—until she had convinced herself that there was nothing more to learn. Esther Fleming's eager repetition: "I lookit to you, Miss Anne, I aye lookit to you," came back upon her, like a call from her father's very grave. She wrote hastily to Lewis, begging him to return immediately; and then sat down to consider her plan.—It might be foolish—it might be Quixotic. Possibly she could do no good—but she must try.

CHAPTER XVIII

Upon the Friday Lewis returned home. Anne had walked out upon the Portoran road, looking for him, and met him a short distance from the gate of Merkland. He looked sulky and out of humor, and leaping from the gig, threw the reins to Duncan, and joined his sister.

"Well?" said Anne, when their first greeting was over, and Duncan out of hearing.

"Well," said Lewis, "we are just where we were. I expected nothing better. We have not advanced a step."

"I understand that," said Anne; "but what of the Aytoun's?—what understanding have you come to?—what arrangement about Alice?"

"Nothing—nothing," said Lewis, hastily; "I tell you we are exactly where we were. My position is not in the least degree better than it was on the first day I knew this history—it is worse indeed, for you buoyed me up with hopes then of the great things we should discover—see what it has all come to."

"You have surely made some arrangement—come to some understanding?" said Anne; "it is a quite useless thing to tantalize me, Lewis. Your engagement has not terminated—you have not given up—"

"'Given up!" Lewis turned round indignantly. "I suppose you would like nothing better, my mother and you; but you're mistaken, I tell you. All the mothers and sisters in the kingdom should not make me give up Alice—a pretty thing!"

"You are quite unreasonable, Lewis," said Anne; "I do not want you to give up Alice—very far from that—I think you have been fortunate in winning so fresh and guileless a youthful spirit; but this impatience and petulance makes you unworthy of Alice Aytoun. At your years men should regard their own dignity more—you are not a boy now, Lewis."

"I should think not," was the angry response. It made him quiet nevertheless; these fits of ill-humor and peevishness were certainly neither dignified nor manly.

"What have you done then? how have you arranged?" said Anne.

"Oh, we must wait, they say. If it had been merely a few months, or even a year, I should not have thought anything of it: but this indefinite delay—to be as patient and dignified as you like, Anne, it is very disagreeable and painful."

"I do not doubt it," said Anne.

"And so, till some further evidence of Norman's innocence can be procured—further! I should say until they can get any evidence—we must wait. James is to keep his eye on the district, he says, and lose no opportunity; that looks all very well, but if there is no evidence to be got, Alice and I may wait till our lives are spent in vain. It's very hard, Anne; I do say so, however boyish you may think it."

"I do not think that boyish, Lewis," said Anne. "We must take measures more active than James's mere watching the district. Lewis, it is my turn to be called childish now. You must let me try—I must go to this place myself."

Lewis opened his eyes in consternation:

"You try! you go yourself! why, what on earth could you do? Anne, you are mad!"

"I am not mad, Lewis, in the least degree, and yet I must go to this place myself; it is not in self-confidence. I have patience more than you, and time less occupied; I never expected that this work could be done easily or soon. Lewis, I must go."

They were entering the house as Anne spoke. Lewis did not answer her. He only shook his head impatiently. There was something humiliating in the very idea that she could accomplish a thing in which he had failed.

He met his mother dutifully and with proper respect and kindness. Mrs. Aytoun's natural, unassuming dignity and entire sympathy with her children; the frank, affectionate, tender intercourse subsisting between them; the seemly regard for her opinion, which was no less apparent in her manly son, James, than in her gentle daughter, Alice, had charmed Lewis unconsciously. The absolute propriety and fitness of that natural honor and reverence made an involuntary impression upon him—an impression which now softened his voice and restrained his temper. With good training, and these righteous influences round him, Lewis was a hopeful subject yet.

"So you have returned as you went away?" said Mrs. Ross, when they had been some little time together.

"Yes," said Lewis, "I should say worse, for I had some hope then, and I have none now."

"I thought it was all nonsense," said Mrs. Ross. "I knew you could make nothing of it."

"You were wrong then, mother," said Lewis, quickly. "We have got no evidence—but I believe now, what I did not believe when we left Merkland, that Norman is innocent."

Anne looked up joyfully.

"Not that my believing it will do much good," said Lewis, "when such a thing as definite proof is not to be had; but that the man, these people spoke of as young Redheugh could do a deliberate and cowardly murder is nearly impossible."

"I thank you, Lewis," exclaimed Anne. "I thank you for myself and for Norman!"

"But what good does it all do?" continued Lewis. "I may believe—but unless you can get other people to believe too, what is the use of it?"

"The use of it!" Anne's lightened heart and shining eye bore witness to its use. "James Aytoun believes it also," she said.

"Yes, James Aytoun believes it; but neither James nor you, Anne, will be satisfied with believing it yourselves. I don't see what we're to do. People judge by evidence—all the evidence is against him, and the only thing in his favor is an impression—well, I will go further—a kind of certainty—one can't give any reason for it, it is the merest indefinite, impalpable thing in the world. There's just a conviction that he is not guilty—there's nothing to support it."

"Well," said Anne, cheerfully; "but the evidence to support it must be got, Lewis. It is foolish to think that a work like this could be done in so short a time, and with so small an expenditure of labor and patience. Your time is otherwise engaged—so is James Aytoun's—he has his business to manage—you, your estate. I have nothing. I am and have been all my life, a very useless person; let me have the satisfaction of being of some service for once in my life."

"Why, Anne," exclaimed Lewis, "are you in your senses? what in the world could you do? Do you think I could ever listen to such a thing? Nonsense, nonsense—mind your own affairs like a good girl, and do not meddle with what is quite out of your sphere."

Anne smiled, but with some pain—another person might have laughed frankly at the condescending superiority of the younger brother. It hurt her a little.

"Lewis, I have even more interest in this matter than you—many hopes there may be, and are, in your life. I have few. This of Norman's return is the greatest of all—and what concerns my brother cannot be out of my sphere."

"No—to wish for it—or to dream about it, or even to scheme for it," said Lewis, "That's all very well; but for anything else—why, what could you do, Anne—what could any woman do? You know nothing of the laws of evidence—you don't know even how to make inquiries. You might go and spend money, and get the thing talked about, and written of in local newspapers. Content yourself, Anne, and leave it in our hands: you could do nothing more."

Alice Aytoun could have done nothing more. Anne Ross felt very certain that she had no gift for spending money and getting herself talked about—that it might be possible for her to do something more. So she said:

"You do not convince me, Lewis. To discover truth, one does not need to be familiar with laws of evidence. I am not a lawyer, and could not go as a lawyer would; but I am Norman's only sister, Lewis, and, as such, might find some fragments of truth favorable to him. I do not ask you to decide immediately—think of it, and then give me your sanction to my enterprise."

"I am perfectly amazed, Anne—quite astonished," exclaimed Mrs. Ross. "What can the girl be dreaming of? you go to collect evidence!—you accomplish what Lewis and Mr. Aytoun, and Robert Ferguson—trained lawyers have failed to do! I never heard of such self-confidence. I cannot comprehend it."

Anne was roused out of her usual patience.

"Mother!" she said, "you have often called me very useless—I grant it, if you choose—I have at least not been undutiful. Hitherto, you know, I have been almost entirely guided by your pleasure. Here is one thing upon which I must exercise my own judgment—must, mother—it is no question of liking or disliking. I also have some affections, desires, wishes of my own. I am not merely an appendage—a piece of goods—forgive me if I speak hastily; but supposing that neither affection nor wish were in this matter, I have even a prior duty to Norman; I have my father's command. Mother, I am no longer a girl—there is some other duty for me now, than mere obedience; I have rendered you that for three-and-twenty years: do not grudge me some exercise of my own faculties now."

Mrs. Ross stared at her in open-eyed astonishment. Lewis had laughed at first—now he was graver. Mrs. Ross, with much obstinacy of her own, was one of those people who sometimes bluster, but always yield and quail before genuine, sober firmness.

"What do you mean? What do you wish to do?" she asked, peevishly. "Dutiful, obedient! ah, I have had a good daughter in you, without doubt! You are your brother's own sister. By all means, devote yourself to Norman. What right have I, who have only been a mother to you all your life, in comparison with this brother Norman, whom you never saw?"

Anne was already sorry for her outburst; yet, in spite of herself, felt indignant and impatient. This thraldom galled her grievously, yet she knew it to be a necessary result of her dependence.

"Stay, mother," said Lewis, "let me be peacemaker, for once. You forget how tired I am. Postpone your discussion till after dinner. We have had civil war long enough; let us have peace now."

Anne withdrew to her own room. So did Lewis; and the discussion was at an end.

What should she do? The few shillings in the end of her purse were all inadequate for the journey, and the expense of residing, perhaps for some considerable time, among strangers. That difficulty there was but one way of overcoming. Anne could not rely upon the generosity of Lewis, or his mother. To tell the truth, the finances of Merkland were in a state of considerable attenuation. But she could rely, without hesitation, upon Mrs. Catherine.

And there were further difficulties: how to go alone, and live alone, in the strange, unknown place: how to forsake her ordinary habits, and take to cottage visiting as indefatigably as an English Lady Bountiful. The first she was rather uneasy about; the second was a trifle. Things which were merely disagreeable, did not much distress Anne Ross: she was by no means in despair even at those which most people called impossible; but shrank with nervous delicacy from any, the very slightest, appearance of evil.

After dinner, the conversation was renewed. Lewis had been somewhat struck by Anne's assertion of some little claim to her own judgment. He certainly did not think her so wise as himself, but he knew her quite equal to various of his friends, whose claim to independent will and action was quite indisputable. Only, she was a woman: that was all the difference. Lewis resolved to be very enlightened and liberal, to let his sister express her opinions freely, and himself to give a final and impartial deliverance upon them.

"Did I mention, in my last letter, the people who had been so intimate with Norman?" he asked, to begin.

"No," said Anne.

"An old woman referred us to them. She said it was a sister of theirs who was the occasion of the dispute between Aytoun and Norman; a poor girl who went to visit some friends in the west, about the time of the murder, and died there of a broken heart. One believes in such things when one hears stories like these. They live alone, in a great, gaunt old house, a brother and sister."

"And what?" said Anne, eagerly.

"Oh, nothing. I have no story to tell. We could gather nothing from them. The sister is a strange, emaciated, worn-out woman. James thought she looked agitated; but save a burst of broken praise of 'poor Redheugh'—I believe she even called him Norman—we elicited nothing more. The brother is an invalid and hypochondriac; we caught a glimpse of him, once or twice, wandering on the beach, but never could address him. They seemed strange people, but had nothing to tell."

Anne did not speak. Her curiosity and interest were awakened.

"What a strange fellow," exclaimed Lewis, "that Norman must have been!"

"Strange!" said Mrs. Ross, "Yes, indeed, I should think he was. I know we had little peace in Merkland, before he came of age."

"How he managed to make the country people all so fond of him," continued Lewis, disregarding his mother's interruption, "one can't tell. And falling in love with a girl, of quite different rank. Altogether, it's a strange story."

"What was their name?" said Mrs. Ross. "I thought you said they lived in an old, great house, Lewis."

"So they do," said Lewis. "It is not their own, though.—They pay some nominal rent, and take care of the place. Their name—what is their name?—upon my word I don't recollect. I don't know that I ever heard the surname. I remember the sister was called Miss Christian: but James will know."

"And you are sure they know nothing?" said Anne.

"Yes; at least the sister gave us no information, and the brother, as I told you, is a poor ailing creature—half crazy, the people say. He had saved an old man from drowning, shortly before we reached the place, and was very much elated about it."

"And their sister?" said Anne.

"Their sister was a very gentle, sweet girl—so runs the story—and was much attached to Norman. The news of his flight was carried to her abruptly by some officious person, and the consequence was, that the poor girl broke her heart, and died. It is a very sad story. Alice seemed to be able for nothing but crying when I told her."

Anne was ruminating in wonder and doubt—who then was the "Marion?" It was impossible that this truthful, upright Norman should have his troth plighted to two! Impossible that he could play one false! The doubt made her heart sink: the weight of one sin is so much heavier than the burden of a hundred misfortunes.

"Now Anne," said Lewis, "what has become of your famous resolution? Has your heart failed you already? I am glad of it: better faint before you enter the wood, than when you are on the way."

"I have no idea of fainting at all," said Anne, "unless, indeed, when we have fairly emerged into the clear air again, with Norman honorably in his own house, and Alice at Merkland—I may have leisure for fainting then. Now, Lewis—listen to me, I beg, mother—I want you to consent that I should go to this place—to Aberford—immediately, or if not immediately, at least soon.—Let me have some one with me—May would do, or old Esther Fleming. I can take quiet lodgings and live there, professedly for the sake of sea air, if, indeed, any pretence is necessary. Once there, with no other claim on my time, and patience enough to bear any ordinary disagreeables, I may make quiet, noiseless unsuspected investigations. Let me try; the matter is of consequence to us all, and the expense will not be great. I beg that I may not be hindered from making this endeavor; it may produce something—and if it does not, there is nothing lost."

"Upon my word you take it very coolly," said Mrs. Ross. "I should like to know why my son's means should be wasted in such an absurd expedition. You will never make anything of it, it is quite nonsense: besides, the idea of a girl going away from home, and living alone, engaged in such a search!—perfectly improper! I am amazed at you, Anne!"

Anne blushed deeply. It might, indeed, be called improper and indecorous, and she was not given to neglect the veriest outer garment and vesture of good fame; but for this, a matter so very dear and precious, involving so many interests, a mere punctilio might surely be disregarded—a ceremonial dispensed with.

"Mother!" she said, "if I were ill, you would not object to this: on the mere order of a doctor, you would have thought it perfectly proper to suffer me to go to the sea-side: how much more now, when interests so great are at stake—Lewis and Norman—your hope and mine! Mother! let me have your consent."

Lewis was touched. This Norman, whom she emphatically called her hope, did not live at all in Anne's remembrance, except in the merest shadow. He began to perceive how void of personal hopes and joys her life was. There were some—deeper, graver, more earnest than his—foremost among them, the deliverance and return of this exile brother; should he, her nearest relative, dim and darken this great hope for her? Lewis forgot himself, and his forgetfulness ennobled him.

"Anne," he said, "let us speak of this hereafter—nay, I mean soon; but not—" he glanced at his mother, "not to-night."

Anne understood, and was satisfied. Lewis had turned peacemaker. Lewis was devising means to turn his mother's ill-humor and undeserved reproofs from her. All honor and praise to that kindly household of Aytoun; the manly son, the gracious mother, the gentle little girl, Alice, who had found out for him, and brought into the pleasant air of day, the hidden heart of Lewis Ross.

The next morning, Lewis himself proposed a consultation with Mrs. Catherine. Anne consented gladly, and they set out. The Oran was frozen hard, and lay, a glittering road of ice, far below the high pathway of crisp snow they were walking on, through which the topmost branches of the buried hedge peered forth like wayside weeds. The snow lay three or four feet deep, and it was intensely cold.

They found Mrs. Catherine in her ruddy inner room, hemming fine cambric still. In the one article of linen, Archibald Sutherland was not likely to find himself deficient for years. Lewis gave in his report. Mrs. Catherine was disappointed.

"But it is no marvel to me, mind, though you yourself, Lewis, are in trouble, as I see, that your skill, and wisdom, and great experience, have failed in the first trial. Take good heart, boy; when you have come to years, you will understand that men are not wont to win the head of the contest, in the first trial. Set your breast to it, man; begin again."

"Why, we have done everything, Mrs. Catherine," said Lewis.

"Ay! you are a clever chield, Lewis Ross. Is it a month since the two gallants went away, Anne? Truly, I had no thought there were two such giants under my roof yon bright January day—done everything!—in four weeks! It is a comfort to folk of an older generation, that have worn out lifetimes at one labor, to hear tell of the like of that."

Lewis did not know whether to laugh, or to be angry: acting on his new notions of manliness, he chose the former. "Of course, Mrs. Catherine, I mean everything we could do."

"Lewis," said Mrs. Catherine, "you are wrong; there is no man in this world—at least, I have never heard name nor fame of him—that did everything he could do in such a space of time; it is a delusion of youth. You have girded yourself for the race, and have run hard for one mile; you think ye have done all. Boy! you are neither footsore, nor weary, nor sick at heart; what ails you to go on? I have known folk struggling hard, that were all the three. Turn back, Lewis Ross, and begin again."

"Mrs. Catherine," said Anne, "if Lewis returned, it would excite curiosity; their investigations have aroused attention already. I think it would not be wise. We came to consult you on a plan of mine. Mrs. Catherine, they say, despairing men venture on forlorn hopes often. I am not despairing, I am only useless; but I want Lewis to entrust this forlorn hope to me."

"And I," said Lewis, "think it is a very foolish idea; but yet have no reasonable defence to offer against it."

Mrs. Catherine looked at Anne earnestly.

"Are you able? that you would endeavor this I never doubted—have you strength for it?"

"I? I am strong," said Anne, "you know that, Mrs. Catherine. I scarcely know what sickness is."

Mrs. Catherine touched, with her fingers, the smooth, clear cheek, which testified the firm and elastic health, both physical and mental, of its owner, and yet was so far removed from robustness.

"Anne, I believe you are able; you have my full consent, and God-speed. Mind you, what I have said to Lewis; it's no one trial, or two, or three—time and patience, thought and labor; you must grudge none of them all. Tell me your plan."

"Must we submit?" said Lewis. "Anne, is Mrs. Catherine's judgment final? is there no appeal?"

"Silence!" said Mrs. Catherine, peremptorily; "who was speaking of appeal or judgment? There is a work to do, Lewis Ross; the thing is to get the fittest workman, and beware how we hinder him of his labor. We have tarried long enough; this is no a time to put further barriers in the road. Child, your plan?"

"I propose going to Aberford," said Anne; "taking some trusty person with me, Mrs. Catherine. It is common, I hear, for people to go there, who seek sea air. I shall attract no attention; it does not matter much how long I stay. I can establish myself under the wing of some matron, and so escape the charge of impropriety. Then I shall go about the district, make acquaintance with every one to whom I can have access, and inquire with all zeal and all quietness. While questions from Lewis, and a lawyer-like person, like James Aytoun, might confuse the people, they will speak frankly to me. I will gossip with them, play with their children; get all possible scraps of recollectings and imaginings, and, perhaps, when the heap is winnowed, something worth going for."

Mrs. Catherine bent her head gravely, and asked: "When?"

"Immediately," said Anne; "at least, I should desire so. We have lost much time already."

Mrs. Catherine rose, and went to the window. The sky was heavy and dark, lowering like some great gloomy forehead. It was laden with snow—large, dilated flakes, like those of fire upon Dante's burning sand were falling one by one, upon the white earth. It was a feeding storm.

"Bonnie weather for the sea-side," said Mrs. Catherine, returning to her seat. "You must go with a good excuse, child, not with an apparent falsehood on your tongue. 'February fills the dyke, either with black or white.' We are getting both of them this month. March is a blustering, wintry time, when there is little to be seen or heard tell of about the coast but shipwreck and disaster. April is pleasant in a landward place. You may go in April; it is too soon, but for the necessity's sake you may go then—not a day sooner, at your peril. You are able and well? I understand your look, child—hold your peace. I would give a good year of my life—and I have few of them to spare, seeing I am trysted to abide in my present tabernacle, if the Lord will tell Archie Sutherland has won back his land—to see Norman Rutherford a free man on Oranside again; but I will not consent to put you in peril, child, for any prospective good. I say you shall go in April. I put my interdict upon you venturing before. I will give you your freedom in the last blast of the borrowing days. Not an hour sooner. Now, will you abide by my judgment, or will you not?"

Anne looked out uneasily. The heavy sky slowly beginning to discharge its load—the earth everywhere covered with that white, warm mantle—the gradually increasing storm. She submitted. Now, at least, it was impossible to go.

Shortly afterwards, Mrs. Catherine took her into another room, and interrogated her concerning her pecuniary arrangements for the journey. Anne evaded the question, laughed at the scanty family of shillings in her own purse, and spoke of Lewis.

"Child, you are a gowk after all," said Mrs. Catherine. "The lad needs all his siller for himself. If there is anything to spare, let him use it on bonnie dies to dress his little bride withal—though the bairn Alison has a natural grace, and needs them less than most. But if you say a word about siller to Lewis, you shall never enter my door again. Mind! It is my wont to keep my word."

Within a week after this conversation, the last half of Mrs. Catherine's prodigal outfit was hurriedly sent to Glasgow, where Archibald Sutherland had made his first beginning with success and honor. The cold lodging, to whose narrow and solitary fireside he returned, night after night alone—the fat, Glasgow landlady, whose broad, good-humored face began to smile upon him with a familiar kindliness, which the broken laird blamed himself for almost shrinking from—the life of strange labor—he was getting accustomed to them all.

The house which he had entered was a great one. The senior partner, Mr. Sutor, a man of good mercantile descent, and capital business head, lived at a considerable distance from Glasgow, in one of those magnificent solitudes of hill and water, whither the merchants of St. Mungo are wont to carry their genial wealth, and their fine houses. It was within convenient distance of the "Saut Water," that irresistible temptation and delight of every genuine Glaswegian. Mr. Sutor came up frequently to business; he was still the active sagacious head of his extensive establishment. The manager, Mr. George Lumsden, was as great a man in his way. He lived in the dignified vicinity of Blytheswood Square. He had a fine house, a well-dressed pretty wife, and beautiful children; gave good dinners; visited baillies and town-councillors, and had baillies and town-councillors visiting him, and was certain in a very short time, to have his respectable name introduced into the firm. He was moreover an active, intelligent man, almost intellectual in spite of those absorbing cares of business, and worthy to call the minister of Portoran brother. Had Archibald chosen, he might have made a tolerably good entre into the society of Glasgow, in the hospitable house of Mr. Lumsden; but Archibald did not choose. His former folly, illness, and repentance had both sobered and saddened him, and he desired to avoid society—a desire which Mr. Lumsden kindly perceived; and after one or two unhappy evenings, during which the sensitive young man had endured in exquisite pain "the pity of the crowd," and suffered the sympathy of indifferent strangers, Mr. Lumsden forbore pressing further invitations upon him.

Messrs. Sutor and Sinclair's office was filled with young men—very young men, most of them—adventurous scions of commercial Glasgow families, foredoomed to push their fortunes, and to push them successfully in every quarter of the globe. Youths who made immense havoc among "grossets," strawberries, and all other delicacies of the luxurious summer-time, sacred to Clydesdale orchards, and radiant with the crowning glory of the Saut Water; nor in the gloomier season did less execution among edibles and drinkables, by no means so delicate or innocent—uproarious, laughter loving, practical-joking youths, among whose noisy conclave Archibald Sutherland sat silent, grave, and sad, in strange solitude.

Thoroughly respectable they would all be by-and-by, on English 'Change and foreign market-place, and home counting-house—men who could lose some few thousands without much discomposure, and whose custom was to win them in tens and twenties. Yet one could pass so lightly over these ruddy faces, to rest upon that pale one among them, with its secret history—its grief—its hope—altogether forgetful that this was a hired clerk, and that the cubs were young gentlemen, taken in at nominal salaries, to learn their craft, and saving Mr. Sutor no inconsiderable annual sum in the salaries of other hired clerks, whose services his great business must have demanded but for them.

But Archibald discharged his duty well: so well, that Mr. Lumsden formally pronounced his satisfaction—shortened his probation—and when he had been but a month in the Glasgow counting-house, bade him prepare immediately for his voyage. Archibald did so: wrote a long letter, and received a short note of leave-taking from his sister Isabel—the much-admired and gay Mrs. Duncombe—packed up his great outfit, placed in his pocketbook Mrs. Catherine's long letter of pithy counsel and tender kindliness; with these few words of grave farewell from Merkland; and on a heavy day in February, took his last look of the fair West Country, and its beautiful Clyde, and set sail for the New World.

CHAPTER XIX

Mr. Lumsden, of Portoran, was seated in his study. The March wind was blustering boisterous and rude without, driving its precious dust, so valuable, as the proverb says, to farmer and seedsman, upon the window. The study of the Portoran Manse was by no means a luxurious place—there were no reclining library chairs in it: the formidable volumes that clothed its walls were such as no dilettanti student would venture to engage withal. Its furniture was of the plainest. One large respectable looking glazed bookcase, and a multitude of auxiliary shelves, were piled to overflowing with books—books worth one's while to look at, though Russian leather and gilding were marvellously scant among them. That glorious row of tall vellum-covered folios—Miss Lumsden tells a story of them—how they were presented to her studious brother John, the day he was licensed, by a wealthy elder (to whom be all honor and laud, and many followers;) and how John, in the mightiness of his glee, forgetful of the new dignity of his Reverend, fairly danced round the ponderous volumes in overbrimming pride and exultation. Miss Lumsden's studious brother John, sits listening the while, with his own peculiar smile upon his face—a smile which gives to that dark, penetrating, intellectual countenance a singular fascination—there is something in the simplicity of its glee, which at once suits so well and contrasts so strangely with his strong and noble character.

For Mr. Lumsden, of Portoran, was altogether a peculiar man; we are sorry that we cannot venture to call him a type of the clergymen of Scotland; he was not a type of any body or profession. You will find rare individuals of his class here and there, but nowhere many. That there were such things as fatigue and weariness, Mr. Lumsden knew—he had heard of them, with the hearing of the ear, and believed in their existence as on good testimony we believe that there are mountains in the moon; but Mr. Lumsden regarded people who complained much of these with a smile, half-pitying, half-incredulous, and met the idea of himself suffering from them with a no less amused burst of open wonder than if it had been suggested to him that he should hold a diet of examination, on some chill hillside of the pale planet over us. The laborious duties of a brave and faithful minister were very life and breath to Mr. Lumsden, of Portoran—obstacles that discouraged every other man did only pleasantly excite and stimulate his patient might of labor. Weary work, from which all beside him turned disconsolate and afraid, Mr. Lumsden swept down upon, his face radiant with all its frank simplicity of glee. Nothing daunted the mighty, vigorous, healthful soul within him—nothing cast down that great, broad, expansive power of Hope, which was with him no fair beguiling fairy, but an athletic spirit, greedy of labor as the elfin serving-man of Michael Scot. In labors manifold the minister of Portoran spent his manly days; foremost in every good work, valiantly at the head of every Christian enterprise, and full of that high religious chivalry which dares all things in the service of the Church and of the Church's Head.

The widow and the fatherless knew well the firm footstep of their faithful friend and comforter; the poor of his parish claimed his kindly service as a public property; no man seeking counsel or help, comfort or assistance, went doubtingly to the Manse of Portoran. The minister—his wisdom, his influence, his genial large heart, belonged to the people; he was the first person sought in misfortune, the first to whom sorrow was unfolded. In a great joy the people of Portoran might forget him—they never forgot to warn him of the coming of grief.

Mr. Lumsden was seated in his study—a great quarto of ponderous Latin divinity, the produce of that busy time after the Reformation, when divines did write in quarto and folio volumes, terrible to look upon in these degenerate days, lay on the table before him. He was not reading it, however; he was pulling on his boot, and looking at an open note which lay upon the book.

One boot was already on—he was tugging at the other indignantly. Mr. Lumsden was particularly extravagant in that article of boots—so much so, as entirely to shock his prudent sister Martha. This one, which would not be drawn on, had been out during the night, upon its master's foot, trudging through all manner of wet by-ways to a sick-bed—it had not yet recovered the drenching. So Mr. Lumsden pulled, and between the pulls looked at the note, and muttered to himself words which his correspondent would not have cared to hear.

Miss Lumsden entered the study. Miss Lumsden had seen out her fortieth winter; for the last ten of these, she had worn one constant dress of black silk, and pronounced herself an old woman; and as it was very much for the benefit of her married sisters and unmarried brothers that she should think so, no one contradicted her. It happened at this time, to be John's turn to have the noted housekeeper of the Lumsden family resident with him. The Manse of Gowdenleas in the rich plains of Mid Lothian, and the Manse of Kilfleurs in the West Highlands, the respective residences of her brothers, Robert and Andrew, were under an interregnum. Mrs. Edie nee Lumsden, in her Fife Manse, had no expectation of a new baby; Mrs. Gilmour the Edinburgh physician's wife, had no sickness among her seven children; Mrs. Morton, the great invalid, whose husband held an office in the Register House was much better than could be expected; so the universally useful sister Martha had time to bestow her care and attention upon the domestic comfort of her brother John.

The boot suddenly relaxed as Miss Lumsden entered, and the shock brought out her brother's muttering in a louder tone than he intended: "A pretty fellow!"

"Who is that?" asked his sister.

Mr. Lumsden looked up, flushed with exertion. "This lord at Strathoran. Take his note—a seemly thing indeed to write so to me; Marjory Falconer is right after all—the man thinks himself a Highland chieftain."

Miss Lumsden read the note, wonderingly.

"Sir.

"My people inform me that you are in the habit of visiting my tenants at Oranmore, and inciting them to a course of action quite subversive of my plans. I am informed that the glen is in the parish of Strathoran, and consequently under the charge of another clergyman—the Rev. Mr. Bairnsfather—whose own good sense and proper feeling have withheld him from any interference between myself and my dependants. I am not inclined to submit to any clerical meddling, and therefore beg to remind you, that as Oranmore is not under your charge, any interference on your part is perfectly uncalled for and officious. I do not choose to have any conventicles in the glen, and trust that you will at once refrain from visits, which may injure the people but can do them no good.

"I am, &c. "GILLRAVIDGE."

"Did ever any mortal hear such impertinence?" exclaimed the amazed Miss Lumsden.

"His people!" said the minister: "they have been his a long time to be so summarily dealt with as goods and chattels. The man must have got his ideas of Scotland from 'Waverley,' and thinks he is a Glennaquoich and at the head of a clan—what absurd folly it is!"

"And just, 'Sir!'" said Miss Lumsden, indignantly; "he might have had the good breeding to call you 'Reverend' at least."

Mr. Lumsden laughed. He rose and changed the long black garment, once a great-coat, now his study-coat and morning-undress, for habiliments better suiting the long ride he was about to commence, twisted his plaid round his neck, and shut his quarto.

"What do you intend to do, John?" asked Miss Lumsden. "Are you going out?"

"I intend to do just what I should have done, had I not received this polite note," said Mr. Lumsden. "I am going to Oranmore, Martha. This lordling threatens to eject these hapless Macalpines, and poor Kenneth, the widow's son, is on the very verge of the grave. I must see him to-day. If they attempt to remove him, it will kill the lad."

"Remove them, John? what are you thinking of?" said Miss Lumsden: "it is nearly three months yet to the term."

The minister shook his head.

"They were warned to quit at Martinmas, Martha. This man, Lord Gillravidge, has his eyes open to his own advantage. He has been advised, I hear, to make one great sheep-farm of these exposed hill-lands. The poor little clachan of Oranmore could not believe that those fearful notices were anything but threats to secure the payment of their rent; but now they promise to turn very sad earnest. I do not know what to do."

"Eject them?" said Miss Lumsden, "bring one of those terrible Irish scenes to our very door—in our peaceable country? John, it's not possible!"

Mr. Lumsden looked still more serious.

"I fear it is nearly certain, Martha. I met Big Duncan Macalpine on the road last night. He says Lord Gillravidge's agent and that fellow with the moustache, have been in the glen several times of late; and the ejectment must be accomplished before their seed is sown. At least if they are permitted to remain till after seed-time, the man will not surely have the heart to remove them then. I do not know—it is a very sad business altogether; but we must try to do something better for them than sending them, friendless and penniless, to Canada. We get a trial of all businesses, we ministers, Martha—this is a new piece of work for me."

The minister's man stood at the door, holding the minister's stout, gray pony. Mr. Lumsden left the room. "And a great comfort it is, John my man," soliloquized his sister, "that your Master has made you able for them all."

Oranmore was not in Mr. Lumsden's parish. Mr. Lumsden was, what in those days was called a "Highflyer," that is, a purely and earnestly evangelical minister—a man who dedicated his whole energies, not to any abstraction of merely beautiful morality—not to amiable respectability, nor temporal beneficence; but in the fullest sense of these solemn words, to the cause and service of Christ. In consequence, Mr. Lumsden was assailed with all the names peculiarly assigned to his class by common consent of the world: sour Presbyterian, gloomy Calvinist, narrow-minded bigot, illiberal Pharisee. The minister of Portoran, like his brethren in all ages, escaped thus the woe denounced by his Master against those of whom all men speak well.

He was a thorough Presbyterian, a sound Calvinist. Men who know, and may rationally judge of these two stately systems of discipline and doctrine, can decide best whether the frank and open pleasantness of Mr. Lumsden's face belied his faith or no. He was a man of one idea—we confess to that; but the mightiness that filled his mind was great enough to overbrim a universe. It was the Gospel—the Gospel in its infinite breadth of lovingness—the Gospel no less in its restrictions and penalties. His hand did not willingly extend itself in fellowship to any man who dishonored the name of his Divine leader and King. His soul was not sufficiently indifferent to prophesy final blessedness to those who contemned and set at nought the everlasting love of God—so far he was narrow-minded and illiberal, a bigot and a Pharisee.

But it happened that Mr. Lumsden's co-presbyters on every side were men called, in the emphatic ecclesiastical phraseology of Scotland, "Moderates;" men who wrote sermons and preached them because it was a necessity of their office, not because they had a definite message to deliver from a Lord and Master known and beloved; men who tolerated profanity, and hushed uncomfortable fears, and were themselves so very moderately religious, as to give no manner of offence to that most narrow-minded and illiberal of all bigots, the irreligious world. We mention this, in explanation of a foible of Mr. Lumsden's, particularly alluded to in the letter of Lord Gillravidge, and the cause of much skirmishing in the Presbytery of Strathoran. Mr. Lumsden had an especial knack of preaching in other people's parishes.

Not to the neglect of his own—of all kinds of dishonor or ill-fame, Mr. Lumsden held none so grievous as the neglecting or slight performance of any part of that honorable and lofty work of his. Dearly as he loved extraneous labor, the minutest of his own especial parochial duties were looked to first. But all his round of toil gone through; his sermons prepared; his examinations held; himself, heart and mind, at the constant service of his people, Mr. Lumsden thought it no longer necessary to confine his marvellous appetite for work within the limits of Portoran.—There was a heathenish village yonder, growing up in all the rude brutality of rural vice, untaught and uncared for. What matter that the privilege of instructing it belonged to the Reverend Michael Drowsihed? The Reverend Michael awoke out of his afternoon sleep one day in wrath and consternation. Mr. Lumsden, of Portoran, had established a fortnightly sermon, and threatened to set down a daily school, in his own neglected village. What matter, that the half-Gaelic colony of Oranmore, belonged of right to Mr. Bairnsfather? The warm heart of the Minister of Portoran was laboring in the cause of the Macalpines, while Mr. Bairnsfather was "sheughing kail and laying leeks," in his own Manse garden.

In consequence of which propensity, Mr. Lumsden made a mighty commotion in that ecclesiastical district. Gratefully to his ears, as he wended homeward, came the voice of psalms from peasant-households, whom his faithful service had brought back to the devout and godly habits of their forefathers. Pleasantly before him stood, in rustic bashfulness, the ruddy village children, for whom his care and labors had procured an education of comparative purity; but by no means either grateful or pleasant were those endless battles convulsing his presbytery, shaking study chairs in drowsy Manses, and sweeping in a perfect whirlwind of complaint and reprimand through the Presbytery House of Portoran.

Mr. Lumsden had his failings—we do not deny it. He had no especial shrinking from a skirmish in the Presbytery. He walked to the bar of that reverend court with so very little awe, that the Moderator was well-nigh shocked out of his propriety. He had even been heard irreverently to suggest to the newly-placed Minister of Middlebury, a young brother, who seemed rather inclined to abet him in his rebellion, that it would be better for him to take his place permanently at the bar, than to be called to it at every meeting. He had been reprimanded by the Presbytery, till the Presbytery were tired of reprimanding. Mr. Bairnsfather had carried the case to the Synod, by appeal. The Synod had denounced his irregularities in its voice of thunder. Mr. Lumsden only smiled his peculiar smile of gleeful simplicity, and went on with his labor.

He was going now to Oranmore. The glen of Oranmore lay among the lower heights of the Grampians, a solitary, secluded valley. A small colony of Highlanders, attached to the Strathoran branch of the house of Sutherland, in feudal times, and bearing the ancient name of Macalpine, had settled there, nearly a century before. The patriarchs of the little community still spoke their original Gaelic; but the younger generations, parents and children, approached much more closely to their Lowland neighbors, whose idiom they had adopted. The glen was entirely in their hands, and its fields, reclaimed by their pains-taking husbandry, produced their entire subsistence. Some flocks of sheep grazed on the hillside. There was good pasture land for their cattle, and the various patches of oats and barley, turnips and potatoes, were enough to keep these sturdy cottar families in independent poverty. Whether in other circumstances they might have displayed the inherent indolence which belongs, as men say, to that much belied Celtic race, we cannot tell. But having only ordinary obstacles to strive against—an indulgent landlord, and a kindly factor—the Macalpines had maintained themselves as sturdily as any Saxon tribe of their numbers could possibly have done; and had, what Saxon hamlets in the richer South are not wont to have, a couple of lads from their little clachan at college—one preparing himself for the work of the ministry, and another aspiring to the dignity of an M. D.

In summer time, these peaceful cot-houses, lying on either side of the infant Oran, within the shadow of the hills, with the fair low country visible from the end of the glen, and the stern Grampians rising to the sky above, were very fair to look upon; and the miniature clan at its husbandry, working in humble brotherhood—the link of kindred that joined its dozen families, all inheriting one name and one blood—the purer atmosphere of morality and faith among them—made the small commonwealth of Oranmore a pleasant thing for the mind to rest upon, no less than for the eye.

Mr. Ferguson had never dealt hardly with these honest Macalpines, in regard to the rent of their small holdings. He knew they would pay it when they could, and, in just confidence, he gave them latitude. Unhappily for the Macalpines, one whole half-year's rent remained unpaid, when the new landlord took the management out of Mr. Ferguson's kindly hands. The year was a backward year: their crops had been indifferent, and the Macalpines were not ready with their rent at Martinmas.

The consequence was, that these fearful notices to quit were served upon them. Big Duncan Macalpine, a man of very decided character and deep piety—one of that class, who, further north, are called "the men,"—perceived the alien Laird's intention of removing them at once. The remainder of the humble people, looked upon the notices only as threats, and set to with all industry to make up the rents, and prevent the dread alternative of leaving their homes. They had come there in the time of Laird Fergus, the great-grandfather of Archibald Sutherland. Their ninety-nine year's lease had expired in the previous year, and had not (for it was Archibald's dark hour) been renewed, so that now they were the merest tenants at will. Mr. Foreman warned Big Duncan that they might be ejected at any time.

The small community became alarmed. The big wheel was busy in every cottage. Sheep and poultry were being sold; every family was ready to make sacrifices for the one great object of keeping their lands and homes. The sharp, keen, unscrupulous writer whom Lord Gillravidge had employed in Edinburgh, where his over-acuteness had lost him caste and character, had been seen in the glen for three successive days. The Macalpines were smitten with dread. Rumors floated up into their hilly solitude of a great sheep-farmer from the south, who was in treaty for these hill-lands of Strathoran. A shadow fell upon the humble households. The calamity that approached began to shape itself before them. To leave their homes—the glen to which they clung with all the characteristic tenacity of their race—the country for which the imaginative Celtic spirit burned with deep and patriotic love—the national faith, still dearer, and more precious—for a cold, unknown, and strange land, far from their northern birth-place, and their preached Gospel!

Mr. Lumsden's strong, gray pony was used to all manner of rough roads, and so could climb along the craggy way that led to Oranmore. The minister rode briskly into the glen. His keen and anxious look became suddenly changed as he entered it into one of grief and indignation. He quickened his pace, leaped from the saddle, fastened his pony to a withered thorn, and hastened forward.

The crisis had come. Mr. Whittret the lawyer, and Mr. Fitzherbert, stood in the middle of a knot of Macalpines; a party of sheriff's-officers hung in the rear, and the youthful Giles Sympelton stood apart, looking on. The high head of Duncan Macalpine towered over the rest. In his moral chieftainship he was the spokesman of his neighbors. He was speaking when Mr. Lumsden approached.

"Your rent is ready, Sir—the maist of us are ready with your rent; but oh! if there is a heart of flesh within ye, spare us our hames! Gentlemen, we have a' been born here. Yon auld man," and Duncan pointed to the venerable white head of a trembling old man, wrapped in a plaid, who leaned against the lintel of the nearest cottage—"and he's past a century—is the only ane amang us that was a living soul at the flitting. For pity's sake, Sir, think o't! Gie us time to make up the siller. We'll pay the next half-year in advance, if better mayna be; but do not bid us leave the glen."

"That's all very well," said Fitzherbert, "very pretty. A set of Scotch cheats, who only want to deceive Lord Gillravidge."

"I want to deceive no man," said the humble chief of Oranmore, indignantly. "I wouldna set my face to a lee for a' his revenues. I am a head of a family, and a decent man, in God's providence, Sir; and I gie ye my word, that if ye'll just give us time, we'll make up the next half-year's rent in advance. His Lordship is a stranger, and maybe, doesna ken whether he can trust us or no. Mr. Ferguson will bear us witness, Sir—the Laird himsel will bear us witness. Mr. Lumsden—Guid be thankit he is here himsel!—the minister will bear us witness!"

Mr Lumsden entered the circle, hailed by various salutations. "Blessings on him! He never fails when he's needed." "He'll bear witness to us that we're honest folk." And one indignant outcry from Duncan's sister: "Ye'll believe the minister!"

"What is the matter, Duncan?" said Mr. Lumsden.

"The gentlemen have come for our rent, Sir; we're ahin' hand. I make nae wonder that folk new to the countryside mayna trust us; but oh! if they would but pit us on trial. I promise, in the name of all in the glen—ye're a' hearing me?—that, though it should take our haill substance, we'll pay the siller just and faithfully, as we have aye dune, if we only can bide upon our ain land."

"You own land!" echoed Fitzherbert. "Fellow! the land is Lord Gillravidge's."

Big Duncan Macalpine's honest face flushed deeply.

"I am nae fellow, Sir; and the land belangs to us by an aulder tenure than can give it to ony foreign lord. We are clansmen of the Laird's. Langsyne our chief sold our land further north—instead of it we got this glen. I say, Sir, that the land is ours.—We were born and bred in it; our fathers fought for it langsyne. We hold it on an auld tenure—aulder than ony lordship in thae pairts. Our forebears were content to follow their chief when he threw his ain hills into the hands of strangers. We got this instead of our auld inheritance. I say, Sir, that the land is ours—that no man has a right to take it from us. Mr. Whittret, ye're a lawyer—am I no speaking true?"

"Bah! You're a cheat!" exclaimed Fitzherbert.

Big Duncan's muscular arm shook nervously. He restrained himself with an effort. Not so his vehement sister Jean.

"Wha daurs say sic a name to Duncan Macalpine? Wha daurs disbelieve his word, standing in Oranmore? A feckless, ill-favored fuil, wi' as muckle hair about the filthy face o' him as wad hang him up in a tree, as the prodigal Absalom hung langsyne.—A cheat! If Big Duncan Macalpine wasna caring mair for his folk and name than for himsel, ye wad hae been spinning through the air afore now, in your road to the low country, ye ill-tongued loon!"

"Whisht, Jean!—whisht!" said her brother. "What needs we heed ill word? We're langer kent it in Oranside than the gentleman."

Duncan drew himself up in proud dignity. The puny "gentleman"—a thing of yesterday—was insignificant in the presence of the cottar of Oranmore—a true heritor of the soil.

"You do not mean, gentleman," said Mr. Lumsden,—"I trust you do not mean to take any extreme proceedings. I rejoice to be able to give my testimony to the sterling honor and integrity of Duncan Macalpine and his kinsmen of Oranmore. Lord Gillravidge cannot have better, or more honorable tenants. I entreat—I beg that time may be given them to make a representation of their case to his Lordship. He is new to the country, and may not know that these men are not ordinary tenants—that they have, as they truly say, a right to the soil. Mr. Whittret, you cannot refuse them your influence with Lord Gillravidge—you know their peculiar claim?"

"They might have a claim upon Mr. Sutherland," said the agent, gloomily. "They can have none upon Lord Gillravidge."

"Lord Gillravidge is bound to preserve ancient rights," exclaimed Mr. Lumsden. "It is not possible he can know the circumstances. These men are not ordinary cottars, Mr. Whittret—you understand their position. For pity's sake do not drive them to extremity!"

"It cannot be helped," said Mr. Whittret, bending his dark brows, and shunning the clear eye of the minister: "I must adhere to my instructions, Sir. These hill-lands are already let to a stock-farmer. I must proceed."

"There can be no need for haste, at least," said Mr. Lumsden. "The new tenant cannot enter till Whit-Sunday. Let the Macalpines stay—let them remain until the term."

Mr. Whittret lifted his eyes in furtive malice, with a glance of that suspicious cunning which perpetually fancies it is finding others out.

"And have Lord Gillravidge called a tyrant and oppressor for removing the people after their seed is sown? You are very good, Mr. Lumsden—we know how clerical gentlemen can speak. We shall take our own plan. Simpson, begin your work."

A detached cottage, the furthest out of the group, stood close upon the Oran—the narrow streamlet, a mere mountain burn so near its source, was spanned there by white stepping-stones. A woman in a widow's cap stood at the cottage-door, looking out with a silent want of wonder, which told plainly enough that some mightier interest prevented her from sharing in the excitement of her neighbors. The men approached the house, and after summoning her to leave it instantly, a summons which the poor woman heard in vacant astonishment, immediately prepared to unroof her humble habitation. The crowd of Macalpines had been looking on in breathless silence. Now there was a wild shriek of excitement and fury—men and women precipitated themselves at once upon the minions of that ruthless law which was not justice.—The ladder was thrown down; the hapless officer who had been the first to mount it, struggled in the hands of two strong young men; and Jean Macalpine, a tall athletic woman, stood before the terrified widow in the doorway, another officer prostrate at her feet. Mr. Fitzherbert and Whittret rushed forward—their satellites formed themselves together for resistance— the Macalpines furiously surrounded the cottage—there promised to be a general melee. But loud above the noise and tumult sounded the united voices of Big Duncan, and his minister.

"Jean Macalpine," shouted the chief of Oranmore, "come out from among this senseless fray. Dugald Macalpine, quit the man: why will ye pollute your hands striving with him? Donald Roy, let go your hold. Gentlemen, gentlemen, haud your hands, and hear me."

There was a momentary truce.

"Beware!" said Mr. Lumsden. "Within that house lies an invalid—if you expose that sinking lad, you will have a death to answer for. I tell you, beware!"

"Gentlemen," said Big Duncan Macalpine, "yon house is mine. I protest, in the name of my people, that ye are doing an unrighteous and unlawful thing. I beg ye, as ye are Christian men, that ken what hames are, to let us bide in our ain glen and country.—In honor, and honesty, and leal service we will pay ye for your mercy; but if ye are determined to carry on this work, unrighteous as it is in the sight of God and man, begin yonder—take my house. I was born in it—I thocht to die in it—begin with my house; but if ye would escape a curse and desolation, leave the hame of the widow."

There was a pause—the invading party were in a dilemma.—The very officials were moved by the manly disinterestedness of Big Duncan Macalpine. He himself strode to the side of the lads who had pulled the man from the ladder, and freed him from their grasp: then he gathered the Macalpines together, spoke a word of comfort to the widow, and placing himself by the door of her cottage, looked calmly towards his own house and waited.

Mr. Whittret stood undecided. Fitzherbert was furious. He had already issued his orders to the men to proceed, when his arm was grasped from behind. He turned round—the Honorable Giles Sympelton was at his elbow, his simple youthful face quivering with emotion.

"Fitz, Fitz," cried the lad, "stop this—I cannot bear it. I wll' not see it; if you destroy that noble fellow's house I will never enter Gillravidge's again. Take care what you do—they are better men than we."

Mr. Whittret looked up. Mr. Lumsden had his note-book in his hand, and was writing. The mean soul of the agent writhed within him. That Mr. Lumsden was writing an exposure of his conduct he never doubted; he would be covered with infamy and shame; at least it should not be without cause. "Simpson," he cried, "take the fellow at his word—proceed with your work."

Vain evil-thinking of the evil-doer! Mr. Lumsden, in fear of the compulsory removal of the invalid, was writing to his sister to send up a chase immediately from Portoran, and in a moment after, had despatched the most ungovernable of the lads to carry his note to the Manse.

Duncan Macalpine stood looking calmly at his cottage. His sister Jean, following his heroic example, had hurried into it, and now returned, leading a feeble woman of seventy—their mother. Duncan's wife stood beside her husband; two of his little boys lingered in childish wonder by the cottage door. The men began their odious work—the straw bands were cut, the heather thatch thrown in pieces on the ground. The children looked on at first in half-amused astonishment. They saw their home laid open to the sky with all its homely accommodations—their own little bed, their grandmother's chair by the fire, the basket of oatcakes on the table from which their "eleven-hours piece" had been supplied. The eldest of them suddenly rushed forward in childish rage and vehemence, and springing upon the ladder, dealt a fruitless blow at one of the devastators. He was thrown off—a piece of the thatch struck upon his head—the child uttered a sharp cry and fell. His mother flew out from among the crowd. The Macalpines were shaken as with a wind, and with various cries of rage and grief were pressing forward again. Again Big Duncan stayed them. "Fuils that ye are, would ye lose your guid fame with your hames? would ye throw everything away? Be still I tell you. Can I no guard my ain bairn mysel?"

The wave fell back: muttering in painful anger, the Macalpines obeyed the king-man among them, and restrained themselves. Big Duncan in his stern patience went forward. Before him, however, was a slight boyish figure, with uncovered head and long fair hair—the child was lifted in the youth's arms, "I will carry him—good woman, come with me—come away from this place. It is not right you should see it—come away."

"I thank ye, young gentleman," said Big Duncan: "it becomes a young heart to shrink from the like of this, but we maun stay. Neither my wife nor me can leave the glen till we leave it with our haill people."

Giles Sympelton hurried on to the widow's cottage with the boy. The child was not much hurt—he was only stunned; and attended by his mother and aunt, he was taken into the house. Sympelton placed himself in front of the Macalpines by Mr. Lumsden's side.

The destruction went on—you could trace its progress by the agonized looks of these watching people. Now a sharp, sudden cry from some distressed mother, that bore witness the destroyers were throwing down the roof under which her little ones had been born. Now a long, low groan told the father's agony. The young men were shutting out the sight with their hands—they could not school themselves to patience; the little children, clinging about their feet, kept up a plaintive cry of shrill dismay and wonder, the chorus of that heart-breaking scene. House after house, un-windowed, roofless, and doorless, stood in mute desolation behind the hirelings of the unjust law, as their work went on. At last it was completed, and they approached the widow's cottage again. There was an instant forgetfulness of individual suffering. Closely, side by side, the Macalpines surrounded the house of the widow. These strong men were dangerous opponents—even these excited women might be formidable to meet at such a time. The officers held back.

"I implore—I beseech!" cried Mr. Lumsden, "spare this house! Leave the sick youth within to die in peace. Leave us this one asylum for the aged and the feeble. If ye are men, spare the widow—spare the boy!"

"Fitz!" cried Giles Sympelton, in a tone of indignant appeal.

Mr. Whittret was enraged and furious.

"Lose no time, Simpson!" he cried. "It is three o'clock already. Make haste and finish!"

Big Duncan Macalpine stood undecided.

"It's a life!" he muttered. "It's lawful to defend a life, at any risk or hazard! Sir—Mr. Lumsden—what will we do?"

Mr. Lumsden made another appeal. It was useless. More peremptorily still the agent ordered the men to proceed.

"Duncan," said Mr. Lumsden, "for the sake of the Gospel you profess, and for your own sake, let there be no resistance! Lift the boy out—protect him as you best can; we must leave the issue in God's hands. Brethren, give way to the officers. You can only bring further evil on yourselves. You cannot deliver the widow. Sirs, stand back till we are ready—we will give you space for your work then. The consequences be upon your own heads!"

The minister entered the cottage, and passed through among the patriarchs of the sorrowful community, who were sheltering from the chill March wind, under the only remaining roof in the glen. In a moment after he reappeared, bearing the sick lad, a helpless burden, in his strong arms. A cry rose from the women—the men clenched their fingers, and gnashed their teeth. The sharp, pale face raised itself above Mr. Lumsden's arm—the feeble invalid was strong with excitement.

"Be quiet, oh! be quiet—dinna do ill for my sake!"

"And now," cried Big Duncan, "I bid ye to my house—all of ye that are Macalpines. Leave the birds of prey to their work—come with me!"

The people obeyed. They formed themselves into a solemn procession: the tremulous old man, whose years outnumbered a century, leaning upon two stalwart grandsons; the aged woman, Duncan Macalpine's mother, supported on her son's arm; strong men restraining by force which shook their vigorous frames the natural impulse to resistance; mothers, with compressed lips, shutting in the agony of their hearts—the train of weeping, bewildered children! The March wind swept keen and biting over them as they passed by their own desolate houses in stern silence, and assembled again, further up the glen. The work was accomplished. The last cottage in Oranmore was dismantled and roofless. The Macalpines were without a home!

CHAPTER XX

Giles Sympelton ran from the glen. The lad was light of foot, and inspired with a worthy errand. Headlong, over burn, and ditch, and hedgerow he plunged on—past the long woods of Strathoran—past the gate where stood some of Lord Gillravidge's household, sheer on to the Tower. The door was open—he darted in—rushed up stairs—and in headlong haste plunged into Mrs. Catherine's inner drawing-room. Mrs. Catherine herself was seated there alone. She looked up in wonder, as, with flushed face and disordered hair, and breathless from his precipitate speed, the lad suddenly presented himself before her.

"I want your carriage—I want you to send your carriage with me—for a dying lad—a sick boy who has no shelter. Give me your carriage!"

"Young man," said Mrs. Catherine, "what do you mean?" She rose and approached him. "You are the lad that was in temptation at Strathoran. Have you seen the evil of your ways?"

"Your carriage—I want your carriage!" gasped poor Giles Sympelton. "Order it first, and I will tell you afterwards."

Mrs. Catherine did not hesitate. She rang the bell, and ordered the carriage immediately.

"Immediately—immediately!" cried the lad. "The cold may kill him."

"Sit down," said Mrs. Catherine, "till it is ready; and tell me what has moved you so greatly."

The youth wiped his hot forehead, and recovered his breath.

"The cottagers up the glen—their name is Macalpine—Lord Gillravidge has evicted them. There is not a house standing—they are all unroofed. The people have no shelter. And the lad—the dying lad?"

Mrs. Catherine rose. Amazement, grief, and burning anger contended in her face.

"What say you? The alien has dared to cast out the Macalpines of Oranmore from their own land! I cannot believe it—it is not possible!"

"The lad is dying!" cried young Sympelton, too much absorbed with what he had seen to heed Mrs. Catherine's exclamation. "They are covering him with cloaks and plaids—they say the cold will kill him. It is a terrible sight!—old men, and women, and little children, and the dying lad! Not a roof in the whole glen to shelter them!"

Mrs. Catherine left the room, and went down stairs. An energetic word sent double speed into Andrew's movements as he prepared the carriage. Mrs. Euphan Morison was ordered to put wine into it; blankets and cloaks were added, and Mrs. Catherine, with her own hands, thrust Giles into the carriage.

"Bring the lad here, to the Tower: come back to me yourself. Bring the aged and feeble with you, as many as can come. Mind that you return to me your own self. And now, sir, away!"

The carriage dashed out of the court, and at a pace to which Mrs. Catherine's horses were not accustomed, took the way to Oranmore.

Fitzherbert and Whittret had left the glen, with their band of attendants. The Macalpines were alone; the shadows of the March evening began to gather darkly upon the hills. In Big Duncan's roofless cottage, on a bed, hastily constructed before the fire, and shielded with a rude canopy of plaids, lay the sick lad, shivering and moaning, as the gust of wind which swept through the vacant window-frame, and burst in wild freedom overhead, shook the frail shelter over him, and tossed the coverings off his emaciated limbs. Mr. Lumsden stood beside him. In the first shock of that great misfortune, the minister endeavored to speak hopeful, cheering words—of earthly comfort yet to come—of heavenly strength and consolation, which no oppressing hand could bereave them of.—Homeless and destitute, in the stern silence of their restrained emotions, the Macalpines heard him; some vainly, the burning sense of personal wrong momentarily eclipsing even their religion; some with a noble patience which, had they been Romans of an older day, would have gained them the applauses of a world. These brief and lofty words of his were concluded with a prayer. The March evening was darkening, the wind sweeping chill and fierce above them. The tremulous old man leaned on the sick lad's bed; the grandmother crouched by the fire upon her grandchild's stool. Big Duncan Macalpine stood on his own threshold; without, close to the vacant window, stood the neighbors who could not find admission into the interior, and from the midst of them the voice of supplication ascended up to heaven, "For strength, for patience, for forgiveness to their enemy."

A consultation followed. Mr. Lumsden was looking out eagerly for the chaise from Portoran. It could not arrive in less than an hour, Big Duncan said; and the minister with his own hands, endeavored to fix up more securely a shelter for the suffering lad.

"What are we to do?" exclaimed one of the Macalpines.—"Neighbors, what is to become of us?—where are we to gang?"

A loud scream from a young mother interrupted him; her infant was seized with the fearful cough and convulsive strugglings of croup. The poor young woman pressed it to her breast, and rushed to her own desolate cottage. Alas! what shelter was there? The roof lay in broken pieces on the ground; window and door were carried away; the fire had sunk into embers. She threw herself down before it, and tried to chafe the little limbs into warmth. Other mothers followed her. All the means known to their experience were adopted in vain. The terrible hoarse cough continued—the infant's face was already black.

"What are we to do?" exclaimed the same voice again. "Are we to see our bairns die before our eyes? Duncan, we let them destroy our houses at your word! What are we to do?"

"If ye had dune onything else," said Big Duncan Macalpine, "we would have had the roof of a jail ower our heads before this time—and it's my hope there is nae faint heart among us, that would have left the wives and the bairns to fend for themsels.—Neighbors, I know not what to do; if we could but get ower this night, some better hope might turn up for us."

His sister brushed past them as he spoke, carrying hot water to bathe the suffering infant—not hot enough, alas! to do it any good. The other women were heaping peats upon a fire, to make ready more; the old people within Duncan's house crouched and shivered by the narrow hearth; the little children clinging to the skirts of their parents, were sobbing with the cold.

"Get ower the night?" said Roderick Macalpine, "we might get along oursels on the hillside; but what's to come of them?" and he waved his hand towards the helpless circle by the fire—the aged, the dying, the children.

"Sirs," said the old man coming forward, fancying as it seemed that they appealed to him, "let us go to the kirkyard. You can pit up shelters there—no man can cast ye out of the place where your forebears are sleeping. If they take all the land beside, ye have yet a right to that."

The listeners shrank and trembled—the old man with his palsied head, and withered face, and wandering light blue eyes, proposing to them so ghastly a refuge. The Macalpines were not driven so utterly to extremity. It remained for these more enlightened days to send Highland cottars, in dire need, to seek a miserable shelter above the dust of their fathers.

The consultation was stayed—no one dared answer the old man—when suddenly Giles Sympelton was seen running in haste up the glen. He had brought the carriage as high as it could come, and now flew forward himself to get the invalid transferred to it. Big Duncan lifted the sick lad in his arms, and carried him away, while Giles lingered to deliver Mrs. Catherine's orders.

"Let me take the old people with me," he said, eagerly, to Mr. Lumsden. "The carriage is large—the old lady said I was to bring as many as could come. It is Mrs. Catherine Douglas, of the Tower—do not let us lose time, Sir: get the oldest people down to the carriage."

The Macalpines did not cheer—they were too grave for that; but the lad's hand was grasped in various honest rough ones, and "blessings on him!" were murmured from many tongues. Three of the most feeble could be accommodated in the carriage—at least, could be crowded beneath its roof, while the sick youth was placed on the cushions, and his mother sat at his feet.

"Is there anything more I can do?" said Giles, looking in grief and pity upon the agonized face of the young mother, sitting within the dismantled cottage waiting while her neighbors prepared another hot-bath for her child.

"Nothing," said Mr. Lumsden. "I thank you heartily, young gentleman, for what you have already done. You may have saved that poor lad's life by your promptitude. Tell Mrs. Catherine that every arrangement that can possibly be made for the comfort of the Macalpines, I will attend to. Good night—I thank you most sincerely. You will never repent this day's work, I am sure."

Giles lingered still.

"How is the child? will it die?" he asked anxiously of one of the women.

"Bless the innocent, the water's hot this time," was the answer; "it's no moaning sae muckle. Eh, the Lord forbid it should die!"

Giles turned and ran down the glen, saw his charge safely deposited in the carriage, and, mounting beside the coachman, drove more leisurely to the Tower.

Before they had been very long away, the chaise arrived from Portoran. The infant's sufferings were abated; it had sunk into a troubled, exhausted sleep. Mr. Lumsden filled the chaise immediately with the feebler members of the houseless community. It was arranged that the rest should walk to Portoran—it was twelve miles—a weary length of way, where the minister pledged himself they should find accommodations. Big Duncan and Roderick Macalpine voluntarily remained in the glen, to protect the household goods of their banished people.

The chaise had driven off—the pedestrians were already on the high road. Duncan and Roderick, wrapped in their plaids, had seated themselves by the peat-fire in Duncan's roofless dwelling.—The stern composure upon the faces of these two men, lighted by the red glow of the fire, as they sat there in the rapidly darkening twilight, told a tale of the intense excitement of that day, and now of the knawing sorrow, the weight of anxiety that possessed them. Mr. Lumsden stood at the door, his pony's bridle in his hand.

"Mind what I have said," he cried, as he left them. "Keep up your hearts and do not despair. You will not need to leave the country—you will find friends—only keep up your hearts and be strong. God will not forsake you."

They returned his good-night with deep emotion. This peaceful glen, that yesternight had slept beneath the moonbeams in the placid sleep of righteous and honorable labor—strange policy that could prefer some paltry gain to the continuance of the healthful homejoy of these true children, and heirs of the soil!

The two Macalpines sat together in silence, their eyes fixed on the red glow of the fire before them. By-and-by Roderick's gaze wandered—first to the numberless little domestic tokens round, which spoke so pitiful a language—the basket of cakes was still on the table, the "big wheel" at which Jean Macalpine had been spinning so busily on the previous night, stood thrust aside in the corner. His eyes stray further—through the vacant window-frame he saw, upon the other side of the Oran, his own roofless house; he saw the cradle from which his child had been hurriedly snatched, lying broken within; he saw the household seat in which, only some five winters since, he had placed bonnie Jeanie Macalpine, a bride then, the mother of three children now. His hearth was black—his house desolate—Jeanie and her heart failed him: "Oh, man! Duncan!" exclaimed poor Roderick, as he hid his face in his hands in an agony of grief.

Big Duncan Macalpine's dark eyes were dilated with the stern and passionate force of his strong resolution; his clear, brave, honest face was turned steadfastly towards the fire.

"Roderick," he said, emphatically, "I daurna trust mysel to look about me. Keep your eyes away from the ruined houses—look forward, man. Have I no my ain share? is my house less desolate than yours?"

In the meantime, Giles Sympelton had arrived with his charge at the Tower; and having seen the sick youth placed in a warm room, with kindly hands about him, and the old people settled comfortably by the great kitchen fire, was finally solacing himself after the labors of this strangely exciting day, at Mrs. Catherine's well-appointed dinner-table, with Mrs. Catherine herself opposite him. She was singularly kind. In spite of much temptation, and many bad associates, Giles Sympelton had remained unsophisticated and simple. The fear of ridicule, which might in other circumstances have induced him to resist the attractions of this stately old lady, with whom he had been brought so strangely in contact, was removed from the lad now—he gave way to the fascination. With natural naivete and simplicity, he told her his whole brief history; how of late he had written very seldom to his father; how he had become disgusted with Fitzherbert, and disliked Gillravidge, and was so very sorry for "poor Sutherland;" how he vowed never to enter Lord Gillravidge's house again, if "that noble fellow, Macalpine," were turned out of his; and, finally, how determined was he to keep his vow—to send for his servant, and his possessions, and to go into Portoran that very night: he was resolved not to spend another night in Strathoran.

"I have houseroom for you," said Mrs. Catherine. "Let your servant bring your apparel here—I am not straitened for chambers. You have done good service to the Macalpines, as becomes a young heart. I rejoice to have you in my house. You should send for your man without delay."

The youth hesitated—met Mrs. Catherine's eye—blushed—looked down, and muttered something about troubling her.

"You will be no trouble to me—I have told you that. What is your name?"

Sympelton looked up surprised and bashful.

"Giles Sympelton," he said.

"Sympelton?" said Mrs. Catherine. "Was the bairn that died in Madeira thirty years ago, a friend to you?"

"My father had a sister," said young Sympelton; "he was very fond of her—who died very long ago, years before I was born."

Mrs. Catherine was silent, and seemed much moved.

"Friend!" she said, "I had one brother who was the very light of my eyes, and there was a gentle blue-eyed bairn, in yon far away island, who went down with him to the grave. The name of her was Helen. He died in the morning, and she died at night, and on the same day her brother and I buried our dead. If you are of her blood, you are doubly welcome!"

"My aunt's name was Helen," said Giles, "and she was only fifteen when she died. I have heard my father speak of her often."

Mrs. Catherine was so long silent after that, that the young man began to feel constrained and uneasy, and to think that, after all, he had better try the accommodation of the "Sutherland Arm's" in Portoran. All the circumstances of Mrs. Catherine's great grief were brought vividly before her by his name. Helen Sympelton!—how well she remembered the attenuated child-woman, maturing brilliantly under the deadly heat of that consumptive hectic, who had accompanied Sholto to the grave.

She spoke at last with an effort:

"I have some country neighbors coming to me this night. You may not be caring for meeting them: therefore do not come up the stair, unless you like. Andrew will let you see your room, and you will find sundry pleasant books in my library; and, till your man comes, Andrew will wait your orders."

Giles intimated his perfect satisfaction in the prospect of meeting Mrs. Catherine's country neighbors; and after some further kindly words, and a beaming sunshiny smile, the old lady left the room.

Mr. Lumsden also had by this time received, and provided accommodation for, his share of the ejected Macalpines. The families of Roderick and Duncan were in his own hospitable Manse. Some of the others had been received, in their way down, into the farm-house of Whiteford. Duncan Roy had stopped to pour his story, in indignant Celtic vehemence, into the ears of Mr. Ferguson, and, with his pretty sister, Flora, had been taken into Woodsmuir. The others were provided for in various houses in Portoran—the most of them in genuine neighborly sympathy and compassion, and some for the hire which Mr. Lumsden offered, when other motives were wanting. They were all settled, in comparative comfort at last; all but those two stern watching men, who sat through the gloom of the wild March night, within the roofless walls of Big Duncan's house, watching the humble possessions of the Macalpines of Oranmore.

His manifold labors over, Mr. Lumsden took a hurried dinner, and proceeded to dress. He had been invited to the Tower, to Mrs. Catherine's quiet evening gathering of country neighbors. His sister endeavored to dissuade him, on the ground of his fatigue. Mr. Lumsden laughed—he always did laugh when fatigue was mentioned. Then it was absolutely necessary that he should see how poor Kenneth Macalpine had borne his removal: and then—probably Mr. Lumsden had some additional inducement, private to himself, which we cannot exactly condescend upon.

Miss Lumsden excused herself from accompanying him. Her brother had done his part for the poor Macalpines—it was her turn now. The gray pony too was not quite so invulnerable as its master. It owned to the fatigue of the day, in a very decided disinclination to leave its comfortable stable, so Mr. Lumsden took his seat beside Walter Foreman in the gig, and proceeded to the Tower.

It was not unusual for Mrs. Catherine to have these gatherings. They were very simple affairs. She liked to bring the young people together; she liked herself, now and then, to have a pleasant domestic chat with the elders. Everybody liked those quiet and easy parties, to which the guests came in their ordinary dress, and enjoyed themselves after their own fashion, without restraint or ceremony; and everybody, who had the good fortune to be on Mrs. Catherine's list of favorites, had most pleasant recollections of the ruddy inner drawing-room, at these especial times.

Giles Sympelton paid another visit to poor Kenneth Macalpine after dinner. He found him sleeping pleasantly in the warm, cheerful, light apartment, his mother watching with tearful joy by his bedside, and Mrs. Euphan Morison sitting in portly state by the fire. Widow Macalpine whispered thanks and blessings, and added, that, "he hadna sleeped sae quiet, since ever they were warned out o' the glen." Giles withdrew with very pleasant feelings, and walking up to the room prepared for him, where his servant already waited, proceeded to dress.

This important operation was performed very carefully, some dreamy idea of "astonishing the natives" floating through his boyish brain the while. Giles, simple lad as he was, was yet a gentleman—he had no flashy finery about him—his dress was perfectly plain and simple. He was satisfied, however, and felt he would make an impression.

Ada Mina Coulter's pretty, girlish face was the first he noticed on entering the room. He did make an impression. Ada knew very pleasantly, as she drooped her brown curls before the glance of the stranger, that the blue eyes from whence that glance came, belonged to a lord's son—an Honorable Giles.

Mrs. Catherine introduced him, with kindly mention of his day's labor, to her elder friends—to Lewis Ross and Anne—and then committing him to their charge, returned to her conversation with the fathers and mothers. Giles by no means made the impression he expected on that party—he had a feeling of old friendship for Anne—a slight idea of rivalry in respect to Lewis—but consoled himself pleasantly half an hour after, by Ada Coulter's side, putting her into a very agreeable state of flutter and tremulousness. Ada was younger than Alice Aytoun—was but a little way past her sixteenth birth-day indeed, and was not yet accustomed to the homage of young gentlemen—and an Honorable Giles!

There was great indignation concerning the ejection of the Macalpines, and as soon as it was known that Giles had been present, a little crowd gathered round him. He told the story with great feeling; described Big Duncan Macalpine's conduct with enthusiasm; touched slightly on his own fears for poor Kenneth; and laughed when he told them of his race. Mrs. Catherine drew near at that point of the story, and extending her hand over Ada's curls, patted him kindly on the head. The Honorable Giles felt rather indignant—it was making a child of him. No matter—Ada Coulter thought him a hero.

A graver group were discussing the subject at the other end of the room. Mr. Lumsden told the story there. Mr. Coulter and Mr. Ferguson were bending forward to him with anxious faces.—The ladies were no less interested. Anne Ross leant on the sofa at Mrs. Coulter's elbow. Marjory Falconer stood apart, with her hand upon the back of a chair, and her strong and expressive face swept by whirlwinds— indignation, grief, sympathy—all mellowed, however, by a singular shade of something that looked very like proud and affectionate admiration—of whom was Marjory Falconer proud?

"Now, gentlemen," said Mr. Lumsden, "you must assist me.—I have set my heart upon it, Mr. Coulter, that these families shall not be sent penniless to Canada. I don't like emigration at all, but in this case it would be nothing less than banishment—what can we do for them?"

Mr. Coulter took a pinch of snuff.

"It is not a bad thing emigration, Mr. Lumsden; if there was no emigration, what would become of these vast waste lands? I suppose we might pour our whole population into the backwoods, and there would still be unreclaimed districts. Depend upon it, Sir, it comes very near a sin to let land, that should be bringing forth seed and bread, lie waste and desolate, when there are men to work it."

"Well," said Mr. Lumsden, "we won't argue about that. It may be right enough—I only say I don't like emigration; and we have abundance of waste lands at home, Mr. Coulter; but in the case of the Macalpines, it could bear no aspect but banishment.—I believe they would almost starve first. What can we do for them?"

There was a pause of consideration.

"Robert," said Mrs. Ferguson.

Her husband looked round.

"When you commence your improvements, you will require many laborers—would not the Macalpines do? We were thinking of taking Flora to be one of our maids at Woodsmuir, you know—other people, no doubt, would do the same. What do you think?"

Mr Ferguson spent a moment in deliberation; then he looked up to Mr. Coulter inquiringly.

"Not a bad idea," said the agriculturist.

"I was thinking of that myself," said Mr. Ferguson. "There is not a very great number of them: we shall surely be able to keep them in the district; and there is always the hope," the good factor endeavored to look very sanguine and cheerful—"there is always the hope of Mr. Archibald's return."

No one made any response; saving himself and Mrs. Catherine, no one was sanguine on that subject: they were very glad to join in good wishes for the broken laird; but saw all the improbabilities in a stronger light than his more solicitous friends could do.

"If he does," said Mr. Lumsden, "if he ever can redeem the estate again, I suppose the Macalpines are safe."

Mr Ferguson looked with gratitude at the minister. It was pleasant to have his hope homologated even so slightly. "Safe? ay, without doubt or fear! there is not a kinder heart in all Scotland. How many men will there be, Mr. Lumsden? how many able men?"

Mr Lumsden entered into a calculation. We need not follow him through the list of Duncans, and Donalds, and Rodericks; there were eleven fathers of families. Duncan Roy and his sister Flora were orphans; besides, there were six or seven young men, and a plentiful undergrowth of boys of all ages and sizes.

"Say sixteen men," said Mr. Ferguson, "the rest could be herds, or—there is always work for these halflin lads. What do you say, Mr. Coulter?"

Mr Coulter's deliverance was favorable. Mrs. Catherine had urgent need of a plough-man, she suddenly discovered. Mrs. Coulter thought she "could do with" another maid. The Macalpines were in a fair way of being settled.

"Mind what I say," said Mrs. Catherine, "its only for a time. They shall recover their ancient holdings, every inch of them; their right to the land is as good as Archie's; the clansman holds it on as clear a title as the chief. Mind, I put this in the bargain; that whenever the estate returns to its rightful owner, the Macalpines return to Oranmore."

Mr. Ferguson's eyes glistened. He seemed to be looking forward to some apocryphal future gladness, which he dared hardly venture to believe in, yet to which his heart could not choose but cling. God speed the adventurer in the new world!

Mr. Lumsden proceeded down stairs immediately, to visit the aged and sick who had been brought to the Tower: in a short time he returned. The guests young and old were more amalgamated than before; they were sitting in a wide circle round Mrs. Catherine's chair. They did not perceive the minister's entrance: for some reason known to himself he stepped behind the window-curtain. He was looking out upon the clear, cold, starry night.

"Bless me," said Mrs. Bairnsfather, "Mr. Lumsden is in high favor with us all. It's a wonder a fine young man like him has not got a wife yet."

Marjory Falconer looked thundery; she had been aware of a private telegraphic sign made by the hand of a certain tall dark figure, which was looking out upon the night.

"All in good time," said Mrs. Coulter, "he is but a young man yet."

"How old would you say?" inquired Mrs. Bairnsfather.

"Oh! one or two and thirty perhaps—not more."

"Not more!" Mrs. Bairnsfather had a vindictive recollection of sundry invasions of her husband's parish. "I'll warrant him a good five years older than that."

"Well, well," said the good-humored agriculturist. "He is not too old to be married yet, that is a consolation."

"What would you say to Miss Ada Mina!" continued Mrs. Bairnsfather. "Miss Jeanie, I suppose, I must not speak of now."

Ada Coulter shook her curls indignantly. She, full sixteen, and receiving the homage of an Honorable Giles, to be "scorned" with a minister of five and thirty!

"Or Miss Ross?" said the mischief-making Mrs. Bairnsfather.—"They would make an excellent couple, I am sure."

"I won't have that," said Lewis. "I have engaged Anne, Mrs. Bairnsfather; if she does not take my man, I'll disown her."

"Anne, I want you," said Marjory Falconer: "come here."

"Or Miss Falconer herself?" said the indefatigable Mrs. Bairnsfather turning sharp round, and directing the attention of all and sundry to Marjory's face, perfectly scorching as it was, with one of her overwhelming, passionate blushes, "and that would secure the contrast which people say is best for peace and happiness."

Miss Falconer tried to laugh—the emphasis on the word peace had not escaped her; she slid her arm through Anne's and left the room. The dark figure behind the curtain, followed her with his eye; laughed within himself a mighty secret laugh, and came out of his concealment, to the immense discomfiture of Mrs. Bairnsfather, and the great mirth of Giles and Ada.

"That abominable woman!" exclaimed Marjory, as they went down stairs.

"Hush," said Anne, "she is the minister's wife."

"The minister's wife! there is never any peace where she is.—She is a pretty person to think she can understand—"

"Who, Marjory?"

"Oh," said Marjory, with a less vehement blush, "it's because John Lumsden is so popular in Strathoran—you know that.—Come, let us go and see Kenneth Macalpine."

They did go; poor Kenneth was feverish and unable for any further excitement, so they spoke a few kirdly encouraging words to his mother, and left the room. Mrs. Euphan Morison had retreated to her own apartment, and sat there by the fire sulky and dignified—the doctor had absolutely forbidden her administering to the invalid a favorite preparation of her own which she was sure would cure him.

Marjory and Anne turned to the great, warm, shining kitchen. The patriarch of Oranmore was dozing in a chair by the fire—the old man's mind was unsettled; he had returned to his native Gaelic, and had been speaking in wandering and incoherent sentences of the church-yard, and the right they had to the graves of their fathers. An aged woman, the grand-aunt of Duncan Roy and Flora, who had brought up the orphans, sat opposite to him, muttering and wringing her withered hands in pain. She had been long afflicted with rheumatism, and the exposure made her aged limbs entirely useless. She had to be lifted into her chair—and aggravating her bodily pain was the anguish of her mind: "The bairns—the bairns! what will become of the bairns?"

The other Macalpine was a feeble woman, widowed and childless, to whom her honorable and kindly kirdred had made up, so far as temporal matters went, the loss of husband and of children. She was rocking herself to and fro, and uttering now and then a low unconscious cry, as she brooded over the ruin of her friends, and her own helpless beggary. The firmament was utterly black, for her—she had no strength, no hope.

Marjory and Anne lingered for some time, endeavoring to cheer and comfort these two helpless women. Mrs. Catherine's maids, carefully superintended by Jacky, had done everything they could to make them comfortable; and before the young ladies left the kitchen, Flora Macalpine had entered, and was at her aunt's side, telling of the reception Duncan and herself had met with at Woodsmuir, and how Mrs. Ferguson had half promised to take her into the nursery to be "bairn's-maid" to the little Fergusons. The old woman was a little comforted—very little; for if Flora was away in service, who could take care of her painful, declining years?

Jacky followed Anne and Marjory out of the kitchen. They were absorbed with this matter of the ejectment, and so did not observe her. Marjory drew her companion to the library.

"Do come in here, Anne. I don't want to go up stairs yet."

They went in, Jacky following—she seemed determined not to lose the opportunity.

"If ye please, Miss Anne—"

"Well, Jacky?"

Jacky hesitated—she did not know how to go on, so she repeated: "If ye please, Miss Anne—" and stopped again.

"What is it, Jacky?" said Anne, "tell me."

"If ye please, will ye let me go with ye, Miss Anne?" said Jacky, in a burst. "I ken how to—to behave mysel, and to attend to a lady, and I'll never give ye ony trouble, and I'll do whatever I'm bidden. Oh, Miss Anne, will ye let me go?"

"What has put that into your head, Jacky?" exclaimed Anne.

Jacky could not tell what had put it into her head, inasmuch as any explanation might have shown Anne that the singular elf before her had, by some intuition peculiar to herself, made very tolerable progress in the study of those important matters which of late had occupied so much of their thoughts, and hopes, and consultations in Merkland and the Tower: so she merely repeated:

"Oh, if ye please, Miss Anne, will ye let me go?"

Anne was somewhat puzzled.

"You are too young to be my maid, Jacky," she said.

"Oh, if ye please, Miss Anne, I ken how to do—and I'm no idle when there's ony purpose for't—and I aye do what I'm bidden, except—" Jacky hung her head, "except whiles."

"But Anne wants a great big woman, like me, Jacky," said Marjory Falconer, laughing, "an old woman perhaps."

"But if ye please, Miss Falconer," said Jacky, seriously, "an old woman wouldna do—an old woman wouldna be so faithful and—and—" Jacky paused, her conscience smiting her: was not the Squire of the redoubtable Britomart an old woman? Whereupon there ensued in Jacky's mind a metaphysical discussion as to whether Glauce or Mrs. Elspat Henderson was the best type of the class of ancient serving-women—remaining undecided upon which point, she had nothing for it but to repeat the prayer of her petition: "Oh, Miss Anne, will you let me go?"

"Do you intend to take a maid with you, Anne?" asked Marjory.

"Yes."

"Then you should take Jacky by all means."

Anne hesitated.

"You forget, Jacky, that it is not I, but Mrs. Catherine, who must decide this."

"Oh, if ye please, Mrs. Catherine will let me go, Miss Anne, if you're wanting me."

"And your mother, Jacky?"

"My mother's no needing me, Miss Anne."

"Well, we will see about it," said Anne, smiling; "as you seem to have quite made up your mind, and decided on the matter. I will speak to Mrs. Catherine, Jacky. We shall see."

Jacky made an uncouth courtesy and vanished.

"Is t Edinburgh you are going to, Anne?" said Marjory, shooting a keen glance upon her friend's face.

"I shall be in Edinburgh," said Anne, evasively.

"Why, Anne!" exclaimed Marjory, "must one not even know where you are going? What is this secret journey of yours?"

"It is no secret journey, Marjory. I am going farther east than Edinburgh—to the sea-side."

"To the sea-side!" Marjory looked amazed. "You are not delicate, Anne Ross. What are you going to do at the sea-side?"

"Nothing," said Anne.

"Nothing! You have not any friends there—you are going away quite by yourself! Is anything the matter, Anne? Tell me what you are going to do."

"I would tell you very gladly, Marjory, if I could. My errand is quite a private one: when it is accomplished, you shall hear it all."

The blood rushed in torrents to Marjory Falconer's face.

"You cannot trust me!" she exclaimed. "Anne, I do not care for Mrs. Bairnsfather's petty insults. I have been too careless of forms, perhaps—perhaps I have made people think me rude and wild, when I was only striving to reach a better atmosphere than they had placed me in—but you, Anne Ross—you to think me unworthy of confidence!"

"Hush—hush, Marjory," said Anne. "Pray do not begin to be suspicious—it does not become you at all. I had a brother once, Marjory—as people say, a most generous, kind, good brother—whose name lies under the blot of a great crime. He was innocent—but the world believed him guilty. I am going to try—by what quiet and humble means are in my power—to remove this undeserved stain. If I succeed, I shall have a very moving story to tell you: if I do not succeed, let us never speak of it again. In any case, I know you will keep my secret."

Marjory pressed her friend's hand, and did not speak. She remembered dimly having heard of some great sorrow connected with Mr. Ross's (of Merkland) death, and was ashamed and grieved now, that she had pressed her inquiries so far. Marjory Falconer, like Lewis Ross, was learning lessons: the rapidly developing womanhood, which sent those vehement flushes to her cheek, and overpowered her sometimes with agonies of shame, was day by day asserting itself more completely. A few more paroxysms, and it would have gained the victory.

CHAPTER XXI

By the beginning of April, the Macalpines were finally settled; the majority of them being employed as laborers on Mr. Ferguson's farms of Loelyin and Lochend. Roderick and his family occupied a cottage in the vicinity of the Tower. He was engaged as ploughman by Mrs. Catherine Douglas. Big Duncan remained with his people—their houses were now far apart—they were restless and ill at ease, feeling their dispersion as the Jews of old felt their captivity. These clinging local attachments are comparatively little known to people confined within the limits of cities, and living in the hired houses, which any caprice or revolution of fortune may make them change. It is not so with the "dwellers of the hills," the whole circuit of whose simple lives for generations have passed under one roof; to whom the sun has risen and set behind the same majestic hills in daily glory, and whose native streamlet has a house-hold tongue, as familiar as the more articulate one of nearest kindred. A hope had sprung up in the breast of the Macalpines—a hope to which their yearning home-love gave vivid strength and power. Their chief would return: he would come back in renewed wealth and prosperity: he would lead them back to their own homes in triumph. This anticipation enlivened the sad pilgrimages, which the banished hillfolk made on those dewy spring evenings to their beloved glen. It needed some such hope to stifle the indignant grief and anger, which might have else blazed up in illegal vehemence, when the ejected Macalpines, in little parties of two and three, returned to Oranmore, to look upon their former homes, now desolate and blackened, with grass springing up on each household floor, and waving already from the broken walls—but they looked away, where, far over the wide-spreading low-country, there shone in the distance, the glimmer of the great sea; and prayed, in the fervor of their hope and yearning, for the home-coming of their chief. God speed the adventurer, landing even now on the sunny shores of the new world! How many hearts beat high with prayers and hopes for his return!

The sick lad, Kenneth, did not die: he lived to hold the name of the youthful Giles Sympelton in dearest honor and reverence, and to do him leal service in an after-time. Giles, with some reluctance, left the Tower, after a week's residence there, to join his father—leaving Ada Coulter with the first sadness upon her, which she had experienced since her happy release from school.

In the middle of April, Anne set out upon her journey. With Mrs. Catherine's full consent, Jacky was to accompany her. Anne's departure excited some attention. There seemed to be a vague conception among the neighbors, that something of moment was concealed under this quiet visit to the south, of the very quiet Miss Ross, of Merkland. Jeanie Coulter wondered if she was going to be married. Mrs. Coulter endeavored to recollect if she had ever heard of the Rosses having relations in that quarter. Mr. Foreman said nothing, but, with that keen lawyer eye of his, darted into the secret errand at once, and already sympathized with the failure and disappointment, which he felt sure would follow.

Anne's farewells were over—all but one—the day before leaving Merkland, she went up to the mill to say good-by to little Lilie. She found Mrs. Melder in ecstasies of wonder and admiration, holding up her hands, and crying, "Bless me!" as she unfolded one by one the contents of a box which stood upon the table. They consisted of little garments beautifully made—a profusion of them. Lilie herself was luxuriating over a splendid picture-book, after viewing with a burst of childish delight the pretty little silk frock which Mrs. Melder, in the pride of her heart, was already thinking would make so great a sensation when it appeared first in their seat in the front gallery (alias the mid loft) of Portoran kirk. Nothing less than a mother's hand could have packed that wonderful box; its gay little muslin frocks, which Mrs. Melder "had never seen the like of, for fineness," its inner garments of beautiful linen, its bright silken sashes, its story books, resplendent in their gilded bindings, its parcels of sweetmeats and toys. Mrs. Melder was overwhelmed—the grandeur and wealth of her little charge fairly took away her breath.

"And now when she's won to an easier speech, Miss Anne," said the good woman aside. "She calls me nurse—what think ye! it's a wonderful bairn—and ye'll hear her say lang words sometimes, that I'm sure she never learned frae me; it's my thought, Miss Anne, that the bairn kent the English tongue afore she came here, and had either forgotten't, or—atweel ane disna ken what to think; but this while she's ta'en to speaking about her mamma. It's a wonder to me that ony mother could hae the heart to part wi' her."

"See," cried Lilie, springing to Anne's side, "look what bonnie things," and she precipitated a shoal of little books upon Anne's knee.

"They are very pretty, Lilie," said Anne. "Who sent you all these?"

The child looked at her gravely. "It would be mamma—it was sure to be mamma."

"Where is mamma?" asked Anne.

"Far away yonder—over the big water—but she aye minds Lilie."

"And why did you come away from mamma, Lilie?" said Anne.

The child began to cry. "Lilie ill, ill—like to die. Oh! if you had seen my mamma greeting." And throwing herself down on the ground, Lilie fell into one of her passionate bursts of grief.

"But yon wasna your mamma that brought ye here, my lamb?" said Mrs. Melder.

Lilie continued to weep—too bitterly to give any answer.

Anne turned over the books—in the blank leaf of one of them a name was written in a boyish hand— "Lilia Santa Clara." By-and-by the child's grief moderated, and, taking up her books again, she ran to the mill to show them to Robert.

"Lilia Santa Clara," it gave no clue to the child's origin.

"Haill three names!" said Mrs. Melder, "if ane only kent what her father's name was; the leddy that brought her here said only 'Lilias,' and I dinna mind if I askit the last ane in my flutter—and bonnie outlandish names they are; 'Lilia Santa Clara'—to think of a wean wi' a' thae grand names putting Melder at the hinder end!—it's out of the question."

"Santa Clara may be the surname, Mrs. Melder," said Anne, smiling at the conjunction.

"Eh! think ye so, Miss Anne? I never heard of folk having first names for their surname; though to be sure they do ca' the English flunky that has the confectionary shop in Portoran, Thomas. Well, it may be sae."

"Does she call herself by this name?" asked Anne.

"Ay, I have heard the words mony a time; and sae far as I can guess, Miss Anne, she maun hae been sent to yon lady frae some foreign pairt. Eh, bless me! there maun be some shame and reproach past the common, afore they sent away a bairn like yon."

Jacky Morison was in a state of intense and still excitement—the fire had reached a white heat before they left Merkland. Barbara Genty, Mrs. Ross's favored maid, cast envious looks at her as she sat perched in the back seat of the gig, which was to convey them to Portoran. Old Esther Fleming, who stood without the gate to watch Miss Anne's departure, regarded Jacky dubiously, as if doubting her fitness for her important post. Jacky rose heroically to the emergency. Her faithfulness, her discretion, her true and loyal service, should be beyond all question when they returned.

From her earliest recollection, Anne Ross had been Jacky's pattern and presiding excellence, less awful and nearer herself than Mrs. Catherine—and of all kinds of disinterested and unselfish devotion, there are few so chivalrous as the enthusiastic and loving service of a girl, to the grown woman who condescends to notice and protect her.

When the coach arrived in Edinburgh, Anne saw from its window little Alice Aytoun's fair face looking for her anxiously. James and Alice were waiting to take her home. Anne had purposed spending the short time she should remain in Edinburgh, in the house of an old companion and former schoolfellow; but Alice clung and pleaded, there was no denying her—so Anne suffered herself to be guided to Mrs. Aytoun's quiet little house.

Mrs. Aytoun received her with grave kindness; the affectionate dependence which Alice had upon the stronger character of Anne, the good report which James had given of her, and even her present undertaking, out of the way and unusual though it was, had prepossessed Mrs. Aytoun in her favor. And Norman—the neglected wife remembered him too, so delicately kind, so generous, so reverent of her weakness long ago, when her husband and he were friends; and though she delivered no judgment in his favor, her heart yet went forth in full sympathy with the brave sister, who was so resolute in her belief of his innocence, so eager to labor for its proof. Mrs. Aytoun's God-speed was music to the heart of Anne.

And Alice, very tremulously joyful, clung about her all night long—now sitting on the stool at her feet, her fair curls drooping on Anne's knee—now leaning on her chair—now seated by her side, clasping her hand. James, too, with brotherly confidence and kindness, advised with her about her plans and future proceedings. Anne felt the atmosphere brighten. Surely these were good omens.

In the meantime, Jacky, we regret to say, had been suffering a good deal from disappointment; it was not from her first glimpse of Edinburgh, but it was from the house in Edinburgh, which was specially honored as being the dwelling of "Miss Alice." Jacky had been struck with awe and admiration as she glanced at it from without. The great "land" looked very stately, and spacious, and commanding, though it did immediately front a street, and had neither grounds nor trees surrounding it—but when the immense house dwindled into a single flat, of which she could count all the rooms at a glance, Jacky felt the disappointment sadly. Then she was taken into the small bright kitchen, where Mrs. Aytoun's stout woman-servant, the only domestic of the household, was preparing tea for the travellers. Jacky was scarcely prepared for this. It might have been difficult, we fancy, for many persons more experienced than Jacky, to ascertain what claim to respect or honor, a young Scottish lawyer, with very little practice as yet, whose house consisted of one flat only, and the wants of whose establishment one woman-servant could supply—could possibly have.

But James Aytoun had not only an excellent claim to respect and honor, but actually received it. It was not any empty pride either which led him to sign himself James Aytoun, of Aytoun. Had it not been for the reckless and extravagant father, whose debts had so hopelessly entangled his inheritance, the territorial designation would have represented many fair acres—a long-descended patrimony. As it was, with only a desolate mansion-house, in a southern county, and some bleak lands about it, James Aytoun, of Aytoun, was still received and honored as a gentleman of good family and blood—neither by descent, education, nor breeding beneath any family in Scotland.

It is but a narrow spirit which endeavors to sneer at a distinction like this, and call it the pride of poverty. James Aytoun belonged to that well-nurtured, manly class, whose hereditary honor and good fame belong to the nation, and whose frank dignity of mind and tone are as far removed as mental loftiness can be from that vulgar and arrogant thing, which mean men call pride.

Jacky was reconciling herself to the little Edinburgh kitchen, and had already entered into conversation with Tibbie, when little Bessie arrived from her mother's humble house in an adjacent back street, to renew her acquaintance with her Strathoran friend.—Jacky had many messages to deliver from Johnnie Halflin, which Bessie received with a due amount of blushing laughter.

"And, Oh, Jacky! how will they ever do wanting you at the Tower?"

Jacky did not apprehend the covert wit—did not even perceive that the rosy little Edinburgh-bred girl, was about to condescend to, and patronise, the awkward rustic one.

"They'll only miss me, for a while, at first—and then maybe, we'll no be long."

"Is't Miss Ross that's with you?" asked Bessie.

"I'm with Miss Ross," said Jacky, quickly "Miss Anne chose me of her own will—after I askit her—and so did Miss Falconer."

"Eh! isna she an awfu' funny lady, yon Miss Falconer?"

"Funny!" Jacky was indignantly astonished. "I dinna ken what ye ca' funny, Bessie. She's like—"

"She's no like ither folk," said Bessie.

"It's you that doesna ken. She's like—"

"Wha is she like, Jacky?"

"She's like Belphoebe," muttered Jacky, hastily. "But ye dinna ken wha she was—and she's a lady, for a' that she does strange thing whiles."

"Is that the lady that throosh the gentleman that was gaun to be uncivil to our Miss Alice?" interposed Tibbie.

"Yes," said Bessie laughing. Little Bessie was not above the vanity of being thought to know these north country magnates.—"And on New-year's night, when all the ladies were at the Tower, (ye mind, Jacky?) Miss Falconer gied me a shilling a' to mysel, for bringing her napkin to her, that she had left in Miss Alice's dressing-room—and nippit my lug, and tell't me to take care o' Miss Alice—she ca'ed her my little mistress. Isna she an awful height herself?"

"She's no so tall as Mrs. Catherine," said Jacky.

"Eh, Jacky! Miss Alice didna come up to her shouther, and she's a haill head higher than Miss Ross."

Jacky did not choose to answer: though why there should seem any slight to Marjory, in an exaggeration of her stature, we cannot tell. Without doubt, Belphoebe was to the full as tall as she.

"Do you ken that Merkland's been in Edinburgh?" asked Bessie. In Strathoran she had called Lewis, Mr. Ross; now she was bent on impressing Tibbie with a deep sense of her own familiarity with these great people. "Eh, Jacky, do you mind what Johnnie Halflin used to say about Merkland?"

Jacky had a high sense of honor. She made an elfin face at her talkative companion, and remained prudently silent.

"What did he say?" asked Tibbie.

"Ou naithing. Jacky and me kens."

"An he said onything ill, I redd him to keep out o' the power o' my ten talents. He's a young blackguard, like maist feck of his kind, I'll warrant—idle serving callants, wi' nought to do in this world, but claver about their betters, wi' light-headed gilpies, like yoursel. I wad just like to ken what he said!"

"It was naething ill," said Jacky.

"Oh, he'll be a lad to some o' ye, nae doubt—set ye up! But I can tell ye, he had better no come here to say an ill word o' young Mr. Ross."

"Miss Anne's Mr. Lewis's sister," said Jacky, decisively.—"Johnnie dauredna say a word ill o' him—only that he was—"

Bessie laughed—she had no honorable scruples, but maliciously refrained from helping Jacky out.

"Only about Miss Alice and him."

"Weel ye're a queer lassie," said Mrs. Aytoun's maid. "Could ye no have tell't me that at first?"

Bessie laughed again.

"And, Jacky, is the wee fairy lady aye at the Mill yet?"

"Wha's that?" cried the curious Tibbie.

"Oh, it's a wee bairn that the fairies sent to Strathoran. She was a' dressed in green silk, and had wings like Miss Alice's white veil, and was riding on a pony as white as snaw; and the miller's wife took her in, and her wings took lowe at the fire, and she would have been a' burned, if Miss Ross hadna saved her—and Johnnie Halflin saw her wi' his ain e'en—and they say she's some kin to Jacky."

Jacky repelled the insult with immense disdain.

"If had Johnnie Halflin here, I would douk him in the Oran."

"Ye might douk him in the water o' Leith, Jacky," said Bessie, laughing; "but the Oran's no here, mind."

Jacky was indignantly silent.

"And wha is she?" inquired Tibbie.

"She's a little girl," said Jacky, with some dignity, "a very bonnie wee foreign lady; and Mrs. Melder keeps her at the Mill, and she speaks in a strange tongue, and sings sangs—low, sweet, floating sangs—ye never heard the like of them, and her name is Lilie."

"Lilie what?"

"I cinna ken. She says her name is Lilia Santa Clara, but neabody kens whether that's her last name or no."

"Losh!" exclaimed Tibbie, "will she be canny, after a'?"

"Canny!—you should look nearer yoursel," said Bessie, with laughing malice.

"Never heed her," said Tibbie. "Sit into the table, and take your tea. She's a light-headed fuil—and ye can tell Johnnie Halflin that frae me."

"Is Miss Anne gaun to bide in Edinburgh?" inquired Bessie, as they seated themselves at Tibbie's clean, small table.

"No—she's gaun to the sea-side."

"Eh, Jacky, where? we'll come out and see ye."

"I cinna mind the name of the place," said Jacky, "but it's on the sea-side."

"And what's Miss Anne gaun to do?"

Jacky paused to deliberate. "She's no gaun to do onything.—She's just gaun to please hersel."

"Ay," said the inquisitive Bessie, "but what is't for?"

"It's maybe for something good," said Jacky, quickly, "for that's aye Miss Anne's way; but she wasna gaun to tell me."

"But what do you think it is, Jacky?" persisted Bessie, "ane can aye gie a guess—is she gaun to be married?"

"No!" exclaimed Jacky indignantly, "Married! It's because ye dinna ken Miss Anne."

"Miss Anne's just like ither folk," was the laughing response; "and there's nae ill in being married."

"Lassie, there'll be news o' you, if you're no a' the better hadden in," cried Tibbie. "Set ye up wi' your lads and your marryings! Maybe the young lady's delicate, or she'll hae friends at the sea-side."

To which more delicate fishing interrogatories, Jacky, who knew that Anne was neither delicate nor had any friend at the sea-side, prudently refrained from making any answer.

The next day, Anne, accompanied by Mrs. Aytoun and Alice, set out for Aberford on a search for lodgings. Mrs. Aytoun had a friend, a regular frequenter of all places of general resort, whose list of sea-bathing quarters was almost a perfect one, and fortified by the results of her experience, they departed upon their quest, leaving Jacky in Bessie's care behind them, to dream at her leisure over that wonderful Edinburgh, whose stately olden beauty the strange girl, after her own fashion, could appreciate so well.

Anne observed, with regret and sympathy, the gloom of silence that fell over the kind mother by her side, as they approached their destination. She observed the long, sad glances thrown through the windows of the coach at the country road, known long ago, when Mrs. Aytoun was not a widow. There were no other passengers to restrain their conversation, and when they were very near the village, Mrs. Aytoun pointed to a house, surrounded with wood, and standing at a considerable distance from the road. "Yonder, Alice, look—you were born there."

Alice looked eagerly out. "You liked this place better than Aytoun, mother? Aytoun must have been very gloomy always."

"Aytoun was a larger house than we needed, Alice—you have heard me say so—and I was in very delicate health then. I was never well while—" your father lived, Mrs. Aytoun was about to say, but she checked herself hurriedly; not even in so slight a way would she reproach the dead.

The coach stopped—they were in the dull main street of the village. Mrs. Aytoun took out her list—at the head of the column stood "Mrs. Yammer"—the sea-bathing friend had particularly recommended the house, whose mistress bore so distressful a name. It was a short way out of the village, close upon the sea-side; they turned to seek it.

The magnificent Firth lay bright before them, its islands standing out darkly from its bosom, and its sunny glories bounded by the fertile shores and distant hills of the ancient kingdom of Fife. The exuberant wealth of these rich Lothian lands was bursting out around into Spring's blythest green—a sunny April sky overhead, and April air waving in its golden breadths about them everywhere—it was impossible to think of sadness there. The shadow of her old woe floated away from Mrs. Aytoun's unselfish spirit—Alice was so gay, Anne so pleasantly exhilarated, that she could not refuse to rejoice with them.

Mrs. Yammer's house promised well. It was seated upon a gentle elevation—its front, at least, for the elevation made a very abrupt descent, and so procured that the rooms which were on the ground-floor before, should be the second story behind. In front ran the road leading to the country town, beyond there were some brief intervening fields, and then the sands. It was not above ten minutes walk from the immediate shore. At some little distance further on, there stood a house close to the water, standing up, gaunt and tall, from among a few trees. In the bright, living spring-day, it had a spectral, desolate look about it. Anne remarked it with some curiosity as she glanced round; but Mrs. Aytoun had already knocked, and she had not time to look again.

The door was opened by an energetic little servant, who ushered the ladies into an airy, lightsome parlor, with which Alice Aytoun was in ecstasies. One window looked out on the sea—the other, in a corner of the room, had a pleasant view of the fresh green country road, and glimpse of the village of Aberford itself in the distance; the furniture was very tolerable—the whole room particularly clean.

"O, Anne!" exclaimed Alice Aytoun, "I will come to see you every week!"

A little woman bustled into the room. She had on an old silk gown, curiously japanned by long service, and possessing in an uncommon degree the faculty of rustling—a comical, little, quick, merry, eccentric face—some curls which looked exceedingly like bits of twisted wire, covered by a clean cap of embroidered muslin, with a very plain border of well-darned lace. Mrs. Aytoun hesitated. To call this little person "Mrs." anything, was palpably absurd; yet they had asked for Mrs. Yammer.

"It's no me, it's my sister," said the brisk little person before them. "I'm Miss Crankie. Will ye sit down ladies? I am very glad to see you."

Mrs. Aytoun sat down—little Alice concealed her laugh by looking steadfastly down the road, at the distant roofs of Aberford, and Anne took a chair beside her.

"Is't no a grand prospect?" said Miss Crankie, "a' the Firth before us, and the town at our right hand—a young lady that was here last simmer said to Tammie (that's my sister, Mrs. Yammer, her name's Thomasine—we call her Tammie for shortness,) 'If it wasna for breaking the tenth command, I would covert ye your house, Mrs. Yammer,'—and so dry, and free from drafts, and every way guid for an invalid. It's uncommonly weel likit."

"It seems a very nice house," said Mrs. Aytoun. "Are your rooms disengaged, Miss Crankie?"

"For what time was ye wanting them, Mem?" said Miss Crankie. "There's young Mrs. Mavis is to be here in July, and Miss Todd was speaking of bringing ower her brother's bairns in August—but I'm aye fond to oblige a lady—for what time was ye wanting them?"

"This young lady, Miss Ross"—Miss Crankie honored Anne with a queer nod and a smile, which very nearly upset the gravity of Alice, and put Anne's own in jeopardy, "desires to have lodgings in the neighborhood for this month, and, perhaps, May.—What do you think, my dear? will you need them longer?"

"I hope not," said Anne, "but still, it is possible I may."

"Miss Ross requires change of air," said Mrs. Aytoun, faltering and endeavoring to excuse her equivocation, by noticing that Anne did look pale.

"Of scene, rather," said Anne, slightly affected by the same hesitation. It was true, however, if not in the usual sense.

Miss Crankie fixed her odd little black eye upon Anne, nodded, and looked as if she comprehended perfectly.

"Will you be able to accommodate Miss Ross and her servant, Miss Crankie?"

"That will I; there's no better accommodation in the haill Lothians; and, for change of scene, what could heart desire better than that—ay, or that either, young Miss, which is as bonnie a country view (no to be the sea) as can be seen. Will ye look at the bed-room?"

Miss Crankie darted out, leading the way. Mrs. Aytoun, Anne, and Alice followed. The bed-room was immediately behind the parlor, resplendent in all the glory of white covers, and chintz curtains, and with an embowered window looking out upon "the green," which was separated from the kitchen-garden by a thick hedge of sweet-briar. Alice was delighted, and Anne so perfectly satisfied, that Mrs. Aytoun made the bargain. The rooms were taken, together with a little den up stairs for Jacky. Miss Crankie faithfully promised in her own name and Mrs. Yammer's, that the apartments should be ready for Anne's reception next day; and when they had partaken of a frugal refreshment—some very peculiar wine of Miss Crankie's own manufacture, and cake to correspond—they left the house.

The day was so very beautiful, and Alice enjoyed the rare excursion so much, that they prolonged their walk. "Do you think I could walk out from Edinburgh, mother?" said Alice. "I should like so well to come and see Anne often; and, Anne, you will be dull alone."

"But you will laugh at Miss Crankie, Alice," said Anne, smiling, "and so get into her bad graces."

Alice laughed. "Is she not a very strange person?"

"I have no doubt you will find her a kindly body," said Mrs. Aytoun; "But I hope Jacky's sense of the ludicrous is not so keen as her poetic feelings. You must take care of Jacky."

"O, mamma," said Alice, "you don't know what a strange good girl Jacky is. People laugh at her, but she would not hurt any one's feelings."

"You do Jacky justice, Alice," said Anne. "She is a strange good girl—she—"

Anne paused suddenly, breathless and excited. Who was that tall, gaunt woman, walking thoughtfully with bent head and lingering foot step, over the sands? She seemed to have come from the spectral dark house, which Anne had noticed before, looming so drearily over the sunny waters. She raised her eyes as they met—the large, wistful, melancholy eyes fell upon Anne's face. It was the unknown relative of little Lilie—the passenger who, six months ago, had lingered to cast that same searching, woeful look upon the house of Merkland.

Anne was startled and amazed. She thought the stranger seemed disturbed also. Her eyes appeared to dilate and grow keener as she looked earnestly at Anne, and then passed on.

"Do you know that person?" said Mrs. Aytoun, wonderingly.

Anne turned to look after her; instead of her former slow pace, her steps were now nervously quick and unsteady. Surely some unknown emotion strong and powerful, had risen in the stranger's breast from this meeting. Anne answered Mrs. Aytoun with an effort. "I do not know her—but I have seen her before—I met her once in Strathoran."

They went on. Anne's mind was engrossed—she could not, as before, take part in the gay conversation of Alice. Mrs. Aytoun perceived her gravity. After some time, she asked again: "Do you know who she is? I see you are interested in her."

"I do not know her at all," said Anne. "You will think me very foolish, Mrs. Aytoun, it is her look—her eyes—she has a very remarkable face."

"Probably she lives here," said Mrs. Aytoun. "Let us look at this house."

The house was no less spectral and gaunt, when they were near it, than at a distance. Many of the windows were closed—the large garden seemed perfectly neglected—only some pale spring flowers bloomed in front of a low projecting window, where there seemed to linger some remnants of cultivation. "It is a mysterious looking house," said Mrs. Aytoun; "she may keep it perhaps—but there certainly can be no family living here."

By-and-by they returned to Edinburgh—where Anne spent the remainder of the day in making some necessary calls. She spoke as little as possible of her intention of remaining in Aberford—those ordinary questions were so difficult to answer.

And who was this melancholy woman who had brought little Lilie to Strathoran? Could she have any connection with Norman's history, or was it only the prevailing tone of Anne's mind and thoughts that threw its fantastic coloring on every object she looked upon?

CHAPTER XXII

Upon the next day, Anne, accompanied by Jacky, left Edinburgh finally for her Aberford lodgings. She felt the isolation strangely at first: being alone in her own room, and being alone in the parlor of Mrs. Yammer's house, were two very different things. She seated herself by the window as these long afternoon hours wore on. Jacky sat at the other end of the room, already engaged on some one of the numberless linen articles, which had been provided by her prudent mother, to keep her occupied. Jacky had already cast several longing glances at the little shelf between the windows, which contained the books of Mrs. Yammer's household, but the awe of Anne's presence was upon her; she sewed and dreamed in silence.

The dark spectral house by the waterside—the melancholy woman who had taken Lilie to Strathoran—Anne's mind was full of these. Now and then a chance passenger upon the high road crossed before her;

once or twice she had seen a solitary figure on the sands. None of these bore the same look. The steady pace of country business, and the meditative one of country leisure she could notice—nowhere the slow lingering heavy footsteps, the wistful melancholy face which distinguished the one individual, whom that fantastic spirit of imagination had already associated with Norman's fate.

Anne had decided upon beginning her inquiries on the next day. She hastily bethought herself now, of a mode of making this evening of some service in her search; and turning to Jacky, bade her ask Miss Crankie and Mrs. Yammer to take tea with her.—Jacky with some hesitation obeyed—she thought it was letting down Miss Anne's dignity. Miss Anne herself thought it was rather disagreeable and unpleasant: nevertheless, it might be of use, and she was content to endure it.

Miss Crankie had a turban, terrible to behold, made of black net, with what looked like spangles of yellow paint upon it, which she wore on solemn occasions. In honor of her new lodger, she donned it to-night. Jacky arranged the tea in almost sulky silence. At the appointed hour, Miss Crankie and her sister sailed solemnly in.

It was the merest fiction to call this pleasant house the property of Mrs. Yammer, as all who were favored with any glimpse into its domestic arrangements could easily perceive. Mrs. Yammer was a woeful, patient, resigned woman, very meekly submitting to the absolute dominion of "Johann," saved for a feeble murmuring of her own complaints, the most voiceless and passive of weak-minded sisters. Miss Johann Crankie was very kind to the woeful widow, who hung upon her active hands so helplessly. She shut her ears to Mrs. Yammer's countless aches and palpitations, as long as it was practicable— when she could no longer avoid hearing them, she administered bitter physic, and mustard plasters; a discipline which was generally successful in frightening away the distempers for some time.

Mrs. Yammer, in a much-suffering plaintive voice, immediately began to tell Anne of the palpitations of her heart. Miss Crankie fidgeted on her seat, shooting odd glances at Jacky, and intelligent ones of ludicrous pity at Anne, who endured Mrs. Yammer's enumeration of troubles as patiently as was possible. The tea was a fortunate diversion.

"What is the name of that house on the waterside, Miss Crankie?" asked Anne.

"That's Schole, Miss Ross," said Miss Crankie, with the air of a person who introduces a notability. "You will have heard of it before, no doubt? It came into the possession of the present Laird, when he was in his cradle, puir bairn, and his light-headed gowk of a mother has him away, bringing him up in England.—She's English hersel: maybe ye might ca' that an excuse. I say its a downright imposition and shame to tak callants away to a strange country to get their breeding, when a'body kens there's no the like o' us for learning in a' the world and Fife?"

"And does the proprietor of the house live in it now?" said Anne.

"Bless me, no—the Laird's but a callant yet. Tammie, woman, what year was't that auld Schole died?"

"It was afore I was married," said Mrs. Yammer, dolefully.—"I was a lang tangle of a lassie then, Miss Ross; and I mind o' rinning out without my bonnet, and wi' bare shoulders, and standing by the roadside, to see the funeral gang by. I have never been free o' rheumatism since that day—whiles in my head—whiles in my arm—whiles—"

"Miss Ross will hear a' round o' them afore she gangs away, Tammie," said Miss Crankie, impatiently, "or else it'll be a wonderful year. It's maybe fifteen or sixteen years ago; and the widow and the bairn were off to England in the first month. Ye may tak my word for't, there wasna muckle grief, though there was crape frae head to fit of her. I mind the funeral as weel as if it had passed this morning—folk pretending they were honoring the dead, that would scarce have spoken a word to him when he was a living man. He was an old, penurious nasty body, that bought a young wife wi' his filthy siller. Ye mind him, Tammie?"

"Mind him!" said the martyr Tammie, pathetically, "ay, I have guid reason to mind him. Was I no confined to my bed, haill six weeks after that weary funeral wi' the ticdouleureux? the tae cheek swelled, and the tither cheek blistered. I ken naebody, Johann, that has guid reason to mind him as me."

"Weel, weel," said Miss Crankie, "it was a strong plaister of guid mustard that cured ye. It's a comfort that ane needs nae advice to prepare that—its baith easy made and effectual."

Mrs. Yammer was cowed into silence. Miss Crankie, with a triumphant chuckle, went on: "And since then there's been no word of them, Miss Ross, except an intimation in the newspapers, that the light-headed fuil of a woman had married again. Pity the poor bairn that has gotten a stepfather over him, for bye being keeped out of the knowledge o' his ain land. I was ance in England mysel. There's no an article in't but flat fields, and dead water, and dreary lines o' hedges. Ye may gang frae the tae end to the tither (a' but the north part, and its maistly our ain,) and never ken ye have made a mile's progress—its a' the same thing ower again—and sleek cattle, beasts and men, that ken about naething in this world but eating and drinking. To think of a callant being keeped there, out of the knowledge of his ain country, and it a country like this!"

"It is a great pity, certainly," said Anne, smiling.

"Pity! it's a downright wrong and injury to the lad—there's nae saying if his mind will ever get the better o't."

"And is the house empty?" said Anne; "does no one live in it?"

"Naebody that belangs to the house—but there are folk in't.—There's a brother and a sister o' them, and they're far frae common folk."

"Is the sister tall and thin—with large, dark, melancholy eyes?" said Anne, anxiously.

"Ay, Miss Ross," said Miss Crankie, casting a sharp inquisitive look at Anne; "where hae ye fa'en in with her? it's no often she has ony commerce with strangers."

"I met her on the sands," said Anne, suppressing her agitation with an effort; "and was very much struck by her look."

"I dinna wonder at that—she never was just like ither folk; and since her sister died—puir Kirstin!"

"Have they a story then?" said Anne; she was trembling with interest and impatience—she could scarcely contain herself to ask the question.

"Ay, nae doubt, ye'll be fond of stories, Miss Ross? the most of you young ladies are."

"I do feel very much interested in that singular melancholy woman," said Anne, tremulously.

Miss Crankie examined her face with an odd magpie-like curiosity. Anne smiled in spite of herself. The strange little head nodded, and Miss Crankie began:

"Ye see, Kirstin and me were at the schule thegither. Ye think Kirstin's younger-like than me? Ay, so she is. I was dux of the class and reading in the Bible, when Kirstin began wi' the question book; but we were at the schule thegither for a' that—there's maybe six or seven years between us. There were three of a family of them; their father had been a doctor—a wild, reckless, dissipated man, like what ower mony were, and the family was puir. I used to take them pieces when they were wee bairns—ye mind, Tammie?"

"Ay," said the doleful Tammie, "ye see Johann has a pleasure in minding thae times, Miss Ross. It's different wi'a puir frail widow woman like me; the last year I was at the schule I was never dune wi' the toothache."

"Kirstin was the auldest," said Miss Crankie, turning her back impatiently upon her sister, "and Patrick was next to her, and there was as bonnie a bit lassie as ever you saw, Miss Ross, that was the youngest of the three—she wasna like the young lady that was here yesterday—she was darker and mair womanlike; but eh! she was bonnie.

"They had nae mother—Kirstin was like the mother of them. We used to laugh at her, when she was a wean of maybe twelve hersel, guiding the other twa like as if they had been her ain bairns; she was aye quiet and thoughtful. I was an uncommon grand hand at the bools mysel, and could throw the ba' as far as Robbie King the heckler—ye mind, Tammie?"

"Ye threw't on my head yince and broke the skin," said the disconsolate invalid. "Eh, Miss Ross, the sore headaches I was trysted wi' when I was a bairn!"

"I am saying there were three of them," interrupted Miss Crankie. "They had some bit annuity that keepit them scrimply, and by guid fortune the father died when Kirstin was about seventeen; so how she guided the siller I canna tell, or if there was a blessing on't like the widow's cruise that never toomed; but she keepit hersel and her little sister decent, and sent Patrick to the college wi' the rest. They had a cottage, and a guid big garden—she used to be aye working in the garden hersel. I believe they lived on greens and taties a' the week, and never had fleshmeat in the house but on the Sabbath-day, when Patrick was at hame. Mind, I'm only saying I think that, for they were aye decently put on, and made a puir mouth to nobody.

"Patrick was serving his time to be a doctor. He was dune wi' his studies, and was biding at hame for a rest, when a young gentleman that was heir of an auld property, on the ither side of Aberford, came into his fortune. Ye'll maybe have heard of him, Miss Ross—the poor, misguided, unhappy young lad—they ca'ed him Mr. Rutherford, of Redheugh."

Anne could hardly restrain an involuntary start; she answered, as calmly as she could:

"I have heard the name."

"Ay, nae doubt—mony mair folk have heard his name than had ony occasion; it was his ain fault to be sure, but he was just a' the mair to be pitied for that."

"I was aye chief wi' Kirstin. I liked her—maybe she didna dislike me. I've weeded her flowers to her mony a time. I was throughither whiles in my young days, Miss Ross—no very, but gey. I yince loupit from the top of our garden wa' wi' her wee sister in my arms—I had near gotten a lilt with it, for I twisted my ancle—and that would have been a misfortune."

"Ye trampit on my fit—it's never been right since," said Mrs. Yammer; "ye never were out o' mischief."

Miss Crankie gave a sidelong look up to Anne, with her odd, merry, little black eyes, and laughed; she took the accusation as a compliment.

"Weel, but that's no my story. Ye see, Miss Ross, they were never like ither folk—there was aye something about them—I canna describe it. Mrs. Clippie, the Captain's wife, was genteeler than them— to tell the truth we were genteeler oursels; but for a' that, there was just something—I never could ken what it was. They keepit no company, but a' the lads were daft about Marion."

"What Marion?" exclaimed Anne, eagerly.

"Oh, just Marion Lillie, Kirstin's sister."

"Marion Lillie!" a wild thrill of hope, and fear, and wonder shot through Anne's frame. What could that strange conjunction of names portend?

"So ye see, the young gentleman, Mr. Rutherford, of Redheugh, came to the countryside—and Kirstin's house is near his gate, and so he behoved to see the bonnie face at the window. It wasna like he could miss it.

"Before lang he had gotten very chief wi' the haill family—they didna tak it as ony honor—they were just as if they thought themsels the young Laird's equals; but they were awfu' fond o' him. I have seen Patrick's face flush like fire if onybody minted a slighting word of young Redheugh—no that it was often done, for there was never a man better likit—and Kirstin herself treated him like anither brother, and for Marion—weel, she was but a lassie; but the Laird and her were just like the light of ilk ither's e'en.

"Ye may think, Miss Ross, there was plenty said about it in the countryside. Rich folk said it wasna right, and puir folk said it wasna right; but Kirstin guarded her young sister so, that naebody daured mint a word of ill—it was only spite and ill-nature.

"Maybe, Miss Ross, your maid will carry ben the tray? or I can cry upon Sarah."

Miss Crankie lifted up her voice and called at its loudest pitch for her handmaiden. Sarah entered, and cleared away the tea equipage with Jacky's tardy assistance. Jacky was by no means pleased to find her attendance no longer necessary; she had managed to hear a good deal of the story, and thirsted anxiously for its conclusion.

"Bring me my basket, Sarah," said Miss Crankie. "Miss Ross, ye'll excuse me if I take my work. I have no will to be idle—it's an even down punishment to me."

Mrs. Yammer crossed her hands languidly upon her lap and sighed. Sarah returned, bearing a capacious work-basket, from which Miss Crankie took a white cotton stocking, in which were various promising holes. "If ye want onything of this kind done, I'll be very glad, Miss Ross—I'm a special guid hand."

Anne thanked her.

"But your'e wearying for the end of my story, I see," said Miss Crankie, "just let me get my needle threaded."

The needle was threaded—the stocking was drawn upon Miss Crankie's arm—the black turban nodded in good-humored indication of having settled itself comfortably—and the story was resumed.

"About that time, when young Redheugh was at his very chiefest with the Lillies, and folk said he was going to be married upon Marion, a gentleman came to stay here awhile for the benefit of the sea-side. His wife was a bit delicate young thing—they said he wasna ower guid to her. They lived on the other side of the town, and their name was Aytoun. Mr. Rutherford and him had gotten acquaint in Edinburgh, and for awhile they were great cronies. Patrick Lillie could not bide this stranger gentleman—what for I dinna ken—but folk said Redheugh and him had some bit tifft of an outcast about him; onyway it made no difference in their friendship.

"But one July morning, Miss Ross, we were a' startled maist out of our senses: there was an awfu' story got up of a dead man being found by the waterside, just on the skirts of yon muckle wood that runs down close by the sea, and who should this be but the stranger gentleman, Mr. Aytoun. Somebody had shot him like a coward frae behind, and when they looked among the bushes, lo! there was a gun lying, and whose name do you think was on't? just Mr. Rutherford's, of Redheugh.

"The haill country was in a fever—the like of that ye ken was a disgrace to us a'—and it was in everybody's mouth. The first body I thought of was Marion Lillie; the day before she had gone into Edinburgh—folk said it was to get her wedding dress. Eh, puir lassie! was that no a awfu' story for a bride to hear?

"They gaed to apprehend Mr. Rutherford the same night, but he had fled, and was away before they got to Redheugh, no man kent whither. I met Christian that day; though I ca' her Kirstin speaking to you, I say aye Miss Lillie to herself. In the one day that the murder was done she had gotten yon look. It feared me when I saw it. Her e'en were travelling far away, as if she could see to ony distance, but had nae vision for things at hand. 'Eh, Miss Lillie!' I said to her, 'isna this an awfu' thing; wha could have thought it of young Redheugh!'

"'I will never believe it!' she said, in a wild away: 'he is not guilty. I will never believe it!'

"'And Miss Marion,' said I, 'bless me, it will break the puir lassie's heart.'

"'I will not let her come home,' said Kirstin, 'I will send her to the west country to my father's friends. She must not come home.'

"She would never say before that there was onything between her sister and young Redheugh—now she never tried to deny it, her heart was ower full.

"Weel, Miss Ross, the miserable young man had gotten away in a foreign ship, and they hadna been at sea aboon a week when she foundered, and a' hands were lost; and there was an end of his crime and his punishment—they were baith buried in the sea.

"But no the misery of them—the puir lassie was taen away somegate about Glasgow, but the news came to her ears there. What could ye think, Miss Ross? It wasna like a common death—there was nae hope in it, either for this world or the next. It crushed her, as the hail crushes flowers. Within a fortnight after that, bonnie Marion Lillie was in her grave.

"Patrick was taen ill of a fever—they say the angry words he had spoken about Mr. Aytoun to young Redheugh lay heavy on his mind. Kirstin had to nurse him night and day—she couldna even leave him to see Marion buried. She died, and was laid in her grave among strangers. When Patrick was able to leave his bed, the two went west to see the grave—that was all that remained of their bonnie sister Marion.

"Since that time they have lived sorrowful and solitary, keeping company with naebody; the sore stroke has crushed them baith. Patrick never sought his doctor's licence, nor tried to get a single patient. He has been ever since a broken-down, weak, invalid man."

"He had a frail constitution like my ain," said Mrs. Yammer, "and Johann maun aye have some great misfortune to account for it, when it's naething but weakness. Eh, Miss Ross, if ye only kent the trouble it is to a puir frail creature like me to make any exertion."

Miss Crankie twisted her strange little figure impatiently:

"When auld Schole died, Christian and Patrick flitted into the house, and let their ain; they couldna bide it after that. It's a bit bonnie wee place, maybe twa miles on the ither side of Aberford; and Redheugh is maybe a quarter o' a mile nearer. They say the King gets the lands when ony man does a crime like that; it's what they ca' confiscate. Redheugh has been confiscate before now. The auld Rutherfords were Covenanters langsyne, and lost their inheritance some time in the eight-and-twenty years—but that was in a guid cause. Ony way, this Mr. Rutherford was the last of his name: if there had been ony heir, I kenna whether he could have gotten Redheugh or no, but it's a mercy the race is clean gane, and there is none living to bear the reproach."

Anne's heart beat loudly against her breast; she remained to represent the fallen house of Rutherford—she was the heir—the reproach: and the suffering must be her's as well as Norman's.

"And was there no doubt?" she asked, "was no one else suspected?"

"Bless me, no; wha in our quiet countryside would lift a hand against a man's life? If he hadna done it, he wadna have fled away; and if Kirstin had ony certainty that he hadna done it, do you think she could have bidden still? Na, I ken Kirstin Lillie better. Patrick was aye a weakly lad, ower gentle for the like of that, but Kirstin could never have sitten down in idleset if there had been ony hope. Mony a heart was wae for him at the time, but the story has blawn by now; few folk think of it. I wadna have tell't ye, Miss Ross, if ye hadna noticed Kirstin first yoursel—but ye'll no mention it again."

"I certainly will not do anything that could hurt Miss Lillie's feelings," said Anne.

"Ye see, she's half housekeeper of Schole the now; she pays nae rent, or if there's ony, it's just for the name, and the house is sae dismal-looking that naebody seeks to see't. You would think they couldna thole a living face dear them; they gang to the Kirk regular, and whiles ye will see them wandering on the sands; but for visiting onybody, or having onybody visiting them, ye might as weel think of the spirits in heaven having commune with us that are on the earth."

"And that minds me," said Mrs. Yammer, breaking in with a long loud sigh, which the impatient Miss Crankie knew by dire experience was the prelude to a doleful story, "of the awfu' fright I got after my man John Yammer was laid in his grave, that brought on my palpitation. Ye see, Miss Ross, I was sitting my lane, yae eerie night about Martinmas, in my wee parlor that looks out on the green; and Johann, she was away at Aberford, laying in some saut meat for the winter—wasna it saut meat, Johann?"

"Never you mind, Tammie, my woman," said Johann, persuasively. "We're dune wi' saut meat for this year."

"Ay, but it was just to let Miss Ross see the danger of ower muckle thought, and how it brought on my palpitation. Eh woman, Johann, if ye only kent how my puir heart beats whiles, louping in my breast like a living creature!"

And the whole story was inflicted upon Anne—of how Mrs. Yammer, on the aforesaid dreary Martinmas night, fancied she saw the shadow of the umquhile John, gloomily lowering on her parlor wall; of how her heart "played thud and cracked, like as it wad burst," as the shadowy head nodded solemnly, darkening the whole apartment; of how at last Johann returned, and with profane laughter, discovered the ghost to be the shadow of a branch of the old elm without, some bare twigs upon the extremity of which were fashioned into the likeness of an exceeding retrousee nose, "the very marrow" of that prominent feature in the face of the late lamented John; of which discovery his mournful relic was but half convinced, and her heart had palpitated since, "sometimes less, and sometimes mair, but I've never been quit o't for a week at a time."

The infliction terminated at last, Miss Crankie carried her sister off when the gloaming began to darken, having sufficient discernment to perceive that Anne's patience had been enough tried for a beginning.

Anne's thoughts were in a maze. She sat down by the window in the soft gloom of the spring night, and looked towards the house, where beat another true and faithful heart which had wept and yearned over Norman—Marion—Marion—was she living or dead? could this Christian Lillie be aware of Norman's existence, and of his innocence? There could not be two betrothed Marions. In the latter part of the story, the countryside must have been deceived. Who so likely to accompany the exile as the sister of this brave woman, who had done the housemother's self-denying duty in her earliest youth? Anne's pulse beat quick, she became greatly agitated; was there then a tie of near connexion between herself and this stranger, whose path she had again crossed? Was Norman's wife Christian's sister? had they an equal stake in the return of the exile?

She could not sit still—cold dew was bursting upon her forehead; she walked from window to window in feverish excitement. Could she dare to ask?—could she venture to make herself known? Alas, she was still no whit advanced in her search for proof of Norman's innocence! If Christian Lillie had possessed any clue, she must, it was certain, have used it before now; and until some advance had been made, these two strangers in their singular kindred would not dare to whisper to one another that Norman lived.

Anne threw herself upon her chair again. And Lilie—who was Lilie? Why was this stranger child brought—of all localities in the world—to the neighbourhood of Merkland? Could it be? could it be? her heart grew sick with feverish hope and anxiety; her mind continued to hover about, and dwell upon this mystery; but she almost forcibly restrained herself from articulate thought upon it—she could not venture yet to entertain the hope.

And Norman! Esther Fleming's story had brought him out clear before her, in the gay light of his generous boyhood.—Graver and more deeply affecting was this. Who might venture to compute the untold agonies of that terrible time of parting—the nervous compulsory strength of the girl-heart that went with him—the stern patience of the maturer one, who above by the sick-bed at home! Grief that must have remained with all its burning sense of wrong, and heavy endurance of an undeserved curse, since ever little Alice Aytoun opened her blue eyes to the light—a lifetime of pain, and fear, and sorrow—too dreadful to look back upon!

And Anne's heart sank when she looked forward—living here, in the immediate spot where the deed was done, with all facility for collecting favorable evidence, and with better knowledge, and a more immediate certainty of Norman's innocence than even Anne herself could have—why had the brother and sister done nothing to remove this stain? She could only account for it by supposing them paralysed with fear—terrified to risk the present security of those so dear to them, for any uncertainty even of complete acquittal—and afraid of making any exertion, lest the eyes of curiosity should be turned upon them.

The Forth lay vast in silvery silence, breathing long sighs along its sands. Opposite swelling soft and full, in the spiritual dimness of the spring night, rose the fair lands of Fife. Still and solemn in its saintly evening rest, lay the beautiful earth everywhere. Only awake and watching, under dusky roofs, and in dim chambers, were the hoping, toiling, wrestling souls of men, nobler and of mightier destiny, than even the beautiful earth.

The next morning, when she entered the sunny little parlor, Anne found Jacky rearranging, according to her own ideas of elegance, the breakfast equipage, which Miss Crankie's energetic little servant had already placed upon the table. Anne smiled, and felt almost uncomfortable, as she observed the solitary cup and saucer on the table—the single plate—the minute teapot.—After all, this living alone, had something very strange in it.

Jacky seemed to think so too: she filled out Anne's cup of tea, and lingered about the back of her chair.

"If ye please, Miss Anne—"

"Well, Jacky?"

"If ye please," said Jacky, hesitating, "do ye ken wha little Miss Lilie is?"

Anne started and turned round in alarm—was this strange, dark maid of her's really an elfin, after all?

"No, Jacky," she said. "Why do you ask?"

"Because—it's no forwardness, Miss Anne," murmured Jacky, hanging down her head.

"I know that, Jacky—because what?"

"Because, Miss Anne," said Jacky, emboldened, "I saw a lady down on the sands. She was standing close by the bushes at yon dark house, and her e'en were travelling ower the water, and her face was white—I will aye mind it—and—"

"And what?"

"It was her that brought little Lilie to the Mill. I saw her once by Oranside at night; and she was on our side of the water; and she was looking across at Merkland."

"Was Lilie with her then, Jacky?"

"No, Miss Anne; but I saw her after, leading Lilie by the hand, and then she was on the Merkland side, where Esther Fleming lives; and she was walking about, canny and soft, as if she wanted to see in."

"And are you sure it is the same lady, Jacky?" said Anne.

"I ken, Miss Anne," said Jacky, eagerly; "because there's no twa faces like yon in a' the world; and, Miss Anne, do ye mind Lilie's e'en?"

"Yes, Jacky."

Anne did recollect them—and how dark and full their liquid depths were!

"Because Lilie's e'en are the very same—only they're no sae woeful—and I kent the lady would be some friend, but Mrs. Melder said it couldna be her mother."

Anne's heart swelled full. Could this little child be as near of kindred to herself as to Christian Lillie? Her mind was overflowing with this. She forgot that Jacky lingered.

"And, if ye please, Miss Anne—"

Anne again turned round to listen.

"She was looking away ower the water, and leaning on the hedge—maybe she lives yonder—and Miss Anne—"

"What is it, Jacky?"

Jacky drew near and spoke very low:

"Do you mind the sang, Miss Anne, that Miss Alice sang on the New-year's night, when Mr. Archibald came home to the Tower?"

Anne started.

"The lady was saying it to hersel very low—the way Lilie sings her strange music."

"What did she say, Jacky?"

"If ye please, Miss Anne, it was a short verse—it was about seeing the stars rise upon the Oran. I can say't a'." And Jacky hung back, and blushed and hesitated.

The connexion became clearer by every word. "The student lad" who wrote this ballad—could it be Patrick Lillie?

"Was it last night you heard this, Jacky?"

"No, Miss Anne, it was this morning very early. I wanted to see the sea," said Jacky, bashfully, "and I saw the sun rise. But I think the lady wasna heeding for the sea. She wasna there at a'. She was in her ain spirit."

"And you are sure you are not mistaken, Jacky?" said Anne.

"Miss Anne!" exclaimed Jacky, "ye would ken yourself, if you saw her. Its just Lilie's e'en—only they are far, far deeper and sadder, and aye searching and travelling, as if something was lost that they bid to find, and were seeking for night and day."

"That they bid to find!" The words roused Anne. "Did you mention this to any one?" she asked.

Jacky looked injured—an imputation on her honor she could not bear.

"I never tell things, Miss Anne. I'm no a talepyet."

"Well, Jacky, remember that I trust you. I have heard that this lady has had great sorrow; and she has some good reason, no doubt, for not keeping Lilie beside her. Mind, you must never mention this to any one—not to Bessie—not even to your mother, when we return. No one knows it, but you and me. I am sure I can trust you, Jacky."

Jacky gave a faithful promise, and went away with secret and proud dignity. She also had entered upon the search—she had begun to co-operate with Anne.

CHAPTER XXIII

Anne had fairly started upon her voyage of discovery. The beginning of it cost her many thoughts. She had half advanced to various peasant wives, whom she saw at cottage doors, screaming to unruly children, or out upon the universal "green," superintending their little bleaching—and had as often shrunk back, in painful timidity, which she blamed herself greatly for, but could not manage to overcome. It was quite different among the well-known cottages of Strathoran, though even with them, Anne would have felt visits of condescension or patronage unspeakably awkward and painful. Now this constitutional shyness must be overcome. Walking along the high road, a considerable way beyond the village of Aberford, she suddenly came upon a desolate mansion-house. The broken gate hung by the merest tag of hinge; the stone pillars were defaced and broken. What had formerly been ornamental grounds before the house, were a jungle of long grass, and uncouth brushwood. Bushes grown into unseemly straggling trees, beneath the shadow of which, thistles and nettles luxuriated, and plumes of unshorn grass waved rank and long, as if in the very triumph of neglect. The house-door hung as insecurely as the gate—the steps were mossy and cracked—the windows entirely shattered, and in some cases the very frames of them broken. Behind, the gardens lay in a like state of desolation. Here and there a cultivated flower, which had been hardy enough to cling to its native soil, marked among wild blossoms, and grass, and weeds, a place where care and culture had once been. Upon a mossed and uneven wall some fruit-trees clung, rich with blossoms: it had been an orchard once. In the midst of another waste and desolate division stood the broken pedestal of a sun-dial; a sloping wilderness ascended from it to the low windows of what seemed once to have been a drawing-room. A spell of neglect was over it all, less terrific than that still horror which a poet of our own time has thrown over his haunted house, but yet in the gay wealth and hopefulness of spring, striking chill and drearily upon the observer's eye. Anne examined it with curious interest; she could suspect what house it was.

A little further on she came upon a cottage of better size and appearance than most, with a well-filled little garden before its door, and knots of old trees about it. It was the house of a "grieve," or farm overseer, a rising man in his humble circle, whose wife aimed at being genteel. She stood in the door, basking in the sun, with her youngest baby in her arms; the good woman had a multitude of babies; the latest dethroned one was tumbling about at her feet. Anne bent over the little gate to ask the name of the forlorn and desolate house she had just past.

"Oh, that's Redheugh," said Mrs. Brock, the grieve's wife.

Anne lingered, and held out her hand to the hardy little urchin scrambling in the garden. Mrs. Brock looked as if she would quite like to enter into conversation:

"Be quiet, Geordie; ye'll dirty the lady's gloves."

"No, no," said Anne, taking the small brown hand into her own. "I am very fond of children, and this is a fine, sturdy little fellow."

"Ye'll be a stranger, I'm thinking?" said Mrs. Brock. "There's few folk in our parish that dinna ken Redheugh."

"Yes," said Anne. "I am quite a stranger; what is the reason it lies so deserted and desolate?"

"Ye'll be come to the sea-side?" pursued Mrs. Brock; "it's no often we have folk out frae Edinburgh sae early in the year. Is't no unco cauld for bathing?"

"I should think it was," said Anne smiling, "but I have never, bathed yet."

"It'll be just for the sea air?" continued Mrs. Brock. "Are ye bideing far frae here, Mem, if yin may ask?"

"I am living a good way on the other side of Aberford," said Anne.

"Oh, and ye have had a lang walk, and it's a warm day. Get out of the road, Geordie; will ye no come in and sit down? ye'll be the better for the rest?"

Mrs. Brock, as we have before said, had an ambition to be genteel. Now Anne Ross with her very plain dress, and quite simple manners, was eminently ladylike, and might be a desirable acquaintance. Anne accepted the invitation, and setting the strong little urchin, whom his mother knocked about with so little delicacy, on his feet, she led him in with her.

Mrs. Brock's parlor was a temple sacred to company, and holidays. Its burnished grate, and narrow mantlepiece, elaborately ornamented with foreign shells; brilliant peacock feathers waved gracefully over the gilded frame of the little square mirror; the carpet was resplendent in all the colors of the rainbow. There were sturdy mahogany chairs, and a capacious haircloth sofa—the two ends of a dining-table stood in the middle of the room, elaborated into the brightest polish—the center piece was placed against the wall, and decorated with a case of stuffed birds. Mrs. Brock paused at the door, and contemplated it all with infinite complacency. It was something to have so grand a place to exhibit to a stranger.

"Take a seat on the sofa, Mem; ye'll be wearied wi' your lang walk. Geordie, ye little sinner, wad ye put your dirty shoon on the guid carpet? Get away wi' ye."

Mrs. Brock bundled the little fellow unceremoniously out, and seated herself opposite her guest.

"You have a fine view," said Anne.

"Is't no beautiful? They tell me there's no a grander sight in the world than just the Firth and Fife. Yonder's the Lomonds, ye ken, and yon muckle hill, even over the water, that's Largo Law. My mother was a Fife woman—I have lived at Colinsbrugh mysel; and we can see baith Inchkeith and the May in a clear day, no to speak o' the Bass. We're uncommonly well situate here; it's a fine house altogether."

"It seems so, indeed," said Anne.

"Ye see the only ill thing about it is, that it's no our ain.—George was uncommon keen to have had the house the bairns were a' born in. He's an awfu' man for his bairns."

"Very natural," said Anne.

"Oh, ay, nae doubt it's natural, but it's no ilka body that has the thought; he wad have gien twa hunder pounds for the house; twa clear hunder—it's no worth that siller, ye ken, but it's just because we've been in't sae lang. But Miss Lillie wadna hear o't; it's no every day she could get an offer like that, and they canna be sae weel off as to throw away twa hunder pounds, ane would think."

"Is this Miss Lillie's house?" said Anne.

"Ay—ye'll ken Miss Lillie it's like?"

"No," said Anne, "I do not know her, but I have heard her name."

"There's bits of conveniences a' through it," said Mrs. Brock, "that had been putten up when they were bideing here themsels; and the garden behint. Miss Lillie beggit George to keep the flowers right, and he takes uncommon pains with them. He's a guid-hearted man, our George; ye'll no often meet wi' the like of him."

"And that house of Redheugh," said Anne; "why is it so neglected and desolate?"

"Eh, bless me!" said Mrs. Brock, "have ye no heard the story?"

"What story?" said Anne.

"Eh, woman!" exclaimed the grieve's wife, forgetting her good manners in astonishment. "Ye maun have been awfu' short time hereabout, if ye havena heard the story of the Laird o' Redheugh."

"I only arrived yesterday," said Anne.

"Weel, it's no ill to tell. The young gentleman that aught it killed a man and was drowned himsel when he was trying to escape: it's just as like the Book o' Jonah as anything out o' the Bible could be. There was a great storm, and the ship he was in sank; he couldna carry the guilt of the pluid over the sea. They say murder wouldna hide if ye could put a' the tokens o't beneath North Berwick Law. It made an awfu' noise in the countryside at the time, but it's no muckle thought o' now, only a'body kens what gars the house lie desolate. Folk say ye may see the gentleman that was killed, and Redheugh himsel in his dreeping claes, like as if he was new come up from the bottom of the sea, fighting and striving in the auld avenue—aye at midnight o' the night it was done—but ye'll no believe the like o' that?"

"No," said Anne vacantly; she did not know what she answered.

"Weel, I never saw onything mysel—but they say the spirit's ill to pacify, that's met wi' a violent death—and I wad just be as weel pleased no to put myself in the way. I have aye an eerie feeling when I pass the gate at night. After a' ye ken, there's naething certain about it in Scripture—maybe the dead can come back, maybe they canna—ane disna ken. I think it's aye best to keep out of the gait."

"It is, no doubt, the most prudent way," said Anne, smiling.

"Ye wad, maybe, like to see the garden, Miss—"

Mrs. Brock was mightily anxious to know who her visitor was.

"Ross," said Anne.

"Weel, Miss Ross, I am sure ye'll be pleased wi' the garden—will ye come this way?"

Anne followed. The garden was in trim order—well kept and gracefully arranged. Spring flowers, with their delicate hopeful fragrance and pale hues, were scattered through the borders. The blossom on the lilac bushes was already budded, and the hawthorn had here and there unfolded its first flowers.

"But the simmer-house, Miss Ross," said Mrs. Brock.

The summer-house was not one of the ordinary tea-garden abominations. It was a knoll of soft turf, the summit of which had been formed into a seat, with a narrow space of level greensward for its footstool. Over it was a light and graceful canopy, with flowering plants more delicate and rare, than are generally seen in cottage gardens, clustering thickly over it, while the foliage of some old trees, growing at the foot of the hillock, made a rich background. From its elevated seat, you could see the slopes of Fife lying fair below the sun, and the gallant Forth between.—Anne stood and gazed round her in silence. She could see the dark trees, and high roof of Redheugh at her other hand; how often might Norman, in his happy years long ago, have stood upon this spot? Yet here it shone in its fresh life and beauty, when all that remained of him, was dishonor and desolation!

But there was in this a solemn, silent hope which struck Anne to the heart. Christian Lillie had entreated, as her tenant said, that these flowers should be carefully tended. Christian Lillie would not part with the house. Was she not looking forward, then, to some future vindication—to some home-coming of chastened joyfulness—to some final light, shedding the radiance of peace upon her evening time?

Anne had to sit down in Mrs. Brock's parlor again, and suffer herself to be refreshed with a glass of gooseberry wine, not quite so delectable as Mrs. Primrose's immortal preparation, before she was permitted to depart. Mrs. Brock had another decanter upon her table, filled with a diabolical compound, strongly medicinal in taste and odor, which she called ginger wine, and which Anne prudently eschewed—and a plate of rich "short-bread," at which little Geordie, tumbling on the mat at the door, cast longing loving looks. Mrs. Brock hoped Miss Ross would come to see her again.

"It's just a nice walk. Ye maun come and tak' a cup o' tea when George is in himsel. He's an uncommon weel-learned man, our George—he could tell ye a' the stories o' the countryside."

Anne had to make a half promise that she would return to avail herself of the stores of George Brock's information, before his admiring wife released her.

She had overcome her repugnance a little—it was a tolerable beginning so far as that went—but how dark, how hopeless seemed the prospect! There was no doubt in that confident expression—no benevolent hope that Norman might be guiltless! She had been told so long before, and had come to Aberford, in the face of that. Yet the repetition of it by so many indifferent strangers discouraged her sadly—her great expectation collapsed. Only a steady conviction in her brother's innocence, a solemn hope of vindication to him, living or dead, upheld her in her further way.

In the evening she wandered out upon the sands. It was a still night, wrapped in the gray folds of a mistier gloaming, than she had before seen sinking over the brilliant Firth. Anne hovered about the enclosure of Schole. The dreary house had a magnetic attraction for her. She stood by the low gate, close to the water, and looked in. The high foliage of the hedge hid her—gate itself was the only loophole in the thick fence, which surrounded the house on all sides. There was light in the low projecting window, which dimly revealed a gloomy room, furnished with book shelves. At a sort of study table, placed in the recess of the window, there sat a man bending over a book. His face was illuminated by the candle beside him. A pale, delicate face it was, telling of a mind nervously susceptible, a spirit answering to every touch, with emotion so intense and fine, as to make the poetic temperament, not a source of strength and mighty impulse, as in hardier natures, but a well-spring of exquisite feebleness— a fountain of pensive blight and beauty. The snowy whiteness of his high, thin temples, the long silky fair hair upon his stooping head, heightened the impression of delicate grace and feebleness. He looked young, but had, in reality, seen nearly forty years of trouble and sorrow. His brow was almost covered by the long, thin white fingers that supported it. He was absorbed in his book.

A strange resemblance to Christian Lillie was in the student's pale and contemplative face. There could be no doubt that he was her invalid brother—and yet how strangely unlike they were!

Anne turned to pursue her walk along the dim sands. A faint ray of moonlight was stealing through the mist, silvering the water, and the long glistening line of its wet shores here and there. In the light, she caught a glimpse of a slow advancing figure. Fit place and time it was, for such a meeting—for the tall dark outline and slow step, could belong to but one person. Anne trembled, and felt her own step falter. They had never yet heard each other's voices, yet were connected by so close a tie—were wandering upon this solitary place, brooding over one great sorrow—perhaps tremulously embracing one solemn hope.

When they met, she faltered some commonplace observation about the night. To her astonishment, Christian Lillie replied at once. It might be that she saw Anne's agitation—it might be that she also longed to know Norman's sister. That she knew her to be so, Anne could not doubt: her melancholy contemplation of Merkland—her evident start and surprise, when they formerly met upon the sands, made that certain.

"Yes," said Christian Lillie, in a voice of singular sadness, "it is a beautiful night."

The words were of the slightest—the tone and manner, the drawing in of that long breath, spoke powerfully. This, then, was her one pleasure—this gentle air of night was the balm of her wearied spirit.

"The mist is clearing away," said Anne, tremulously. "Yonder lights on the Fife shore are clear now—do you see them?"

"Ay, I see them," was the answer. "Cheerful and pleasant they look here. Who knows what weariness and misery—what vain hopes and sick hearts they may be lighting."

"Let us not think so," said Anne, gently. "While we do not know that our hopes are vain we still have pleasure in them."

"I have seen you more than once before," said Christian Lillie. "You are not, or your face is untrue, one to think of vain pleasure at an after-cost of pain. Hopes!—I knew what they were once—I know now what it is to feel the death of them: what think you of the vain toils that folk undergo for a hope? the struggle and the vigils, and the sickness of its deferring? I see light burning yonder through all the watches of the night—what can it be but the fever of some hope that keeps them always shining? I saw yours in your window last night, when everybody near was at rest but myself. What is it that keeps you wakeful but some hope?"

"You know me then—you know what my hope is?" said Anne, eagerly.

"No," said Christian. "Tell it not to me. I have that in me that blights hope—and the next thing after a blighted hope, is a broken heart. It is wonderful—God shield you, from the knowledge—how long a mortal body will hold by life after there is a broken heart within it! I think sometimes that it is only us who know how strong life is—not the hopeful and joyous, but us, who are condemned to bear the burden—us, who drag these days out as a slave drags a chain."

"Do not say so," said Anne. Her companion spoke with the utmost calmness—there was a blank composure about her, which told more powerfully even than her words, the death of hope.—"There can be no life, however sorrowful, that has not an aim—an expectation."

"An aim?—ay, an aim! If you knew what you said you would know what a solemn and sacred thing it is that has stood in my path, these seventeen years, the ending of my travail—an expectation! What think you of looking forward all that time, as your one aim and expectation—almost, God help us, as your hope—for a thing which you knew would rend your very heart, and make your life a desert when it came—what think ye of that? There are more agonies in this world than men dream of in their philosophy."

"Are we not friends?" said Anne. "Have we not an equal share in a great sorrow that is past—I trust and hope in a great joy that is to come? Will you not take my sympathy?—my assistance?"

Christian Lillie shrank, as Anne thought, from her offered hand.

"An equal share—an equal share. God keep you from that—but it becomes you well: turn round to the light, and let me see your face."

She laid her hand on Anne's shoulder, and, turning her round, gazed upon her earnestly.

"Like—and yet unlike," she murmured. "You are the only child of your mother? she left none but you?"

"Except—"

"Hush, what would you say?" said Christian, hurriedly.—"And you would offer me sympathy and help? Alas! that I cannot take it at your, hands. You have opened a fountain in this withered heart, that I thought no hand in this world could touch but one. It is a good deed—you will get a blessing for it—now, fare you well."

"Shall I not see you again?" said Anne.

Christian hesitated.

"I do not know—why should you? you can get nothing but blight and disappointment from me, and yet—for once—you may come to me at night—not to-morrow night, but the next. I will wait for you at the little gate; and now go home and take rest—is it not enough that one should be constantly watching? Fare you well."

Before Anne could answer, the tall, dark, gliding figure was away—moving along with noiseless footstep over the sands to the gate of Schole. She proceeded on herself, in wonder and agitation—how shallow was her concern for Norman in comparison with this; how slight her prospect of success when this earnest woman, whose words had such a tone of power in them, even in the deepness of her grief, declared that in her all hope was dead. It was a blow to all her expectations—nevertheless it did not strike her in that light. Her anticipation of the promised interview, her wonder at what had passed in this, obliterated the discouraging impression. She was too deeply interested in what she had seen and heard, to think of the stamp of hopelessness which these despairing words set on her own exertions. That night she transferred her lights early from her little sitting-room to the bed-chamber behind. That was a small matter, if it gave any satisfaction to the melancholy woman, the light from whose high chamber window she could see reflected on the gleaming water, after Miss Crankie's little household had been long hours at rest.

The next day was a feverish day to Anne, and so was the succeeding one. She took long walks to fill up the tardy time, and made acquaintance with various little sunbrowned rustics, and cottage mothers; but gained from them not the veriest scrap of information about Norman, beyond what she already knew—that he had killed a man, and had been drowned in his flight from justice—that now the property, as they thought, was in the king's hands, "and him having sae muckle," as one honest woman suggested, "he didna ken weel what to do wi't. Walth gars wit wavor—It's a shame to fash him, honest man, wi' mair land that he can make ony use o'—it would have been wiser like to have parted it among the puir folk."

On the afternoon of the day on which she was to see Christian Lillie again, Anne lost herself in the unknown lanes of Aberford. After long wandering she came to the banks of a little inland water, whose quiet, wooded pathway was a great relief to her, after the dust and heat of the roads. She stayed for a few minutes to rest herself; upon one hand lay a wood stretching darkly down as she fancied to the sea. She was standing on its outskirts where the foliage thinned, yet still was abundant enough to shade and darken the narrow water; a little further on, the opposite bank swelled gently upward in fields, cultivated to the streamlet's edge—but the side on which she herself stood, was richly wooded along all its course, and matted with a thick undergrowth of climbing plants and shrubs and windsown seedlings. The path wound at some little distance from the waterside through pleasant groups of trees. Anne paused, hesitating and undecided, not knowing which way to turn. A loud and cheerful whistle sounded behind her, and looking back, she saw a ruddy country lad, of some sixteen or seventeen years, trudging blythely along the pathway; she stopped him to ask the way.

"Ye just gang straight forenent ye," said the lad, "even on, taking the brig at Balwithry, and hauding round by the linn in Mavisshaw. Ye canna weel gang wrang, unless ye take the road that rins along the howe of the brae to the Milton, and it's fickle to ken which o' them is the right yin, if ye're no acquaint."

"I am quite a stranger," said Anne.

"I'm gaun to the Milton mysel," said the youth. "I'll let ye see the way that far, and then set ye on to the road."

Anne thanked him, and walked on briskly with her blythe conductor, who stayed his whistling, and dropped a step or two behind, in honor of the lady. He was very loquacious and communicative.

"I'm gaun hame to see my mother. My father was a hind on the Milton farm, and my mother is aye loot keep the house, now that she's a widow-woman. I've been biding wi' my uncle at Dunbar. He's a shoemaker, and he wanted to bind me to his trade."

"And will you like that?" said Anne.

"Eh no—I wadna stand it; I aye made up my mind to be a ploughman like my father before me; sae my uncle spoke for me to the grieve at Fantasie and I'm hired to gang hame at the term. So I cam the noo to see my mother."

"Have you had a long walk?" said Anne.

"It's twal mile—it was eleven o'clock when I started—I didna ken what hour it is noo. It should be three by the sun." Anne consulted her watch; it was just three; the respect of her guide visibly increased—gold watches were notable things in Aberford.

"I thought yince of starting at night. Eh! if I had been passing in the dark, wadna I hae been frighted to see a leddy thonder."

"Why yonder?" said Anne, "is there anything particular about that place?"

"Eh!" exclaimed the lad, "do ye no ken? there was a man killed at the fit of thon tree."

Anne started. "Who was he?" she asked.

"I dinna mind his name—it's lang, lang ago—but he was a gentleman, and my father was yin 'o the witnesses. Maybe ye'll have seen a muckle house, ower there, a' disjasket and broken down. George Brock, the grieve lives near the gate o't—it's no far off."

"Yes, I have seen it," said Anne.

"Weel, the gentleman that killed him lived there—at least a'body said it was him that did it—I have heard my father speak about him mony a time."

"And what was your father a witness of?" said Anne.

"Oh, he met Redheugh coming out of the wood—only my father aye thought that he bid to be innocent, for he was singing, and smiling, and as blythe as could be."

"And your father thought him innocent?" said Anne eagerly.

"Ay—at least he thought it was awfu' funny, if he had killed the man, that he should be looking sae blythe. A' the folk say there was nae doubt about it, and sae does my mother, but my father was aye in a swither; he thought it couldna be. Here's the Milton, and ower yonder, ye see, like a white line—yon's the road—it's just the stour that makes it white; and if ye turn to the right, and haud even on, ye'll come to the toun."

Anne thanked him, and offered some small acknowledgment, with which the lad, though he took it reluctantly, and with many scruples, went away, whistling more blythely than ever. How little did the youthful rustic imagine the comfort and hope and exhilaration which these thoughtless words of his had revived in his chance companion's heart!

There had been one in this little world, who, in the midst of excitement, and in the face of evidence, and the universal opinion of his fellows, held Norman innocent. Anne thanked God, and took courage—there was yet hope.

She waited nervously for the evening; when the darkness of the full night came stealing on, she glided along the sands to the gate of Schole.

The projecting window was dark; there seemed to be no light in the whole house. She looked over the gate anxiously for Christian—no one was visible—dark ever-green shrubs looking dead and stern among the gay spring verdure, stood out in ghostly dimness along the garden; the house looked even more gloomy and dismal than heretofore, and the night was advancing.

Anne tried the gate; it opened freely. She went lightly along the mossed and neglected path to the principal door. It was evidently unused, and in grim security barred the entrance; she passed the projecting window again, and with some difficulty found a door at the side of the house, at which she knocked lightly.

There was evidently some slight stir within; she thought she could hear a sound as of some one listening. She knocked again—there was no response—she repeated her summons more loudly; there was nothing clandestine in her visit to Christian.

She fancied she could hear steps ascending a stair, and echoing with a dull and hollow sound through the house. Presently a window above was opened, and the face of an old woman, buried in the immense borders of a white night-cap, looked out:

"Eh! guid preserve us. Wha are ye, disturbing honest folk at this hour o' the night; and what do ye want?"

"Is Miss Lillie not within?" said Anne in disappointment.

"Miss Lillie! muckle you're heeding about Miss Lillie; its naething but an excuse for theftdom and spoliation; but I warn ye, ye'll get naething here. Do ye ken there's an alarm-bell in Schole?"

"I am alone," said Anne, "and have merely come to see Miss Lillie, I assure you. You see I could do you no injury."

"And how div I ken," said the cautious portress a little more gently, "that ye havena a band at the ither side of the hedge?"

"You can see over the hedge," said Anne, smiling in spite of her impatience, "that I am quite alone. Pray ask Miss Lillie to admit me; she will tell you that I came by her own appointment."

"A bonnie like hour for leddies to be visiting at," said the old woman; "and how div ye ken that Miss Lillie will come at my ca'?"

"Pray do not keep me waiting," said Anne, "it is getting late. Tell Miss Lillie that I am here."

"And if I were gaun to tell Miss Lillie ye were here, wha would take care o' the house, I wad like to ken? Ye're no gaun to pit your gowk's errands on me. If I had the loudest vice in a' Scotland, it wadna reach Miss Lillie, an I cried till I was hoarse."

"You don't mean to say," exclaimed Anne, "that she is not at home!—that Miss Lillie has left Schole?"

"Ay, deed div I—nothing less. Mr. Patrick and her gaed away last night' to see their friends in the west country. Is that a'? If ye had a hoast like me, and were as muckle fashed wi' your breath, ye wadna have keeped your head out of the window sae long as I have done."

"Did she leave no word?" said Anne, "no message—or did she say when she would return?"

"Neither the tane nor the tither: she never said a word to me, but that they were gaun to the west country to see their friends. What for should they no? They are as free to do their ain pleasure as ither folk."

Anne turned away, greatly disappointed and bewildered.

"Be sure you sneck the gate," screamed the careful guardian of Schole, "and draw the stane close till't that ye pushed away wi' your fit."

Anne obeyed, and proceeded homeward very much downcast and disappointed. She had expected so much from this interview, and had looked forward to it so anxiously. Why should they avoid her? For what reason should the nearest relatives of Norman's wife, flee from Norman's sister? She herself had hailed, with feelings so warmly and sadly affectionate, the idea of their existence and sympathy— perhaps of their co-operation and help. Now Christian's words returned to her mind in sad perplexity. She could find no clue to them. The house of Schole looked more dreary and dismal than ever. She felt a void as she looked back to it, and knew that the watcher, whose light had fallen upon the still waters of the Firth through all the lingering night, was there no longer. She left her watch at the window early, and, with a feeling of blank disappointment and loneliness, laid herself down to her disturbed and dreaming rest—very sad, and disconsolate, and unsettled—seeing no clear prospect before her, nor plan of operation.

CHAPTER XXIV

The bright weeks of May stole on rapidly, and Anne had made no advance in her search. Little Alice Aytoun, when she came to visit her, clung round her neck anxiously, lifting up beseeching eyes to her face, but Anne had no word of hopeful answer to give. Her own heart was sinking day by day; the window of Patrick Lillie's study was still shut up and dark; the old servant whom they had left behind them could give no information as to their return. Anne was compelled to confess to herself that her plan had failed—that except for her dim and mysterious knowledge of these singular Lillies, she had not made a single step of progress.

Then Lewis wrote letters, slightly querulous, requiring her presence at home—and Mrs. Catherine sent one characteristic note promising, "if ye will be a good bairn and come back, maybe to go with ye myself, when the weather is more suiting for the seaside." She was doing no good in Aberford; so with a heavy heart Anne returned home.

The first day after her arrival at Merkland, she visited the Mill. With what strange feelings swelling in her heart did she draw the child to her side, and take into her own its small soft hand. The little strange exotic Lilie, the wonder of the quiet parish—was she indeed a Lilias Rutherford?—a daughter of the banished Norman?—her own nearest kin and relative?

"Jacky Morison's been up this morning already, Miss Anne," said Mrs. Melder. "Indeed, and ye may think muckle o' yoursel, Lilie my woman—baith leddy and maid comin anceerrant to see ye, the first thing after their home-coming. She's an awfu' strange lassie yon, Miss Anne; ane would think she had gotten some word o' the bairn that naebody else kens. She was aye unco fond o' her, but now it's Miss Lilie every word."

Strange indeed! these intuitive perceptions of Jacky's puzzled Anne greatly.

"That was what they called Lilie at home," said the child thoughtfully.

"Ay, listen till her; I dinna misdoubt it, Miss Anne—the folk that sent a' yon bonnie things, maun be weel off in this world."

"Will you come and walk with me, Lilie?" said Anne: "see what a beautiful day it is."

The child assented eagerly, and trying on her bonnet, Anne led her out. They went to the foot of the tree on which were carved the names of those two exiles—Norman and Marion. It was a fit resting-place for their sister and their child. Anne seated herself on the turf, and placed Lilie by her side.

"Can you tell me where your home is, Lilie?"

"Away yonder," said Lilie, "far away, over the sea."

"And what like is it?" said Anne, "do you remember?"

"A bonnie, bonnie place—where there's brighter light and warmer days; and grand flowers far bigger than any in Strathoran; but its lang, lang to sail, and whiles there were loud winds and storms, and Lilie wasna weel."

"Would you like to go home, Lilie?" said Anne.

"I would like to go to mamma. I would like to go to my own mamma; but—mamma doesna call yon place home."

"What does she call it, Lilie?"

"When mamma was putting Lilie into the big ship, she said Lilie was coming home; and maybe she would come hersel for Lilie."

"And how did she look when she said that?" said Anne.

The child began to cry.

"She put down her head—my mamma's bonnie head—down into her hands, this way; and then she began to greet, like me—oh, my mamma!"

Anne drew the little girl's head into her lap, and wiped away the tears. "You would be very glad to see mamma, Lilie, if she came here? she will come perhaps some day."

"Do you ken my mamma?" said Lilie eagerly. "Did she tell you she was coming?"

"No," said Anne, "but when she comes, you will take my hand, and say, 'Mamma, this is my friend;' will you not, and introduce me to her?"

The child looked brightly up:

"Eh, Lilie will be blythe! blythe!—but if mamma were coming, what would Lilie call you?"

"You would call me aunt," said Anne, her eyes filling as she looked upon the little face lying on her knee. "Your Aunt Anne that found you out, when you came a little stranger to the Mill."

Lilie rose to wind her small arms round Anne's neck.

"But you're no Lilie's aunt—I wish you were Lilie's aunt—then you would take me to live at Merkland."

"Would you like to live at Merkland, Lilie?"

"Whiles," said the child; "no in bonnie days like this, but whiles—Jacky says I'm a lady—am I a lady?"

"Not till you are old, like me; you will be a lady then."

"But Jacky says I'm a young lady," reiterated Lilie; "does Jacky no ken?"

"We will ask mamma when she comes," said Anne.

The little face became radiant:

"Eh! when mamma comes!—will you be glad too, like Lilie?—and will they a' be there? Papa and Lawrie? What way do you put your head down? then your eyelashes come upon your cheek, and then you grow like—"

"Like whom, Lilie?"

"My papa. If mamma comes, will they a' come—papa and Lawrie?"

"Who is Lawrie, Lilie?" The name was a still further corroboration; there was something touching in the exi e calling his son by his father's name.

"Lilie's brother. He is near as tall as you, and he's like papa."

"And you think I am like papa," said Anne, tremulously.

"Whiles, when you hold down your head, and look sad."

"Does papa look sad?"

"No," said Lilie, "but when you look as if you would greet, then you grow like him; and Lawrie never greets, and yet he's like him, too. What way is that?"

"And do they call you Miss Lilie at home?" said Anne, at once to evade the difficult question submitted to her, and to ascertain something of the worldly comforts of her banished brother. Mrs. Melder's guess was no doubt correct: the box which had been sent to Lilie could come from no poor house.

"No papa, or mamma, or Lawrie, but the maids and English John, and Jose—for papa's no like Robert Melder; he's a rich gentleman."

"And why did they send you here?" exclaimed Anne, more as expressing her own astonishment, than addressing the child.

"Lilie was very ill—had to lie in her bed—mamma thought I would die, and it was to get strong again. See," Lilie disengaged herself from Anne, and ran away along the bank of the Oran, returning ruddy and breathless, "Lilie's strong now."

"And why did you not tell me this before?" said Anne.

"Lilie didna mind—Lilie didna ken how to speak;" and the child looked confused and bewildered. By means of her broken sentences, however, Anne made out that Lilie had been brought home by a Juana, a Spanish nurse, and had been accustomed to hear the servants in her father's house speak the liquid foreign tongue, which she was already beginning to forget. That being suddenly brought into the rustic Scottish dwelling, and seeing, with the quick perception of a child, that its inhabitants were of the same rank as her former attendants, the child had naturally fancied that their language must also be, not the cultivated English, the speaking of which was an accomplishment, but the more ornate tongue which she had been accustomed to hear among their equals in her own country. Then Mrs. Melder's dialect still further puzzled the lonely child, who, under the care of Juana, had spoken nothing but Spanish during the voyage, which she thought so long a one, so that the ideas of the little head became quite perplexed and ravelled; and it was not until she had mastered in a considerable degree this new Scottish tongue, that the more refined words learned from "mamma" began to steal once more into her childish memory.

But Anne's attempted questioning, respecting the person who brought Lilie to the Mill, produced no satisfactory answer. The remembrance had become hazy already; and save for a general impression of discomfort—one of those vague indefinite times of childish suffering and unhappiness, which are by no means either light or trivial, howsoever we may think of them, when we are involved in more mature calamities, Lilie's memory failed her. She could give no account of the interim, between her voyage under the government of Juana, and her transference to the rule of Mrs. Melder.

To Mrs. Catherine, Anne had said little of the Lilies—to Lewis nothing. Their connexion with Norman had nothing to do with the proof of his innocence, and though Christian Lilie's strange words had occupied her own mind night and day since she heard them, she yet did not think it either necessary or prudent to make them a matter of conversation.

Again, she remained in so much doubt about this singular brother and sister—their strange seclusion, and grief, and inactivity—their mysterious and abrupt removal, which evidently was to avoid meeting her, perplexed herself so much that she did not venture to confide even in Mrs. Catherine. She brooded over her secret by herself; she slept little—rested little—took long, solitary, meditative walks, and much exercise, and felt herself more than ever abstracted from the busy little world about her. She was becoming a solitary, cheerless woman, cherishing in silent sadness one great hope; a hope with which strangers might not intermeddle—which was foolishness to her own nearest friends—which might never be realized upon this earth—nevertheless a hope in which her whole nature was concentrated—the very essence and aim of her being.

She did not even reveal to Mrs. Catherine her suspicion her hope, that Lilie was the child of her banished brother. She cherished it in her own mind as a secret strength and comfort. She endeavored in all gentle ways to supply the want of the mother after whom the little heart yearned, and she was successful. Lilie began to call her aunt—to watch in childish anxiety for her daily visits—to wander about anywhere, unwearied and joyous, so long as Anne was leading her, and to look to her at all times as her dearest friend and protector. Then these childish confidences—these snatches, of dear remembrance of the far-away mamma—these glances into the household of the exile! Anne drew new invigoration, strength, and hope from these, in the darkest time of her depression.

Yet all endeavors for her great end were stayed—no one lifted a hand in the cause of the injured man—no one made any exertion to deliver him. In the bright sunshine of that leafy month of June her heart sickened within her. She longed to return again to the place where something might be done, where with a prospect of success, or without it, she might still labor; she might still engage in the search.

In the meantime, everything went on peaceably in the parish of Strathoran. Jeanie Coulter and Walter Foreman had made up their mind, and were speedily to be married. Ada Mina, in the glory of being bridesmaid and bride's sister, had almost forgotten Giles Sympelton. Marjory Falconer was very remarkably quiet; she was "beginning to settle." Mrs. Bairnsfather said, maliciously, "and it was high time." Mr. Ferguson's work was advancing in the bleak lands of Lochend and Loelyin. Mr. Coulter and he were very busy, and in high spirits. Lord Gillravidge had left Strathoran. The fair country, in the height of its summer beauty, had no attractions for Lord Gillravidge. There was no game to slaughter, and other kind of excitement, the quiet Norland parish had never possessed any.

Mr. Fitzherbert was left behind; he was now lord paramount at Strathoran, and a very great man, intensely detested by the Macalpines of Oranmore, and spoken of with bitter derision and disdain by all the other inhabitants of Strathoran. He had displeased Lord Gillravidge by being the occasion of Giles Sympelton's desertion, and was left behind half as a punishment for that offence, and half as a promotion for counter-balancing good offices. Mr. Fitzherbert's feelings concerning it were of the same mixed description. He was immensely bored with the intolerable weariness of the country, while at the same time he enjoyed his temporary lordship, and ordered and stormed magnificently in the desecrated house of the Sutherlands.

We should not have intruded ourselves into his disagreeable presence had that been all. But Mr. Fitzherbert in his dreariness, when he had exercised his petty despotism to its full extent—had cursed the servants, bullied Mr. Whittret, and asserted his predominance in various other pleasant and edifying ways—was forced to invent further amusement for himself. Surely, there never was an unhappy individual with small brains and a craving for excitement more miserably placed.

It chanced one day that Flora Macalpine, Mrs. Ferguson's very pretty and very bashful nurserymaid, unwarily entered the contested by-way, while walking with the Woodsmuir children. Mr. Fitzherbert met her there, and the first harsh sound of his command to leave the road, was very much less disagreeable than the softening of tone which followed. Mr. Fitzherbert began to admire the pretty Highland girl, and to venture to express to her his admiration—to her, a Macalpine! Flora hurried from the by-way with her charge, in burning shame and indignation.

But Mr. Fitzherbert was not to be got rid of so easily. Flora did not know the might of ennui which made him seek out her quiet walks, and waylay her so perseveringly. She avoided him in every possible way; but still he found means to persecute her with his odious flattery and attentions. Flora was engaged, moreover, and tall Angus Macalpine, her handsome bride-groom elect, and Duncan Roy, her brother, were equally irate, and equally contented to have a decided personal plea for punishing the obnoxious jackal of Lord Gillravidge. So Flora reluctantly suffered herself to be made a party in a plan, which should ensnare her tormentor, and pour out upon him, in full flood, the rage and contempt of the Macalpines.

It was a beautiful evening in June: Mr. Fitzherbert had just received from Lord Gillravidge the much wished-for call to London.

In great glee he put the letter in his pocket, took his hat, and sallied out. His splendid hair, his magnificent whiskers and moustache were in the most superlative order. Flora Macalpine had intimated to him bashfully that she would be in the contested by-way, near the stepping-stones, at seven o'clock; it is always pleasant to be victorious. Mr. Fitzherbert had no doubt that the power of his fascinations had smitten the simple cottager, and accordingly in perfect good-humor with himself, and very much disposed to accept Flora's homage, with the utmost condescension, he set out for the stepping-stones.

Close by the trysting place, in the slanting June sunlight, screening himself with the thick foliage of a "bourtree-bush," stood tall Angus Macalpine watching for his prey. Flora, nervous and trembling, stood beside him; she felt she was very much out of place, and did not at all like her position, but that strong, thickset little brother of hers, Duncan Roy, was squatting at her feet, concealing the flaming red head, which might have alarmed their victim, among the surrounding leaves, and Angus, bending down his handsome head with its curling fair hair, and healthful, good-looking face, was very carefully supporting her, and guarding against her running away. So, after all, there was nothing improper in it, and she could not help herself. The idea of the compulsion comforted Flora.

Footsteps approached by-and-by. It was not Mr. Fitzherbert. It was George, the Falcon's Craig groom, and Johnnie Halflin, to whom Duncan Roy had communicated some hint of his intention. The punishment was far too just, the fun far too good, for these mischief-loving lads to let it slip. They had come to assist the Macalpines. George was making horrible faces. His veins were perfectly swoln with the might of his suppressed laughter. Johnnie had a little pink pocket-handkerchief—a keepsake from Bessie—thrust bodily into his capacious mouth. The Macalpines were graver; a quiet glee was shooting from the eyes of Duncan Roy, and Angus sometimes smiled—but the smile was an angry one.

"But, Angus," whispered Flora; "mind, you maun promise that you'll no hurt him?"

"I'll try," was the emphatic response.

"Eh! but Duncan—Angus! Dinna hurt him, for ony sake.—Just fear him, or I'll rin away this moment."

It was easier said than done. That mighty arm of Angus Macalpine's might have restrained a man of his own inches without any particular strain.

"We'll no hurt him, Flora," said Duncan encouragingly,—"We'll only douk him, forbye—Listen! There he is—in behint the bush, lads. Angus, let Flora go."

It was indeed Fitzherbert. They could hear his swaggering step as he advanced, whistling gaily.

"I'll whistle ye!" exclaimed the angry Angus, in a strong undertone. "If ye were ance in my hands, my lad, ye'll whistle or ye get out again!"

Flora had only time to speak another earnest remonstrance, when her admirer appeared.

The ambush had been skilfully contrived. The unsuspected Fitzherbert advanced gaily. Poor Flora trembled and shrank back—the instinctive delicacy of her simple womanly nature overpowering her with shame. To meet this odious man at all, if it were but for a second, was a disgrace to her, even though Angus and Duncan were waiting at her side.

Mr Fitzherbert began a gallant speech—he attempted to take Flora's hand. The girl shrank back to the shelter of the bourtree-bush—and in another moment, Fitzherbert was struggling in the stalwart arms of Angus Macalpine—an embrace as unexpected as it was overpowering.

"Haud the ill tongue of ye!" exclaimed Duncan Roy, as he seized the struggling legs of the unhappy adventurer, and held him fast. "If ye say another word, ye shall rue it a' your days."

"Do you want to rob me?" cried Fitzherbert. "I haven't my purse on me, good fellows. Let me go, or you shall suffer for it."

"Rob ye!" Tall Angus Macalpine seized his collar with an exclamation of disgust, and shook him violently. "Rob ye! Ye pitiful animal, wha would file their fingers with your filthy siller! Duncan, give me the plaid."

The other two auxiliaries were standing by expending their pent-up laughter, Johnnie Halflin bestirred himself now, to hand to Angus one of the plaids that lay on the grass beside him.

Threats, entreaties, vociferation, rage, all were in vain. The plaid was bound tightly round the unhappy Fitzherbert, strapping his arms to his side. Then Duncan confined in like manner his struggling feet. Then they laid him down on the grass.

"Hushaba!" sung Johnnie Halflin as, with laughter not to be suppressed, they viewed the ludicrous bondage of their foe. "Eh, man, ye're a muckle baby to lie there, and do naething but squeal."

"What gars ye no fight wi' your neives, like a man?" cried George.

"Do you no see? He's putting a' his strength into the feet of him. See, woman Flora, he's walloping like the fishes in the Portoran boats when they're new catched. He's new catched, too. Gie him a taste o' the water."

"If ye had dune what ye had to do against us, like a man," said Angus Macalpine, solemnly, addressing the miserable captive, who lay prone before these shafts of rustic wit, upon the grass at their feet, "we might have throoshen ye like a man, and gi'en ye fair play; but because ye're a vermin that have creeped in to quiet places, where there was nae man to chastise ye—and because ye have tried to breathe your ill breath into the purest heart in a' Strathoran, ye shall hae only a vermin's punishment. Duncan, ye can get your shears. I'll haud the sheep."

Duncan advanced in grim mirth, holding a pair of mighty shears. Angus knelt down upon the grass, and held Fitzherbert with his arm. The operation commenced. The punishment was the bitterest they could have chosen. Duncan Roy squatting at his side, with methodic composure and malicious glee, began to clip, and cut away, in jagged and uneven bits, his cherished whiskers, his beautiful moustache, his magnificent hair. The victim roared and groaned, entreated and threatened, in vain—the relentless operators proceeded in their work—the scissors entered into his soul.

A light, quick step came suddenly along the path. They did not hear it, so overwhelming was the laughter of the lookers-on, till Marjory Falconer stood in the midst of them. Duncan's scissors suddenly ceased. The victim looked up in momentary hope, and again shrank back despairing. He by no means desired to throw himself upon the tender mercies of Miss Falconer.

"What is the matter?" cried Marjory. "Flora, are you here! What is the matter? what are they about?"

"Oh! Miss Falconer," exclaimed Flora who, between shame and laughter, was now in tears, "it's the gentleman from Strathoran—and it's Duncan and Angus—and he wouldna let me be, and they're—"

An involuntary burst of laughter choked Flora's penitence.—The lifted head of her brother, with its look of comic appeal, as he held up his shears before Miss Falconer, and silently asked her permission to proceed—the grim steadfastness with which Angus continued to hold the victim on the grass—the vain attempt of Miss Falconer to look gravely displeased and dignified—the fierce struggles of Fitzherbert—Flora could not bear it: she ran in behind the bourtree-bush.

Marjory stood undecided for a moment. She had great influence with the Macalpines and their class, as a strong and firm character always has. She thought for an instant of what people would say, almost for the first time in her life. Then she looked at the ludicrous scene before her—the just punishment of poor Flora's persecution. The prudent resolution faded away—she yielded to the fun and to the justice. She could not put her veto upon it.

"George, do you go home—you are not wanted. Duncan, have you finished?"

"Na," said the rejoicing Duncan, beginning with double zeal to ply his redoubtable shears. "He's a camstarie beast, this ane—he tak's lang shearing—but we're winning on, Mem."

George reluctantly turned away. His mistress's orders were not to be trifled with, he knew. Little Bessie's pink handkerchief was in Johnnie Halflin's mouth again. Flora remained behind the bourtree-bush, terrified to look upon her tormentor's agonized face. Marjory Falconer looked on.

The blood was rushing in torrents to her hot cheeks already.—She could have put an end to this if she would: instead of that she had encouraged it. She had yielded to the mirthful impulse: now she was paying the penalty in one of her overpowering agonies of shame.

"Now—now!" she exclaimed, as Duncan, with methodic accuracy, finished his operation on one side of Mr. Fitzherbert's fiery countenance, "that will do now—let him go."

The operators looked up in disappointment.

"Do let him go; let me see him released before I leave you."

Duncan and Angus looked at each other.

"Weel," said Angus, smiling grimly, "he's gey weel; ye'll think again, my lad, before ye offer to lay your filthy fingers on a Macalpine, or ony ither lass in the countryside. Now, Duncan—"

They began to free him from his bondage. Angus took one end of the plaid which confined his arms—Duncan the other. The process was satisfactory, but by no means gentle; over and over they rolled him, and when the hapless Fitzherbert found himself at last at liberty, he was lying within the green verge of the Oran—the soft waters embracing him. His first struggle threw him further in; and when he rose at last, spluttering with wrath and water, his clothes wet, his face scarred with the pebbles, and shorn of its hirsute glories—all his tormentors were gone. Light of foot, and conversant with all the by-ways, they had dispersed, considerably against the will of the Macalpines, but in obedience to the command of Miss Falconer, and the entreaties of Flora.

In burning rage and mortification Mr. Fitzherbert stalked back to Strathoran. In the distance, upon the other side of the river, he could see the retreat of the Macalpines; it was a fruitless thing vowing vengeance upon them. He had done his worst; they were out of his power.

But Mr. Fitzherbert's mortification and rage reached a climax when he looked upon his sad mutilation—cruel as Hanun the son of Nahash, and his artful counsellors of the children of Ammon, the scissors of the remorseless Duncan had swept away one entire half of Mr. Fitzherbert's adornments. It must all go, cherished and dearly beloved as it was—the flowing luxuriance of the one side must be sacrificed to the barbarous stubble of the other.—Alas the day! How should he meet Lord Gillravidge! how account for the holocaust! Mr. Fitzherbert was fitly punished—he was in despair.

Marjory Falconer hurried along the road to Merkland, little less despairing than Mr. Fitzherbert. She was bitterly ashamed; her face was burning with passionate blushes. She needed no one to remind her of her loss of dignity; the strong and powerful vitality of her womanhood avenged itself completely. Like Jeanie Coulter, or Alice Aytoun, or even Anne Ross herself, she knew Marjory Falconer could never be!— nor like the cheerful active sister Martha of the Portoran Manse. Marjory did not blush more deeply when that last name glided into her memory; that was impossible—no human verdict, or condemnation would have abashed her so entirely as did her own strong, clear, unhesitating judgment; but she looked uncomfortable and uneasy. Another person now might be involved in the blame of her misdoings; the reflected shadow of those extravagancies might fall upon one, of whom many tongues were sufficiently ready to speak evil. It did not increase the scorching passion of her shame—but it deepened her repentance.

"Is Miss Ross in, Duncan?" she asked as she entered Merkland.

"Ou ay, Miss Falconer, Miss Anne's in," said Duncan, preceding her leisurely to Mrs. Ross's parlor. "She's in her ain room—according to her ain fashion. There's nae accounting for the whigmaleeries of you leddies, but an she disna live liker a human creature and less like a bird, ye may tak my word for't she'll no live ony way lang."

"What do you mean?" exclaimed Marjory. "Is Miss Ross ill?"

"Na. I'm no saying she's ill," was the cautious answer; "but taking lang flights her lane, up the water and down the water, and when she comes in eating a nip that wadna ser a lintie, and syne away up the stair to pingle her lane at a seam; I say it's a clear tempting o' Providence, Miss Falconer, and I have tell't Miss Anne that mysel."

Marjory ran up stairs, and tapped at the door of Anne's room. "Come in," said Anne. Marjory entered.

The window was open—the full glory of the setting sun was pouring over the beautiful country, lying like a veil of golden tissue, sobered with fairy tints of gray and purple upon the far-off solemn hills, and gleaming in the river as you could trace its course for miles, where its thick fringe of foliage was parted here and there. Anne leant upon the window-still, looking out. It was not the fair heights and hollows of her native district that she saw; her eyes were veiled to these. The dim shores of the Forth in the still evening-time—the long, low, sighing of the waters—the desolate, gloomy house behind—the tall, gaunt figure stealing shadowlike over the glistening sand—these were before her constantly, in dream and vision, shutting out with their gray tints and sad colouring all other landscapes, how fair soever they might be.

She did not look up when Marjory entered, but waited to be addressed, thinking it May or Barbara. At last, finding the new-comer did not speak, she turned round.

"Marjory, is that you?"

"What are you thinking of, Anne?" said Marjory. "What makes you dream and brood thus? There you have been gazing out these two minutes, as fixedly as if you saw something of the greatest interest. I am quite sure you don't know what you are looking at, and, had I come forward suddenly, and asked you what river that was, you would have faltered and deliberated before you could be certain it was the Oran. I know you would. What is it all about?"

Anne smiled.

"It is not so easy to tell. You put comprehensive questions, Marjory."

"And here are you making yourself ill!" exclaimed Marjory, impetuously; "dreaming over something which no one is to know; walking alone, and sitting alone, and defrauding yourself of proper rest and relaxation, and altogether, as plainly as possible endeavoring to manufacture a consumption. I say, Anne

Ross, what is it all about? I have a right to know—we all have a right to know; you don't belong to yourself. If you were not Anne Ross, of Merkland, I should begin to suspect we had some love-sickness on our hands."

"And if you were any one else but Marjory Falconer, of Falcon's Craig, I should be very angry," said Anne, smiling.

"Never anything reasonable from you since you came home; never a call upon any one but Mrs. Melder. Nothing but patient looks, and paleness, and reveries! I don't see why we should submit to it, Anne Ross. I protest, in the name of the parish—it is a public injustice!"

"Very well, Marjory," said Anne. "Pray be so good as sit down now, and do not scold so bitterly. Did you come all the way from Falcon's Craig for the sole purpose of bringing me under discipline?"

Marjory Falconer put up her hands to her cheeks to hide the vehement blushes which rushed back again; then, as she recalled the story she had come to tell, its ludicrous points overcame the shame, and she laughed with characteristic heartiness. There was not, after all, so very much to be ashamed of; but, as everybody exaggerated the extravagance of everything done by Marjory Falconer, so Marjory Falconer felt herself bitterly humiliated in the recollection of escapades which young ladies of much greater pretensions would only have laughed at.

"What is it, Marjory?" said Anne.

The fit of shame returned.

"Oh! not much. Only I have been making a fool of myself again."

Anne expressed no wonder; she only drew her friend into a chair, and asked:

"How?"

"I am going to tell you. I came here at once, you see, lest some one else should be before me with the news. Ah! and there you sit as cool and calm as though I were not entering my purgatory!"

"I don't want to tease you further," said Anne, "or I should say that when people make purgatories for themselves, it behoves them to endure patiently."

"Very well: you don't intend to be sympathetic. I am quite satisfied. Now for my confession. Most unwittingly and innocently, I premise, was I led into the snare. Anne Ross! turn away from the window, and keep your glances within proper bounds. If your eyes wander so, I shall forget my own foolishness in yours—and I don't choose that."

Anne obeyed, and Marjory told her story—sometimes overwhelmed with her own passionate humiliation, sometimes bursting into irrepressible mirth. It was very soon told. Anne looked annoyed and vexed. She did not speak. It was the sorest condemnation she could have given.

"You have nothing to say to me!" exclaimed Marjory, the hot flood burning over her cheek, and neck, and forehead. "You think I am clearly hopeless now. You think—"

"I think," said Anne, "that Marjory Falconer, whom malicious people blame for pride, is not half proud enough."

"Not proud enough!"

It was difficult to believe, indeed, when one saw the drawing-up of her tall, fine figure, and the flashing of her eye.

"Yes, I understand. You would be proud enough were you Ralph; then, for everything brave, and honorable, and true, the fame of the Falconers would be safe in your hands: but you are not proud enough, being Marjory. I fancy we should inhabit a loftier atmosphere than these boyish frolics could find breath in, Marjory; an atmosphere too pure and rare to carry clamorous voices, whatever may be their burden."

"Gentle and mild," said Marjory, attempting a laugh, which would not come; "perfumed and dainty. I am no exotic, Anne; I must breathe living air. I cannot breathe odors."

Anne rose, and lifted her Bible from the table.

"The sublime of mild and gentle belongs to One greater than us; but I don't want to compel you to these. Look here, Marjory."

Marjory looked—read.

"'Strength and honor are her clothing,'" and bowed her head, in token of being vanquished.

"You have nothing to oppose to my argument," said Anne, smiling. "You are obliged to yield without a word. Let me convince you, Marjory, that we stoop mightily from our just position, when we condescend to meddle with such humiliating follies as the rights of women—that we do compromise our becoming dignity when we involve ourselves in a discreditable warfare, every step in advance of which is a further humiliation to us. I forgive you your share in this exploit with all my heart. I am not sorry the man is punished, though I would rather you had not been connected with his punishment. It is not very much, after all; but I do declare war against these polemics of yours—all and several.—I would have you more thoroughly woman-proud: it is by no means inconsistent with the truest humility. I would have you like this portrait; men do not paint in such vigorous colors now. Strength and honor, Marjory; household strength, and loftiness, and purity—better things than any imaginary rights that clamor themselves into mere words."

Marjory was half angry, half smiling.

"Very gentle, and calm, and proper, for an example to me; and so nobody does us any injustice—nobody oppresses us? Very well: but I did not know it before."

"Nay," said Anne, playfully; "that is not what I said. But:

"'The good old rule Sufficeth me, the simple plan, That they should take who have the power, And they should keep who can.'"

"Anne!"

"I am quite serious. There are few amongst us who are ruled more than we need to be, Marjory. The best mind will always assert itself, in whomsoever it may dwell—we are safe in that.—The weak ought to be controlled and guided, and will be, wherever there is a stronger, whether man or woman."

"Strange doctrines, these!" said Marjory Falconer. "I acknowledge myself outdone. I give up my poor little innovations. Why, Anne Ross, what would the proper people say? What would the Coulters—the Fergusons—the whole parish?"

"Perfectly agree with me," said Anne, "when it had time to think about it, without being shocked in the least. The proper people. You forget that I am a very proper person myself."

"So I did," said Marjory Falconer, shrugging her shoulders, "so I did. Patronised by Mrs. Bairnsfather, highly approved by Mrs. Coulter and Mrs. Ferguson—I almost thought, just now, that you were as improper as myself."

CHAPTER XXV

The summer had reached its height—the fervent month of July was waning, and Anne Ross's cheek growing paler every day.—Very hard to bear this time of waiting was, harder than any toil or labor, more utterly exhausting than any weight of care and sorrow, which had opportunity and means of working! She hardly ventured to speak of returning to Aberford, for Mrs. Ross's peevishness at the merest hint of such a wish, and the impatience of Lewis, were perfectly natural, she acknowledged. Her former journey, undertaken in opposition to their opinion, had produced nothing; she could not expect that they would readily yield to her again.

In the meantime tidings had come from Archibald Sutherland. He had reached his destination safely, and, under circumstances much more favorable than he could have hoped, had commenced his work. He had been able to render some especial service, the nature of which he did not specify, to his employer's only son, a very fine lad of fourteen or fifteen, which within a few days of his arrival brought him into Mr. Sinclair's house on the footing of a friend. Mr. Sinclair himself was, as common report said, a man of great enterprise in business, and notable perseverance, whose fortune was the work of his own hands; and blending with this, Archibald found a singular delicacy of tone and sentiment which pleased him greatly. A man of strong mould, whose "stalk of carle hemp," was invested with rare intellectual grace and refinement—a household which, under the fervent skies of that strange Western World, remained still a Scottish household, looking back with the utmost love and tenderness to its own country and home—in the atmosphere of these, the broken laird found himself not long a stranger.

Mr. Sinclair had some knowledge of the North country—had heard of Archibald's family, and on some long past occasion, had seen Mrs. Catherine. This was an additional bond. The family of the merchant lived a very quiet life in a country house in the vicinity of the town, having scarcely any visitors: Archibald Sutherland, with his attainments and abilities, was an acquisition to them.

His prospects were pleasant; they brightened the inner room at the Tower, and shed a ray of light even upon Anne's reveries. Something more was needed, however, to shake off the lethargic sadness that begun to overpower her. Mrs. Catherine applied the remedy.

Upon a drowsy July afternoon, when one could fancy the earth, with her flushed cheek and loose robes, lying in that languid dreamy state, half way between asleep and awake, which in Scotland we call "dovering," Mrs. Catherine in her rustling silken garments, went stately down under the shadow of the trees, to Merkland. It was a very unusual honor. Mrs. Catherine was wont to receive visits, not to pay them.

Anne went to the gate to receive her. Lewis who, with characteristic prudence, had already begun to devote himself to the careful managing of his lands, put away the papers that lay before him, and left the library with much wonder, to ascertain Mrs. Catherine's errand. Mrs. Ross rose very peevishly from the sofa on which she had been for the last hour enjoying her usual sleep. It was enough to make any one ill-humored to be disturbed so unexpectedly.

"Now, Madam," said Mrs. Catherine, when Mrs. Ross had greeted her with great ceremony and politeness, "you may ken I have come for a special purpose; I am going to Edinburgh."

"To Edinburgh!" exclaimed Mrs. Ross; "you, Mrs. Catherine. How shall we manage to get on at all without you?"

"You will contrive it in some manner doubtless," said Mrs. Catherine, drily.

"I may, perhaps, for I am a great house-keeper; but for Anne and Lewis, nothing goes right if a week passes without two or three visits to the Tower."

"Ay, Lewis, is it so?" said Mrs. Catherine. "I thought not I had kept the power, now that I am past threescore, of drawing to my dwelling gallants of your years."

"I have not been at the Tower for a month," said Lewis, bluntly; "I mean I have been very much occupied."

"As you should be," said Mrs. Catherine. "I am not seeking excuses, Lewis; I am but blythe that it is not my memory that is failing me—seeing I should like ill to suffer loss in that particular, till this world's affairs are out of my hands—be careful of your lawful business, Lewis, as becomes your years. If you were a good bairn, I might maybe do my endeavor to bring folk back with me, that your leisure would be better spent upon: in the meantime, I have a suit to your mother."

Mrs. Ross looked astonished.

"To me?"

"Yes; this bairn Anne, Mrs. Ross, as you see, has been misbehaving herself. My own gray cheek, withered as it is, has stronger health upon it than is on her young one. I have a doctor of physic among my serving woman; I see no reason why I should not undertake to work cures as well as my neighbors—send her with me—I will bring her back free of her trouble."

"Oh, I beg you will not refer to me," said Mrs. Ross, angrily. "Anne is quite able to judge for herself."

"I beg your pardon, Madam. I say this bairn Anne has no call to judge for herself. Is it your pleasure that I should try my skill? I came to make my petition to you, and not to Anne."

"She is an excessively unreasonable girl," said Mrs. Ross, tossing her head; "if you know how to manage her, it is more than I do. I assure you, Mrs. Catherine, Anne's conduct to me is of the most undutiful kind. She is a very foolish, unreasonable girl."

Poor Anne had been laboring these three or four weeks to please her stepmother, as assiduously as any fagged governess or sempstress in the land. The honorable scars of the needle had furrowed her finger; she had been laboring almost as hardly, and to much better purpose than the greater portion of those "needlewomen, distressed or otherways," whose miserable work done for miserable wages attracts so much sympathy and benevolent exertion in these days. She was somewhat astonished at the undeserved accusation. If she did wander for long miles along the course of the Oran, it was in the dewy morning, before Mrs. Ross had left her room. If she did brood over her secret hope and sorrow, it was when Mrs. Ross was sullen or asleep. She said nothing in self-defence, but felt the injustice keenly, notwithstanding.

"That is what I am saying," said Mrs. Catherine. "She has been misbehaving herself, and we have noticed her pining away, in silence. So far as I can see, it is high time to take note of it now; therefore my petition is, that you suffer her to go with me. It is not my wont to pass over ill-doing; let me have the guiding of her for a while."

"I think you ought to take advantage of Mrs. Catherine's invitation, Anne," said Lewis. "You do not look well."

Mrs. Ross tossed her head in silence.

"Truly, Anne," said Mrs. Catherine, "I have worn out of the way of asking favors; maybe it is want of use that makes me prosper so ill. Am I to get your daughter, Mrs. Ross for company on my travel, or am I not? I must pray you to let me have your answer."

"Oh, if you choose to take her, and if Anne chooses to go, my consent is of little consequence," said Mrs. Ross: then softening her tone a little, she added, "I have no objection, unfortunately Anne is not of sufficient importance in the household, Mrs. Catherine, to make us feel the want of her greatly. Certainly I have no objection—she can go."

A harsh reply rose to Mrs. Catherine's lips; but for Anne's sake, she, suppressed it—the permission, ungracious as it was, was accepted, and Mrs. Catherine made arrangements with Anne for their journey; she had settled that they should leave the Tower that week.

Mrs. Catherine travelled in her own carriage. She had an old house, grand and solitary, in an old quarter of Edinburgh, whose antique furniture and lofty rooms strangers came to see, as one of the lesser wonders of the city, which boasts so many. Mrs. Catherine's horses were proceeding at a good pace along the southward road, within sight of a dazzling sea, and very near the dark high cliffs, and scattered fisher villages which formed its margin. Johnnie Halflin sat beside the coachman, Jacky Morison and her grandmother were behind. Mrs. Catherine within was explaining her plans to Anne.

"It is my purpose, child, to set you to your labor again; I see there is neither health nor peace for you until you have got some better inkling of this matter. Am I not right?"

"Perfectly," said Anne. "I cannot rest, indeed. I shall be of little use to any one, until some light is thrown on this."

"Then, child, it is my meaning to dwell in my own house in Edinburgh, where you can find me, if I am needed. I cannot be in the house of a stranger, or I would have gone with you. I am not ill-pleased that this necessity has come, for there are many in Edinburgh, that it is meet I should say farewell to, before I depart to my rest. Forbye this, child, there is another cloud rising upon the sky of that ill-trysted house of Sutherland."

Anne started.

"Archibald is well—is there any further intelligence, Mrs. Catherine?"

"Archie's sister is not well, Gowan. Did I not tell you that her fuil of a man was dead?"

"No, I never heard it before."

"I meant to tell you—it has passed from my mind, in the thought of the travel. He has been killed—how, or for what reason, I have not asked. I have written to Isabel Sutherland to come home. I cannot trust her without natural guard or helper, her lane in the midst of strangers. She is a light-headed, vain, undutiful girl—I know her of old—and farther shame must not come upon the house, Gowan, if it is in my power to ward it off. If she will not come, I have made up my mind—I will go, and bring her home."

"Go!" exclaimed Anne. "To England?—you are not able for the journey."

"Hold your peace, child! I am able for whatever is needful, as every mortal is, that has a right will to try. It's my hope Archie Sutherland is in a fair way of recovering his good fame and healthful spirit. If Isabel is in peril, it is deadly and beyond remedy—for the sake of the fuil herself (she bears Isabel Balfour's name and outward resemblance,) and for the sake of Archie, I am bound to do my endeavor, if it should be by the strong hand. Child, you may think me distrustful beyond what is needed. Maybe I am. She left her mother's sick-bed for the sake of a strange man. And when he was sent to a solitary place, she left him, also, for the sake of vanities. If you had done the like, I would have distrusted you."

Anne could not realize the cause of distrust. She deprecated, and thought Mrs. Catherine's fears uncalled for—shrinking from the idea of danger to Isabel, almost as she would have done from any suspicion of herself.

When she had seen Mrs. Catherine settled comfortably in her spacious and grand Edinburgh lodging, and the bustle of arrival fairly over, Anne, with her attendant Jacky, proceeded to Aberford.

Miss Crankie and Mrs. Yammer were at tea. Their energetic little servant ushered Anne into the small parlor, looking out upon the green, in which they usually sat. They had blue cups and saucers of the venerable willow pattern, arranged above the red and yellow lady on the tray—a teapot, belonging to the same set, with a lid, the sole relic of a broken black one—a comfortable plate of tolerably thick bread-and-butter, and two or three saucers, containing various specimens of jellies. Mrs. Yammer sat languidly in a great, old elbow-chair. Miss Crankie was perched upon a low seat before the tray, making tea.

Anne's entrance caused a commotion. There were a great many apologies, and expressions of wonder and pleasure at seeing her again; and then she was begged to take a seat, and a cup of tea. Anne sat down, and kindly looked out at the window, while Miss Crankie abstracted the lid from the teapot, and, from the depths of an adjoining cupboard, produced another one more resembling it in color.

"Ye see," said Miss Crankie, nodding her wiry little curls at the ruddy-colored compounds in the saucers, "we've been making our jelly, and were just trying it. I can recommend the rasps, Miss Ross—the red currants would take a thought mair boiling, and the gooseberries are drumlie—but I can recommend the rasps."

"If Miss Ross is no feared for her teeth," sighed Mrs. Yammer. "I got cauld mysel on Sabbath at the Kirk, and was trying the jam for my throat. I'm a puir weak creature, Miss Ross: the wind gangs through me like a knife."

"I have returned to you for accommodation, Miss Crankie," said Anne. "Are the rooms unoccupied now?"

"Eh, bless me! isna that an uncommon providence," exclaimed Miss Crankie. "Mrs. Mavis is gaun away the morn!"

"But what can you do with me to-night?" said Anne.

"Oh, nae fear o' us—we'll do grand," said Miss Crankie. "I'm blyth ye're come back Miss Ross, and yet I'm sorry to see you so shilpit. Ye'll find the sea-air do ye mair guid noo. Ye're no looking half sae well as ye did when ye gaed away."

"Ah! Miss Ross," said Mrs. Yammer, dolorously, "I hope ye'll use the means and get right advice in time. Ye'll be fashed wi' a pain in your side? For mysel, it's little use saying what I have to thole—there's scarce an hour in the day, that I havna stitches through and through me."

"Hout, Tammie, ye're aye meat-hale," responded her brisker sister. "Ye've come at a better season now, Miss Ross, the haill town is full of sea-bathers. I was saying to auld Marget, that she might win a pound or twa for her ain hand, with letting some o' thae muckle rooms, in Schole, and naebody, be the waur—it's sae handy for the sea—if Kirstin Lillie and her brother, hadna come hame sae suddenly."

"They are at home, then?" said Anne.

"Oh, ay! they came hame about a month ago, in as great a hurry as they gaed away; ane scarce ever sees them noo, even on the sands—they're strange folk."

The next day, young Mrs. Mavis and her two blooming children left their sea-side lodgings, and Anne took peaceful possession of her former rooms. The tall gaunt outline of Schole, as it stood out against the deep blue of the evening sky, dismal and forlorn as it was, looked like a friend; but though she lingered about its vicinity all the night, and watched eagerly within sight of its little gate, no one ventured forth. The low projecting window had light within it, but it was curtained carefully. She could see no trace of Christian. Why did they avoid her? why was there so much additional secrecy and seclusion?

The second day after their arrival in Aberford, Jacky had a visitor. It was little Bessie, Alice Aytoun's maid. Bessie was living with an aunt, the wife of a forester, whose house was within three or four miles of Aberford. Jacky, by Anne's permission, returned with her to spend the afternoon in the aunt's house.

The two girls set out very jubilant and in high spirits, with much laughing mention of Johnnie Halflin, whom Bessie had already seen in Edinburgh, and from whom she had received a very grandiloquent account of the chastisement of Mr. Fitzherbert, and of the mighty things which the said Johnnie would have done, had not Miss Falconer put her veto on his valor.

The forester's house was in the bosom of the wood under his charge. A narrow foot-road, winding through the trees, ran close to the bounding hedge of its well-stocked garden, and nestling warmly below the thick foliage, the house stood snug in the corner of its luxuriant enclosure, presiding in modest pride, like some sober cottage matron, conscious of decent comfort and independence, over its flourishing cabbages, and stately bushes of southern-wood, ripe gooseberries, and abounding roses. Within, it was as clean and bright as forest cottage could be, and with its long vistas of noble trees everywhere, and the one thread of communication with the outer world that ran close to its door, was a pleasant habitation—homelike and cheerful. Bessie's aunt was, like her cottage, soberly light-hearted, kind and motherly. Upon her well scoured white deal table, she had set out a row of glancing cups and saucers, flanked with delicate bannocks of various kinds, and jelly more plentiful than Miss Crankie's. It was early in the afternoon. Mrs. Young, honest woman, hospitably purposed entertaining her guests with a magnificent tea before her husband and stalwart sons came in to their ruder and more substantial meal. She gave her niece's friend a hearty welcome; the two girls, after their dusty walk of four miles, by no means thought the kindly auntie's preparations unseasonable; but after Mrs. Young had turned a deaf ear to two or three hints from Bessie, she explained her delay at last.

"Ye see, lassies, there's an auld neighbor coming this gate this afternoon. Her and me served in one place before I was married, and she's been lang in a gentleman's house, south—near Berwick. She's an auld lass; a thrifty weel-doing carefu' woman, wi' a guid wage, and siller to the fore; but she's come to years when folk are lone, if they have nae near friends, and Rob Miller, her brither, has a housefu' o' weans; and I'm no sure that his wife can be fashed fyking about a pernickity single woman. So ye maun see and be ceevil, and take note o' Jean—how weel put on and wise-like she is—and tak a pattern by her; it's a' her ain doing; she's been working for hersel' a' her days."

Bessie drummed upon the table—looked at the tea "masking" before the fire, the smooth, well-baked bannocks, and beautiful red currant jelly upon the table—and became impatient.

"I wish she would come then, auntie. It's awfu' stourie on the road."

"Yonder's somebody in among the trees," said Jacky, glancing out.

It was Mrs. Young's friend at last, and the good woman bestirred herself to complete her table arrangements, while Bessie conveyed the mighty Leghorn bonnet and wonderful Paisley shawl, which Rob Miller's eldest daughter already looked forward to as a great inheritance, into the inner room. Mrs. Young's friend was a tall, bony, erect woman, with a thin brown face, and projecting teeth, and sandy hair carefully smoothed beneath a muslin cap, modestly, tied with a scrap of blue ribbon. She was a very homely, unhandsome-looking person, yet had an unassuming simplicity about her, not common in the upper servant class. Jean Miller had known evil in her day. The long upper lip pressing above these irregular ill-shaped teeth of her's had quivered with deep griefs many times in the painful and weary past years, which had left no record of themselves or of her course in them, save that most deeply pathetic one engraven in her own solitary high heart—a high heart it was, humble and of slight regard as was the frame it dwelt in—much stricken, sorely tried, and with an arrow quivering in it still.

Jean's hands were rigidly crossed in her lap; she was never quite at ease in idleness. Mrs. Young good-humoredly drew her chair to the table, called Bessie, placed the teapot on the tray, and began her duties. There was a simple blessing asked upon the "offered mercies," according to the reverent usage of peasant families in Scotland, and then the dainties were discussed.

"And how is Andrew winning on wi' his learning, Jean?" said Mrs. Young.

There was a slight quivering of the thin upper lip—very slight—no eye less keen than Jacky's could have perceived it.

"They tell me very weel," said Jean, meekly; "he's been getting some grand books in a prize, and they're unco weel pleased wi' him at the college."

"He's a clever lad," said Mrs. Young.

"Ay, I'll no say but he's a lad of pairts," said Jean, "if he but makes a right use o' them."

"Ay," said Mrs. Young, sympathetically, "they're no ower guid company for that, thae young doctor-lads. Eh, keep me! Jean woman, if this callant was taking to ill courses like his faither, ye wad never haud up your head again."

Jean's lip quivered again—more visibly this time—the discipline of her self-denying life had been a stern one. The prodigal of her family, the gayest, handsomest, and cleverest of them all, a good workman, and an idle one, had hung upon her, a heavy, painful burden, falling step by step in the ruinous downward course of reckless dissipation, until he ended his days at last, shorn of all the gaiety and cleverness which had thrown a veil at first upon his sin—an imbecile, drivelling drunkard. With mighty anguish, which few comprehended or could sympathize with, she had prayed, entreated, remonstrated, forgiven, and supported him through all his sad career. He left an orphan boy on her hands. With the tenderest mother-anxiety, Jean Miller had brought up this child—with genuine mother-ambition, had, at the cost of long labor, and much self-denying firmness on her own part, sent him to college when he reached proper years, eager to raise him above the fear of that terrible stain and sin which had destroyed the first Andrew—her once gay and clever brother. But of late insidious voices had whispered in her ear that the second Andrew had taken the first step in that descending course. In agony unspeakable, the youth's watchful guardian hastened to Edinburgh to ascertain the truth of this. She found it false; there was yet no appearance of any budding evil, but her heart, falling back upon its sad experience, sank within her, prophetic of evil. She said nothing in return to the ill-advised sympathy of Mrs. Young—her lip quivered—it was more eloquent than words.

"You're new to this country, I'm thinking?" she said, addressing Jacky.

"Yes," said Jacky, bashfully.

"She's frae the north country," said Mrs. Young. "Ye've been lang out o' this pairt yoursel, Jean."

"Ay," was the answer, "it's eighteen year past the twenty-first o' June—I mind the day weel."

"That would be about the time the gentleman was killed," said Mrs. Young.

"Yes," said Jean; "the very morning. I'll ne'er forget it."

"Eh, auntie!" exclaimed Bessie. "Whatna gentleman?"

Jacky did not speak, but her thin, angular frame thrilled nervously, and she fixed her keen eyes upon Jean.

"Deed a gentleman ye've heard o' often enough, Bessie," said her aunt. "Miss Alice's father—ye've heard your mother telling the story about Mr. Aytoun mony a time, nae doubt. Ye see, Jean, my sister was Mrs. Aytoun's right-hand woman. I dinna ken how the puir lady would have won through her trouble ava, when Miss Alice was born, if it hadna been for our Bell—no that he was ower guid a man, if a' tales were true, but nae doubt it was an awfu' dispensation. Ane forgets ill and wrang when the doer o't's taen away—and a violent death like that!"

"Weel," said Jean Miller, "a'body's dear to their ain. But he wasna muckle worth the mourning for."

"And how was he killed?" asked Jacky, with some trepidation.

"Anither gentleman—a fine, cheery, kindly lad as ye could see—shot him wi' a gun. It was an awfu' disgrace to the parish, as weel as a great crime; but, sae far as I could hear, the folk were mair wae for young Redheugh than they were for Mr. Aytoun."

"And were they sure he did it?" asked Jacky, breathlessly.

"Sure! Lassie, what could be surer? They found his gun, wi' his name on't and they saw him himsel leaving the wood; and unco easy he had ta'en it, as the folk say, for he was gaun whistling and singing at a fule sang, and the man's bluid on his hand."

"If he took it easy, it's mair than his friends did," said Jean Miller, significantly.

"I never heard tell of ony friends he had in this part," said the matter-of-fact Mrs. Young. "He was nephew to the auld family, and no son. I mind hearing ance that he was frae some place away in the Hielands—but maybe that was a' lees."

"But maybe you werena meaning a relation?" adventured Jacky, addressing Jean.

"Na, lassie, it was nae relation. I ken naething about his kin: it was a friend—ane that was uncommon chief wi' him. He was a student lad at that time, that had served his time to be a doctor like my ain nephew Andrew, only he was done wi' the college; and if ever mortal man was out o' his mind wi' trouble and fricht and sore grief for an unhappy reprobate, it was that lad, the morning o' the murder."

"Did you see him?" exclaimed Jacky, anxiously.

"Ay, lass, I saw him. I was gaun hame that very day to my place that I'm in yet—I've been eighteen year past wi' the same mistress—and it happened I was by that waterside between eight and nine in the morning. I was but a young lass then, and I had reason for't—it's nae matter now what it was. I was coming round the howe o' the brae where the road turns aff to the Milton, when I met that lad. That white apron had mair a life-like color than he had on his face; but, for a' that, he was wiping his brow for heat. The look of him was like the look of a man that had the bluid standing still in his veins. He neither saw me, nor the road he was gaun on, but just dashed on right before him, as if naething could stop him in the race. Ye may tak my word, it's nae little grief like what men ca' sympathy or pity, that could pit a man into a blind madness like that. I ken mair about it noo than I did then."

"Woman—Jean!" exclaimed Mrs. Young; "what for did ye no come forrit at the time—it might have helped the proof? Losh! would the tane be helping the tither? would there be twa o' them at the misfortunate man?"

"Na; he was an innocent, pithless callent, that Maister Patrick," said Jean. "He could have nae hand in't. A' that day I couldna get his face out o' my mind; but I had mony things to trouble me, sorting at my mother, and putting things right for Andrew—he was doing weel then, puir man!—and getting my ain kist ready for my journey, and I gaed away early in the day, and so I didna hear o' the murder. And my mother was nae hand at the writing, and Andrew, puir man, was aye a thocht careless, and I never saw ane belanging to my ain place, to tell me the news. So a' the trying that there was, was dune, and poor young Redheugh was lying at the bottom of the sea, before I ever heard tell o't—but I've aye minded sinsyne Maister Patrick Lillie's awfu' face—I've had a kindness for him frae that day, for of a' the sair troubles in this world, I ken nane, like murning ower a sinner that ye canna mend, and yet that ye would gie your ain life for, as blythe as ever ye gaed to your rest. I ken what it is—and sure am I, that if ever there was a man distracted with the crime o' anither, it was Maister Patrict Lillie, for young Redheugh."

"And was Redheugh an ill man?" said Jacky, in a half whisper.

"I never heard an ill word o' him till then. He was as weel likit as a man could be—and a kinder heart to puir folk there wasna in the countryside."

"And that's true," said Mrs. Young. "Ye should take it to yoursels, lassies—you that are young, and havena got the rule o' your ain spirits. There was a fine young gentleman, ye see, wi' routh o' a' thing, as grand as heart could desire, and yet he tint baith life and name, in this world and the next, a' for an evil anger in his heart. It's an awfu' warning—it's our pairt to improve it for our ain edification."

"And what for was the gentleman angry at Mr. Aytoun?" asked Bessie.

"Oh! the adversary has aye plenty spunks to light that fire wi'. Some folk say yae thing, and some anither. I've heard it was for speaking lightly of a young lady that was trothplighted to Redheugh."

"And what for did he no fecht him, the way folk fecht in books?" said Bessie.

"Nae doubt because the enemy thought he had fa'en on an easier plan of putting an end to them baith. Nae mortal in this world, let alane a bit lassie like you, can faddom the wiles o' the auld serpent, or the weakness o' folk's ain treacherous hearts. It's no what folk should do, to be making a wark about a criminal like that, that shed blood wi' a wilful hand—but there was mony a heart in the parish wae for Redheugh."

"And him that ye saw coming out of the wood?" said Jacky, tremulously, turning to Jean Miller again: "how would he ken?"

"I canna tell," said Jean. "It was my thought he had met Redheugh, or seen him, when the deed was new done—and it stunned the very soul within him, so that he scarce kent in his extremity what it was, that was pitting him distracted. I was asking Rob's wife about him last night: she says his sister and him are living their lane in an unco quiet way. Puir lad!—but he'll be a man of years now."

"And ye didna speak to him?" said Jacky.

"Speak to him! Lassie, if ye havena a lighter weird than ither folk, ye'll ken before lang, that sore trouble is not to be spoken to. I wad rather gang into a king's chamber unbidden, than put mysel forrit, when I wasna needed, into the heavy presence of grief."

"For grief is a king, too," murmured Jacky.

"And so it is," said Jean Miller, with another emphatic quiver of her lip—the little narrow Edinburgh attic, in which her student nephew toiled, or ought to toil, rising before her eyes, and her heart yearning over him in unutterable agonies of tenderness—"and so it is—and kenning that there's sin in ane ye like weel, or fearing that there's sin, in ane whose purity is the last hope o' your heart, that's the king o' a' griefs. But, mind, ye mauna say a word of this ower again. I never tell't onybody before now, and I would like ill to add a trouble to a sair heart. Mind, ye mauna mention this again."

"Yonder's my uncle!" exclaimed Bessie, whom this grave episode had wearied mightily, "and Jamie, and Michael, and Tam. We've twa good hours yet, Jacky, before, ye need to gang hame, and Miss Anne winna be angry if you're a thocht late. We'll gang and let ye see the Fairy Well—it's at the ither end o' the wood. Eh, woman, ye dinna ken how bonnie it is!"

But Jacky had no heart for the Fairy Well, or the rude gallantry of Tam, and Michael, and Jamie. She was too full of the great intelligence she had gathered for her mistress. She drew her own conclusions, quickly enough, if not very clearly, but she saw at once that Anne would think it of the highest importance. How she knew so much we cannot tell—she could not have told herself. These electric thrills of intuition, which put the elf into possession of the most secret and guarded desires and wishes of her superiors, were as much a mystery to herself as to others. There were various mysteries about her—not the least of these being the reason why the spirit of a knight errant, of as delicate honor, and heroic devotion, as ever adorned the brightest age of chivalry, should have been endued with the singular, and by no means elegantly formed garment, of this girl's dark elfin frame and humble place.

So Jacky with much weariness, physical and mental, endured the visit to the Fairy Well; and then under the safe conduct of Tam, Mrs. Young's youngest son, and "convoyed" half way by Bessie and Michael, returned to Aberford. The night had fallen before she reached Miss Crankie's house. Anne, newly returned from a long and ineffectual survey of Schole, had passively submitted to have candles placed upon her table by Miss Crankie's servant. She still sat by the window, however, looking out upon that centre of mysterious interest. It was perfectly still—only a faint reflection of light upon the dark water told of a watcher in the high chamber of the desolate house.

Jacky entered, and Anne turned to ask her kindly how she had enjoyed her visit. "I dinna ken, Miss Anne," said Jacky, "but if ye please—"

"What, Jacky?"

"Would ye let me draw down the blind, and put in your chair to the table, because I've something to tell you, Miss Anne."

Anne consented immediately. The room looked, as dusky parlors will look by faint candle-light in the evenings of bright summer days, very dull and forlorn and melancholy. Anne seated herself smiling by the table; she expected some chronicle of little Bessie's kindred, or at the utmost some confession of petty ill-doing, which burdened Jacky's conscience. Jacky's conscience was exceedingly tender; she did make such confessions sometimes.

"If ye please, Miss Anne," began Jacky earnestly, "Bessie's aunt kens Jean Miller."

"And who is Jean Miller, Jacky?" said Anne, smiling.

"And if ye please, Miss Anne, Jean Miller was in the wood by the waterside, at the brae, where the road goes to the Milton farm, eighteen years ago, on the twenty first of June."

It was Anne's turn to start, and look up anxiously now. Jacky went on in the firm steadiness of strong excitement.

"And if ye please, Miss Anne, she saw a man; and it wasna Mr. — it wasna the gentleman they ca' young Redheugh—"

"Who was it, Jacky?"

"His face was whiter than white cloth, and he was like as if the blood was standing still in his veins, and he was running straight on, as if he neither saw the road nor who was looking at him; and as he ran, he wipit his brow, for a' that he was whiter than death."

Anne was walking through the room in burning agitation; she could not rest—now she came up to Jacky, as the girl made a pause for breath, and grasped her arm.

"Who was he, Jacky—who was he?"

"If ye please, Miss Anne, it was the gentleman at Schole. She called him Mr. Patrick Lillie."

Anne put her hands up to her head, dizzy and stunned; she felt like one who had received a mighty shock, and scarcely knew either the instrument or the reality of it in the first extremity of its power. She did not say a word—she did not think—she sat down unconsciously on her chair, and pressed her hands to her head with some vague idea of crushing the dull indefinite pain out of it. Jacky stood beside her, pale, self-possessed, but trembling violently; the girl's excitement had reached a white heat—intensely strong and still.

Deadly light and deadly darkness struggling for hopeless mastery—a goal so nearly won, and yet so utterly removed. A long, low cry of pain came from Anne's parched lips; she had not strength or heart to inquire further; a fearful possibility came upon her now, which had never struck her mind before.

At length, when the violence of the first shock was moderated, she began again to question Jacky. Jean Miller's explanation of the haggard looks and wild bewilderment of Norman's friend composed, though it could not convince her. She must see him, this mysterious sufferer, must ascertain—standing before him face to face—what of this dark dread might be true, and what false. It would not leave her: before she had been alone for ten minutes, the deadly bewilderment had returned, and what to do she knew not!

CHAPTER XXVI

The next morning rose, dim, hot, and oppressive, suiting well, in its unnatural stillness and sultry brooding, with the terror of bewilderment and darkness which had fallen upon Anne. The tossings and wild restlessness of that mental fever, the gloomy clouds that had settled upon the future, the sad significance with which Christian Lillie's words came burning back upon her memory—bore her down in dark blinding agony as those heavy thunder clouds bore down upon the earth. She wandered out:—with eyes keen for that one object, and veiled to all things else, she hovered about Schole. Once as she lingered by the hedge, she saw an upper window opened, and the pale head which she had seen once before, with its high snowy temples and thin hair, and delicately lined face, looked out steadfastly upon the gloomy weltering water. The eyes were blue, deep, and liquid as a summer evening sky—the face, with all its tremulous poetry, and exquisite delicacy of feebleness, was gazing out with a mournful composure, which made its extreme susceptibility and fluctuating language of expression, more remarkable than ever. Calmly mournful as it then was, you could so well see how the lightest breath would agitate it—the faintest whisper sway and mould these delicate facile features. One long, steadfast sad look was thrown over the darkly silent water, and brooding ominous sky, and then the window was closed. Anne remained upon the sands nearly the whole day—but saw nothing more of the mysterious inhabitants of Schole.

Wild whispers of wind curled along the dark Firth as the evening fell. All the day, the earth had been lying in that dread, bewildered pause which comes before a thunder storm. Now, as Anne sat looking out into the darkness, the tempest began; the night was very dark—the whole breadth of the sky was covered by one ponderous thunder-cloud, through which there suddenly shot a sheet of ghastly light. Anne was still at the window—she started back, but not before the scene revealed by that flash, had fixed itself in its terrific gloom and unearthly colors upon her memory. The dismal outline of the house of Schole—the sea beyond, plunging and heaving in black wrath—and on its troubled and gloomy bosom, a drifting, helpless ship, the broken masts and rigging of which seemed for the moment flaming with wild, phosphoric light. Anne shrank from the window; but in a moment returned in intense anxiety, too thoroughly aroused and absorbed to think of fear.

Another flash, and yet another—and still the helpless, dismantled ship was drifting on; she fancied she could see dark figures, specks in the distance, clinging to the yards; she fancied she could discern the black waves weltering over the buried hull, as the light fell full upon the vessel—there was a blind incompetency in its motions which showed that its crew had lost command of it.—She saw the falling of some spar—she fancied she could hear a terrible shrill cry; she threw open her window. The thunder was pealing its awful trumpet-note into the dense darkness:—gazing eagerly through the gloom she waited for another flash.

"For guid sake come in—for pity's sake come in," cried Miss Crankie, pulling her from behind. The sisters, their maid, and Jacky had crowded together into Anne's room in the gregarious instinct of fear.

Bursting over the mighty gloom of waters flashed that death-like illumination. There were figures on the yards of the drifting ship—there were wild cries of sharp despair and anguish; you could fancy there were even agonized hands stretching out in vain for help, and there were—yes, there were also figures upon the sands. "God preserve us!" exclaimed Miss Crankie in overwhelming awe and excitement as the flash shone over their faces. "Miss Ross for pity's sake come in."

Anne did come in—she snatched a shawl which hung upon a chair, and hurried blindly forward to the door.

"Where are ye gaun?" exclaimed Miss Crankie.

It was echoed in different tones by all the others, as they crowded together in awe and terror.

"To the sands—to the sands," said Anne: she made her way through them in spite of remonstrance and entreaty: she extricated herself from the detaining grasp of Miss Crankie, and leaving the house, ran hastily towards Schole.

It was a fearful night; the wind had risen imperceptibly from the wild whispers which crept over the Firth in the earlier evening to a shifting, coarse, impetuous gale. The lightning, as it burst in sheets over the earth, revealed strange glimpses of the shivering summer foliage and verdure, which bore so strange a contrast to the storm raging above. Anne saw nothing but the black, weltering water—the helpless drifting ship—the deadly danger of some souls—the help that might be rendered them.

Before she reached Schole, Miss Crankie and Jacky overtook her—none of them spoke. All were agitated, excited, and anxious—all were looking eagerly towards the sea.

Another flash—the black waters were dashing high up on those feeble spars. Clinging to them in the wild vehemence of despair were several men, and one slight shadow bound as it seemed to the mast—could it be a woman in that extremity? The hull was covered—the waters appeared to rise higher every moment.—There was a little knot of people on the sands—was there no help?

Again the deadly illumination bursts over sea and sky. There is a figure struggling through the surge—you catch a glimpse of him—now fighting through the foam—now buffeting with the black waves. Anne and her companions are already on the sands; they see a strong rope trailing over the wet shore—the other end is fastened round the body of this brave man. The little knot on the shore is sternly silent—fearfully anxious. No one looks in the face of his neighbor they are watching with intense, unswerving gaze, the progress of that adventurer across the gloomy water. Even Anne scarcely notes that the gates of Schole stand open, and there are lights within!

They see him again further in, when the next flash comes, fighting vigorously through the waves; the dark figures on the yards of the helpless ship have ceased to cry—they too are watching (who can tell with what agonies of fear and hope?) the speck that fights towards them through the turbid gloom of that dark sea.

There is a long pause this time, between the lightning and its accompanying thunder. In the dense gloom they can discover nothing of his progress. They wait in intense anxiety for the next flash.

The water is bathed in light again: he is returning. He carries an indistinct burden in one arm, guiding himself painfully as they can discern by the tightened rope. The men on shore assist him warily—another long buffeting—another breathless watch, and he has reached solid land again.

Who is this man? Anne Ross's eyes are strained eagerly to discover. The light from a lantern streams on a woman carried in his arms; he did not wait to bring her fully to the land, but placing her in the hold of one of the lookers on, turned instantly back again—back through the gloomy, heaving, turbid water, to save more lives—to complete the work he had begun.

Anne watched him toiling back again through surge and foam, so anxiously that she scarcely noted the burden he had brought from the wreck in his arms. Now a faint cry recalled her attention; the saved woman was a young mother clasping an infant convulsively to her breast. Two or three female figures were already kneeling round her—Miss Crankie, Jacky, and another.—Anne joined them; the third person was Christian Lillie.

They could scarcely draw the child from the strained arms that clasped it; it was alive—nothing more. The agonized hold relaxed at last, and Miss Crankie received it from the mother.

"Let us take her in," said Christian Lillie raising the young woman in her arms.

She resisted feebly.

"No—no till they're a' safe; no till I see Willie."

Miss Crankie carried the child into Schole. Christian and Anne wrapped the young mother in a shawl, and supported her.—Her limbs were rigid with the terrible vigil. She gazed in agony towards the ship, and murmured:

"He'll no leave it till the last; he'll no save himsel till a'body else is saved. Oh! the Lord keep him—Willie!—Willie!"

And there they remained till six heroic voyages had been made to the helpless vessel. They were all saved at last. The last, the husband of the young woman, and captain of the ship, fighting his own way to the shore; he had more strength or nerve than the rest.

And who had done it all? The light from the lantern streamed for a moment on his face—that pale susceptible face, whose delicate features spoke so eloquently the language of expression—the thin hair clung to his white temples; his eyes were shining with unnatural excitement—with something which looked like an unnatural vehemence of hope. It was Patrick Lillie!

The bystanders and the saved men alike poured into Schole; they were all assembled in the large old-fashioned kitchen. Their deliverer had disappeared. Miss Crankie, alert and active, went about, briskly helping all. Christian was there, and Anne.—Seven lives in all had been saved by Patrick Lillie. The young wife of the captain lay almost insensible in an easy chair; she had borne the extremity of danger bravely, but now she sank—the over-strained nerves gave way—she could hardly answer the inquiries of her husband.

By and by, under Christian's directions, he carried her to a small room upstairs, where a bed had been hastily prepared for her. Anne volunteered her attendance, and rendered it with all care and tenderness; she was left alone with the young mother, Christian and the captain of the ill-fated vessel in the meantime arranging for the accommodation of the men.

The rigid limbs of Anne's patient relaxed at last; the chill was gradually overcome, and about an hour after they had been brought within the sheltering walls of Schole, Anne received the infant from Miss Crankie to satisfy the eager mother. The strangers by this time were gone; the shipwrecked men were accommodated as well as might be in the comfortable kitchen.—Miss Crankie herself, when there remained nothing further to be done, departed also—only Anne continued with her patient—she had not seen either Patrick or Christian again.

Drawing the baby to her breast, the young mother soon fell into a refreshing sleep. Anne sat thoughtfully by her bed-side—now and then she heard a footstep below testifying that the household was still astir. She was anxious to remain as long as possible—to endeavor to open some communication with this singular brother and sister. For the moment she had forgotten Jean Miller's history, and shuddered and trembled as she remembered it—would they avoid her still?

The room she occupied had a faded red curtain drawn along the further wall; she fancied she heard a low murmur as of some voice beyond it, and rose to see. The wall was a very thin partition which had evidently been put up in some emergency to make two rooms of one—immediately behind the curtain was a door standing ajar. Anne could see through into another room guarded like this by a curtain, placed there for some simple purpose of preventing a draft of air as it seemed, for each of the rooms had another door, and both entered from a gusty, windy gallery.

And there was a voice proceeding from that outer room—a solitary voice, low-toned, and strange—it was reading aloud as it seemed, although its owner was evidently alone. "Behold, Lord, the half of my goods I give to the poor, and if I have taken anything from any man by false accusation, I restore him fourfold."—Anne glanced back to see that her patient slept; she was lying in a calm slumber, luxuriously peaceful, and at rest. The low voice went on:

"Not fourfold but sevenfold. Lord! Thou seest the offering in my hand. Thou who didst not reject this sinner of old times.—Thou who didst tread wearily that way to Jericho for this publican's sake, who was a son of Abraham. Lord, Lord, rejectest Thou me?—seven for one—wherefore did I toil for them, but to lay them at Thy feet—seven saved for one lost. Oh, Thou blessed One, where are Thy tender mercies—Thy loving kindnesses—wilt Thou shut thy heaven only to me?"

There was a pause; the voice was broken and unsteady; the strange utterance passionate and solemn; it was resumed:

"Not thy heaven, unless it be Thy will—not Thy glory or Thy gladness—only Thy forgiveness, merciful Lord, only one uplifting of Thy reconciled countenance. There is no light. I grope in the noonday, like a blind man, I cannot see Thee—I cannot see Thee! Lord, I confess my iniquity before Thee. Lord, I restore Thee sevenfold. Look upon my offering—seven for one! I bring them to Thy feet—seven saved for one lost! Lord of all tenderness—of all compassion, Thou most merciful—most mighty—is it I—is it I? Wilt Thou reject only me?"

Anne stood fixed in silent, eager interest—she could not think of any evil in her listening. She was too deeply moved—too mightily concerned for that!

"Thou knowest the past. Thou, who ordainest all things, dost know these fearful years. Blood for blood. Lord, thou hast seen mine agonies—Thou knowest how I have died a thousand times in this fearful, blighted life: look upon mine offering—I bring thee back sevenfold. Lord of mercy, cast me not away for evermore!"

The voice ceased. Anne cast a tremulous glance from the edge of the curtain. He was sitting by a table, a Bible lying open before him. Large drops hung upon his thin, high forehead—his delicate features were moving in silent agonies of entreaty—a hot flush was on his cheek. He suddenly buried his face in his hands, and bowed it down upon the open Bible. Very fearful was this to see and hear! This living death of wakeful misery—this vain struggling to render with his own hands the atonement which he, of all men, needed most—while the great Evangel of divine love and tenderness, with its mightier offering and all-availing sacrifice, lay unapplied at his hands.

Anne drew back in awe and reverence, and carefully closed the door—it was not meet that she should pry further into the secret agonies of this stricken and sinful spirit, as it poured itself forth before its God. She returned to the bedside, her head throbbing with dull pain, her heart full of darkness and anguish. Was it true?—was it indeed true?—a haunting fear no longer, but a deadly and hopeless reality!

At intervals she heard the murmurings renewed, and watched in breathless anxiety then, lest her patient should wake—at length it ceased altogether. The young mother slept peacefully with her infant nestling in her arms—a strange contrast there was between the sleeper and the watcher—the one in delicious safety and rest, after deadliest peril—the other wading through a restless sea of grief and pain, to which there seemed neither shore nor boundary, involving agonies mightier than death.

The night wore swiftly on—the morning rose as calm and sunny as if storms had never raged in the soft atmosphere which it gilded with its early sunbeams. Anne rose to look from the window—the Firth lay broad before her, still something moved and unquiet—rolling long waves upon the shore, and specked like the breast of some war-horse, with spots of foam. At a little distance, dashed against a bold, projecting cliff, the masts of the hapless vessel appeared through the dark water. Anne shuddered when she saw the white spars, rising so very short a way above the broad surface of the Firth. A little longer delay last night—a paroxysm of desperate energy a little less bold, and these hapless seamen, and this youthful mother, had been lying, far from all consciousness of earthly pain or pleasure, in the dark graves of the sea!

Sevenfold—seven saved for one lost! Alas, was this all?—had he no hope but this?

Anne's patient waked—she began to look about her confusedly—then she recollected herself: "Willie, Willie, where is he—is he safe?"

Anne hastened to reassure her; but finding that she only partially succeeded, and hearing as she thought some one stirring below, she left the room to seek "Willie," to satisfy his anxious wife.

In a small bare parlor below she found the serving-woman of the Lillies and Jacky—they had just made a fire, and Marget, with considerable grumbling, was preparing tea. Jacky, looking very dark, and pale, and wakeful, was moving about in her own intense stillness of nervous activity, discharging various pieces of work entrusted to her, and returning instantly to seek more.

"I declare," exclaimed Marget, peevishly, as Anne reached the door, "ye're enough to pit a body daft. Afore ane can think ye're weel begun wi' ae turn, ye're seeking anither. Have ye washen a' the cups?"

"Yes."

Marget looked back—the long array of gleaming earthenware spoke for itself. In anticipation of so many stranger guests, Marget had collected a dusty congregation of cups and saucers, out of the corners of a dark old pantry.

"Do ye aye do your work as cleverly? Ye're a strange speerit o' a creature to get through a turn at that rate. Are ye aye as fast?"

"Ay," said Jacky, bashfully, "when there's ony need."

"I wadna like to be trysted to haud ye gaun. Ye wad be as ill to ser as Michael Scot's man. Get out yon muckle tray, and tak the dust aff't, and set down the cups—it's aye something. Eh, Mem, I beg your pardon!"

This was addressed to Anne, whom Marget descried for the first time standing behind her. Anne asked where the young captain was.

"Ye see, they're a' lying in the kitchen, puir creatures. It was the warmest place, and we made shake-downs to them as well as we could; and no to disturb them, I kindled my bit fire in here—and your lassie is very handy, Mem, and I'm muckle obliged to ye for letting her help me. Ye see I'll hae plenty on my hands wi' a' thae strangers, and trouble in the house forbye."

"Is any one ill?" asked Anne, eagerly.

"Ye see, it's just yin o' Mr. Patrick's ill turns. What was onybody to expect after the way he exposed himsel last night?—a frail man like him fighting through the sea as if he had been a giant—and he's waur than ordinar the day."

"Can I see Miss Lillie?" said Anne.

"Miss Kirstin's been at his bedside close, since ever we got the men sorted in the kitchen. She had to wile him out o' his ain room, because the young Captain's wife was in the next, and she was feared he would disturb her, and he's lying up in the west room. He'll no hear o' a doctor—maybe it's because he kens about physic himself—ony way he'll no have yin near him."

"But Miss Lillie would see me perhaps, if you asked her," said Anne.

"She's no fond o' onybody fashing her, when she's no wanting them," said Marget, "and it's ill my pairt to anger my mistress.—I've been here even on wi' her this sixteen year—I come frae Falkirk mysel, and dinna belang about this place—and a guid mistress she is, if she's no just like ither folk, And it's a lang trail up that weary stair when ane's breath is as short as mine—and—if ye have nae objection, Mem, I wad rather ye would wait till she comes down hersel. She'll be wanting something for Mr. Patrick before lang."

"Will you ask the Captain of the ship to come to me then?" asked Anne.

Marget went with some reluctance, and returned in a few minutes with the stalwart young Captain. Anne begged her to guide him to his wife's room, and then opening the outer door, stepped out herself into the garden for a moment's refreshment in the cool morning air.

Fresh, bright, healthful, tinged and gilded with their young sunbeams, while everything around rejoiced in its lightsome breadth and purity, Anne almost fancied it strange that the joyous air did not shrink from these gray walls—so full of sin and grief—sorrow, remorse, and pain, that shrank from the eye of man, as they were.

When she again entered the room where she had found Marget and Jacky, the young captain of the wrecked ship was there, somewhat tremulous and unsteady, poor fellow, after his meeting with his wife. They had been looking together from the window at the lost vessel with mingled thankfulness and regret. Anne began to speak to him.

"The boat was a schooner—the William and Mary of Kincardine—homeward bound from the Baltic, with a cargo of timber. We've been water-logged for three weeks; drifting very much where the wind likit to drive us. If it had not been for the summer weather and lown winds, we must have perished before now; we've had a dreadful time—no that I care for a while of hardship myself—it like comes natural to a seafaring life—but Mary and the infant! I was saying to her the now, that she had better make up her mind, to let me go alone after this; I durst not put her in such peril again."

"She seems to have borne it bravely," said Anne.

"Ay, that she has," said the young man, his eyes glistening.—"It's often no the strongest and roughest like that can bear the most. For the bairn's sake and mine, and her mother's at hame, I believe she could have held out as long as myself. To be sure, we sheltered her, while shelter was possible, but that has not been for a while—and now she's less worn out than the men. It's a strange thing that, but I've seen the like of it before. They can stand work—plenty of it—but they canna both work and thole—and we have needed both."

"It is very strange," said Anne, "almost all of them were stronger than their deliverer."

"Ay it's no that," said the captain of the William and Mary, "it's the spirit that ever does anything. My men were stunned and helpless, worn out with the terrible watch they have kept for three weeks bye-past. The gentleman scarce so much as felt he had a body clothing him, when he saw our peril. It was the keen spirit that did it."

Anne sighed. This unhappy man, borne down by his fearful secret, his life desolated by a great hidden crime, was a very angel of bravery and goodness to the men whose lives he had saved.—She asked:

"Will the loss be great?"

The young man's countenance fell.

"No doubt it'll be heavy upon us. It's part my father's, and part mine. We built it just before I was married, as you would, maybe, notice by the name. My mother had aye a great wark with Mary, and she would have it called after us both. When the tide's out, we'll see better what's lost, and what may be saved. It's a mercy the cargo can take no scaith, being timber. Onyway it must be a heavy loss, but we may be thankful we're to the fore ourselves."

Anne did not answer. At any other time, she would have sympathized warmly with this prepossessing, youthful couple. At present, her interest and thoughts were so engrossed, that any other feeling was faint within her.

"Mary was speaking of coming down herself," said the young captain, "to thank you for your goodness. And the gentleman—I have not seen the gentleman!"

"I hear he is ill," said Anne. "I am only a—a neighbor: but I hear Mr. Lillie's exertions have hurt him—he has been long an invalid."

The young man said some words of respectful regret, and then left her to attend to his men. He wished to remove them as soon as possible—especially now, when he heard that there was sickness in the house.

Marget, with a good deal of grumbling, was preparing a breakfast for them. Anne opened the door of a room on the opposite side of the hall—it was Patrick Lillie's study—and went in. She felt she had a right. In all the world, there was no family so closely connected with her as this.

Upon the table, in the recess of the low projecting window, lay an old Latin book—others of a like nature were scattered round. Anne was sufficiently acquainted with old literature to see that some of these were rare and strange. A small pile, which she could fancy the daily and beloved companions of their owner, lay at one side. The upper one of the pile, was the "Imitatione Christi," of Thomas a Kempis, in the original Latin—the others were of the same contemplative cast. Old emblematic poems, full of devout conceits: old dialectic philosophy, subtle and shifting—a strange atmosphere for that fragile mind, with its sensitive beauty and feebleness, to breathe and dwell in.

She was thinking of him—with her hands clasped over her eyes, and her head bowed down, she was trying to think what she could do—"looking forward as the aim and expectation of your life—almost, God help us—as your hope—for a thing which you knew would rend your heart, and make your life a desert when it came." The words returned before her constantly, blinding her mind and stilling it. She could do nothing.

A hand was laid upon her shoulder. She looked up hastily—it was Christian Lillie. Her eyes were fixed upon Anne with a look of wistful inquiry: her tall figure was slightly bent. Anne saw more clearly than she had ever done before, how attenuated and worn out she was. Yet, in the melancholy face and shadowy frame, there was no trace of greater weariness than usual. She had been watching by a sick-bed all the night—and such a sick-bed!—but she thought of no rest, she evidenced no fatigue. You could fancy the soul within, so constantly awake and watching, that its thin robe of earthly covering needed not the common sustenance of feeble humanity.

"What do you here?" said Christian Lillie, "this is no air for you to breathe—no roof to cover you. Let us bear our own burden as we best can; you must not try to render help to us—no, nor even sympathy—you must go from this fated house."

Anne took into her own the thin hand which rested on her shoulder.

"You must let me stay," she said eagerly. "I can take no dismissal—you must let me stay—no one else in this wide world could be beside you as I can be—save one. I must remain with you; I must share your labors—you cannot watch continually."

"Watch!" said Christian, "I have watched continually, without ceasing night or day. You can rest who are young—you who have known no deadly evil—what rest is there for me? Leave me to my own weird. God knows, who sent it, that He has sent patience also to bear its bitterness. It was long before that came, but I watched, and waited, and prayed for it dry-eyed: tears are not for me, unless it be the terrible ones that the heart weeps when it is wrung. You must go from this place; let us not throw the shadow of our desolation over another of your blood. You must go before you are blighted."

"Do not fear me," said Anne, anxiously; "do not fear to trust me. Is not our sorrow the same—our hope the same? let me stay beside you."

"The same—the same! God forbid that you knew what you were saying. There are agonies that folk may not lay the light name of sorrow upon. Be thankful that you know nothing sorer than grief; and if you would keep your hope alive, leave the house that contains us."

"I cannot leave you; you must not ask me," said Anne; "I have a claim upon you. Do not you know better than I the bond that there is between us? I will not leave you."

Christian Lillie walked through the room slowly, sadly, heavily; she made no answer; she seemed to acquiesce at last.

For a time they both continued silent. Then Anne asked:

"Is he ill? they told me he was ill."

"He!" Christian paused; over the steadfast whiteness of her face there flushed an unnatural color. She gazed upon Anne; her wistful melancholy eyes dilating as it seemed in eager inquiry. "He!" she checked herself; it appeared to have flashed upon her that Anne knew something of their mighty secret greater than she had before thought. She controlled herself with an effort—"yes, he is ill; what can he be else but ill?"

"I must return to him," she resumed, after an incoherent pause. "Stay with us, since you will stay; but mind I have warned you, that with us there can be nothing but desolation, and blight, and hopelessness. What depths you may fathom before we are parted, I know not. It may be that you are sent thither for that end. We walk darkling, but He sees the beginning and the end: let His will be done."

She left the room—in a short time, Anne also quitted it. Marget was arranging in the kitchen the breakfast for the shipwrecked seamen. There was no scant or niggardly provision. The men, gaunt and famished-like, an uncouth company, were gathered about the table. In the little parlor sat the captain and his wife.

"Miss Kirstin said I was to see they had plenty to their breakfast," said Marget, deprecatingly, "and there wasna bread enough in the house; and I'm no sae young as I hae been mysel, forbye having a fashious hoast, and a sore shortness in my breath, sae I took the freedom to send your lass, because she was willing to gang, and I hope, Mem, ye'll no be angry."

"By no means," said Anne. "Jacky will be glad to help you, I am sure."

"She's a willing lassie," said Marget; "but if it werena that she's discreet, and does what she's bidden, I wad maist think she wasna canny. Preserve me! there she is already rattling at the gate; if she's been at Aberford, she maun hae flown."

Jacky had only been at Miss Crankie's; she returned laden with provisions sent by Anne's kind, active, odd little landlady—there was a full supply. Anne herself joined the young captain and his wife in the little parlor.

In the course of the day the forlorn crew of the "William and Mary," considerably revived by their night's rest and shelter, left Schole—with much gratitude expressed and unexpressed. William and Mary themselves proceeded, with their infant, to the house of the husband's father. The men dispersed to their various homes.

Anne remained—only once again during that day she saw Christian. Then she spoke less incoherently, with something indeed of singular gentleness, and an endeavor for the moment to forget her individual burden, as though her heart began to yearn for the sympathy of this younger sister. Patrick was very ill; he could not leave his bed.

The next day told the same tale, and so did the next—and the next again. The illness increased. The fever and agitation of that night had wrought their due effect upon the delicate, enfeebled frame whenever the desperate tension and rigid strength of its nervous excitement failed. On the fourth day, Christian, who all this time had watched unceasingly, called the medical practitioner of the little town to her brother's bedside. Anne saw him as he passed down stairs, and asked eagerly for his patient; the doctor shook his head—he could give no hope.

Anne spent the greater part of the day in Schole, returning to Miss Crankie's only for the night. Now, when Patrick's illness had increased so alarmingly, she could only exchange a passing word with Christian on the stair, or at the door of the sick-room. She had pleaded vainly for permission to help her in her tendance of the sufferer: failing in that, she gradually assumed the management of the household matters below. She lightened Christian's hands, at least so far.

A week after the shipwreck, Anne entered Christian's room—the high turret chamber from which so often she had seen the reflected light gleaming upon the dark waters of the Firth—to wait for her coming. It was a still, dim, balmy night, soft and melancholy. There was always a great attraction in that broad Firth at their feet—a kind of wandering freedom for the overcharged heavy hearts gazing forth upon it. The rounded window was veiled by an old-fashioned, faded curtain: within this there was a seat which Christian Lillie had occupied for more lingering woeful nights than we could count or record. Anne seated herself there, and looked out in the dim gloaming upon the silent land, and gleaming sea.

By-and-by she heard the slow, sad footstep enter, and sat still, in expectation of being joined immediately—for Christian, like herself, continually sought these windows; continually calmed her sorrow in the wide tranquillity and balmy peace that lay around.

"Give him to me for a prey. Lord, give him to me for a prey," were the strange words that came to Anne's ear, falling low through the tremulous darkness; "I ask not for his life. Thou knowest that I ask not for his life. My Father, wilt Thou not hear? wilt Thou forget the prayers that have risen to Thee day by day and night by night since Thou didst hide Thy countenance from us? My Lord! hast Thou said any word in vain? shall any promise be forgotten before Thee?"

The listener sat still in awe; she dared not interrupt this agony of supplication with any token of her presence.

Christian was pacing the room quickly, with tremulous step, and passionate low voice, too mightily absorbed to think of form or posture.

"If it be Thy will—Thy will—and Thy will is to seek and save the lost; and this is lost in sin, in blindness, and the deep gloom of unbelief, and it was such that Thou camest to save—such, and not the righteous. It is Thy will—it is Thy will. Grant me Thy will of salvation to this sinner—Lord! Lord!"

She paused; she threw herself on her knees; there was an indefinite sound of entreaty—groaning that could not be uttered.—Then she started to her feet again, and the words poured forth aloud, as one who finds a new argument and can scarce pause for language in which to state and plead it.

"Thou who art a man! Thou who bearest a human heart in Thy high heaven! Thou who hast entreated, and yearned, and wept over sinful brethren, whom the adversary sifted as wheat! Thou, O Lord! who wearest Thy humanity upon Thy throne!—he is a sinner—so were they whom Thou didst call Thy friends.—He hath denied Thee—so did he, for whom Thy holy lips prayed, that his faith might not fail. My Lord!—my Lord!—thou hearest always. Look down upon us, and send us deliverance."

She sat down; she put back her wet hair, and wiped the heavy dew from her forehead. Then she clasped her hands over her brow.

"Not life—not joy—not temporal deliverance—whatsoever is in Thy hands is well—be it to us as seemeth good to Thee. But light, O, my Father! light to this darkness—deliverance to this bondman—the grace of Thine infinite mercy—the touch of Thy divine compassion. Lord, if Thou wilt, Thou canst deliver him."

There was a faint call from another room. Christian Lillie paused for a moment to compose her agitated features, and then hastened to the restless sick-bed. Anne Ross sat still at the high turret window, looking out through silent tears upon the dim country, and the gleaming sea.

That sky serene, and calm, and boundless, beholding all beneath its infinite extent—that mighty eye above, looking down amid the countless myriads of its universe, as certainly upon the untold agonies of this house as if all humanity were centered there—that One, at the right hand of the Father, who, in the might of His eternal Godhead, doth dwell in heaven—a man! The appeal of the broken heart was to these; and they do not fail to answer.

CHAPTER XXVII

Wearily, mocking sick hearts with their floods of brightness, the summer days stole on. The house of Schole gaunt and melancholy, stood shrined in the full glory of that sunshine. The dark figures within wandered about in restless pain, like ghosts uncongenial to the light, or gazed forth with vacant eyes upon the rejoicing country, and dazzling sea. In the sick chamber lay that restless, suffering man, wending unconsciously nearer and nearer the valley of the shadow of death.

The doctor from the little town had visited him repeatedly.—Nearly a fortnight after the wreck, he had a final conversation with Christian. Anne was watching eagerly in Patrick Lillie's study. Christian accompanied the doctor to the door, and answered his subdued and sorrowful farewell; then she entered the study. Anne looked up anxiously in her face.

"The time has come," said Christian, solemnly, "there is no hope of his life. He has but a little way to go, and yet he knows not the only entrance. God succor us—what can we do alone? Come with me—now there is no longer any obstacle or hindrance—come with me."

Anne followed her silently. The room in which Patrick lay was high, and had also windows looking on the water—that broad placid, noble Firth, the sole companion of the watcher.

Wan and wasted, with only the hectic spot burning on his cheek to distinguish it from the pillow on which it uneasily rested, lay the dying man. Cold, wasting, death-like perspiration lay heavily upon his brow; his long, white hand and emaciated arm were stretched upon the coverlet with a power of nervous motion in them, which contrasted strangely with their color and form of death.

On a small table beside him lay a paper closely written. Near at hand were writing materials. His eyes were fixed upon the manuscript—he did not seem to notice the entrance of Christian and Anne. He was speaking in broken sentences, with incoherent intervals between.

"Sevenfold—sevenfold. Thou God of mighty justice! Thou Lord of holy revenge! What can a sinful man do more? Not an old man, O, Lord! not a little child; seven lives in their prime—seven full of health, and strength, and hopefulness—seven saved for one lost. Lord of mercy, wilt Thou accept them! what can I more?"

"Patrick," said Christian Lillie, "if the whole world had lain perishing at your feet, what more than urgent need was it to save them all; the seven will not atone for the one. If ye have no other atonement to offer, then the blood is still crying upon God for vengeance."

"Christian," exclaimed the dying man, "what can I do?—what shall I do? They tell me I am near the hour of judgment; will you thrust away my last plea?—will ye deny me my last hope? Did He not accept the publican who restored fourfold? Behold my offering, O, Lord, and be merciful—be merciful! I have toiled through all this terrible life—labored, and groaned, and fainted for the uplifting of Thy countenance—and shall I go away in darkness, and wilt Thou show me no more light at all for ever? Lord! Lord!"

The thin, worn arms were lifted in passionate appeal—the long white fingers clasped—the wasted face convulsed with despairing earnestness. Christian Lillie knelt by her brother's bedside.

"Mercy and light, Patrick—mercy and light! our Father in heaven does not give them for a hire. Take them out of a gracious hand that has paid a bitter price for the gifts—take them, Patrick. Take them from Him who has made the sole sacrifice that can stand in the sight of God. Blood for blood."

"Blood for blood!" said Patrick Lillie, with a wild shudder. "Blood for blood! has it come to this end? Christian, I have been laboring to make amends—I have labored in vain: let me pay the price now at last—there may be peace then. Let me away—let me away—I will pay the price—a life for a life!"

He was struggling to rise—his emaciated features shining wildly with his desperate purpose. Christian's arms were stretched over him, subduing the frenzy.

"Patrick," she said, solemnly, "in a little while the Lord will recall the life He has sent so fearful a shadow on. A day or two—maybe only an hour or two—and in this ghastly noon of ours, which is more terrible than the darkest midnight, the sun of your life must go down. The Lord is taking the price with his own hand. Patrick, let me but know that you are grounded on the one rock—that ye can see the one sacrifice."

The unhappy sufferer sank back exhausted.

"'Whoso sheddeth man's blood, by man shall his blood be shed.' Christian, it is a just sentence—take me away—I see it—I see it—it is what no mercy can wipe out—no grace forgive—it must be atoned for. Ye hear me, Christian! the price must be paid. If ye would have hope in my death, take me away."

"It is a just sentence," said Christian Lillie, firmly. "Just in the sight of God and man—I say not that there needs no public atonement; but ye cannot pay it now—and I say that for your life, your higher life, Patrick, an atonement has been made. Do you forget Him that died at Jerusalem? they ranked him with murderers—was He one? He was accursed for the shedders of blood. Throw but your sin upon Him—rest but your soul upon Him, and I will have hope in your death—ay! such hope as will cover all the by-gone darkness with a mist of radiance; only let me know that you are safe in His shadow—strong in His faith, and I am content."

"I have slain a man to my bruising, and a young man to my hurt," murmured the dying man, "and I should—God forgive me that I have shrunk and trembled from this fearful penalty—I should pay back blood for blood in the sight of man. Christian, hear me: I acknowledge Him, my Saviour—my Lord—my King. I acknowledge His work—only not for this—for this I must render justice in the sight of men. Let me go—I have trembled for it all these dreadful years—I have hid me from the very sunshine for its fear—I have doomed them—God bless them! God, out of his gracious heaven, send down the blessings of the covenant upon them! whom I shall never look upon in this world again—to exile and shame for me. Christian, let me go—I see it all now—my eyes are opened. Let me pay the price—then there may be peace; whoso sheddeth man's blood—Christian, let me go!"

"Patrick," said Christian Lillie, "you have told me when your mind was clear that this deed was not wilful, nor springing from a heart of evil against him that is gone. Tell me again. Patrick!—do you mind how he fled into the sacred city in the ancient Israel, who had shed blood unawares, and there was safe? Can you see? is there no shadow before your eyes? Can you tell me? Patrick, you shed this blood unawares."

A wild gleam shot over the sick man's death-like face. His lips moved—he shut them convulsively as though to keep down some thrill of agony.

"I cannot tell—I cannot tell. God help me—there is nothing clear; that I did it—that I took away the divine mysterious life which all the universe could not give back again—Christian, Christian, it will make me mad—the remembrance of it has gone near to make me mad a thousand times. Oh, that my life had been taken instead! oh, that he had slain me, and not I him!"

Christian knelt by his bedside holding his hand—he became calmer.

"Lord, show it to me—show me the past—show me what is to come. I was angry with my brother in my heart—I cannot see—I cannot tell, if the fiend was within me then. Christian, have they not suffered a death for me?—have I not slain them in cold blood with my fear and cowardice! I will do them justice—I will bear my own sin. Let me go."

He sat up in his bed, his excitement giving nervous strength to his wasted frame; as he rose he saw Anne for the first time—she stood awed and wondering by the door.

The unhappy man threw himself back upon his pillow, covering his face.

"Send her away. Do you want to kill me—do you want to betray me, Christian? Send her away."

Christian Lillie made a motion with her hand, and Anne withdrew. Most strange, and sad, and terrible was this scene; this unhappy sufferer enduring in those agonies so intense a retribution—eager to do justice on his death-bed, and yet shrinking from the sight of her who might bring that justice speedily upon him—her, the sister of the injured Norman, who would not have inflicted another pang upon the man for whom her generous brother had sacrificed his all.

She did not see Christian again that day: during all its long, weary, sunny hours, Christian remained constantly by that sick-bed—through the shorter watches of the balmy and tranquil night her vigil continued; those melancholy wistful eyes never closed in slumber; that gaunt, attenuated frame sought neither rest nor nourishment; the agony of eighteen years had come to a climax; the heroic work of all her desolate lifetime was drawing to an end.

Anne did not leave the house till late that evening; she could hear the sound of voices in the sick chamber, and Christian's slow step sometimes traversing it, when she went away. In the morning she returned early. Christian was in her own room, as Anne could hear, while she sat in the apartment below—sometimes kneeling—sometimes pacing it slow and heavily as was her wont, and sometimes with the agitated quick step, which she had heard before during the short time in which she witnessed Christian Lillie's supplications. Her patient was for the time asleep. She was there, not resting nor seeking rest, absorbed in the unutterable earnestness of her pleadings, wrestling with God for a blessing.

The day glided on, so slow—so wearily, with but the drowsy ripples of the sea, the steady, cold, immovable beating of that strange pulse of Time, whose sound fatigues the anxious ear so miserably, and the irregular, agitated throbs of her own heart, to fill its languid lingering hours, that Anne sickened when she looked abroad upon its cloudless radiance. Then those books of Patrick Lillie's fascinated while they irked and pained her—the pensive, contemplative tone—the microscopic, inward-looking eye—the atmosphere of monastic quietude and meditative death! She was in no mood for studying character, yet she felt how strangely constituted the spirit must have been which found its daily ailment in these.

Had he done that deed and yet was he not guilty? Did he stand in the position of the manslayer, for whom God's stern law of olden vengeance, in one of those exquisite shadings of mercy, which mark the unchanging unity of our Gospel Lord and Saviour—ordained through ancient Palestine, the sacred cities of refuge? Had he shed this blood unawares? and whence then came the terrible mist which had gathered in his memory about the deed? Was it possible that he could be uncertain of himself?—that he could have forgotten those momentous circumstances? or had his long-diseased brooding over them made imagination and fact stand in his remembrance side by side?

At last, the weary day declined. Christian Lillie came to her at sunset, and with few words, bade her follow to the sick room again. Anne obeyed.

It was very near now, that awful peace of Death. The emaciated face was sharp and fixed—the stamp was upon his forehead. A little time now, and all earthly agony would be over for him.

But there was a tranquil shadow on his face, and the large caverns of Christian's eyes were full of dew, which did not fall, but yet had risen to refresh the burning lids which had kept watch so long. The manuscript was upon the table still—the thin arm lay quietly on the coverlet. A slight shudder passed across his frame as Anne entered; an involuntary thrill of that coward fear which had overwhelmed his nature. Then he turned his eyes upon her with a steadfast, melancholy, lingering look, failing sometimes for a moment as the slow blood crept coldly to his heart in another pang of terror; but renewed again—a sorrowful look of lingering, clinging tenderness, as though he saw in her face the shadow of another—the generous glance of one dearly beloved long ago, who had given up name, and wealth, and honor for his sake.

"Christian," he said, "Christian, it comes. I feel that I am entering the dark valley. What I have to do, let me do quickly.—Raise me up."

She lifted him in her arms—in her strong devotion she might have borne a threefold weight—the dying man was like an infant in her hands.

He took the pen she offered him into his unsteady fingers, and began, in feeble characters, to trace his name at the bottom of the manuscript. While he did so, he murmured broken words.

"I am guilty—I am guilty! I only. Lord, Thou knowest who hast saved me! Only his tenderness, like Thine—only his gracious heart, Thy true follower, has screened me, a miserable sinner, from the doom of the slayer! It is I only—my Lord, Thou knowest it is I!"

He had signed his name. Christian laid him back tenderly upon the pillow. With a firm hand she placed her own signature at the side of the document, and then gave the pen to Anne. The sister of the man who had done the deed, and the sister of him who had suffered for it—it was meet their names should stand together. Anne added hers. She could form some idea, of what this paper was. She signed it as a witness.

The words of the dying man ran on—a feeble, murmuring stream.

"Christian! he is alive—he is safe! No evil has come upon them! Tell me again—tell me again! They do not curse me—they forgive the miserable man who has made them exiles? It is over now, Christian. All your anguish—all your vigils: their disgrace and banishment—it is over now. God knows, who has visited me with His mercy and His light, why this desolation has fallen upon you all for my sin. I have been a coward. Christian, Christian! when they are home in their joyous household—when they have forgotten all their grief and dishonor, when they are tranquil and at rest—they will never name my name; my memory will be a thing of shame and fear: they will shrink from me in my grave."

The thin hands met in silent appeal. There was a wistful, deprecating glance thrown upon Anne and Christian.

"Patrick," said Christian, "can we ever shrink from you, who have been willing, for your sake, to endure the hardest calamity that could be thrown upon man? Can they forget your name, who have lost their own for your sake, and never murmured? Patrick! look upon his sister. She has come to us in our sorest trouble; she has clung to us with her tenderest service, as if we had blessed him, and not blighted. Take your comfort from her. As for me, my labor is over. I will live to see Marion. I must, if it be the Lord's will—but for forgetfulness, or shame, or shrinking, ye never thought of me!"

Anne stood by the bedside. The eyes of the dying man, so intensely blue, and strangely clear, were shining wistfully upon her. She could not find words to speak to him.

"Mind them of me," said Patrick Lillie, faintly. "Tell them, that if they have suffered pain for me, they never can know what agony, bitterer than death, I have endured within this desolate house. Bid them mind me as I was, in yon bright, far away time, that I have been dwelling in again this day. Tell them, the Lord has given me back my hope, that He gave me first in my youth. Tell them, I am in His hand, who never loses the feeblest of His flock. Tell them—"

He was exhausted—the breath came in painful grasps.

"Do not fear," said Anne, gently. "We will remember you in all tenderness, with sorrow and with reverence. I will answer for Norman."

"For Norman!" said the dying man. "All blessings on the name that I have not dared to say for years! The blessing of my God upon him, who has been separated from his brethren. Norman! Marion! They have suffered in exile and in grief for me. Tell them, that with my last breath, I bade God bless them—God bless them! They have done as my Lord did—they have suffered for the guilty—and He will acknowledge His own."

There was a pause. His breath came painfully. The hectic on his cheek flushed deeper. Christian made a gesture with her hand to Anne, dismissing her. He saw it.

"Stay," he said, "stay—my work is not yet done. Christian, hear me; when I have said this, I will take my journey in peace. My eyes are clear now. I dare look back to that terrible time. I did it unawares. The blood on my hand was not wilfully shed; ye hear me, ye trust me, Christian! I had that deadly weapon in my hand; my mind was far away as it often was. I was thinking of the two, and of their bright lot; my eye caught something dark among the trees. I thought it was a bird. Christian, it was the head of Arthur Aytoun, the man that I was hating in my heart! I came home; my soul was blinded within me. I was as innocent of wish to harm him as was the water at my feet; but yet in my inmost heart long before, I had been angry with my brother! My soul was blind; now I see, for the Lord has visited me with His mercy. You know all now. I have sinned; but I did this unawares, and into His city of refuge, my Lord has received my soul."

The shadows were gathering—darker, closer—the face becoming deadly white. His breath came with less painful effort, but the end was at hand. He made a sign which Christian knew. She lifted a Bible, and began to read. Anne stood behind in silent awe, as the low voice rose through that dim room, whose occupant stood upon the eternal brink so near an unseen world. "There is, therefore, now no condemnation." Wondrous words! spanning all this chaos of human sin and feebleness with their heavenward bridge of strong security.

Christian read on calmly, solemnly while the slow life ebbed wave by wave. She had reached the end.

"Who shall separate us from the love of Christ? shall tribulation, or distress, or persecution, or famine, or nakedness, or peril, or sword? Nay, in all these things we are more than conquerors through Him that loved us. For—"

She was stayed by the outstretching of that worn and wasted hand. A strange shrill voice, unnaturally clear, took up the words:

"I am persuaded that neither death, nor life, nor angels, nor principalities, nor powers, nor things present, nor things to come, nor height, nor depth, nor any other creature, shall be able to separate me from the love of God, which is in Christ Jesus my Lord."

Christian sprang forward to support him. He needed no support. In the might of that one certain thing, of which he was at last persuaded, the spirit of Patrick Lillie had ascended into his Saviour's heaven.

A pale, feeble, worn-out garment, over which no longer the fluctuating fever of a wavering mind should sweep and burn—a fair, cold face, whose gentle features could answer no longer to the thousand changes of that delicate and tremulous soul, Christian laid back upon the pillow—no longer restless, or ill at ease, or fearful, but sleeping peaceful sleep—tranquil and calm at last!

And she stood by his bedside who had borne, through all these dreadful years, the strong tenacious life of deadly agony for him. As pale as his, was the thin, worn face bending over him; for a moment she listened with that intensest pain of watching, which seems to make the listener blind, and concentrates all the senses in that one—listening for the faint fall of his breath. It was in vain: those pale lips, until the great day of resurrection, should draw breath again—never more.

"I thank God," said Christian Lillie, in the solemn calm of that death-chamber; "I thank God, Patrick, my brother, that you are safe, and at rest. Safe after perils greater than time could wear out. At rest after the hourly warfare and deadly travail of a lifetime—I thank God. My Father!—my Father! I thank Thee, who rejectest no petition, that Thou hast heard my cry!"

Her hands were clasped. Anne feared they were becoming rigid in the attitude of supplication so common to them. She laid her hand upon Christian's arm.

"Ay, I will not linger," said Christian, "but look at him—look at him at peace, and blessed at last. Do you see my tears? I have not shed one since yon June morning, but now I can weep. I will not linger; but can you not feel the blessedness of seeing his salvation—his rest in the fair haven—his solemn peace at last? I thank God, Patrick—I thank God!"

"You are worn out," said Anne, gently; "come now and take rest—leave the further cares of this sad time to me."

The tears were falling from her eyes like large soft rain-drops; there was a quivering, woeful smile about her lip.

"Ay, ay, I will go; I have one work yet for his sake, and theirs. At peace in the pure heaven of our Lord and Saviour—at rest. In hope and certainty that nothing can shake again, look how he has begun his tranquil waiting for the second coming. He is with his Lord, and I—yes, I will go and rest. Here I take up again the human hope that has been dead within me for eighteen lingering years; it died by him, and by him it is alive again. I will go and take rest for my labor. I trust him to your hands; I have never trusted him before in the care of any mortal. Now, I must rest for Norman's sake, and you will watch for Patrick's; I trust him to you."

And so, at last Anne was able to lead her to her own chamber. The tension of mind and frame had been so long and stern, that now, when it was relaxed, Anne trembled for the issue; but Christian had borne all the vicissitudes of mental agony too long to sink now when there still remained labor to do "for his sake, and theirs." She suffered Anne's attendance with a strange child-like gentleness, as of one whose own long task is over; and while she lay down upon her bed, continued to speak of that blessed rest and peacefulness with a tremulous quivering smile, and wandering of thought which brought the tears fast from Anne's eyes.—Deeply pitiful and moving was this pathetic garment of her grief.

At last, sleep was mercifully sent, such sleep as God gives to His beloved—calm, serene, and child-like—the sad smile trembling upon her lip—the mild tears stealing from under her closed eyelids, and her soul the while carried back to times of past tranquillity—the peace and gentle joyousness of the old cottage home.

From Christian's bedside, Anne proceeded to a sadder work; a work too painful and repugnant for anything but callous habit, or deep tenderness. She called up the old serving-woman, and together they rendered the last offices to the dead.

The solemn, calm, majestic, awful dead, in whose still presence, were he in life the meanest, the princeliest soul of earth must stoop and bow. Strange doom which, with its sad mysterious ending, can make the meanest lifetime a sublime, unequalled thing! Strange death which, in its ghostly silence, can thrust so lightly the vain speculations of man aside, and make our mortal flesh shrink and tremble from the thrilling power of unseen life, that moves behind the curtain of its gloom. What man shall stand in its presence, and dare to say that this is the end? What man shall look upon its majesty, and tell us that is the mere death at which he thrills and shivers? It is not so—mightier, more terrible and great—it is the supernatural glow of an unseen life beyond that thus appals us.

The moonbeams glided over the Firth in spiritual stillness.—The necessary offices were done, and Anne and Marget sat down in a small adjoining room to watch. The old woman began to nod in her chair; this was to her but an ordinary death, and death to those who are accustomed to assist at its dread ceremonials, loses its awe and solemnity. Anne opened the window as the sun rose, and bathed her pale face in the delicious air of the morning. Under her sadness and awe a solemn joy was trembling.—Her work was accomplished—now for the exile's home-coming—for household rest and companionship—for communion with the near and dear kindred over whom her heart had yearned so long.

The country was beginning to awake: the early morning labor of those rural people had commenced. She could see smoke rising from the indistinct dim towns on the Fife coast.—She awoke her companion, and then went softly into Christian's room.

But Christian was gone; her Bible lay open upon the table, where she had sought its comfort when she rose. Her plain black silk cloak and bonnet had been taken away. Anne began to be alarmed; where could she be?

In the chamber of death she was not. Anne fancied she could perceive some trace of her having entered the room, but they had watched in the adjoining apartment, and Anne knew that she had been wakeful. She hurried down stairs and searched the rooms below: Christian was not to be found.

Looking through the low window of the study, she saw Jacky standing at the gate, and hastened to admit her. The girl was shivering with intense anxiety, and alarm—she had been standing there for more than an hour. On the previous night, she had haunted the precincts of Schole in fear and trembling for her mistress, and had been abruptly dismissed by Marget, with a fretful explanation that "Maister Patrick was in the deadthraw"—since then she had been watching at the window of Miss Crankie's parlor. Now, she was awe-stricken, speaking below her breath, and letting fall now and then silent, solitary, large tears. She had never been in the shadow of death before, and her imaginative spirit bowed before its majesty.

"Jacky," said Anne, "he is dead."

Jacky did not answer—she only glanced a timid, wistful, upward look out of those keen, dark eyes of hers, dilated and softened with her sympathy.

"You will come in and stay with me, Jacky," said Anne. "I must remain here for some days—you are not afraid?"

Afraid! no. Jacky was stricken with awe and sad reverence, but not with fear.

"I do not well know what to do, Jacky," said Anne, thoughtfully. "Miss Lillie seems to have wandered out: I cannot find her."

"If ye please, Miss Anne, I saw her."

"Where, Jacky?"

"I was standing at the window looking out—it was just at the sun-rising—and I saw the gate of Schole opened canny, and Miss Lillie came out. She was just as she aye is, only there was a big veil over her face, and she took the Aberford road; and she didna walk slow as she does at common times, but was travelling ower the sands as fast as a spirit—as if it was a great errand she was on; naebody could have walkit yon way that hadna something urging them, and I thought then that Mr. Patrick was dead."

Anne did not observe Jacky's reflections and inferences—she was too much occupied in speculations as to Christian's errand.

"If ye please, Miss Anne, would ye no go up to your ain room and lie down? I'll stay and keep a'thing quiet."

"I must see Miss Crankie," said Anne. "The air will revive me, Jacky, and I could not rest. In the meantime, you must stay at Schole, and see that no one disturbs the stillness that belongs to this solemn vicinity. We should have reverenced him living—we must reverence him more sadly dead."

Jacky was overcome—her eyes were flooded—she needed to make no promise. Anne's charge to her was given in consequence of some grumbling threat of Marget's to "get in some o' the neighbors—no to be our lane wi' the corp." Anne was determined that there should be no unseemly visits, or vulgar investigation of the remains of one who had shrunk from all contact with the world so jealously.

"If ye please, Miss Anne—"

Anne had put on her bonnet, and stood at the gate on her way out.

"What is it, Jacky?"

Jacky hung her head in shy awkwardness.

"It was just naething, Miss Anne."

Anne comprehended what the "just naething" was, and, understanding the singular interest and delicate sympathy of this elfin attendant of hers, knew also how perfectly she was to be trusted.

"Jacky," she said, "what I tell you, you will never tell again, I know: this gentleman who died last night was nearly connected with us—if Marget asks you any questions, you can tell her that; and my work is accomplished here—accomplished in sorrow and in hope. By-and-by my brother of whom you have heard, will come home I trust, in peace and honor, to his own house and lands.—The work we came here for is done."

Jacky was tremulously proud, but she had yet another question.

"And if ye please, Miss Anne—little Miss Lilie?"

A radiant light came into Anne's eye. It was the first time she had dared to speak of the near relationships with which she now hoped to be surrounded.

"Lilie is my niece—my brother's child—I believe and hope so, Jacky."

Jacky's first impulse was to turn her back on Schole, and flee without a moment's delay to Oranside. She recollected herself, however; she only sat down on the mossy garden-path, and indulged in a fit of joyous crying—pride, and exultation, and affection, all contributing their part. "For I kent," said Jacky to herself, tremulously, when Anne was gone, "I aye kent she was like somebody—a' but the e'en—and it would be her mother's e'en!"

But Jacky recollected her charge—recollected the solemn tenant who lay within those walls, and became graver. Marget was sitting in the kitchen when she entered, refreshing herself with a cup of tea. Their salutations were laconic enough.

"Is that you, lass?" said Marget.

"Yes, it's me," said Jacky. "Miss Anne said I was to come in and stay; and she'll be back soon hersel."

"And wha's Miss Anne that's taking sae muckle fash wi' this puir afflicted family?" said Marget. "Are ye ony friend to us, lassie? or what gars your mistress and you come into our house, this gate?"

"Miss Anne says Miss Lillie is a friend. I think it's maybe by ither friends being married, but I dinna ken—only that they're connected—Miss Anne said that."

"And what do they ca' ye?" continued Marget.

"They ca' me Jacobina Morison—I was christened that after my uncle—but I aye get Jacky at hame; and they ca' Miss Anne, Miss Ross, of Merkland."

"She'll be frae the north country," said Marget. "I never heard o' ony Norland freends Miss Kirstin had. Onyway it maun be for love ony fremd person taks heed o' us—for it canna be for siller. They're a strange family. Ye see the breath was scarce out o' Maister Patrick, puir lamb—he was liker a bairn, than a man of years at ony time—when Miss Kirstin she gaed away. I saw your leddy seeking her—whaur she's gane, guid kens."

"Did she ever do that before?" asked Jacky.

"Eh, bless me, no: she was aye ower feared about him, puir man, wha has won out o' a' trouble this night. Maybe ye wad like to see him? He's a bonnie—"

Jacky interrupted her hurriedly. In that imaginative, solemn awe of hers, she could not endure the ghastly admiration which one hears so often expressed by persons of Marget's class for the dead, about whom they have been employed.

"Ye'll be wearied?" said Jacky, hastily.

"Ay, lass, I'm wearied: it's no like I could be onything else wi' a' that I have to do—and that sair hoast, and the constant fecht I hae wi' my breath—it's little the like o' you ken—forbye being my lane in the house. If ye'll just bide and look to the door, I'll gang an get some o' the neighbor wives to come in beside me: there's nae saying when Miss Kirstin may be hame."

"Miss Anne's coming hersel," said Jacky, eagerly. "And if ye would lie down and get some rest, I'll do the work—and I'm no feared to be my lane—and if ye had a guid sleep, ye would be the better o't."

"I'll no' say but what I would," said Marget, graciously; "and ye're a considerate lass to think o't. Tak a cup o' tea—it's no right to gang out in the morning fasting—and I daresay I'll just tak your counsel. It doesna do for an auld body like me to be out o' my bed a' night."

So Jacky got Marget disposed of, and remained with much awe, and some shadow of superstitious fear, alone within the house of Schole—supported by the sunshine round about her as she lingered at the door—for Marget, in decent reverence, had drawn a simple curtain across the window. The other rooms were shuttered and dark—the natural homage of seemly awe and gravity in the presence of death.

Anne had no difficulty in inducing Miss Crankie to take upon her those matters of sad external business, which she herself was not qualified to manage. With more delicacy than she expected, Miss Crankie undertook them immediately. Mrs. Yammer was "in sore distress with rheumatics in my back, and my head like to split in twa wi' the ticdoloureux—and it's a' yon awfu' nicht—and I dinna believes Miss Ross, I'll ever get the better o't.—Johann and you, that are strong folk, fleeing out into the storm, and me, a puir weak creature, left, to fend my lane—forbye being like to gang out o' my judgment wi' fricht, for you and the perishing creatures in the ship. Eh! wha would have thought of a weak man like yon saving them—and so he's ta'en to his rest! Weel I'm sure, Miss Ross, you've been uncommon kind to them—they canna say but they've found a friend in need."

"They are my relatives," said Anne: "I mean we are nearly connected."

Miss Crankie opened her little dark eyes wide. Mrs. Yammer began, with an astonished exclamation, to recollect the pedigree of the Lillies, and acquaint herself with this strange relationship.—Her sister stopped her abruptly.

"Take your breakfast, Tammie, and dinna haver nonsense. Is Kirstin content, Miss Ross, to have ye biding in her house?"

"Quite content," said Anne.

Miss Crankie's eyes opened wider. She began with a rapid logic, by no means formal, but which had a knack of arriving at just conclusions, to put things together. She had a glimmering of the truth already.

"Miss Lillie is out," said Anne. "I fear, in her deep grief, she wandered out, finding herself unable to rest; but neither she nor I are able for these details. You will greatly oblige me, Miss Crankie, and do your old friend a most kind service, if you will undertake this."

Miss Crankie promised heartily, and Anne returned to Schole. Again there passed a long, weary, brilliant summer day, but Christian did not return. The night fell, but the roof that covered the mortal garment of Patrick Lille, sheltered no kindred blood. Anne had taken Christian's place—she was the watcher now.

CHAPTER XXVIII

Another day, as bright, as weary, and as long, and still there were no tidings of Christian. Anne became alarmed. She sent out Jacky to make inquiries; Jacky ascertained that Miss Lillie on the previous morning had gone by the earliest coach to Edinburgh. The intelligence was some relief, yet perplexed Anne painfully; the arrangements were going on, but what could she do, if Christian remained absent, thus left alone with the dead?

In the middle of the day, Miss Crankie brought her a letter from Mrs. Catherine. Anne's conscience smote her; during Patrick's illness, she had scarcely written to Mrs. Catherine at all; and her brief notes had only intimated his illness, and her hope of obtaining some further information through the Lillies. Mrs. Catherine's letter had an enclosure.

"My Gowan,

"What has come over you? I have been marvelling these past mornings whether it was success or failure—a light heart or a downcast one, that made you forgetful of folk to whom all your doings are matters of interest, and have been since you could use your own proper tongue to testify of them. Think you this lad Lillie has any further knowledge than you have yourself? I count it unlikely, or else he is a pithless laggard, not worthy to call Norman Rutherford friend, and Norman was not one to choose his friends lightly, or be joined in near amity with a shallow head and a faint heart. So I would have you build little on the hope of getting good tidings from him, seeing that if he had known anything, he must have put it to its fitting use before now. You say it gave him a fever? I like not folk, child, who are thrown into fevers by sore trouble and anguish, and make themselves a burden and a cumbrance, when they ought to be quickened to keener life—the more helpful and strong, the greater the extremity; it augurs a narrow vessel and a frail spirit in most cases—it may be other in his. Certain he bore himself like a man in the night you tell me of. Let me see his sister, if you can bring her; there, seems—if ye draw like the life—to be no soil in her for the cowardice of sickness to flourish on, from which I take my certainty, that if she had kent any good word concerning this dark mystery, she must have put it to the proof before now.

"To speak about other matters, I send you a letter—worthy the light-headed, undutiful fuil from whose vain hand it comes. You will see she will have none of my counsel, and puts my offer of an honorable roof over her, and a home dependent on no caprice or strange woman's pleasure, in the light of a good meaning—will to do kindness without power. If it were not for Archie's sake, and for the good-fame of their broken house, she should never more say light word to me. He has been but a month dead, this miserable man of hers—that she left her mother's sick-bed for—and look at her words! without so much as a decent shadow on them, to tell where the sore gloom of death had fallen so late. I am growing testy in my spirit, child; though truly sorrow would set me better than anger, to look upon the like of a born fuil like this—her brother ruined, and her man killed. Archie, a laboring wayfarer, with his good name tarnished, and his father's inheritance, lost; the husband for whose sake she brought down her mother's gray hairs with sorrow to the grave, taken away suddenly from this world by the red grip of a violent death, and the wanton fuil what can I call her else?—as if she had not gotten enough to sober her for a while, returning in haste to her vanities—feared to leave the atmosphere of them—singing songs over the man's new grave, and giving long nights to strangers, when she can but spare a brief minute to say a kind word to her one brother—a kind word, said I! I should say a bitter one, of folly and selfishness,—not comfort to him in his labor, but records of her own sinful vanities.

"You will say I am bitter, child, at this fuil—so I am—the more that I cannot be done with her, as I could with any other of her kind. She is still the bairn of Isabel Balfour—in good or in evil I am trysted to keep my eye upon her. I have been asking about the household she is in. The mistress of it, her friend, is at least of pure name; a scheming woman as I hear from one of their own vain kind—who has a pride in yoking the fuils about her in the unstable bands of marriage. Isabel has her mother's fair face; they will be wedding her again for some passing fancy, or for dirt of siller. I scarce know which is the worst. I will have no hand in it, however it happens. Since she will be left to herself, she must. If deadly peril ever comes, I must put forth the strong hand.

"You will come to me with all speed when you can win. If you have any glimpse of good tidings, or if you have none—I am meaning when you come to any certainty—let me know without delay, that I may make ready for our home-going. To say the truth, I am weary at my heart of this place, and sickened with anger at the fuil whose letter I send you. Let me look upon you soon, lest the wrath settle down, and I be not able to shake it off again; which evil consequent, if you prevent it not, will be the worse for you all.

CATHERINE DOUGLAS."

Mrs. Duncombe's letter was enclosed.

"My dear Mrs. Catherine,

"It is so good of you to think of troubling yourself with me at the Tower, and must have put you so much out of the way, coming to Edinburgh, that I hasten to thank you. Poor dear Duncombe was taken away very suddenly; you would be quite shocked to hear of it. I was distracted. They had been quarrelling over their wine. Poor Duncombe was always so very jealous; and it was all for the merest word of admiration, which he might have heard from a thousand people beside. So they fought, and he was wounded mortally. You may think how dreadful it was, when they brought him home to me dying. I went into hysterics directly, I believe I needed the doctor's care more than he did: before he died I was just able to speak to him, and he was so very penitent for having been sometimes rude to me, and so sorry for his foolish jealousy. Poor dear Edward!—I shall never forget him.

"I am staying here with a dear friend of mine, Mrs. Legeretie. She has got a delightful house, quite out of town, and they have come here just for my sake, to be quiet and away from the gay world, which of course I could not bear just now. We have quite a nice circle of friends, besides our visitors from London, and just with quiet parties, and country amusements, get on delightfully. Dear Eliza is so kind, and gives up her engagements in town, without a murmur, just to let me have the soothing quietness of the country, which the doctors order me—with cheerful society—for if it were not for that, my poor heart would break, I am sure—I have suffered so dreadfully.

"You will have heard that dear Archibald has arrived safely at that horrid place in America. What could induce him to do such a thing, when he might have gone into the army, or got into Parliament, or something? and the friends of the family would have helped him, I am sure. It's just like Archie; he's always so hot and extreme. I thought he would have killed himself that dreadful time at Paris, before he took the fever; and what a shocking thing that would have been for me, with all my other misfortunes. To be sure, it was a horrid, foolish business—that of losing the estate—and if it had not been that dull old Strathoran, where papa and mamma managed to vegetate all the year through, I don't know how—I should have been broken-hearted. I am sure, considering that dear Archie was only my brother, there was nothing I was not willing to do for him; but to go away a common clerk, into a horrid mercantile office! I must say he has shown very little regard for the feelings of his relatives, especially as he knows how I detest these ogres of commercial people. One can only bear with them if they are very rich, and I am afraid dear Archie is not likely ever to become a moneyed man.

"They are so fond of me here, and dear Eliza has done so much to make me comfortable, that I should be very ungrateful to run away, else I should have been delighted to spend a week or two at the Tower. Mr. Legeretie has a shooting-lodge in the Highlands, and dear Eliza talks of going down with him this year to give me a little change; if we do, we shall come by dear old dreary Strathoran just to look at it again. I hope the Rosses, and all the other old friends, are well. I used to think a good deal of Lewis. I suppose Anne is never married yet; she must be getting quite ancient now.

"My dear Mrs. Catherine, "Very sincerely yours,

"ISABEL DUNCOMBE."

It was a strange contrast—with Christian Lillie's desolate life before her—with her own heart throbbing so anxiously for the stranger, Norman, whom, in her remembrance, she had never seen—to hear this Isabel, her play-mate long ago, talking of Archie as "only" her brother. The effect was very singular. What had become of the sad sufferer who lay within these walls in the tranquil rest of death, if for Christian, and Marion, and Norman there had been any "only" stemming the deep tide of their self-denying tenderness?

Anne wrote a brief note to Mrs. Catherine, announcing Patrick Lillie's death, and saying that her mission was now accomplished; and that in a day or two she would return to Edinburgh to explain the further particulars of this long mystery. The day was waning again; in weary sadness and solitude she sat in Patrick Lillie's study. From the kitchen she could hear the subdued voices of Marget and Jacky: above, the stealthy step of Miss Crankie, as she arranged the sad preliminaries of the funeral. The second evening had fallen since he departed to his rest; and where was Christian?

A dark shadow flitted across the window. She heard a footstep enter, and pass quickly up the stair. Anne rose and followed. The footstep was quicker than Christian's, but it went steadily to the chamber of death.

Anne paused at the door. The lonely dimness of the evening air gathered shadowy and spiritual round the bed, a dark background, from which that rigid marble face stood out in cold relief. A deadly stillness—a dim, brooding, tremulous awe—which carried in it a vague conviction of watching spirits, and presences mysteriously unseen, was hovering in the room.

And kneeling at the bedside, her veil hanging round her white, thin face, like a cloud over the tearful pallor of a wan November sky, was Christian Lillie, the quivering smile upon her lip again, and the words of sad thankfulness falling from her tongue.

"Ye are thanking God in His own heaven, Patrick, my brother; the justice is done, the cloud is taken away. Henceforward, in the free light of heaven, may Norman bear his own name; and now there remaineth nothing but to lay you, with hope and solemn thanksgiving into your quiet grave."

Anne stood still; there was a long pause. Christian knelt silently by her dead brother's side, in darkness, in silence, in the presence of death, thanking God.

At last she rose, and turned to leave the room. Anne's presence did not seem to excite any wonder; she took her offered arm quietly and kindly.

"I have been very anxious," said Anne.

"Ay," said Christian; "did you think I could rest, and that blight remaining on their name? Did you think there was any peace for me till all my labor was accomplished? Now—you heard me speak—Norman Rutherford may bear his own name, and return to his own country with honor and blessing upon him, in the open sunshine of day. My work is ended: I must but tarry for one look upon them, and then I wait the Lord's pleasure. His call will not come too soon."

"You have taken no rest," said Anne, anxiously: "remember, there is one trial yet remaining. Let me get you some refreshment, and then try to sleep. This constant watching will kill you."

Christian suffered herself to be led down stairs. Into the little parlor Anne hastily brought tea, and, considerably to Jacky's horror, insisted upon rendering all needful services herself. It was evident that Christian felt the delicacy which kept strange eyes from beholding her grief. She took the tea eagerly, removed her cloak and bonnet, and met Anne's anxious look with a tremulous, tender smile, inviting, rather than deprecating, conversation now.

"Let me go with you to your own room," said Anne; "you have been in Edinburgh, and are quite exhausted, I see. You will be better after you have slept."

"Sit down, I need no sleep," said Christian: "I scarcely think now, after my long watching, that I can begin to think of rest.—Sometimes—sometimes—"

She rose and stretched out her thin arms, like one who complains of some painful void within, drawing them in again wearily to her breast.

"Sometimes, when I do not think of them, and mind that he is gone, I could be content to bear it all again, were he but back once more. God aid us, for we are weak. Patrick, my brother, are ye away at last? are ye at peace? And I am ready to lament and pine, and not to thank God! God be thanked! God be thanked! that he is away in blessedness at last."

She paced the room slowly for a while, and sitting down by the window, drew the curtains aside, and looked out in silence upon the sea—the placid, wakeful sea—with which so often in her misery she had taken counsel.

"The morning after he went home," she said at last, turning to Anne abruptly, "I saw you looking out upon the Firth, when I departed on my needful errand. You mind the soft fall of the air, like the breath of a young angel—a spirit in its first joy—the latest born of heaven? You mind the joy and gentleness that were in the air?"

"Yes," said Anne.

"On such a morning—as soft, as joyous, and as bright—he came to me, who is now in heaven at peace. There was no peace about him then. Within his soul, and in his face, was an agony more bitter than death. You know the reason. He had done the deed, for which, through eighteen lingering, terrible years, Norman Rutherford has been a banished man.

"I took him in, and closed the door: he fell down upon the ground, at my feet. From the terrible words of his first madness, I gleaned something of the truth. Think of it—think of that.—The horror of great darkness that fell on me that day has scarce ever been lightened for an hour, from that time to this.

"I sent for him, for Norman, your brother, and mine. He came to me, into the room where Patrick lay, in a burning fever of agony and madness. By that time a breath of the terrible story was abroad. It was his gun it was done with. He had parted from Arthur Aytoun in just anger. There were but two ways—either to give up the frantic, fevered lad that lay there before us, knowing neither him nor me, to a death of shame and horror, or for him—him, in his honorable, upright, pure youth—to sacrifice honor, and home, and name.

"He did not hesitate—the Lord bless him!—the Lord send the blessings of the convenant upon him, promised and purchased!—he made up his mind. And to us, as we stood there in our first agony, with Patrick stricken down before us, there was no consolation of innocence. We knew not but what the blood had been wilfully shed: we thought the torture he was in was the just meed of a murderer.

"I gave him a line to Marion: she was at a friend's house, between Edinburgh and Glasgow. She had gone, a joyous light-hearted girl, with as fair a lot before her as ever lay at mortal feet, to get apparel for her bridal. I bade her go with Norman. When I wrote that, I was calmer than I am now. I, that was parting with them both—that was left here alone with this stricken man and his blood-guiltiness.

"They went away, and he was still lying unconscious on my hands. Then I had to hear the unjust stain thrown upon the noble and brave heart that was bearing the burden. I had to hear it all—to listen to the certainties of his guilt—to hear them tell how he had done it like a coward; and with my heart burning within me, I dared not say to them that he was pure and guiltless as ever was righteous man. I turned from the scorching summer light, and the false accusation, in to the bedside of my raving, maddened brother, and he was the man. Oh, Lord! oh, Lord! how did I live?

"Then there came the word that they were lost; and a calm, like what you will see in storms, came over the miserable heart within me. I defied my misery: I dared it to add to me another pang.

"Then I said that Marion was dead—my bird—my light—my little sister! When I said that, I knew not it was false; I believed she was gone out of her new grief; I believed I was alone in the world.

"Then the secret news came to me that they were safe, and then the life struggled through that time of horror, and Patrick rose from his bed. One solemn still night I told him all, and in his agony he said he was innocent. Since that time through all this life of desolation, he has repeated that at times, when his mind was clear; but his soul was frozen within him in terror. When I spoke of justice to Norman, he shrank and trembled, and bade me wait. What could I do? I could not give him up as a shedder of blood—he was in my hand. To my own heart, and to my Father in heaven, I had to answer for him; and when I dared hope that he had shed this blood unawares, I became strong."

She paused. She had been speaking rapidly, without stop or hesitation, almost without breath. Anne endeavored to soothe and calm her.

"Last year, they sent me their child. He had called her Lilie. He himself, whom our unhappy name had blighted. The child was pining under the hot sun of yon strange land. I could not keep her in our desolate house. I took her to Norman's country. I was to place her with his nurse, near to his old home. When we got there, I feared to enter; I trembled to betray the secret I was burdened with. I thought a heart that he was dear to, could not fail to discover his bairn, and so I took her to a stranger.

"When I left her there—you mind?—I met you, and we looked upon each other face to face: I did not need to hear the name that the blue-eyed girl by your side was saying. I knew you were Norman's sister—I felt that his spirit was within you, and that we would meet again.

"Now we have met, and you know it all. The history is public now. The ban is off Norman's name—your brother and mine. I will see them again—my bird Marion—my bairn, that my own hands nurtured!"

"Christian," said Anne, "for her sake, and for us all, you must rest. There are quiet days in store—tranquil days of household peace and honor. You have done your work nobly and bravely, as few could have done; for Marion's sake, who is my sister as well as yours, and for the sake of the dead, for whom you have watched so long, take rest now. Your work is over."

Christian drew the curtain aside again, and gazed out upon the sea. "For him—for Marion—for Norman; for Thy mercy's sake, O, Lord! and for Thy beautiful world, which Thou hast given to calm us, I will be calm—give me now what Thou willest, and Thy rest in Thine own heaven, when Thy good time shall come."

And so peacefully, in chastened hope and with gentle tears, refreshing with their milder sorrow the weary eyes that had burned in tearless agony so long, they laid the innocent shedder of blood in his quiet grave.

On the evening after the funeral, Christian wandered out alone. "She goeth unto the grave to weep there," said Anne, as it was said of the Mary of the Lord's time; and she made no attempt either to detain or to accompany her. To Christian, the balm of Anne's sisterly care and sympathy was evidently very dear; but she was not wont to lean upon any mortal arm, and it was best that she should be left with her sorrow alone.

The house had the exhausted, worn-out look which is common after such a solemn departure. Marget sat, dressed in her new mourning, in the kitchen, in languid despondent state, telling Jacky traits of the dead Master, whom, now that all excitement was over, she began to miss and lament, and weep some natural tears for. Jacky was half-listening to these, half-buried in an old volume of "Quarles' Emblems," which she had recently brought from the study. Anne had opened the low projecting window, and sat in the recess with one of those devout contemplative books in her hand; she was reading little, and thinking much—feeling herself affected by the listless weariness that reigned around her.

She saw a lad come in at the gate, without observing who he was. In a minute after Jacky entered the study.

"If ye please, Miss Anne, it's Johnnie Halflin."

Anne started.

"Has he come from Mrs. Catherine?"

"If ye please, Miss Anne, Mrs. Catherine's at Miss Crankie's."

Anne rose immediately, and proceeded up the lane to Miss Crankie's house. Mrs. Catherine's carriage stood at the door. Mrs. Catherine herself was in the parlor, where Miss Crankie stood in deferential conversation with her—keenly observant of all the particulars of her plain, rich dress and stately appearance, and silently exulting over the carriage at the door—the well-appointed, wealthy carriage, which all the neighborhood could see.

"Anne!" exclaimed Mrs. Catherine, as Anne in her deep mourning dress entered the room. "What is the matter?"

Miss Crankie sensibly withdrew.

"He is dead, Mrs. Catherine," said Anne.

"Who is dead? Who is this lad?"

"The brother of Marion—the brother of Norman's wife."

"Anne," said Mrs. Catherine, "you have not dealt ingenuously and frankly with me in this matter. Who is this lad, I ask you? Have you a certainty that Norman's wife was his sister, that you are thus mourning for a fremd man?"

Anne sat down beside her.

"What I knew formerly was so dim and indistinct that I feared to tell you. They avoided me—they went away from their own home to shun my presence. In the confusion of my imperfect knowledge, I felt that I could not speak of them. Now I am sure. There is a most sad story to tell you, Mrs. Catherine—Patrick Lillie is Marion's brother—he is more than that."

"Speak out, child. Who is he?"

"He is the man for whom Norman sacrificed all—he is the slayer of Alice Aytoun's father."

Mrs. Catherine started—in her extreme wonder she could say nothing.

"An innocent man, Mrs. Catherine; this dreadful deed was done unawares, and in a life of agony has it been avenged."

Mrs. Catherine remained silent for a moment.

"And he let Norman, the honorable, generous, just lad, suffer a death for him—suffer the death of a lifetime? Anne—Anne, is it a coward like this you are mourning for? A faint heart and a weak spirit—what could it be other that would let a righteous man bear this for him?"

"There is justice done," said Anne, "it is over now. I acknowledge the weakness, Mrs. Catherine; but he has suffered dreadfully. A gentle, delicate, pensive spirit, unfit for storms and trials—altogether unfit for doing any great thing: one to be supported and tenderly upheld—not to take any bold step alone."

"Suffered!" Mrs. Catherine rose and walked through the room, till the boards, less solid than those of the Tower, quaked and sounded below her feet. "Wherefore did he not come forth in the light of day, and bear his own burden? Good fame and honor—land and home—what was he that a just man should lay down these for him?"

"He was a feeble, delicate, dependant spirit," said Anne: "one of those whom it is our natural impulse to defend and suffer for. That was his only claim; but you know how strong that is."

Mrs. Catherine did know, but she felt no sympathy for the shrinking weakness which could suffer another to bear its own just punishment.

"I know? Yes, I know; but what claim has the like of such a weakling to call himself a man? Eighteen years—eighteen long, slow years—all Alice Aytoun's lifetime. Anne, I marvel you can bear with his memory, or lift up your face to me, and speak of him as kindred. He shed this blood unawares, said you? Did he doom Norman to this death unawares? was it without his knowledge that he laid this blight upon the two that have borne banishment for him? Speak not to me of this coward, child. I say, mention not his name to me."

"Mrs. Catherine," said Anne, "bear with me till you hear his story. If you had seen him as I have seen—if you had listened to Christian as I have listened, you too would mourn over this blighted, broken man, less in his death than in his life. When Norman fled, he was in an agony of fever and madness, unconscious of what was passing round him—only aware in his burning horror and grief that he had shed blood. When he recovered—and most strange it was that he should have recovered—most strange the tenacious life and strength of his feebleness—he heard of Norman's sacrifice; and then I acknowledge he ought to have done justice, had not his weakness overpowered him. He dared not face the terror and the shame; perhaps the dreadful death due to his blood-guiltiness, and so he lived on—such a life as few have ever lived in this world—a life of despair, and gloom, and misery: terrible to hear of—more terrible to see."

Mrs. Catherine seated herself again.

"And the sister and the righteous man, his friend, bearing a dark name for him over the sea; and the sad woman at home, that you have told me of, wearing out her days for him. Was his miserable life worth that, think you? Should that not have been worse than any death?"

"Should have been," said Anne; "but I do not speak of what should be, Mrs. Catherine. Why this shrinking, feeble spirit was conjoined with such a lot, who can tell? It had a strange, feverish, hysteric strength, too. When he battled through yon dark waves to save the perishing seamen, you would not have said that Patrick Lillie was a coward."

There was a pause. Mrs. Catherine's manner softened. Anne took advantage of it to repeat to her Christian Lillie's story. The stern, stately old lady was moved to very tears.

"And so at last justice is done," she said. "Anne, it is meet that this worn woman, after her travail, should have light in her evening-time. If she will come with you, bid her come to my house. The like of her would do honor to any dwelling, were it a king's. And she left him at his grave's brink, whenever he was at rest, to render what was just to the banished man? She did well. It behoves that all who known this history should render reverence. I say she did well."

There was again a momentary pause.

"And where is he?" asked Mrs. Catherine. "Where, and in what condition is Norman Rutherford?"

"I have never asked yet," said Anne. "I was anxious to soothe her; she has been so worn out with watching and grief. I will ask her now, when all excitement is over, and she has only to bear her gentle sorrow for Patrick's death."

"Ay—ay," said Mrs. Catherine, slowly; "ay—and yet you do not know, Gowan, the terrible, dreary calm that is left by that shadow of death. I speak of the death that carries home a godly, honorable, righteous man, whose life was a joy and a blessing.—This is a grief sorer than mine. I bow my head to this tribulation. I cannot fathom all the depths of its bitterness; it is greater than mine."

And with her large gray eyelid swelling full, Mrs. Catherine Douglas bowed her stately head. Yes! the solitary, desolate, dumb might of anguish with which her strong spirit quivered, when she left all that remained of Sholto Douglas sleeping peacefully in his calm island grave, overwhelming as it was, became a gentle sorrow in presence of the life of wakeful agony which Christian Lillie had borne silently within the desolate walls of Schole.

Mrs. Catherine began to speak of the possibility of remaining for the night. It was a very strange idea for her, who had not slept under a strange roof for more than thirty years. Since Patrick's death, Anne had passed both night and day at Schole, and the pretty little clean bed-room behind was unoccupied. Miss Crankie herself was called in to be consulted on the subject.

Miss Crankie had scarcely entered the room, when there was a rush in the passage. The door flew violently open, and Mrs. Yammer, her head bound up with mighty rolls of flannel, and a newspaper trembling in her eager hand, stood before them.

"Eh, Johann!—Eh, Miss Ross!" she could articulate no more.

"What in the world has come ower the woman now?" exclaimed Miss Crankie, peevishly. "If ye will be a puling, no-weel fuil, ye may keep your ailments to yoursel at least. For guid sake, Tammie, haud your tongue; dinna deave the ladies."

"Eh, Miss Ross!—Eh, Johann!" exclaimed the aroused and excited Mrs. Yammer, "if it wasna for the stitch in my side, I wad read it to ye mysel. Look at this."

Anne took the paper wonderingly. She glanced down a long paragraph, headed "Romance in real life," with hurried half attention, and little interest. Her eyes were arrested by the concluding words: they seemed to shine out from a mist. Unconsciously, in her sudden excitement, she read them aloud: "This most honorable vindication of Norman Rutherford, of Redheugh—"

"Gowan," exclaimed Mrs. Catherine, hastily, taking the paper from her powerless hand, "what is that you say?"

"Ye see," said Mrs. Yammer, following up briskly her unwonted independent movement, "we get it atween us. Mr. Currie, the saddler, and Mrs. Clippie, the captain's widow, and Robert Carritch, the session-clerk, and Johann and me; and I was just sitting ower the fire, trying if the heat would do ony guid to my puir head, when I saw that about young Redheugh—and I'll be out o' my wits the morn wi the draft frae that open door."

"Gae way to your fireside again, and haud your tongue," said Miss Crankie, bundling her sister unceremoniously out of the door before her. "Wits!—woman, if ye had as muckle judgment as wad lie on a sixpence, ye wad see that the ladies have mair concern in that than either you or me."

Anne had been looking at them vacantly with a vague, unconscious smile upon her lip. Now, when the door was shut, she suddenly knelt down at Mrs. Catherine's knees, scarce knowing what she did, and leaning there, burst into tears. She was conscious of Mrs. Catherine's hand laid caressingly upon her hair; she was conscious of an indistinct mist of joy and thankfulness. It overpowered and weakened her; she could not stay these tears.

In the meantime, Mrs. Catherine read:

"We have just had communicated to us the particulars of a very moving story, another of the many examples that truth is strange, stranger than fiction. We believe that many of our readers, who are acquainted with the neighborhood of our city, may have remarked a desolate house, standing in the midst of a very rich country, within sight of the Firth, and presenting a very singular contrast, in its utter neglect and ruin, to the prosperous and flourishing appearance of everything about it. The story current in the neighborhood is, that its last proprietor perished miserably in the sea, while flying from the doom of a murderer, with the blood of a friend shed deliberately and in cowardice on his hand. Other more ghostly rumors of sights seen and sounds heard in its immediate neighborhood are of course current also.—The account we have now to give of this dark transaction reveals something almost as strange as the re-appearance on this earthly scene of spirits long ago departed. It seems the very triumph and perfection of generous self-sacrifice and 'godlike amity,' and as such we are happy to have an opportunity of presenting it to our readers.

"A few days since, the Lord Advocate received from a lady a full exculpation of Mr. Rutherford, of Redheugh, in the shape of a confession made by the real criminal upon his death-bed. We do wrong in applying the name of criminal to this unhappy man.—According to his death-bed declaration, made in the presence of witnesses, and to which full credence may be given, the death of the late Arthur Aytoun, Esq., of Aytoun, so long regarded as a murder, falls under the lighter title of an accident. A dreamy student had been spending an hour of a brilliant summer morning shooting upon the sands, and on his return home fired an inadvertent shot, while resting in a wood, when, instead of the bird which he fancied he aimed at, the unhappy young man heard a cry of mortal agony, and beheld the death of a fellow-man. Distracted and maddened, he rushed home; made some wild confession to his sister of the fact alone, without telling her that it was accidental, and immediately fell into the wild delirium of fever. Mr. Rutherford, of Redheugh, was the most intimate friend of the family, and betrothed to the younger sister. The fowling-piece, which had fallen from the young man's hand when he discovered the fatal effects of the shot, belonged to Mr. Rutherford. Mr. Aytoun and Mr. Rutherford had parted the night before in anger: every circumstance directed suspicion to the Laird of Redheugh. In her first terror, the sister of the unhappy shedder of blood, naturally sought counsel from the friend who was so shortly to enter into the most intimate relation with the family; and Mr. Rutherford, with a generosity never in our knowledge paralleled, resolved at once to divert attention from his helpless friend by his own flight. The younger sister accompanied him, after a secret marriage. By universal consent he was pronounced guilty: the fact of his flight settled that beyond dispute in the judgment of the world.

"The vessel he sailed in was lost; himself in it, as has to this hour been universally believed. But the strange eventful history of this unfortunate gentleman has not had so abrupt a termination. He still lives, and will long live, we trust, to expend in a larger circle the rare generosity of which he has given so remarkable a proof.

"The unhappy man, by whose inadvertent hand Mr. Aytoun fell, and for whom Mr. Rutherford has suffered, is lately dead.—Without a moment's delay, after his death, his sister immediately brought his confession to the proper quarter, so that now there remains nothing but to give to the world this most honorable vindication of Norman Rutherford, of Redheugh. In the consciousness of an act of singular goodness, bravely done, and in the universal applause of all good men, our heroic countryman, on his return to his own land, will, we doubt not, find himself abundantly rewarded."

And thus it was made known to the world—the work of the two sisters was accomplished. Free from all stain and disgrace, radiant in the honor and blessing of generous work and life, the sentence of justice, and the universal voice of good men, should welcome to his long-lost home and country Norman Rutherford, of Redheugh.

CHAPTER XXIX

The next day, after a long interview with Christian Lillie, and granting the further delay of a week to Anne for Christian's sake, Mrs. Catherine returned to Edinburgh. At the week's end, when she had rendered what service and assistance she could to Christian, Anne was to join Mrs. Catherine, and they were to proceed home.

But the invitation of Mrs. Catherine, and Anne's entreaty that she should accompany them, was steadily and quietly negatived by Christian. The day before Anne left Schole, they sat together in the study— Anne was renewing her solicitations.

"No," said Christian, calmly, "no, I cannot leave his grave. I cannot give up my watch of Patrick. You do not know—I pray God you never may—when folk have watched and waited for a lifelong like me, how hard it is to break the old wont, even though it be one of the sorest pain that ever oppressed mortal spirit. I am calm now—you know how calm I am—but I must tarry by his grave."

"And will you stay here," said Anne, "here in this desolate house?"

"At this time I must—my desire is to return to our old home, before Marion comes back to me—I forget she has been a mother long, and a grave tried woman. I only mind her as my bird Marion, my little sister; I would like to have her chamber for her, as it was before this cloud fell. You shall go with me to-morrow, and we will see what they say—the people who are in the house."

"And where are they?" said Anne, "will you not tell me, Christian, where they are?"

Christian's countenance changed: "They will be home in due time. Your brother Norman will reveal himself to you himself, and you will not ask me further. It is a weakness—a remembrance of my old bondage—but you will wait, Anne, my sister.—Let him carry you his own secret himself."

Anne was silent. It was a singular hesitation this, but she could not press her question further. "And will you not come to Merkland—to see us—to see Lilie?"

"I will come when Marion comes," said Christian. "Let me stay until then. By the time this year is ended, as I calculate, they will be home, and till that time I will rest."

Anne rose, a stranger was at the gate: through the window she descried the good-humored round face of Mrs. Brock, her earliest acquaintance in Aberford. "Here is your tenant, Christian," she said: "shall I see her? it may fatigue you."

"No," said Christian, "let her be brought in, Anne; it will save us our walk to-morrow."

Anne went out, and met the Grieve's wife, who was greatly astonished to see her. "Eh, preserve me! is this you, Miss Ross? and ye never came back to tak a cup o' tea; and I've been looking for ye ilka fine day; and sae muckle as wee Geordie had to tell his father about the leddy yon night; and ye'll hae been biding close a' this time at Aberford?"

"No," said Anne, "I have been in the North since I saw you."

"And sae ye ken Miss Lillie? She'll be sair put out o' the way, it's like, about her brother. Losh! do ye ken Miss Ross, our George says there's something in the papers about it being Maister Lillie that killed the man, and no young Redheugh. Is there onythiug in't, think ye? ane couldna ask Miss Lillie."

"By no means," said Anne, "she is in great grief for her brother, and you must not allude to it."

"It' I be true then? Eh! to think of a delicate looking man like thon doing the like o' that."

"It was an accident," said Anne, quickly; "he was a gentleman, who would not have harmed any living thing. Do you wish to see Miss Lillie?"

"Ou, ay, it was just about the house, ye ken. George thought we micht maybe come to a settlement about the house. Ye see there's a new yin building at the back end o' the toun, nigher the water—a guid twa story house, and we've a big family, and George would like to be off or on at yince."

Anne ushered the visitor into the study. Mrs. Brock, honest woman, expended upon Christian some piece of common-place consolation, which made the pale lip quiver. Then she entered upon her business.

"Ye see, we've reason to be thankfu', we've won on no that ill in the world; and George says its a daftlike thing to us to be paying rent for a house, and us has lying siller that could buy mair than yin. Sae if ye're agreeable, he'll make ye his auld offer ower again—twa hunder pounds, and us to get it as it stands, all and haill."

"I am sorry, Mrs. Brock," said Christian, "when you like it so well, that I cannot part with it; but I must keep the house in my own possession."

"Weel," said Mrs. Brock, "of course it's your ain to do what ye like wi't—and ye see there's John Tamson, he began to build a twa story house, down by the back end o' the toun—and he's broke. Its nae wonder—his wife wearing silk gowns, and gowd earrings ilka day, less wadna ser her, and her was only a ewemilker fræ the Lammermuir! Sae George thinks we micht maybe buy John Tamson's house—its stickit in the building e'enow, but we could sune hae it begun again; and maybe since ye'll no sell yours, ye wad hae nae objection to quit us at Martinmas."

"I shall be very glad," said Christian. "I expect friends home who have been long absent, and this house is not pleasant to me. I will be glad to release you when you choose."

Mrs. Brock was satisfied; and after various other attempts at conversation, in which Anne bore the brunt as well as she could, and did all in her power to prevent their visitor from recurring to the death of Patrick, Mrs. Brock at last intimated, "that she bid to be thinking o' gaun hame—though it was an awfu' hot stourie day, and she was bye ordinary tired."

Roused by this hint, Anne hastened to bring a glass of wine, and at last their visitor departed.

"So there will be time to restore all," said Christian, as Mrs. Brock left the house. "It is well, I will have a pleasure in it. It is the first time I have said that word since yon June day! Do I look like a woman dead? Is there something in my voice, and face, that speaks of death?"

"Christian," said Anne in alarm, "why do you ask that?"

"Because I feel it, Anne—a dead unnatural calm, like the stillness of the Firth before yon storm—not peace but death; I feel it in myself. When I go about, I think I can hear no sound of my footsteps; when I breathe, I think the air seems to cleave before me; when I speak, the voice has a dull, cold modulation, that is not human. I can think of them all—of Patrick in his agony—of myself so short a time ago, as feverish shadows—I feel this calm oppress and envelop me like a shroud—I feel like one dead."

"This should not be, Christian," said Anne, "it is but the reaction of stillness after all your labor and watching. How much have you to live for!"

"I have no further work," said Christian Lillie, in her old composure of melancholy, "no further watching—no one now to care and labor for. You do not know my life; when I was a girl, in the days when others are gay and light of heart, beloved, and served, and cared for, I was fighting with a household shame and sin—a miserable, sensual, earthly sin, in the one man to whom I should have looked up for support and guidance: striving to hide it—to keep it from the knowledge of the bairns—the two that were depending more upon me, their sister, than upon him their father; striving, too, with weary cares of poverty, to keep them from want—real want and not mere meagreness. From that a death relieved me—and then, with only eighteen years over my head, I was left the mother of these two; to protect, and defend, and bring them up, the only near kindred they had in the world. Since then my hands have been full—there has been no lack of vigils or labors in this past life of mine. Now it is over; I have carried Patrick safely to his grave, and seen him laid down there in sorrow and in hope; and now Marion will come again to a bright household in joy and honor. Do you marvel that I think my work over?—the need of me in this world past."

"I do not marvel," said Anne, "but I wish that it should be otherwise, Christian. I would not have your sky overcast with this dull calm; I would have it free to receive God's sunshine; the light he sends upon it, in the evening time."

"God forbid," said Christian Lillie rising, and pressing her hands painfully to her breast, "God forbid that I should hide my head, from His mercy of joy; God forbid that I should shut my eyes to His sunshine, or sin His mercies; only I am blinded with this cold calm, and my heart is dead within me. When I am in my own house, bring the child to me—Marion's bairn, that he called by our unhappy name; and come yourself, my sister Anne, that I may begin to live again. Till then, in my own fashion let me rest."

And so they arranged. At the term of Martinmas, or sooner, if John Tamson's house, the newly-acquired property of George Brock, should be sooner completed—whenever Christian had regained possession of the old home cottage, Anne was to visit her with Lilie. At present, all was done for her that affectionate care could do, and on the next day Anne left Aberford.

When in the evening she entered Mrs. Catherine's Edinburgh drawing-room, in its stately pride of olden furniture, gracefully not stiffly antique, she found James Aytoun and his mother waiting to meet her. Mrs. Aytoun gave her a tremulous welcome, which was half an embrace, and would have been wholly one, had Mrs. Aytoun been at all a demonstrative person. James shook hands with her with respectful kindness and friendship. The good opinion of such a mother and son was worth having. Anne felt enlivened and exhilarated.

"Alice has gone out," said Mrs. Aytoun: "she will be with us very soon again. They were to watch for your coming, but I fear these young people become engrossed in their own matters sometimes."

"They?" said Anne.

"Ay, she has a gallant with her you have seen before," said Mrs. Catherine, "be patient—you will find out who he is before long."

"Is it Lewis?—is Lewis here?" asked Anne.

"Mrs. Catherine wishes to take Alice from us again," said Mrs. Aytoun. "I am afraid, Miss Ross, I can hardly thank you for the barrier you have removed. Alice is so young—little more than a child yet."

James Aytoun took up a book, and went away smilingly to a window. He saw that a consultation matrimonial and maternal was impending.

"I do think she is too young. I do not approve of too early marriages," said Mrs. Aytoun, shaking her head. "Why, many girls are but leaving school at Alice's age—she is not quite eighteen yet."

"She is in no peril," said Mrs. Catherine. "It's my hope, kinswoman, that you do not think you are sending her into a savage country, where there will be but barbarous people to show kindness to the bairn. There is no fear of her—I warrant her in as careful hands, when she is in Lewis's, as she could be under the shadow of my very sel; I would not just have advised you to wed her—a bairn as she undoubtedly is—to the like of Archie Sutherland; but she is in no peril with Lewis."

The slightest possible additional color wavered over Anne's face. She did by no means perceive any connexion, logical or otherwise, between the marriage of little Alice Aytoun and Archie Sutherland.

"I am not afraid for her," said Mrs. Aytoun: "it is not peril that I mean; but so young a girl entering upon the care of a house—the management of a family—besides the pain of losing her. If it had not been for your mother's presence, and your own, Miss Ross, I should never have consented—at her age."

Mrs. Aytoun expressed something of what she felt, but not all. She did not like the idea of Alice entering another family, not as its mistress, but as a younger daughter. She felt sure of Anne; but Alice was by no means so exuberant in her praise of Mrs. Ross.

"I do not know what arrangement my mother may make," said Anne, "but, of course, whether we remain in Merkland or not, it must make a very great, and a very pleasant change to us."

Mrs. Aytoun smiled a dubious smile—she was not reconciled to it. In any way, parting with the girl-daughter was a great venture, but to send her into the rule of a husband's mother, while even the husband himself was comparatively unknown! Mrs. Aytoun was jealous and afraid for her little clinging Alice, whose life hitherto had been so carefully guarded.

"And so you are demurring to the lad's petition?" said Mrs. Catherine. "Well, I do not marvel; but a month or two can make little odds, and you bid to have parted with her soon or syne."

"Certainly, that is a consolation," said Mrs. Aytoun, with her faint smile. "It is selfish of me, I am afraid, to be so loath to think of parting with Alice; and part I must one time or other, that is true, but still—a little longer, I think, she may be left to me. Your brother has been pressing an early time upon us, Miss Ross. I do not object that he should wish it—but you must do us the kindness to help me in deferring this a little."

"I believe," said Anne, "that my brother Norman may be home—that we may expect him at the end of the year. I should like exceedingly that he could be present—that it were deferred until that time."

Mrs. Aytoun pressed her hand gratefully—Alice, radiant with smiles and blushes, looked in at the door. "Oh! Anne is here—she has come," she exclaimed as she ran to Anne's side—Lewis was behind her.

"So my mother has been bringing you over to our side," said James Aytoun, when the evening was considerably advanced, as he took a seat near Anne. "Mrs. Catherine is wavering. I fear to find her throw her mighty forces into alliance with the active, serviceable, energetic troops whom Lewis himself brings into the field. We are by no means pleased to have our little Alice carried off from us so rapidly. I begin to fear Mrs. Catherine is anything but a safe guardian for young ladies; I certainly shall not advise any client of mine to send favorite daughters or sisters to the Tower, if he wants to keep them out of harm's way."

"What is that you say?" said Mrs. Catherine, "do you make light of my good name, James Aytoun? and do you, Anne, sit still and hear? you are an irreverent generation! Never you heed, Alison. It is because you are overlooking the rule of Laban, the son of Bethuel, and cheating him of his elder right."

"If you will come to Merkland, James," said Lewis, "I will say a good word for you to Marjory Falconer. By the bye, I forgot my great news—have you heard about Marjory, Anne?"

"What about her?"

"In the first place, she has made a silent recantation—if one may guess from appearances. A hint of Walter Foreman's the other day, about the rights of women, instead of setting her off at a tangent, as such a thing used to do, threw her into an agony of blushing, and made her dumb. That is great enough for one report; but I have another. Marjory Falconer—listen to me all who know Strathoran—Marjory Falconer is about to be married!"

"To be married!" echoed little Alice, with a look of laughing wonder and dismay. These two, Lewis and his betrothed, had not got the slightest glimpse of Marjory Falconer yet, well though they fancied they knew her; Anne looked slightly puzzled, and a little anxious: Mrs. Catherine smiled.

"Who is it? who is it?" cried little Alice.

"Anne can guess," said Lewis: "I see his name upon her lips. It seems my news is no such wonder, after all.'

"Who is she going to marry, Lewis?" asked Anne, hastily, "it is rather a wish than a guess with me. Marjory does not give confidences of that kind—is it Mr. Lumsden?"

"May all your wishes, sister Anne," said Lewis, with mock gravity, "be as fully realized. It is the mighty minister of Portoran. Ralph, they say, rebelled, and had a swearing fit when he heard of it, which Marjory promptly checked, however, and sent him down stairs to the congenial society of his horses and grooms. It will be a serious matter for Ralph though, for Marjory, with all her whims, kept things going at Falcon's Craig."

"I am very glad to hear it," said Anne. "It is one of the few marriages that have no drawback; one can feel that Marjory, with her strength and good sense, is safe now, in a pure healthful atmosphere, where she will grow and flourish. I am very glad."

Lewis and Alice exchanged glances and laughed.

"Lewis," said Mrs. Catherine, "hold your peace. It becomes the like of you—gallants that have a while to grow before they reach their full stature—to take heed that you meddle only with things within your power of vision. Ay! you are lowering your bit forehead on me, Alison Aytoun; but truly, after all, there are wiser men in this world, to my own certain knowledge, than this gallant that calls himself of Merkland."

"But Miss Falconer figures very largely in Alice's reminiscences," said James, smiling. "To whom shall I apply for an account of her? to you, Mrs. Catherine, or to Lewis."

"I bid you come yourself and see, James Aytoun," said Mrs. Catherine. "As for Lewis, he does not know, and therefore it is not likely he can tell; but truly, I think you would be better employed telling my Anne, whom you have set yourself beside, the issue of the plea, that Robert Ferguson and you have been working at so long."

James obeyed: with signal disgrace and utter discomfiture, Lord Gillravidge's defence had been overpowered. The road through the Strathoran grounds, by the omnipotent voice of the Court of Session, was proclaimed free as the sunshine to all and sundry, its natural proprietors and heirs. Henceforward the pulling down of barricades was a legal and proper enforcement of the law, and the erection of the same entirely useless, for any other purpose than that of keeping the well-disposed lads of Strathoran in glee and mischief. Mrs. Catherine was victorious, and triumphed moderately in her victory.

"If it were not that I hope in my lifetime to see Archie Sutherland back to his own lands, I would hazard a trial with that English alien, of his title to take their old inheritance from the clansmen whose right it is. You shake your head, James Aytoun—I will uphold it in the face of a whole synod as learned in the law as yourself, that the clansman has the same natural right of possession as his chief; that it comes to him by the same inheritance; that in no way is the laird more certain in his tenure than the humble man, except in so far as he is chief of both land and men, natural protector, ruler and guardian of the same. You forget the ancient right and justice in this drifting unsettled generation. If it were not that you pleaders of the law, have a necessity of spinning out the line of a plea, past the extremity of mortal life, and I hope to see Archie home within the course of mine, I would see that this was tried without delay, let the whole parliament-house of you shake the heads of your wisdom if ye likit."

"I am afraid," said James, "we might get the theoretic justice of it approved—but as for any practical result to follow—"

"You do not know," interrupted Mrs. Catherine: "so far as I have seen in my life, a thing does not commonly succeed till it's tried; ay, tried with labor, and zeal, and longwaiting; and it's a poor work that is not worth that. I know not but what for the sake of the coming race, there is a clear call to try it. If the first bit petty tyrant that took their right inheritance from clansmen, whose fathers won it by the strong hand, had been resisted in his ill doing, this pang English lordling would not have dared to turn the Macalpines out of Oranmore."

"But we dont all hold our lands by the strong hand," said Lewis Ross.

"Lewis, you are a loon; how often have I told you to hold your peace; and what better tenure could the man have for his lands, I would crave to know, than just the tenure of the strong hand? Your fathers knew better, and what they won by their sword and by their bow, was well won I say! won by clansmen and chief together, and by clansmen and chief, in their degree, to be lawfully and justly held—in peace, if the Almighty ordained it so, and if not, in honorable holding of the land they had won, against all aliens and incomers; whether they came by open war, or with courtesies of craft and falsehood, as men do in this time!"

In a few days after, Mrs. Catherine and her train, including Alice Aytoun and her maid Bessie, left Edinburgh for the Tower. In consideration of the six months' delay to which Lewis had reluctantly submitted, Mrs. Aytoun as reluctantly consented that her little daughter should pay a brief visit to Mrs. Catherine—a visit which was by no means to exceed the limits of a month.

Jacky and Bessie, under the safe-conduct of Johnnie Halflin, were to travel by the coach. When the youthful trio reached the starting-place in high glee, an early coach had just arrived from one of the many village-towns in the vicinity of Edinburgh. Jacky's quick eye discerned, among the little knot of bystanders, a tall lad of some nineteen or twenty years, engaged in superintending the collection of boxes belonging to an elderly woman, who stood with a slightly fluttered, agitated look upon the pavement below. The large Paisley shawl, the mighty leghorn bonnet—Jacky threw over them a glance of hasty recognition. Their owner turned her head. The thin, long upper lip was not quivering now—a glance of troubled joy was in the eye—Jacky hastily ran to speak to her. It was Jean Miller. Bessie drew near also. In Johnnie Halflin's presence, Bessie would have had no objection to a slight flirtation with the young doctor, Jean Miller's genteel nephew. The tall, slight lad drew himself up, however, with the slightest possible recognition. He had a soul above flirtation with maid-servants.

"Andrew's maister, I'm meaning the doctor he's serving his time wi', has ta'en in a daft gentleman to board wi' him," said Jean Miller, aside to the sympathetic Jacky, "and so there wasna room for the callant, and it was needful he should get up-putting in a strange house. Sae it chanced, when I was in seeing him, that I saw some mair neighbors o' his, collegianers, and ae young doctor, that was unco chief wi' him; and it appears Andrew—he's a kindly callant, and has been a' his days—had been telling them o' his auntie, and how I was anxious about him in the strange place, where he had nae mother's e'e ower him, nor onybody to keep him right. Sae what did they do—the young doctor and the auldest o' the students, but they said, that if Andrew would get his auntie to come in and take a house, they would a' bide wi' me, and that they would be mair comfortable a'thegither, and could help ane anither in their learning. Sae ye may think Andrew was blythe to come out to tell me, and seeing I'm wearing into years, and a'body likes to have a house o' their ain, and in especial for the laddie's sake, that he may be wiled to care mair for hame, than for the vanities that have ruined lads of promise by the hunder before him, as I ken ower weel, I didna swither; and the house is ta'en, and the plenishing's bought, and I'm gaun hame the day. It's a great change to me, but—Andrew, my man, yon blue box is mine too—it'll be a great ease to my mind to hae my laddie aye in my ain e'e; and I hope the Lord will send a blessing on't. It's a' for the lad's guid I'm anxious. Guid kens, I would have little thought o' mysel that am withered, and auld, and past my strength, if it werena for him."

The journey was accomplished in safety. Little Alice was established again at the rounded window of that pretty bower of hers, looking over, through the golden air, to the quiet house of Merkland, with no phantom of grief or pain or sorrow, throwing its shadow now between; but everything around and before, throwing out that sunny light of hope and promise, beautiful to see.

The day after their arrival, Anne set out to visit Esther Fleming. Lewis had not thought of any anxiety of Esther's; unfortunately, very much as his intercourse with the Aytouns had improved him Lewis was still by no means given to any great consideration of other people's anxieties, and therefore he had suffered the paper which Anne sent specially for her, containing the first public notice of Norman's innocence, to lie useless in his library without the least remembrance of Esther. He had not the same bond to her as Anne had, it is true, for Esther had never bestowed any great share of her patronage upon "the strange woman's bairn."

A little way from the gate of Merkland, Anne met Marjory Falconer. Marjory had the slightest possible air of timidity hanging upon her, with a singular grace. She was a little afraid of Anne's reception of her intended marriage—whether she already knew—and if she would lecture, or rally her.

"Come with me to the Tower first," said Marjory, drawing Anne's arm within her own. "I want to see little Alice Aytoun—and I have a great deal to say to you."

"I am glad you have the grace to acknowledge that," said Anne, smiling; "but I do think, Marjory, that some of it should have been said sooner."

"Anne!" exclaimed Marjory Falconer, with one of her violent blushes, "you would not have had me speak to you, the way young ladies speak in novels."

"Many young ladies in novels speak very sensibly, Marjory," said Anne.

"Very well—never mind, that is all over now. Tell me of your own matters, Anne—you have not returned to Merkland as you went away; there is to be no more brooding, no more unhappiness?"

Anne told her story briefly, as they went up Oranside. Marjory was much affected. To her strong, joyous spirit, in its vigorous contendings with mere external evil, and now in the prospective strength and honor of its new, grave, happy household life, the mention of these agonies came with strange power. Nothing like them, as the fair promise of her future went, should ever enter the healthful precincts of the Manse of Portoran, yet her heart swelled within her in deep sympathy as the hearts of those swell who feel that they themselves also could bear like perils and miseries—the true fraternity.

In the inner drawing-room they found little Alice alone, and there ensued some gayer badinage, which Marjory bore with wonderful patience and a considerable amount of blushing laughter, inevitable in the circumstances. "The only thing is," said Marjory, with a look of comical distress, "what I shall do with Ralph—I wish somebody would marry him—I do wish some one would do me the special favor of marrying Ralph!"

Little Alice Aytoun looked up in wonder. It was Alice's wont to be greatly puzzled with those speeches of Marjory's, and quite at a loss to know how much was joke, and how much earnest.

"Yes, indeed," said Marjory, laying her hand on Alice's shoulder. "I think it would have been a very much more sensible thing for you, little Alice Aytoun, to have fallen in love with my poor brother Ralph, who needs somebody to take care of him, than with that rational, prudent Lewis of Anne's who can take such very good care of himself."

Alice drew herself up, and was half inclined to be angry; but glancing up to Marjory's face, ended in laughing, blushing and wondering.

"And yet that must have been very unsatisfactory too," said Marjory, smoothing Alice's fair hair as she would have done a child's, "for then, I had been certainly thirled to Falcon's Craig to take care of you both—to see that Ralph was not too rough with you, and that you were too gentle with him. No, we must have some one who can hold the reins. Altogether you have chosen better for yourself, little Alice—Lewis will take care of you. But who shall I get to manage Ralph?"

"Perhaps Anne will," suggested Alice wickedly.

Anne was full three-and-twenty, and she was not even engaged! Little Alice, with a touch of girlish generosity, felt the superiority of her own position almost painful.

"Hush, little girl," said the prompt Marjory. "Anne is not a horsewoman; besides I won't endanger a friend's interest, even for the sake of getting Ralph off my hands. Anne is—"

"Oh! is Anne engaged?—is Anne engaged?" cried little Alice, clapping her hands. Alice had been a good deal troubled by this same want of an engagement for Anne, and had even been secretly cogitating, in her own mind, whether it might not be possible to direct the attention of her grave brother James to the manifold good qualities of Lewis's sister.

"Now, pray, do you two brides leave me undisturbed in my humble quietness," said Anne, good-humoredly. "Why there is Jeanie Coulter to be married next week—and then yourselves—if I do not hold my ground, there will not be a single representative left of the young womanhood of Strathoran and that is a calamity to be avoided by all means. I must really go to Esther Fleming's now. Do you go with me, Marjory?"

Marjory assented, and they left the Tower; instead of going directly to Esther Fleming's house, Anne went round by the mill. On reaching Mrs. Melder's, they found that good woman standing, with a puzzled look, before her table, on which lay a parcel, which Anne had sent with Jacky, of mourning for the child. Lilie herself stood by, regarding the little black frock, in which she was dressed, with a look of childish gravity. The mourning chilled the little heart, though after being convinced that nothing ailed papa, mamma, or Lawrie, Lilie, in Anne's bed-chamber, the previous night, had heard of her uncle's death, with only that still awe natural to the blythe little spirit, "feeling its life in every vein." She did not know the strange uncle Patrick, who was dead. It only subdued the gay voice a very little, and sent some sad speculations into the childish head—a place where grave speculations are rife enough sometimes, whether we of the elder generation discern them or no.

When Anne and Marjory approached the door, the child ran to meet them. "Oh, aunt Anne—my aunt Anne!"

Marjory Falconer looked puzzled—she had not heard this part of Anne's story.

"This is my niece," said Anne, with a slight tremor. "This is Lilias Rutherford, my brother Norman's child."

"Anne!" exclaimed Marjory, in amazement, "what do you mean?" Mrs. Melder pressed forward no less astonished.

"This little stranger," said Anne, holding the child's hand, "is the daughter of my brother Norman, of whom you have heard so much, Marjory—my niece, Lilias Rutherford."

Marjory Falconer, in the extremity of her astonishment, snatched up Lilie in her arms, and ran out with her into the open sunlight, as if to satisfy herself that Anne's new-found niece was indeed the little Spanish Lilie, whose strange coming to the mill had been so great a wonder to the countryside.

"Ye're no meaning you, Miss Anne?" exclaimed Mrs. Melder, anxiously, "it's only a joke wi' Miss Falconer—ye're no meaning it?"

"Indeed I am," said Anne, "Lilie is truly my niece, Mrs. Melder; the daughter of a brother who has been long lost to us, but whom we have now found again."

"Eh!" cried Mrs. Melder, "that'll be the auld leddy's son that was said to have killed anither man—and ye wad aye ken it, Miss Anne? Keep me! To think of me telling ye about the leddy, and you kenning a' the time wha the bairn was."

"No, you do me injustice," said Anne, eagerly. "At that time I had not the slightest idea who Lilie was, and it is only a week or two since I was certain."

Mrs. Melder did not look perfectly contented. "Weel, nae doubt it's my pairt to be thankfu' that the bairn has friends o' her ain, that can be better for her than me—and it's like ye'll do taking her to Merkland, Miss Anne?" Mrs. Melder lifted the corner of her apron to her eye, and tried to look offended and indifferent.

"I want to take her down with me to-day," said Anne, "and we can arrange about that afterwards. Lilie, come here, I want you to go with me to Merkland."

Mrs. Melder took Lilie's little bonnet, and drew the child to her knee to put it on. "And they're gaun to take ye away frae me, my lamb! but ye'll aye mind us, Lilie? and when ye're a grand laddy, ye'll no forget the wee house at the mill, that ye lived in when ye were a bairn?" Mrs. Melder's eyes were over-flowing.

"Dinna greet," whispered Lilie, clinging to her kind nurse, "if my aunt Anne takes me to stay at Merkland, I'll come down every day—me and Jacky—and when mamma comes, she'll come and see you. Eh!" cried Lilie, forgetting her sympathy with Mrs. Melder in her remembrance of one dearer than she; "you never saw a lady so bonnie as my mamma!"

"Ay, but, Lilie," said the good woman, applying the apron to her eyes again, "ye dinna think how we'll miss ye here. There'll aye be the wee bed empty at nicht, and aye the wee facie away in the morning. Oh! Lilie, my lamb!"

"But I'll come down every day," said Lilie, in consolation; "and when mamma comes, I'll bring her to see you, and papa, and Lawrie; and Jacky will bring me every day, and when I'm a big lady, I'll come my lane."

They went down Oranside together, Lilie holding a hand of Anne and Marjory, and skipping gaily between them. Marjory Falconer spoke little: she had not yet overcome her surprise.

Esther Fleming sat by the door of her cottage, knitting a stocking, and enjoying the sunshine. Her young niece was going lightly about within, "redding up" the lightsome clean apartment. The old woman looked very cheerful, neat and comfortable, her snow-white muslin cap covering her gray hair, and closely surrounding her sensible, kindly face. She started from her seat as she saw Anne.

"Eh, Miss Anne, are ye come at last?" but her face darkened with disappointment as she perceived Marjory and the child.

"I would have come sooner, Esther," said Anne, "but that I thought you had been told."

"Told what?" Esther staggered back to her seat, and sitting down there, supported her head firmly between her hands. "For guid sake, Miss Anne, say it out, whatever it is. Let me hear it at once. Young lady go away, and let my bairn tell me her tidings."

"I may tell them before all the world Esther," said Anne. "Norman is innocent, known and declared to be so, in the face of all men, free to return to his own house and name, in honor and peace, and good fame. All our sorrow and trouble for him are over. He is safe, Esther. He is justified in the sight of the world."

The old woman uttered a cry—a low, wild, unconscious cry. She might have done the same had it been bitter sorrow that overwhelmed her, instead of a very agony and deluge of joy and thankfulness. She threw her apron over her head—under its covering they could see the motion of her hands, the bowing of her head. Prayers innumerable, offered by night and day for eighteen years, that had lain unanswered till this time, before yon Throne in Heaven, were pouring back upon her now in a flood of blessedness. It was meet that they should stand apart in silent reverence, while thus, in the presence of the Highest, His old and faithful servant rendered thanks, where so long she had poured forth her petition for mercy.

At last she raised her head—her clear and kindly features trembling yet with the storm of joy that had swept over them; her eye fell upon the child. She had seen Lilie once or twice before, but never before in this strong light which tinged everything with a remembrance of Norman. She started to her feet: "Wha are ye, bairn? wha are ye?—for ony sake, Miss Anne, tell me wha this is?"

Anne took Lilie's hand, and led her to Esther's side; the child looked up wonderingly with those large dark wistful eyes of hers, almost as Christian Lilie had been wont to look—Anne placed her in the arms of her father's devoted, loving friend. "Esther, you have a better right to her than I—she is my brother's child—she is the daughter of Norman, for whom you have sorrowed and prayed so long."

And Marjory Falconer stood apart, repeating to herself in a low voice, which trembled sometimes, that Psalm, the blessing of the good man, sung by the Hebrew people in the old time, as they journeyed to Jerusalem, and familiar now to us in Scotland, as the household words of our own land—

"Behold each man that fears the Lord, Thus blessed shall he be, The Lord shall out of Sion send, His blessing unto thee, Thou shalt Jerusalem's good behold, While thou on earth dost dwell, Thou shalt thy children's children see, And peace on Israel!"

CHAPTER XXX

The months travelled on peacefully; Jeanie Coulter and Walter Foreman were married with all due mirth and rejoicing. Ada Mina was reigning now, in the absence of all rival powers, acknowledged belle and youthful beauty of Strathoran; and had been thrown into an immense flutter, to the great dismay and manifest injury of a young Muirland laird from the west, who had come to take lessons in agriculture from Mr. Coulter, and was very assiduously paying court to Mr. Coulter's daughter—by a hint from Mrs. Catherine, of a possible visit to the Tower of the Honorable Giles. Little Harry Coulter, the Benjamin of Harrows, was more desperately in love than ever with the stranger Lilie, now living at Merkland, in her full dignity as Merkland's niece; and with his first knife had already constructed, with mighty deliberation and care, a splendid model of a patent plough, to be laid at the small feet of his liege lady, who unfortunately had no manner of appreciation of patent ploughs, and greatly preferred Charlie Ferguson's present, a boat—a veritable boat with little white silken sails, elaborated in the Woodsmuir nursery by Mary Ferguson and Flora Macalpine, and which could actually, with a fairy cargo of moss and ruddy autumnal wild-flowers, make genuine voyages upon the Oran, to the delight of Lilie and the Woodsmuir party, and the immense disgust of Harry Coulter. Lilie was becoming a great pet at Merkland, "evendown spoiled," as Mrs. Melder said, with the slightest possible tinge of jealousy; the constant companion and pupil of Anne, the plaything of Lewis, and even—so great was the witchery of the fair fresh childhood—a favorite with Mrs. Ross herself, whom aunt Anne taught Lilie to approach with the greatest reverence, and to call grand-mamma—mamma would not do. Lilie stoutly resisted the bestowal of that sacred name upon any individual except the one enthroned in the loyal little heart, the bonniest of all existent ladies; the especial mother of the loving child.

In the beginning of winter, Anne paid her promised visit to Christian, carrying little Lilie with her. New life was budding again in the large melancholy heart which had lived through a lingering death for so many years. A deep sorrow, and tender remembrance of the dead carried about with her in religious silence, shunning common sight and common comment, did not prevent this. It was not meet that the griefs of such a spirit should pass lightly away, or was it possible; but bordering the deep stillness of that lasting sorrow were other holds on life. Hope for Marion, the little sister of her happier days; reverent enjoyment of God's mercies, which one who had bowed to His chastisements so long was not like to hold lightly; a sympathy, exquisitely deep and tender, with everything of nature, and much of humanity—all swelling up from the strong vitality, healthful and pure and heaven-dependant, which God had placed, as a fountain in his servant's heart, before He laid her mighty load upon her.

Anne and the child remained for a considerable time with Christian. She had settled again in the old cottage, and was already making arrangements for the repair of Redheugh. When Anne parted with her, it was in the confidence of meeting her again in the end of the year, when Norman and Marion should have returned; a light passed over the wan face, as Christian said those words, but still she did not say from whence the exiles were to return. Anne could not press the question, and the time was not very long to wait. Lilie returned with her to Merkland.

The year waned; the December days again darkened over the sky of Strathoran. Mr. Lumsden of Portoran had refurnished his Manse, in a style which utterly scandalized Mrs. Bairnsfather.—Some one presented him with a whole library of additional books—the same individual that had lately put into his hand money enough to build a school-house in the hamlet at Oran Brig, at which already masons and joiners were working merrily, and under whose shelter Mr. Lumsden himself had vowed to preach, let the Presbytery storm as it pleased. Mrs. Bairnsfather moved her husband to appeal the case to the Assembly this time, if the Synod's thunders proved unavailing. Mr. Bairnsfather, very much disgusted as he was—was dubious. A certain mighty man in an obscure Fife parish, lying on the south side of the Tay—a wondrous visionary man, who seeing the first experiments made with gas in the streets of the mighty cities, had tubes laid for the conveyance of the same to the pleasant parlors of that rural Manse of Kilmany, had discovered a mighty truth by that time, and was beginning to throw the rays of it from that marvellous lamp of his, over the Tay, to be over all Scotland ere long. The truth that preaching proprieties would not do; that ministers of Christ's holy evangel must preach Christ—nothing less, and that the name of the Lord was the strong Tower—it and no other—in which purity of soul and life could be kept unsullied and undimmed for ever. And vigorous athletic forces, whose front rank, among other sons of Anak, stood that restless man of might and labor, so long called fire-brand and fanatic, the Rev.

John Lumsden of Portoran, were pressing into the highest places of the Church, with this greatest of Scottish men at their head. So Mr. Bairnsfather sagaciously, over his gardening, resolved that it might be well to proceed with caution in this matter, and that the eye of a General Assembly in this great renewing of its youth, might see shortcomings in his own ministerial life and conversation, not particularly adapted for the light of the day; in consequence of which prudent doubts Mr. Lumsden escaped a call to the bar of the supreme judicatory of the Church.

He was not married yet, however, for Marjory Falconer was still disconsolately, and in vain, looking out for some one who would do her the especial favor of marrying Ralph.

Mrs. Ross was becoming reconciled to the inevitable marriage of Lewis. It was to take place some time about the new year—the special period depending upon the looked for arrival of Norman. Little Alice, with her girlish kindness of heart, had put a decided negative upon Lewis's proposal, that his mother should leave Merkland. Surely they could all dwell together in unity. Alice had considerable confidence in her own powers of charming. To a little bride of eighteen, whom all the stronger natures round her instinctively conspired to guard and defend from evil, the confidence was natural and becoming enough.

In the meantime, Alice had been plotting somewhat ineffectually to direct the especial attention of that grave brother James of hers to Anne, and Anne's to him. It by no means succeeded.—They were the best friends in the world, but clearly, even to the solicitous eye of Alice, as comfortably indifferent to each other as it was possible for very good friends to be.

Mr. Ferguson's work went on prosperously in the bleak lands of Loelyin and Lochend. The sides of the glen of Oranmore were covered with the flocks of the Southland farmer. In the glen itself, those roofless walls stood still desolate and silent, the end of many a stern pilgrimage made by the ejected Macalpines, who from their cottages in the low-country, and from fishing-boats on the wide seashore beyond Portoran, looked forward constantly with silent prayers, and stern onwaiting for the return of their chief, and the recovery of their homes.

He, this hapless chief of theirs, had heard ere now of their calamity, and in an agony of bitter earnestness had plunged again into his labor, his hope swelling within him, in a burst of force which made it almost painful—for them—also like himself heirs of the soil—and for their inheritance. It had been some relief to his burning eagerness, could he have cried his war-cry as his ancestors did, and rushed on—

To the rescue! There never was deed of olden arms, or bold knight-errantry more instinct with chivalrous honor and energy than this, though the battle-field was counting-room and market-place, and the wrestler a broken man!

Lord Gillravidge had returned to Strathoran, greatly to the chagrin of his useful friend, Mr. Fitzherbert, who had been, through all the intervening time laboriously endeavoring to convince his Lordship of the insupportable ennui of this out-of-the-world place of his. His Lordship was more than half convinced; nevertheless there was excellent shooting, and Lord Gillravidge filled his house with sportsmen, to the defiance of ennui, which reigning supreme in presence of one bore, seems to be expected to dissipate itself in the society of twenty.

One evening late in the year, Mr. Fitzherbert chanced inconsiderately to pass through the little hamlet at the Brig of Oran, after the darkening. It was a beautiful, clear, frosty night.—Hardy, strong, red and blue children, were sliding on the frozen Oran; young men and douce fathers, had been tempted to join them. Cottage doors were open on all sides, revealing homely interiors, partially lighted by the kindly firelight; grandmothers seated by the firesides; mothers stirring with care and pains-taking the mighty pot of wholesome "parritch" for their evening meal; elder sisters, eager to be out upon the slide, rapidly, and with much noise, putting upon the table bowls and plates to receive the same; while some who had finished the process stood at the door calling impatiently to boys and men, to "come in afore the parritch cules." Through this peaceful place, Mr. Fitzherbert inconsiderately passed alone. He had scarcely entered it, when he was recognised by a band of children on the ice. The youngsters of the Brig of Oran were just in such a state of exhilaration, as made them ready for mischief in all its possible varieties. "Eh!" cried out a stout lad of fourteen, at the top of his considerable voice, "younder's the man that Angus Macalpine shore like a sheep at the stepping stanes!"

"Great cry and little woo!" shouted another, adding also the latter line of the proverb, in all its ludicrous expressiveness.

"Eh man!" continued a third, "I wadna hae lain still, and gotten my head cuttit when I wasna wanting it."

Mr. Fitzherbert was perfectly blind and dumb with rage; in the midst of a chorus of laughter he hurried on.

"Never you heed, my man," said the shoe-maker's wife, known as "a randy" beyond the precincts of the Brig of Oran, "ye've gotten new anes—they're grown again."

"Grown again!" ejaculated a little old wifie, whose profession was that of an itinerant small-ware dealer, and who was privileged as an original, "grown again!" and she lifted her quick little withered hand to Fitzherbert's face, as she glided in before him; "let-abee shearing—I wad a bawbee the new anes wadna stand a pouk."

And secure in the protection of the hardy mason, under whose roof-tree she was to receive shelter for the night, the old wifie extended her fingers to the graceful ornament of hair which curled over Mr. Fitzherbert's lip. We cannot tell what dread revelations might have followed, had not Lord Gillravidge's unfortunate friend dashed the old woman aside, and saved himself by flight. Poor old Nannie paid for her boldness by a slight cut upon her withered brow—her host growled a thundery anathema, and the well-disposed lads of the hamlet pursued the fugitive with gibes and shoutings of revengeful derision up to the very gate of Strathoran.

After which stimulating adventure, Mr. Fitzherbert's arguments became so potent and earnest, that Lord Gillravidge was moved by them, and finding likewise that Mr. Whittret turned out by no means the most honorable of stewards, and that this great house was enormously expensive, his Lordship took it into his serious consideration whether it might not be the wisest course to get rid of Strathoran.

December passed away—the new year came, and still there were no tidings of Norman. Anne became anxious and uneasy; but Christian's letters said, and said with reason, that the delay of a week or so, was no unusual matter in a long sea voyage. Where was he then, this exile brother?

Lewis was not to be put off so easily. He did not see why a matter of so much importance as his marriage should be delayed for the uncertain arrival of Norman. So the day was determined on at last;

the ceremony was to be performed at the Tower, by Mrs. Catherine's especial desire—in the end of January; if Norman came before that time, so much the better; if not they would go on without him.

A fortnight of the new year was gone already; the Aytouns had arrived at the Tower. Mrs. Aytoun and her son, under the escort of Lewis, had gone down to Merkland to pay a formal visit to Mrs. Ross. Anne was at the Tower with Lilie. She had been there of late, even more than usual. It was Mrs. Catherine's desire that her favorite should remain with her permanently, when Alice had taken her place in Merkland. It pleased Anne greatly to have the alternative, but until the return of Norman, she made no definite arrangement.

The afternoon was waning—Alice was in very high spirits, a little tremulous and even something excited. Her wedding-day began to approach so nearly.

She had been sitting close by Anne's side, engaged in a long and earnest conversation, wherein the elder sister had many grave things to speak of, while the younger, leaning on her in graceful dependence, listened and assented reverently, forgetting for the moment what a very important little personage, she herself, the future Mrs. Ross of Merkland, was.

Mrs. Catherine entered the room suddenly, with a newspaper in her hand, and a triumphant expression in her face. "Here is news, Anne, news worth hearkening to. Did I not know the cattle would not be suffered to do their evil pleasure long in the house of a good man? Now in a brief hour, we will be clear of the whole race of them—unclean beasts and vermin as they are. Look at this."

Anne started when she did so; it was a long advertisement setting forth, in auctioneer eloquence, the beauties and eligibilities of the desirable freehold property of Strathoran, which was to be offered for sale, on a specified day in spring, within a specified place in Edinburgh.

"What think you of that?" said Mrs. Catherine. "We have smitten the Philistines and driven them out of the land—a land that it is my hope will be polluted with the footsteps of the like of them never more in my day, though truly I am in doubt how we can get the dwelling purified, to make it fit for civilized folk."

"And what do you mean to do?" said Anne, eagerly. "It may be bought by some other stranger: it may be—"

"Hold your peace, Anne," said Mrs. Catherine; "are you also joining yourself to the witless bairns that would give counsel to gray hairs. It may be! I say it shall be! The siller will aye be to the fore, whether I am or no, and think you I will ever stand by again, and let a strange man call himself master of Strathoran—the house that Isabel Balfour went into a bride, and went out of again, only to her rest? It has been a thorn in my very side, this one unclean and strange tenant of it. Think you I will ever suffer another?"

"And what then?" said Anne, with anxious interest.

"We must get it bought, without doubt," said Mrs. Catherine. "You are slower of the uptake, Anne, than is common with you. Whether I myself have, or have not, sufficient siller is another matter. There are folk in Scotland, who know the word of Catherine Douglas, and can put faith in it. Before three months are over our heads, an it be not otherwise ordained, Archie Sutherland shall be master of his land again."

"Oh! Anne, are you not glad?" exclaimed little Alice: "we shall have Mr. Sutherland back again."

Anne did not feel herself particularly called upon to express gladness, but she looked up inquiringly into Mrs. Catherine's face.

"I said nothing of the lad coming home," said Mrs. Catherine firmly. "Alison Aytoun, you are but a bairn, and will never be tried, so far as I can see the lot before you, by thoughts or purposes of a stern and troublous kind. It is other with you, Anne, as I know. This Archie Sutherland, has wasted with his riotous living the substance given in charge to him from his father, and from his father's God. It is not meet he should come back unscathed to this leisure and honor; it is right he should clear himself by labor and toil, not of the sin before God, which is atoned for in a holier way, but of the sin in the sight of man. I say, I also would be sinning against a justice, which neither fails nor alters, and discouraging strong hearts that held upon their warfare manfully, when he fell under the hand of the adversary, were I bringing back Archie Sutherland at this time to the full honor and possessions of his father's house. I will let him stay in his trial and probation, child, till he can show labor of his own hands, bravely done and like a man. The gallant is nearer to my own heart than ever man was, but Sholto my one brother; but it is meet he should render due justice after he has done evil."

Anne bowed her head in silent acquiescence: she did not speak. Mrs. Catherine was right.

"But this must be looked to without delay," said Mrs. Catherine, seating herself in her own great chair, while the gloaming shadows gathered darkly in the room; "we must buy his land back for him now. I will speak of it to Mr. Foreman this very night. Alison, go your ways, and sing to me the ballad of the wayfaring man."

And in the soft shadowy gloaming, little Alice seated herself at the piano, and began to sing. You could scarcely perceive her fair head in the dreamy gloom of the large apartment. Further in, the red glow of the fire flickered ruddy on the stately form of Mrs. Catherine, bringing out with momentary flashes sometimes the shadow of her strong face in bold relief against the wall. Still more in the shade sat Anne, very still and thoughtful, looking at the old friend, and the young beside her, and thinking of others far away. Over them all were these low floating notes of music hopeful and sad—

Thy foot is weary, thy cheek is wan, Come to thy kindred, wayfaring man!

Down stairs in the snug housekeeper's room, a little party was assembled, merrier and younger than were wont to be seen within that especial sanctum of the famous Mrs. Euphan Morison. Mrs. Euphan herself had gone to Portoran, to make provision of many things necessary for the jubilee and festivities, which in the ensuing week were to be holden in the Tower. She was not to return till late that night, and Jacky had taken advantage of her absence.

Round the fire, in the early winter gloaming, sat little Bessie, Johnnie Halflin, Jacky herself and Flora Macalpine. There was to be a quiet reunion in the Tower that night, and Flora came, in attendance upon little Mary Ferguson, who was gaily engaged at that moment, in the hall, playing hide and seek with Lilie Rutherford.

The little company in the housekeeper's room were very merry. Jacky was repeating to them that sad adventure of Sir Artegall, which ended in his captivity to the most contemptuous of Amazons, the warlike Radigund; with whispers innumerable, and stifled laughter, her companions listened, or pretended to listen.

At that time, the gig from the Sutherland Arms, which had formerly conveyed James Aytoun to the Tower, was tumbling along the high-road in the same direction again. At some little distance from the entrance to Mrs. Catherine's ground, two gentlemen alighted, and dismissing it, ascended to the Tower.

One of them—he was bronzed by the beating of a sun more fervid than that of Scotland—was casting keen glances of joyous recognition round him—at the Tower—at Merkland—at a light in a high window there, which he fancied he knew, and still more eagerly at Strathoran in the dim distance. Its name had rung strangely in his ear from the tongue of the "crooked helper" at the inn, who drove their humble vehicle—"mony thanks to ye, Strathoran." It sent a thrill to the heart of Archibald Sutherland.

Yes, Archibald Sutherland! it was no other!

An older man leaned on his arm. In the darkness you could not distinguish particularly either his face or form; he was tall, with an elastic buoyant footstep, and was looking about him in a singular abrupt way, now here, now there, like a man in a dream.

They approached the Tower door—it was closed. Archibald's friend had been eager hitherto, but now he lingered and seemed to wish delay. Archibald was entirely in the dark as to the reason. There was a ruddy light gleaming from a low window near at hand. The stranger drew near to look in, almost as if he knew it.

The room was full of the ruddy fire-light—the two dark figures at the window were quite unseen by those merry youthful people about the fire. Some one had slightly opened the window a little while before, for the room was very hot, and the door had been closed, that graver ears might not hear their laughter.

Jacky sat in the midst, her dark face glowing keen and bright. She was reciting vigorously that doleful adventure of the luckless Sir Artegall. The woman's weedes put upon him by the disdainful Amazon; the white apron—the distaff in his hand, "that he thereon should spin both flax and tow;" his low place among the brave knights, whom he found "spinning and carding all in comely row;" and

"—forst through penury and pyne,
To doe these works to their appointed dew,
For nought was given them to sup or dyne,
But what their hands could earn by twisting linen twyne."

A very sad thing, doubtless, for the hapless Sir Artegall, and furnishing very sufficient occasion for the "deep despight" and "secret shame" of his lofty and royal Lady Britomart, but by no means calculated to impress any deep feeling of pity or compassion upon that somewhat ungovernable knot of youngsters. Flora Macalpine, too kindly and good-humored to hurt Jacky's feelings, had bent her head down upon her knee to hide her laughter; Johnnie Halflin leaned against the mantelpiece, shaking with secret earthquakes; Bessie had her head turned to the door, and was gazing at it steadily, and biting her rosy lip. They had all an awe of Jacky. It would not do, however. That picture, with its gradual heightening; at last the sad honor of the unfortunate knight, steadily spinning in his woman's weedes, because his word was pledged to the despightful Radigund,—there was a general explosion—it was impossible to withstand that.

Jacky stopped suddenly, and withdrew from the laughters in lofty offence. She herself had a perception of the allegory, and was hurt and wounded at its reception, as we see greater people sometimes, whose myths a laughing world will persist in receiving as rather grotesque than sublime.

Jacky was almost sulky; she sat down in the shade, and turned her head resolutely away. Flora drew near to her in deprecatory humbleness. Jacky resisted and resented proudly.

Just then the door opened; the tall man, leaning on Archibald Sutherland's arm, gave a nervous start. Archibald had begun to weary of his station here, at the window of the housekeeper's room. His friend and employer, Mr. Sinclair was exhibiting a singular fancy to-night. He looked in wonderingly to see the reason of the sudden start.

It was only the entrance of two little girls; one of them blooming and ruddy, with radiant golden hair. The other paler, with a little frock of black silk, and eyes like the night—wistful, spiritual, dark.

"What ails Jacky?" said the new comer.

"Oh, if ye please, Miss Lilie," said Bessie eagerly, "we werena meaning ony ill; we only laughed."

Lilie slid gently within Jacky's arm—drew down the hand which supported her head, and whispered in her ear—the arm of Mr. Sinclair quivering all this time most strangely, as it leaned upon his friend's.

"Dinna be angry," whispered Lilie; "I want you to say Alice Brand. Mary never heard it; never mind them. Say Alice Brand to Mary and me."

"Oh! ay, Jacky," echoed Bessie and Johnnie together, "say Alice Brand; it's a real bonnie thing."

Jacky was mollified; after a brief pause, caressing Lilie, she began the ballad. Little Mary Ferguson, with the fire-light gleaming in her golden hair, stood, leaning on the shoulder of her favorite Flora. Lilie was at Jacky's knee, lifting up her face of earnest childish interest, and listening with all her might. Without, in the darkness stood the stranger, eagerly looking in, and holding Archibald's arm.

The first notes of Alice Aytoun's song were sounding up stairs. Archibald Sutherland stood still, but with eyes that wandered somewhat, and a considerable weariness. This was a most strange freak of Mr. Sinclair's—he could not comprehend it.

Her story possessed Jacky and inspired her. She rose as it swelled to its climax, and spoke louder.—

"It was between the night and day When the Fairy folk have power That I fell down in a sinful fray, And twixt life and death was snatched away, To the joyless, elfin bower.

But wist I of a woman bold, Who thrice my brow durst sign, I might regain my mortal mould As fair a form as thine.

She crossed him once, she crossed him twice, That lady was so brave; The fouller grew his goblin hue, The darker turned the cave,

She crossed him thrice, that lady bold, He rose beneath her hand, The fairest knight on Scottish mold, Her brother, Ethert Brand!

'Tis merry, 'tis merry, in good greenwood."—

The quick elfin eye shot a glance out into the darkness, and saw the listening figures there; the well-known face of young Strathoran! Jacky steadily finished the verse—committed Lilie into the hands of Flora Macalpine, and shutting the door of the house-keeper's room carefully behind her, opened the outer one, and admitted the strangers.

She conducted them up stairs in her own still, excited, elfin way; the fumes of the ballad hanging about her still. Mr. Sinclair grasped Archibald's arm, as they reached the door of the inner room, and held him back. The plaintive hopeful music was floating out again upon the soft shadows of the darkening night.

"Speed thy labor o'er land and sea, Home and kindred are waiting for thee."

They entered, Jacky gliding in before them to light the candles which stood upon the table. Mrs. Catherine started up in overwhelming surprise—so did Anne and Alice. There was a loud exclamation, "Whence come you, gallant and what brings you home?" and a confused uncertain welcoming of Archibald. Then they became calmer, and he introduced Mr. Sinclair. At this stranger, Jacky when she brought the lights, had thrown a long, keen scrutinising glance. There seemed an agitated uncertainty about him, which contrasted strangely with his firm lip and clear eye. They were seated again at last. A mysterious agitation had fallen upon them all, which Archibald could not comprehend. To this new-comer Mrs. Catherine's large gray eyes were travelling continually. Anne, with nervous timid glances, turned to him again and again. Mr. Sinclair himself, generally so frank, and full of universal sympathies, was confused and tremulous, speaking incoherently, and saying things which had no meaning; Archibald was greatly astonished—even little Alice Aytoun began to steal shy glances at the stranger.

Archibald made a sign to Anne, and rising went out—Anne followed. He was in high spirits, great in hope, and with prospects more cheering than he had ever dreamt of. He began to speak of them as she met him at the door.

"Who is he? who is he?" exclaimed Anne eagerly.

Archibald looked at her in amazement. "My employer and friend, Mr. Sinclair, Anne. What is the matter? I have come home with him at his own special desire. He intends—"

Jacky had been hovering on the stairs. She came up to the door where they were standing, and looked at them wistfully, "Oh if ye please, Miss Anne—"

"What is it, Jacky?"

Jacky could not tell what it was. She sat down on the stair, and put her hands up to her face, and began to cry—her excitement overpowering her.

"I cannot bear this," said Anne, wringing her hands nervously. "Jacky," she whispered in her ear—the girl shot down stairs like a spirit.

"Anne!" exclaimed Archibald, "something ails you. I beg you to tell me what it is."

"Afterwards—afterwards—" said Anne, hastily. "Go in now, Archibald. Jacky, come—"

Jacky returned, leading little Lilie by the hand. Archibald in silent amazement, went in again to the inner drawing-room. Anne followed him with the child, her face deadly pale, her form trembling.

Mrs. Catherine had changed the position of the lights on the table—one of them threw the profile of the stranger in clear shadow on the wall—she was looking with a singular scrutiny on the face, and on the shade of it. Little Alice Aytoun looked almost afraid. Mr. Sinclair was as confused and agitated as ever.

Lilie came in—she drew near Archibald timidly, with some remembrance of having seen him before; behind her, Anne stood in stiff excitement, watching her motions.

Suddenly the child's quick eye caught the stranger. Mr. Sinclair's arms moved tremulously. Lilie looked—wavered—turned back—looked again, her dark eyes dilating—her face full of childish earnestness. The time—the distance—the slight child's-memory—these did not make darkness enough, to veil from her remembrance the well-known face. The child sprang forward to the arms of the strong man, who sat trembling there under her simple scrutiny; she uttered a cry—Anne only could distinguish the latter words of it—they were enough, "My papa!"

And Mrs. Catherine rose, drawing up her stately figure to its full height, in solemn, judicial dignity, and advanced to the side of the father and child, "I bid you joyous, righteous, peaceful welcome; Norman Rutherford, I bid you welcome to your own name and land!"

And this was he! after eighteen years of labor and pain and banishment—an assumed name, a strange country, a toilsome life—in joy and peace and honor, Norman Rutherford had returned again to his own fatherland.

But their joy was too deep and still to bear recording; the manner of their rejoicing, the forms of their thankfulness were not such as we can dwell on. The serenity of deep and holy happiness, the exuberance of new-found blessings!—we cherish those things too deeply in our inmost hearts to speak of them; for we are very still, when we are very blessed, in Scotland!

At Portoran he had left Christian, Marion, and his son. He had promised to return to them immediately, with Anne and Lilie. Mrs. Catherine's carriage was ordered for them, and they drove round by Merkland. Anne sat, her heart beating joyously, by the side of her new-found brother. Little Lilie was nestling in the darkness in her father's arm, pouring forth a stream of questions about mamma and Lawrie. All the three were half weeping yet, in the tumult and excitement of their joy. The past, with all that was dark and painful in it, was lost in the present brightness; peace, security—the bond of tender and near relationship no longer a secret thing, but recognised now in joy and triumph, an abiding gladness all their days. The brother and sister united now for the first time in their lives, felt no restraining chillness of new acquaintanceship. They knew each other, and rejoiced, with tender pride and thanksgiving, in their kindred.

They stopped at Merkland—leading his child by the hand, and supporting Anne on his arm, Norman Rutherford entered the house of his fathers. His naturally buoyant step was restrained by a grave dignity; the memory of the dead hung over these walls—a thousand sad and potent remembrances were rising in the in the exile's heart—but withal he had been doubted here. He knew that, as it seemed instinctively, and drawing his sister's hand more closely through his arm, they entered Mrs. Ross's sitting-room together.

He stood gravely at the door waiting for his welcome. Lilie looked up wonderingly in his face; he held her hand with such gentle firmness, that she could not run to the wondering grand-mamma, who sat there staring suspiciously at the new comers. Mrs. Aytoun rose—neglected wives, sad and sorrowful, remember those who feel for their hidden troubles delicately. She came forward, she looked at him, she held out her hands, "Welcome, welcome home."

Mrs. Ross was looking at him now eagerly. James and Lewis had both risen—so did she. "Who is this, Anne?" exclaimed Lewis: "Lilie, who is this gentleman?"

Mrs. Ross's better angel visited her for that white moment. She advanced before either Anne or Lilie could answer. "It is your brother, Lewis—your brother Norman; Norman, you are welcome home."

And then a subdued and tender radiance came shining from the eyes of the returned son. He led Mrs. Ross to her chair—he called her mother. In the revulsion of his generous heart, thinking he had done her wrong, he forgot the dark wedding-day long ago which had brought her, a strange ruler, to Merkland, and which he spent by his own mother's grave. With Lilie on the little stool at her feet, and Norman doing her reverence, and all the rest joyous and glad about her, Mrs. Ross forgot it also.

He was to return to Merkland, she insisted, with his wife, their sister, and their son. The old house would hold them all. Norman's dark eyes brightened into deep radiance. He kissed the harsh step-mother's hand—he had done her wrong.

Then he drew Anne's arm through his own once more, and leaving Lilie in the carriage, in charge of Mrs. Catherine's careful coachman, went down Oranside to Esther Fleming's cottage; but in Esther's recognition there was neither pause nor doubt. The manly bronzed cheek, the dark hair with its streaks of grey—she did not linger to look at these. She heard the light elastic step, the voice so dearly known of old—and it was her beautiful laddie, her bairn, her son—not the grave man, who had more than reached the highest arch of his life—about whose neck the old woman threw her withered arms, as she lifted up her voice and wept.

At last they reached Portoran. The Marion, the little sister of Christian Lillie, had a face of thoughtful gracious beauty, such as gladdens the eye and heart alike; a saintly peaceful face, in which the strength of Christian and the weakness of Patrick were singularly blended, for she was like them both. The plough of sorrow had not carved its iron furrows on her fair brow, as it had done on Christian's. The sunshine of her smile was only chastened with natural tears for the dead brother who had gone to his rest; he was not her all in all as he had been Christian's.

No, for the little girl rejoicing in a childish exuberance of joy and tenderness already in her arms; the beautiful, bold, gallant boy, who stood beside her chair; the radiant dark face of the father and husband looking upon them with tremulous delight and pride—had all a share. Christian too, whose heroic work was done, and the new-found sister Anne; there was warm room for them all in the large heart of

Marion Rutherford. The burning fire of bitter grief had not intensified her love upon one—she was the family head, the house-mother—full of all gracious affections and sympathies, hopes and happiness.

CHAPTER XXXI

Mrs. Ross was inspired—how or by what means we are not sufficiently good metaphysicians to be able to specify—but inspired she was! It might be that all the court that had been paid to her of late had softened the adamantine heart: it only concerns us to know that softened it was. She took immediate counsel with May; she had fires lighted in half a dozen bed-chambers. Then the wainscotted parlor was made radiant—a fire in its grate "enough," as Duncan said with an involuntary grumble, "to keep the decent folk at the Brig of Oran in eliding frae this till Canlemas"—and additional candles upon its table. Then Mrs. Ross did something more wonderful than all this—the very climax and copestone of her unwonted melting of heart. She sent Duncan mysteriously up stairs to the attic lumber-room with secret instructions. May and Barbara lingered in wonder to what was coming.

A great thing was coming—covered with dust, and grumbling audibly, Duncan re-appeared in ten minutes, carrying in his arms a picture—the portrait of the lost son of the house of Merkland—the boy's face of the exiled Norman, dethroned from its standing in his father's house for eighteen weary year.

It was restored again now, and when Mrs. Ross having dismissed the servants sat down alone in her bright room, through the dark polished walls of which the warm lights were gleaming pleasantly, to wait for her guests; the unclouded sunshine of the bold, frank, fearless boy's face shone upon her for the first time. It had enough of the indefinite family resemblance, to bring her own Lewis before her mind. Lewis had gone up to the Tower, but was to return immediately. His mother sat in the parlor alone, more cheerily than was her wont, for the blood was warming about her heart.

And then they arrived—the whole of them, with all their different manifestations of joy; the mother Marion starting in delight at what she thought the portrait of her own bright Lawrie, and Norman himself heaping up in such generous measure his delicate amends of honor and attention to the step-mother, whom he fancied he had wronged. She remembered him so different once, in his impetuous youth, that the compliment was all the greater now.

Christian and Anne sat by the fire in a quiet corner. Lawrie, proud of his new kindred, and bashfully exultant over them all, hovered between them and the uncle Lewis, whose good looks and independent young manhood already powerfully attracted the boy: while on either side of Mrs. Ross herself sat Norman and Marion, and Lilie loyal to the newly-come mamma, joining her childish talk to theirs; and all so willing and eager to do honor to the head of the household—the sole remnant of an older generation. Deep peace fell upon Merkland that night in all its many chambers—deeper than had been there before for years.

The evening was not far spent when Archibald Sutherland stole in among them, not unwelcome, and with him to the gate of Merkland—no further—came Marjory Falconer; she had one word to say to Anne. Anne went to her at the gate; it was almost a relief in all this gladness to have a minute's breathing time.

"I came to congratulate you, Anne," said Marjory breathlessly. The moon was up, and at some little distance a tall dark shadow fell across the Oran, which Anne smiled to see. "To wish you manifold joy of all the arrivals—all, Anne. If I come down to-morrow, will you introduce me to your brother?"

"Surely, Marjory," said Anne, "but why not come to-night?"

"I might have come if you had married Ralph," said Marjory laughing, "but as it is, a stranger must not intermeddle with your joy. No, no—but I shall come to see them all to-morrow. By the by—"

"What, Marjory?"

"Oh, not much—only speaking of Ralph—I have found her at last; I have fairly laid my hands upon her. To-morrow I shall have her safely housed in Falcon's Craig!"

"Who is it?—what do you mean?"

"The daughter of Nimrod! the mighty huntress! I have got her all safe, Anne. I invite you to a wedding at Falcon's Craig in three months. I give them three months to do it in."

"You should know the necessary time," said Anne smiling.—"Shall there not be two, Marjory?"

"Hush," said Marjory gaily, "or I will retaliate. Now I must go. Mrs. Catherine is quite out of sorts for the want of you, Anne; and Alice is drooping as prettily as possible. Why did not your Norman come last night, and then we might—all of us—have rejoiced over him at the Tower?"

The next morning, the first excitement of their joy over, the three sisters sat together in the Merkland parlor. Mrs. Ross was superintending various domestic matters. Lewis was at the Tower. Norman had gone out with his son. Christian, Marion, and Anne were sitting together, with Lilie on her stool at their feet, communing "of all that was in their heart"—and that was much.

"It was very strange to us," said Marion, "I cannot tell you how strange, to hear from Mr. Sutherland—of Merkland, of you, of ourselves. He told us our own story—so much as he knew of it, and sought our sympathy and pity for his friends. Strangely—most strangely—did we feel as he spoke."

"I did not think Archie would have spoken of a thing so private," said Anne.

"Nay, do not blame him," said Marion. "He saved our Lawrie's life a few days after his arrival; and that of course, even if he had possessed fewer good qualities of his own, must have at once opened our hearts, and our house to him. But we liked him for himself, and he seemed to like us; and then as we knew him better, the home he spoke of, the names he mentioned, were very music to Norman's ears. I cannot tell you, Anne—you cannot fancy—how your brother has longed and yearned for the home we dared not return to."

There was a pause.

"And then," continued Marion, "as he gradually became, a member of our family, and a very dear friend, we gradually received his confidence. He spoke one night of 'little Alice Aytoun.' The name startled us both. Norman asked who she was—and then, Anne—by degrees we heard our own story—very sad and mysterious he thought it, although he knew not, Christian, the half of its sadness. But Anne, he said, was convinced of the innocence of her dead brother, and was full of hope for the vindication of his memory. 'Who is Anne?' I asked. Mr. Sutherland looked astonished for a moment, and then slightly embarrassed. He seemed to think it strange that there should be any one who did not know. Anne; and, sister Anne, he did you justice. We were strangely excited that night, Norman and I. I could not prevail upon him to go to rest. He walked about the room with a mixture of joy and fear on his face, that only people who have known such a position as ours could realize, repeating to himself, 'Anne—the child—my little sister Anne!' It was balm to him to think that you had faith in him, and hope for him; and yet he was full of fear lest he should endanger"—

Marion paused—the tears came into her eyes; she looked at Christian.

"Go on, Marion," said Christian, leaning her head upon her hand. "Go on—he is safe now, and past all peril."

"Our poor Patrick!" exclaimed his younger sister, "my gentle, broken-hearted, sad brother! At that time when the eighteenth year was nearly past, Norman was afraid—Norman was full of terror, lest any exertion made for him should disturb the peace of Patrick. He was as willing to suffer for him then, as he was when he went away—that terrible time!"

"Do not think of it," said Christian. "We are all at peace now, Marion, living and dead; and he the safest, peacefullest, most joyous of us all."

"And then he told us of Lilie," said Marion after a long silence. "And how you, Anne, became attached to the little stranger child; and we listened, endeavoring to look as if we did not know or care—I wonder at myself how I succeeded."

"And did you never tell him?" said Anne.

"No. Norman reserved it as a surprise to him when they should reach Strathoran. He wondered, I could see, why we were so anxious to come here, but he did not ask. Norman regards him almost as a younger brother. He is very anxious that he should have a situation more suitable for him, than the one he held at Buenos Ayres; but he will tell you his arrangements himself;—where is Norman?"

He was out, no one knew where he was.

He was at that moment stooping his lofty head, to enter the door-way of a solitary cottage—a very mean and poor one—at some distance from the Brig of Oran. Its inhabitant in former days had known Mr. Norman of Merkland well. She had been an old woman when he left home—she was a very old woman, decrepid and feeble, now; yet on the first day after his return, his kindly remembrance of old days carried the restored Laird, the great merchant, to the cottage of the "old Janet," who had given him apples and bannocks in his youth.

And in the long walk they took, the father and son made many similar visits, to the great amazement of Lawrie, who knowing his father a reserved grave man, called proud by strangers, was very greatly at a loss how to account for these many friendships. The hearty kindliness of these old cottage people, in which there was fully as much affection as awe, and the frank familiarity of his father, puzzled Lawrie mightily. He did by no means understand it.

They had begun with Esther Fleming's house—they ended with the Tower. Between these two, besides the cottage visitations we have mentioned, with all the joyful wonder of their recognitions, they visited a grave—a grave which had received another name since Norman Rutherford left his fatherland, and on which Lawrie read with awe and reverence, names of his ancestry the same as his own, and near the end, that of "Lawrence Ross, aged 15," his own age, who was his uncle.

In the meantime, at a solemn private conference in the little room, Mrs. Catherine was receiving Archibald's report.

"Mr. Sinclair's proposal to me," said Archibald, "is of so liberal a kind that I feel almost ashamed to accept it. Mr. Lumsden, the manager at Glasgow, has been received as junior partner into the firm, and is intended to succeed Mr. Sinclair at Buenos Ayres. Mr. Sinclair offers me Mr. Lumsden's situation in Glasgow, in the meantime, as he says, with a speedy prospect of entering the house. He himself intends to withdraw, and he talks of my chance of taking his place in the firm. This for me, who went out a poor clerk only a year ago, looks ridiculously Utopian; but the managership—Mr. Lumsden's situation, is sure—and it is higher than, in ordinary circumstances, I could have hoped to rise for years."

"I am glad of it—I am heartily glad to hear it, Archie," said Mrs. Catherine. "That you should leave your lawful labor is no desire of mine; but I have that to tell that concerns you more than even this. Have you heard any tidings yet, of the cattle you left in Strathoran?"

Archibald changed color, and said "No."

"Then it has not been told you that your father's house is within your reach again; that Strathoran is to be sold."

"To be sold!" Archibald started to his feet; his temples began to throb, his heart to beat—within his reach and yet how very far removed, for where could he find means to redeem his inheritance. "To be sold!"

"Yes. Archie Sutherland, to be sold—what say you to that?" He did not say anything to it; he pressed his hand to his brow and groaned.

"What ails you? sit down upon your seat this moment, and hearken to me; what say you to that?"

"I have nothing to say, Mrs. Catherine; it takes from me my great hope. There is no possibility of recovering it now, and what chance is there of any opportunity again. It is not likely to change hands thrice in one life-time."

"Archie," said Mrs. Catherine, "you are but a silly heart, after all. I thought not to have seen the beads on your brow for this matter. Sit down upon your seat I bid you, and hearken to me. I am not without siller as you know, seeing it is no such great space of time since a Laird of Strathoran made petition to me, to serve him in this Mammon; that you should have forgotten. I was slow then, for you were in the way of evil, Archie; but ill as you were, you know I was nearly tempted to cast away my siller, into the self-same mire in which you lost Strathoran, for the sake of Isabel Balfour and him that was her trysted bridegroom.—Now, Archie Sutherland, it is my hope that your eyes are opened to see the right course of man; which is not idleset and the mean pleasures of it, but honorable work and labor that the sun may shine upon, and God and your fellows see. Think not that I mean the making of siller; I mean a just work, whatsoever, is appointed you, to be done in honor and bravery, and in the fear of God. So as it is my hope you perceive this at last, you shall have your lands again, Archie. Not, that I desire you to return to Strathoran, as if you had never done ill. Go your ways and labor: you will return a better and a blyther man, that you have redeemed your inheritance with the work of your own hands. In the meantime, I myself will redeem it for you; I give you back the name your fathers have borne for ages. See that it descends to your bairns for their inheritance, Strathoran. And now I see Norman Rutherford at the door; go and take counsel with him for your further travail and leave me to my meditations."

And with kindly violence Mrs. Catherine shut the door of her sanctuary upon the bewildered Archibald—then she seated herself opposite the portrait of her brother, and gazed upon it long and earnestly. "Ay, Sholto Douglas, he is Isabel's son, and what would you have left undone for the bairn of Isabel?—and if he had been yours also, what is there within the compass of mortal might, that I would have halted at for him? He is Isabel's son—and it had not been ordered in a darker way, he would have been your first-born, Sholto Douglas; the shadow of your tenderness is upon the youth—he has none in this earth so near to him as me."

That day, there were various visitors at Merkland—Mrs. Catherine, the Aytouns, Marjory Falconer; they met together at night in the Tower, all joyous, hopeful, and at peace.

But in the vicinity of the Tower, that evening, there hovered a knot of stalwart men, uncertain as it seemed whether to enter or no. The younger ones were for pressing forward; the most eager among them was Angus Macalpine, himself longing to become the head of a household, and remembering Flora's limit "no till we get back to the glen;" but the highest and most potent of the group hung back.

"Man, Duncan, we're no wanting to vex him. I've as muckle honor for the Laird as on a' man o' my name—only it's our right to have an answer. If he's no gaun to buy back the land, maybe we could make favor wi' whaever does. We belong to the ground, and the ground to us, Duncan—we've a right to seek an answer at the hands of our chief."

"It a' sounds very just that, Angus," said Big Duncan Macalpine; "but the Laird's a distressed man, that hasna siller to give for the redemption of his inheritance and ours. Think ye onything but extremity could have garred him time the lands as he did? or think ye there can be siller enough gathered in ae year to buy back Strathoran? I tell ye, lads, I ken the Laird, and if he's maybe wasted his substance like a prodigal—I dinna dispute he has, and we're a' bearing the burden—he keeps aye a kind heart. Now, here are we, coming to him, young men and auld of us, that have been hunted from our hames. He kens it's his wyte, and he kens he canna mend it; and what can we do but gie him a sair heart, and what can he say but that it grieves him? If he had the power we wad be hame again the morn; but he hasna the power, and wherefore should we make his cup bitterer wi' putting our calamity before him and saying it's his blame?"

The reasoning of Big Duncan was strong like himself—the men fell back—but Angus was still eager.

"The auld man at the ingleside wrestles night and day to get quiet deein' in his ain house in the glen. He's wandered in his mind since ever yon weary day—aye, when he's no at his exercise—he's clear enough then; and if ye heard him, just to get hame that he may fa' asleep in peace, ye wadna be sae faint-hearted. I'm no meaning that you're faint-hearted either; but the Laird hasna had sae muckle thought o' us, that we should be sae mindfu' o' him."

"You're an inconsiderate lad, Angus," said Big Duncan; "but for the auld man's sake we may wait a while here. Maybe the Laird may pass this gate—yonder's somebody."

"It's the Laird," exclaimed Angus—forward as he had been before, he shrank back now. The man who had opposed the measure was left to be the spokesman.

Archibald had observed them from a window, and came towards them rapidly. Duncan lifted his bonnet—no servile sign, as smaller spirits in the arrogance of their so-called equality would assert, but the independent respect of an honorable poor man, who in his chief's good fame had an individual stake, and was himself honored. He was at some loss how to frame his speech.

"I trust," said Archibald, hastily, "I trust I shall have it in my power very shortly to redress your wrongs. You have suffered innocently—I justly; but we have both had some trials of faith and patience since we last met. Trust me the power shall not be in my hands a moment sooner than the will, to make amends to you for your loss—the bitterest hour of all this bitter twelvemonth was the one in which I heard of your wrong. There are two months yet between us, and the time which shall decide the proprietorship of Strathoran. I hope then, through my friend's help, to be able to redeem my inheritance and yours—if I succeed, have no fear—I will not spend an hour in unnecessary delay till you again enter Oranmore in peace."

These men did not cheer him—we are by no means loud in our demonstrations in Scotland—but their rough features moved and melted, and some eyelids swelled full. Archibald was a little excited too.

"So far as I have caused this, Macalpines, you forgive your chief?" He held out his hand—it was grasped with a silent fervor which spoke more eloquently than words. Tall Angus Macalpine, who touched his chief's hand last of all, could have thrown himself down at his feet, and craved his pardon. He did not do that; but would have rejoiced with mighty joy, as he flew down Oranside that night, to tap at the nursery window of Woodsmuir and carry Flora the news, to have had an opportunity of douking, knocking down, or in any way discomfiting "ony man that daured to mint an ill word of the Laird!"

Upon the appointed day little Alice Aytoun was married—Ada Mina Coulter, as having experience of the office, serving her in the capacity of bridesmaid, while Anne and Marjory were merely lookers on; the latter not without consideration of the proprieties of this same momentous ceremony, so soon to be repeated in a case where she could not be merely a spectator.

For Marjory's bold experiment was succeeding beautifully. Her visitor, Sophy Featherstonehaugh, the mighty huntress over whom she exulted, was half a Northumbrian, and half a maiden of the Merse—the daughter of a foxhunting Squire, a careless, good-humored, frank, daring girl, who could guide a vicious horse, or sing you "a westerly wind, and a cloudy sky," with any sportsman in the land. Poor Sophy was an only child—motherless from her infancy; the lands of her weak, boisterous, indulgent father were strictly entailed, and he seemed to have deadened any fatherly anxieties he might have had for leaving his daughter penniless, by fooling her to the top of her bent, so long as he remained lord of his own impoverished acres. But he died at last—and with an immense mastery over horses, and sufficiently cunning in all sports of the field to have filled the place of huntsman to some magnifico, and withal with a dowry of two hundred pounds, Sophy Featherstonehaugh, the daughter of an old and honorable family, was thrown upon the charities of the world.

A precise aunt in Edinburgh, with a great nursery-full of children, gave her a reluctant invitation. The innocent lady fancied Sophy's services might be turned to good account as a sort of unpaid nursery-governess. She was not long in discovering her mistake. Sophy had not been a week in charge, when the walls of the nursery rang with a shrill "Tally-ho!" of many juvenile voices. The next morning, Master Harry demanded from his astonished papa a horse, and coolly proposed turning over his pony to his sister, little Sophy, who earnestly seconded the embryo sportsman. Their mother was dismayed. She resolved to have a solemn forenoon conference with her unpaid nursery-governess, to ascertain what all this meant. When she reached the schoolroom door, she paused to listen. Alas! it was not any lesson that kept that little group so steadily round their teacher. It was one of those barbarous ballads with which a "northern harper rude" horrified the ears of the cultured Marmion, in Norham's castled keep, celebrating the exploits of a Featherstonehaugh. The aunt stood horror-stricken at the door—not long, however, for Sophy, with her loud, frank, good-humored voice, was already transgressing still more unpardonably, and in a moment after the boisterous chorus of "A hunting we will go—eho—eho—eho!" pierced the ears of the hapless mother, ringing from the shrill, united voices of all her children.

There was no more to be said after that: in unutterable wrath, poor Sophy was sent off immediately, in spite of her indignant remonstrances, and her twenty years, to a boarding-school in the neighborhood of Strathoran, the principal of which was informed of her past riotous behavior, and begged, with much bitterness by the aunt, to do what she could to make the girl human.

The girl's bold spirit rose at this—she, a Featherstonehaugh? But she had no kindred in the wide world to turn to, and even her poor two hundred pounds was mulcted for the payment of the year's stipend to the boarding-school. In these circumstances, Marjory Falconer became acquainted with her, and in a week thereafter, free from all governesses, or attempts to humanize, the bold Featherstonehaugh was triumphantly reining the wildest horse in the Falcon's Craig stables, while Ralph rode in delight and admiration by her side, and Marjory, standing at the door, said joyously, within herself:

"She has a firm hand—she can hold the reins—she will do!"

Marjory was by far too wise, however, to trust Ralph with her intention; but she made much of the frank, good-humored Sophy, and looked forward in good hopes.

The day arrived for the re-purchase of Strathoran, and Mr. Foreman and Mr. Ferguson, in the absence of all competitors, joyfully redeemed the inheritance of Archibald Sutherland, at a price considerably below its real value.

"Come light—gang light," said the lawyer, emphatically. "We give them more for it than they gave us."

There had been negotiations entered into with the Southland sheep-farmer, whose farm comprised the glen of Oranmore, and he readily accepted in lieu of it, for the justice sake, and to oblige the Laird, an equal extent of land elsewhere. In wild eagerness, the Macalpines threw themselves into their glen, and wrought so furiously at their dismantled houses, that in a very short time after the sale the longed-for homes stood complete again, ready for the joyful flitting.

And then, upon a balmy day of early April the clansfolk returned, in solemn procession, to their home. The bustle of removal was over—the lofty tone of those mountain people made a grave ceremonial of their return. In the glen, beneath the soft, blue sky, and genial spring sunshine, they gathered together to thank God; and, with the blue heights rising over them, and the fair low-country swelling soft and green at their feet, and the peaceful cottar houses round, with fire upon their hearths, and lowly, protecting roofs once more, they lifted up their voices in psalms:

"Lord, Thou hast been our dwelling place In generations all, Before Thou ever hadst brought forth The mountains great and small. Ere ever Thou hadst formed the earth, Or all the world abroad, Even Thou from everlasting art To everlasting God."

And then, their minister standing by the while, Duncan Macalpine the elder, of Oranmore, rendered thanks to God.

Archibald Sutherland denied himself this gladness. It invigorated him in the dingy manager's room of the Glasgow counting-house to hear of it, but he felt he had no claim to the triumph. Mr. Ferguson was there, radiant with honest glee, and Mr. Lumsden from Portoran, his face covered with a dark glow of simple delight and sympathy. And there was little Lilie, and Mary Ferguson, solemnly invited to take tea with Flora and Angus, on their first entry into their new house, and Anne and Marjory, with Lawrie for their gallant, were in charge of the children and a straggling back-ground of well-wishers from Merkland and the Tower, filled up the rear.

The months wore peacefully on. Esther Fleming's son had returned to her, and only did not become captain of a schooner, which called Norman owner now, because he had enough, and preferred comfortably dwelling at home, greatly honored by his foster-brother, and very proud of the relationship, while, withal, his mother's little housekeeper-niece did so seriously incline to hear his stories of sea perils and victories, that the rustic neighbors already in prophetic anticipation, had some half dozen times proclaimed the banns of William Fleming.

Norman Rutherford and his family were settled peacefully in the now bright and cheerful house of Redheugh. Anne was with them. Little Alice, the blythest of young wives, kept Merkland bright and busy. There was word in Edinburgh of some rich young Indian lady, who had thrown her handkerchief on James.

And before the three months were fully expired, Anne Ross accepted Marjory Falconer's invitation, and was present at a wedding-party in Falcon's Craig. A double wedding—at which Mr. Lumsden, of Portoran, placed in the stout hand of Sophy Featherstonehaugh the reins of the ruder animal Ralph Falconer, of Falcon's Craig, and immediately thereafter submitted in his turn to the same important ceremony, performed in his case by the brother Robert, of Gowdenleas, in the midst of an immense assemblage of kindred, Andrew of Kilfleurs standing by.

And prosperous were these weddings. Good-humored, kindly, and of tolerable capacity, the bold Sophy had improved under her sister-in-law's powerful tutorage. She had a firm hand. The boisterous Ralph felt the reins light upon him, yet was kept in bounds, and by-and-by Sophy left the management of wild horses entirely in his hands. She got other important things to manage—obstreperous atoms of humanity, wilder than their quadruped brethren, and scarce less strong.

And with her old chimeras scattered to the winds, in lofty lowliness, and chastened strength, Marjory Falconer entered her Manse, the minister's stout-hearted and pure-minded wife. One hears no more of the rights of women now—bubbles of such a sort do not float in the rare atmosphere of this household—there is nothing in them congenial with the sunshine of its blythe order and freedom.

For granting that our Calvinism is gloomy, and our Presbyterian temperament sour, one wonders how universal this household warmth and joyousness should be beneath the roof-trees of those strong, pure men, whom the intolerant world upbraids with the names of bigot, hypocrite, and pharisee. One could wish to have this same intolerant bigot world make a tour of these Scottish Manses, from which it might return, perchance, able to give a rational judgment on the doctrine and order of Christ's Holy Evangel, as we have held it in Scotland from the days of our fathers until now; at least might have its evil speaking hushed into silence before the devout might, which labors for the hire, not of silver and gold, but of saved souls—and the sunny godliness which is loftiest gain.

There is a rumor in the Lumsden family that, upon one evening shortly after the marriage, a certain chapter of the Epistle to the Ephesians, containing a verse which married ladies do mightily stumble at, was read in regular course: on which occasion, says the mirthful Sister Martha of the Portoran Manse, one could detect the shadow of a comic inflection in the voice of the household priest, while his wife with a certain grave doggedness, slightly bowed her strong head before the unpalatable command.

We cannot tell how the truth of this story may be, but Sister Martha laughs when she tells it, and Marjory blushes her violent blush, and the minister looks on with his characteristic smile of simple unsophisticated glee. But we can vouch for it, that Mrs. Lumsden of Portoran has become a renowned church-lawyer, mighty in the "Styles," and great in the forms of process; whose judgment maintains itself triumphantly in face of a whole Synod, and whose advice in complicated matters, of edicts, or calls, or trials, youthful reverends scant of ecclesiastical jurisprudence, would do well to take.

Only there is growing up in the Manse of Portoran a host of little sun-burnt, dark-haired heads—all prosperity and increase to the sparkling eyes and bold brows of them!—over whose rejoicing band a little fairy sister, the joy of the minister's heart, exercises her capricious sway, and sovereign tyranny. They are growing up, all of them, to call Marjory blessed—already for their generous nurturing "known in the gates" as hers—and hereafter still more to rejoice in the strong, gladsome, sunshiny nature to which they owe their healthful might and vigor. The prophecy and hope of her friend and counsellor is fulfilled in full: "Strength and honor are her clothing. She opens her mouth with wisdom, and in her lips is the law of kindness."

The months passed on, and lengthened into years. Archibald Sutherland, after good work in the manager's room, entered the firm triumphantly as Norman's successor; before that, he had succeeded to the well-ordered house in the vicinity of Blythswood Square, which had been occupied by his predecessor Mr. Lumsden. People said it certainly needed a mistress, and very wonderful were the rapidity of those successive occasions, on which the Laird of Strathoran, clear-headed as men called him, found it absolutely necessary to repair to Redheugh to seek counsel of his friend.

His sister Isabel had made a brilliant marriage; they had scarcely any intercourse—unless some new misfortune should befall her she was lost to her early friends. Mrs. Catherine and Mr. Ferguson, under Mr. Coulter's advice, were managing his estate. Sentences oracular and mysterious were sometimes heard falling from Mrs. Catherine's lips, in which the names of "Archie" and "Anne" were conjoined. The house of Strathoran had been thoroughly purified. Mrs. Catherine had made sundry important additions to its plenishing; it was always kept in such order, that its now prosperous and rising possessor might return to it, at once. Anne was resident at the Tower sometimes, and knew of these processes. They tended to some new change in the eventful life of Archie Sutherland.

The Rosses of Merkland were visiting the Rutherfords of Redheugh. In the large sunny drawing-room, from whose ample windows sloped a lawn of close and velvet greensward, the whole family were assembled. The elder Mrs. Ross was mollified and melted; the younger gay and rejoicing. Lewis was in high spirits—under the regimen approved and recommended by Mr. Coulter, Lewis hoped to raise the rent-roll of Merkland a half more than it had ever been. You could see now in the large wistful dark eyes of Christian Lillie, only the subdued and serious tone proper to those who have borne great griefs without brooding over them. There was an aspect of serene peace and healthful pleasure over all the house. The three sisters, Marion, Christian, and Anne, were sisters indeed.

Without was a merrier group. Lilie Rutherford, with her youthful gallant, Charlie Ferguson, now a High School boy, lodged in a closet of his brother Robert's rooms, and frequent in his Saturday visits to Redheugh; and Lawrie, growing a young man now, as he thought, and dubious as to the propriety of keeping company with lesser boys and girls, to whom he was very patronizing and condescending, stood by the sun-dial; while in the background was Jacky, now waiting gentlewoman to Miss Lilias Rutherford, a very great person indeed, and little Bessie, young Mrs. Ross of Merkland's own maid.

Lilie was coquettishly making inquiries of Bessie, touching the welfare of Harry Coulter, whereat Charlie Ferguson grew irate and sulky.

"And the young gentleman's biding at the Tower," said Bessie; "he's a lord noo his ainsel—and he's been twice at Harrows."

"Who is that?" said little Lilie.

"Oh, if ye please, Miss Lilie," said Jacky, "it's a young gentleman that was a lord's son, and now he's a lord himsel—and he's gaun to be married to Mr. Harry's sister."

"Eh, Jacky, what gars ye say such a thing?" cried Bessie. "If ye please, Miss Lilie, naebody kens—only he's been twice at Harrows; but maybe he's no courting Miss Coulter for a' that."

"I should think not," exclaimed Charlie Ferguson, indignantly. "Ada Coulter married to a lord! Yes, indeed—and they can't talk of a single thing at Harrows but fat pigs, and prize cattle, and ploughing matches. Why, Lilie, do you mind what Harry gave you when you were at Merkland—a plough! what can ladies do with ploughs?"

"Mrs. Catherine has a great many ploughs, Charlie," said Lilie, gravely—"and it was very good of Harry; and Mary and me might have played with it all our lane, and we would not have needed you. I dinna like boats—folk can plough at hame—but in boats they go over the sea."

"And, eh, Jacky!" exclaimed Bessie, curiously, as Charlie followed his capricious liege lady, to efface if he could this unfortunate recollection of Harry Coulter and his gift—"isna young Strathoran awfu' often at Redheugh?"

"He's here whiles," said Jacky, briefly.

"Johnnie Halflin says," said Bessie, "and it's a' through the parish—and folk say Mrs. Catherine's just waiting for't, and that it's to be in the Tower, and Mr. Lumsden is to do it, and Mrs. Lumsden kens a' about it—"

"About what?"

"Oh, ye just ken better than me for a' you'll no say—just that young Strathoran's coming out of yon muckle reekie Glasgow, hame to his ain house, and then he's to be married to Miss Anne. Tell us, woman, Jacky—I'll never tell a mortal body again, as sure as I'm living."

Jacky's dark face lighted up—she knew this secret would bear telling, even though Bessie broke faith.

"We're a' gaun to the Tower at the New year—like the time Redheugh came hame; Miss Lilie and Miss Anne, and a' the house—and young Strathoran's to be there too. And Miss Anne has gotten a grand goun, a' of white silk, shining like the snaw below the moon, and a shawl—ye never saw the like o't—it's as lang as frae Merkland to the Tower. And maybe something will happen then, and maybe no—Miss Anne wasna gaun to tell me!"

Margaret Oliphant – A Short Biography

Margaret Oliphant Wilson was born on April 4th, 1828 to Francis W. Wilson, a clerk, and Margaret Oliphant, at Wallyford, near Musselburgh, East Lothian.

She spent her childhood at Lasswade, near Dalkeith, Glasgow before moving to Liverpool.

Her youth was spent in establishing a writing style so much so that, in 1849, she had her first novel published: Passages in the Life of Mrs. Margaret Maitland based on the Scottish Free Church movement. It met with some success and was a good start to her career.

Two years later, in 1851, her third book Caleb Field was published. It was also now that she met the publisher William Blackwood in Edinburgh and was asked to contribute to his well-received Blackwood's Magazine. It was to be a lifetimes endeavor. Over the course of the relationship she would have well over 100 articles published.

In May 1852, Margaret married her cousin, Frank Wilson Oliphant, at Birkenhead, and they settled at Harrington Square, Camden, London. He was an artist working primarily in stained glass. With the marriage she became Margaret Oliphant Wilson Oliphant.

Their marriage produced six children but three tragically died in infancy.

When her husband developed signs of the dreaded consumption (tuberculosis) they moved, on the advice of doctors, to warmer climes. In January 1859 it was to Florence, and then to Rome where, sadly, he died.

Margaret was naturally devastated but was also now left without support and only her income from her writing. She returned to England and took up the task of supporting her three remaining children by her literary activity.

By now she was being published both as an established novelist and regularly in Blackwood's Magazine, amongst others. Her incredible and prolific work rate increased both her commercial reputation and the size of her reading audience.

Against this her domestic life continued to be tragic, full of sorrow and disappointment.

In January 1864 her only remaining daughter Maggie died and was buried in her father's grave in Rome. Her brother, who had emigrated to Canada, was shortly afterwards involved in financial ruin. Margaret generously offered a home to him and his children, adding another demand to her already heavy responsibilities.

In 1866 she settled at Windsor to be closer to her sons, who were being educated at near-by Eton School. That year, her second cousin, Annie Louisa Walker, came to live with her as a companion-housekeeper. Windsor was now to be her home for the rest of her life.

Her literary career for three decades was one of constant delivery and success. Whether she wrote historical works or across several genres in fiction: domestic realism, historical, romance or supernatural she was successful.

For more than thirty years she pursued a varied literary career but family life continued to bring problems.

The literary ambitions she wished for her sons were unfulfilled. Cyril Francis, the eldest, died in 1890, leaving a Life of Alfred de Musset, incorporated in his mother's Foreign Classics for English Readers. The younger, Francis, who she nicknamed 'Cecco', collaborated with her in the Victorian Age of English Literature and won a position at the British Museum, but was rejected by Sir Andrew Clark, a famous physician. Cecco died in 1894.

With the last of her children now lost to her, she had but little further interest in life. Her health steadily and inexorably declined.

Margaret Oliphant Wilson Oliphant died at the age of 69 in Wimbledon on 20th June 1897. She is buried in Eton beside her sons.

At her death, Margaret was still working on Annals of a Publishing House, a record of Blackwood's Magazine with which she had enjoyed such a successful relationship.

Her Autobiography and Letters, which present a thoughtful picture of her domestic anxieties, was published in 1899. Only parts were written with a wider audience in mind: she had originally intended the Autobiography for her son, but he died before she could finish it.

Opinions on Oliphant's work are split, with some critics seeing her as a 'domestic novelist', while others recognize her work as influential and important to the Victorian literature canon. Critical reception from her contemporaries is also divided. John Skelton took the view that Oliphant wrote too much and too quickly. Writing a Blackwood's article called 'A Little Chat About Mrs. Oliphant', he asked, "Had Mrs. Oliphant concentrated her powers, what might she not have done? We might have had another Charlotte Brontë or another George Eliot." However not all of the contemporary reception was negative. The esteemed M. R. James admired Oliphant's supernatural fiction, concluding that "the religious ghost story, as it may be called, was never done better than by Mrs. Oliphant in 'The Open Door' and 'A Beleaguered City'. Mary Butts lavished praise on Oliphant's ghost story 'The Library Window', describing it as "one masterpiece of sober loveliness".

More modern critics of Oliphant's work include Virginia Woolf, who asked in Three Guineas whether Oliphant's autobiography does not lead the reader "to deplore the fact that Mrs. Oliphant sold her brain, her very admirable brain, prostituted her culture and enslaved her intellectual liberty in order that she might earn her living and educate her children."

Whatever the merits of their cases Margaret Oliphant has been shamefully neglected in modern years. She is now becoming more widely recognised as a leading writer of her day.

Margaret Oliphant – A Concise Bibliography

A canon of more than 120 works, including novels, travel books, histories, and volumes of literary criticism.

Novels

Margaret Maitland (1849)
Merkland (1850)
Caleb Field (1851)
John Drayton (1851)
Adam Graeme (1852)
The Melvilles (1852)
Katie Stewart (1852)
Harry Muir (1853)
Ailieford (1853)
The Quiet Heart (1854)
Magdalen Hepburn (1854)
Zaidee (1855)
Lilliesleaf (1855)
Christian Melville (1855)
The Athelings (1857)
The Days of My Life (1857)
Orphans (1858)
The Laird of Norlaw (1858)
Agnes Hopetoun's Schools and Holidays (1859)
Lucy Crofton (1860)
The House on the Moor (1861)
The Last of the Mortimers (1862)
Heart and Cross (1863)
Salem Chapel (1863)
The Rector (1863)
Doctor's Family (1863)
The Perpetual Curate (1864)

Miss Marjoribanks (1866)
Phoebe Junior (1876)
A Son of the Soil (1865)
Agnes (1866)
Madonna Mary (1867)
Brownlows (1868)
The Minister's Wife (1869)
The Three Brothers (1870)
John: A Love Story (1870)
Squire Arden (1871)
At his Gates (1872)
Ombra (1872
May (1873)
Innocent (1873)
The Story of Valentine and his Brother (1875)
A Rose in June (1874)
For Love and Life (1874)
Whiteladies (1875)
An Odd Couple (1875)
The Curate in Charge (1876)
Carità (1877)
Young Musgrave (1877)
Mrs. Arthur (1877)
The Primrose Path (1878)
Within the Precincts (1879)
The Fugitives (1879)
A Beleaguered City (1879)
The Greatest Heiress in England (1880)
He That Will Not When He May (1880)
In Trust (1881)
Harry Joscelyn (1881)
Lady Jane (1882)
A Little Pilgrim in the Unseen (1882)
The Lady Lindores (1883)
Sir Tom (1883)
Hester (1883)
It Was a Lover and his Lass (1883)
The Lady's Walk (1883)
The Wizard's Son (1884)
Madam (1884)
The Prodigals and their Inheritance (1885)
Oliver's Bride (1885)
A Country Gentleman and his Family (1886)
A House Divided Against Itself (1886)
Effie Ogilvie (1886)
A Poor Gentleman (1886)
The Son of his Father (1886)
Joyce (1888)

Cousin Mary (1888)
The Land of Darkness (1888)
Lady Car (1889)
Kirsteen (1890)
The Mystery of Mrs. Biencarrow (1890)
Sons and Daughters (1890)
The Railway Man and his Children (1891)
The Heir Presumptive and the Heir Apparent (1891)
The Marriage of Elinor (1891)
Janet (1891)
The Cuckoo in the Nest (1892)
Diana Trelawny (1892)
The Sorceress (1893)
A House in Bloomsbury (1894)
Sir Robert's Fortune (1894)
Who Was Lost and is Found (1894)
Lady William (1894)
Two Strangers (1895)
Old Mr. Tredgold (1895)
The Unjust Steward (1896)
The Ways of Life (1897)

Short stories
Neighbours on the Green (1889)
A Widow's Tale and Other Stories (1898)
That Little Cutty (1898)
The Open Door (1918)

Selected Articles

Mary Russel Mitford (Blackwood's Magazine, Vol. 75, 1854)
Evelin and Pepys (Blackwood's Magazine, Vol. 76, 1854)
The Holy Land (Blackwood's Magazine, Vol. 76, 1854)
Mr. Thackeray and his Novels (Blackwood's Magazine, Vol. 77, 1855)
Bulwer (Blackwood's Magazine, Vol. 77, 1855)
Charles Dickens (Blackwood's Magazine, Vol. 77, 1855)
Modern Novelists—Great and Small (Blackwood's Magazine, Vol. 77, 1855)
Modern Light Literature: Poetry (Blackwood's Magazine, Vol. 79, 1856)
Religion in Common Life (Blackwood's Magazine, Vol. 79, 1856)
Sydney Smith (Blackwood's Magazine, Vol. 79, 1856)
The Laws Concerning Women (Blackwood's Magazine, Vol. 79, 1856)
The Art of Caviling (Blackwood's Magazine, Vol. 80, 1856)
Béranger (Blackwood's Magazine, Vol. 83, 1858)
The Condition of Women (Blackwood's Magazine, Vol. 83, 1858)
The Missionary Explorer (Blackwood's Magazine, Vol. 83, 1858)
Religious Memoirs (Blackwood's Magazine, Vol. 83, 1858)

Social Science (Blackwood's Magazine, Vol. 88, 1860)
Scotland and her Accusers (Blackwood's Magazine, Vol. 90, 1861)
The Chronicles of Carlingford (Blackwood's Magazine 1862–1865)
Girolamo Savonarola (Blackwood's Magazine, Vol. 93, 1863)
The Life of Jesus (Blackwood's Magazine, Vol. 96, 1864)
Giacomo Leopardi (Blackwood's Magazine, Vol. 98, 1865)
The Great Unrepresented (Blackwood's Magazine, Vol. 100, 1866)
Mill on the Subjection of Women (The Edinburgh Review, Vol. 130, 1869)
The Opium-Eater (Blackwood's Magazine, Vol. 122, 1877)
Russian and Nihilism in the Novels of I. Tourgeniéf (Blackwood's Magazine, Vol. 127, 1880)
School and College (Blackwood's Magazine, Vol. 128, 1880)
The Grievances of Women (Fraser's Magazine, New Series, Vol. 21, 1880)
Mrs. Carlyle (The Contemporary Review, Vol. 43, May 1883)
The Ethics of Biography (The Contemporary Review, July 1883)
Victor Hugo (The Contemporary Review, Vol. 48, July/December 1885)
A Venetian Dynasty (The Contemporary Review, Vol. 50, August 1886)
Laurence Oliphant (Blackwood's Magazine, Vol. 145, 1889)
Tennyson (Blackwood's Magazine, Vol. 152, 1892)
Addison, the Humorist (Century Magazine, Vol. 48, 1894)
The Anti-Marriage League (Blackwood's Magazine, Vol. 159, 1896)

Biographies

Edward Irving (1862)
Francis of Assisi (1871)
Count de Montalembert (1872)
Dante (1877)
Cervantes (1880)
Life of Sheridan in the English Men of Letters series (1883)
John Tulloch (1888)
Laurence Oliphant (1892)

Historical & Critical Works

Historical Sketches of the Reign of George II (1869)
The Makers of Florence (1876)
A Literary History of England from 1760 to 1825 (1882)
The Makers of Venice (1887)
Royal Edinburgh (1890)
Jerusalem (1891)
The Makers of Modern Rome (1895)
William Blackwood and his Sons (1897)
The Sisters Brontë. In: Women Novelists of Queen Victoria's Reign (1897)

www.ingramcontent.com/pod-product-compliance
Lightning Source LLC
Chambersburg PA
CBHW052015020726

47501CB00004B/1078